JIM & RACHEL BRITTS

ALL OR NOTHING

Britts Books.

All or Nothing

Copyright © 2012 by Jim and Rachel Britts

Published by Britts Books in partnership with New Song Pictures.

Britts Books, Oceanside, CA

This novel is a work of fiction. Names, characters, and incidents are the
product of the author's imagination and are used fictitiously. Any resem-
blance to actual events, organizations, or persons living or dead is entirely coincidental and beyond the intent of the authors or the publisher.

ISBN: 978-0-9850626-0-6

Cover Design: Alexia Garaventa
Graphic Design and layout: Alexia Garaventa

Printed in the United States of America

ALTHOUGH 2200 MILES OF ASPHALT still lay between him and home, Jake could almost taste the salty Oceanside air as he pulled onto I-64 away from Louisville, Kentucky. His stereo blared a random mix of songs, courtesy of his roommate Grant, and Jake couldn't help but let his shoulders bop to the unfamiliar yet catchy beats. After a year and a half, Jake was finally going home. He was so excited.

According to his mom's meticulous planning, the grueling thirty-some hour drive should take him three days; she had carefully plotted out detailed dining and sleeping suggestions on a map for Jake and expected him home by late Sunday night. Jake appreciated his mom's efforts but was more interested in the check that came with it. She had sent more than enough to cover basic expenses and had even included some fun money for random tourist attractions like the Cadillac Graveyard in Bushland, Texas. As fascinating as that sounded, the only points of interest Jake was interested in were the ones he could see from his car at seventy-five miles per hour. He was determined that the trek should take no more than two days, with brief roadside pit stops only when necessary and convenient. Of course, who knew? Maybe in a thousand miles, even an eccentric man's Caddy collection would sound interesting.

In spite of it being a Friday morning, freeway traffic was still light at 5 a.m., so Jake set his cruise control and let his truck race away from the rising sun. They sped by a billboard that boasted "We love our Cardinals!" in bold red and white and Jake couldn't stop the smile that crept onto his face.

Jake loved his team, too. What a season they'd had this year! It had been over for nearly two months already, but Jake relived it as if it were yesterday. If he were honest, his favorite part, of course, was the downfall of Nate Williams. Jake and the starting point guard had been rivals on and off the court since the day Jake arrived at Louisville, and even though Jake never wished anything bad on the guy, it had seemed like well-timed justice when Nate sprained his ankle in their first game of the NCAA tournament. Jake finally was given his chance to shine and he had carried the team to victory that night. Goosebumps raised on his arms as Jake clutched the steering wheel remembering how good that had felt.

Since Nate had still been sidelined for their second game two days later, Jake was given a second chance to lead the team, and again he wrangled in a win. They had made it to the Sweet Sixteen! And how sweet indeed it was. In that game, even though Nate tried to start, Jake got most of the minutes, and his seventeen points, nine assists and three steals had the entire Cardinal fan club on their feet cheering. He could still hear the thousands of Louisville faithful chanting his name, "Taylor! Taylor! Taylor!"

Unfortunately, even with that performance, they couldn't topple top-ranked Duke. In a nail-biting double overtime, the Blue Devils finally prevailed and sent Jake and his teammates packing. The loss had been disappointing, but the knowledge that they had pushed the inevitable national champion to the edge of elimination was at least some consolation.

Jake's reminiscing was interrupted by the absurdity of the song currently playing. A folksy-sounding duet crooned about how their love for each other was like an old pair of jeans: "I don't care about the rips, baby. With a little love, we can patch it up."

Where does Grant find this stuff? Jake wondered as he chuckled. Regardless of his roommate's unique taste in music, Jake had to concede that Grant was the best friend Jake had ever had. *Besides Roger.*

It had been quite awhile since Jake had thought much about Roger, and he was surprised to find his eyes stinging a little as he remembered that horrible day their senior year when Roger had shot himself right in front of Jake. Jake had worked through the what-ifs so many times before—there were tons of things Jake wished he could have done differently. But instead of re-hashing those regrets, today Jake found his mind wandering to how his own life might have been different if Roger had never killed himself.

It was an interesting thought to consider. Some things would probably still be the same. Jake was pretty sure he'd still be at Louisville, but he probably wouldn't have missed that first season by staying home with Amy. *Amy...*

Jake let his mind linger on her for a moment before he realized that even if Roger's death had never rocked his world, there was still probably zero chance that they would currently be together. Jake realized with shame that he had been too self-centered, too immature to make it last. Even *with* everything he learned through Roger's tragedy, *I still let her slip away!* Jake lamented.

Steering his brain away from her, Jake turned instead to think about how his basketball experiences would be different if he hadn't missed that first semester. Maybe Nate Williams would be the one clamoring for his spot, instead of the other way around. Maybe Jake could have led his team all the way to the championship this year. Maybe he'd even have a shot at the NBA draft this summer.

Some sort of mutant combination of country and techno brought Jake back to reality, and he thought of Grant again. If it weren't for Roger, there's no way Jake would still be friends with Grant. When everything turned sour after Grant revealed his homosexuality, Jake was quick to want to withdraw his friendship like he had with Roger. It was just too easy to stick with the rest of his friends. But after Grant called him out on it, Jake knew he couldn't make the same mistake again. With some help and encouragement from Chris and Buddy, Jake had made it right, and in spite of their many differences, the two had settled into a deeper friendship than Jake had ever experienced.

With no more early morning practices to wake up for, the last two months had provided Jake and Grant just the fertile soil they needed to let their camaraderie grow. Nearly every night, they ended up talking until the wee hours of the morning, about everything from their futures in the NBA to the existence of God. They disagreed on many things, but they shared a mutual respect and an unspoken appreciation for each other.

Jake prayed for his friend, thanking God for bringing them together and asking for God's continued hand in his life. Grant had been home for a few weeks now, and it had been rough. His family put the funk in dysfunctional. One of his brothers was back in jail, and the other was back sleeping on the couch of their mom's one-bedroom apartment, usually too stoned to mind. Jake wasn't even sure where Grant slept. His mom drank far too much, and, desperate that her third son would not fail her like the others had, she pushed Grant every chance she got. But nothing Grant did ever seemed good enough. Jake wondered how his friend would survive the summer. Jake had offered Grant the option of staying with him out in California, but Grant had said he needed the time and space to figure some things out on his own. *God, please help him out and give him strength!*

Just thinking about Grant's awkward family situation made Jake appreciate his own that much more. Sure, his parents had their problems. But at least they both loved him. For years, Jake wasn't sure if he could say that about his dad, but things had improved significantly between them, ever since their long drive out to Louisville a year and a half ago. Glen was still far too obsessed with work, and stayed far too busy to maintain quality relationships, but at least they talked more and Glen tried to be genuinely interested in his son's life.

Unfortunately, he didn't exert that same effort with Jake's mom. After almost two years of separation, Glen had just recently filed divorce papers. Jake wasn't sure what exactly had triggered that next step, but obviously counseling hadn't worked. Jake didn't expect to be able to bring his parents back together during his time home, but it couldn't hurt to ask God for a modern day miracle. Maybe he could just get his dad to come to church with him sometime. *Talk about a modern day miracle!* Jake spent some time talking to God about them, until his thoughts turned to church and another unavoidable smile crept onto his face.

He caught himself pressing the accelerator and found his truck doing ninety-five down the Interstate. *Oops!* He grinned as he let the cruise control take over again. His thoughts were getting ahead of him. If he could stick to his rigorous driving plan, he would pull into Oceanside late Saturday night...which meant he could attend New Song Community Church on Sunday morning, something he'd been looking forward to for weeks. Preferring to keep it a surprise, Jake had intentionally neglected to mention this plan to anyone, especially Chris. But Jake couldn't wait to see the look on his youth pastor's face when he strolled into the church lobby unannounced.

How things had changed in the last few months! Whereas for most of the last year, ashamed of the life he had been living, Jake had guiltily avoided all contact with Chris, now he was excited to share everything with him. He had been learning and growing so much, thanks in large part to his eighty-four-year-old friend Buddy. Ironically, Jake had met Buddy at the first church Chris had encouraged him to check out his freshman year—one to which Jake had planned to never return. Since then, the choir at Grace Fellowship certainly hadn't improved much—nor had the preaching. But now that Jake was starting to get more involved, it was actually starting to feel a little more like a home away from home.

About two months ago, Buddy had talked Jake into being an usher with him. Together, they made it their goal to greet every single person to walk through the doors of their church each week with a smile and a hug. After a few weeks of that, Jake decided that they really needed those donuts and coffee that he had missed on his first visit. So after presenting his plan to the elder board, Jake got permission to start a hospitality table in the lobby.

Fresh coffee and donuts gave people an excuse to stand around and chat longer, and increasing friendliness was in the air.

Then, Jake was asked to help out with Grace Fellowship's Vacation Bible School. As one of very few young people in the church, they needed his energy and stamina and quickly assigned him the role of Games Leader. Hanging out with a bunch of kids this past week had definitely stretched Jake's comfort zone, but by yesterday morning, he was in his element playing "Hot Potato" and "Steal the Bacon" and "Over Under." Who knew how much fun could be had with a bean bag?

Volunteering had required Jake to stick around Louisville for a few extra weeks after finals, which was fine, since he had nothing better to do back home. Buddy and his wife Yvonne were quick to offer their home to Jake after the dorms closed, and Jake felt like their spoiled grandkid. But when Buddy told him last night that, due to a sudden heat wave, they were only going to show a movie during game time today and that Jake's game skills wouldn't be needed, Jake was quick to do the math and realize that he could still make it home for Sunday morning at New Song. Buddy only smiled, and a twinkle danced in his eyes as he'd helped Jake pack his truck. His final words to Jake at 4:30 this morning were "Good luck!"

Truth be told, Chris wasn't the only person Jake was looking forward to seeing at New Song, and Buddy knew it. Jake had just "happened" to notice that Stanford finals were over this week, which meant that a certain someone might also likely be back for a visit this weekend. Jake had mentioned that to Buddy yesterday afternoon, only a few hours before Buddy got the official call that VBS games were being canceled today.

Ha! What a coincidence! Jake shook his head and smiled in appreciation of his friend and mentor, and then sighed as his thoughts flew to Amy once again. And as much as he tried not to let them linger there, they just wouldn't budge. Goosebumps raised the hairs on his forearms at the thought of seeing her in two short days, and again, he found himself pushing the accelerator. But then reality swarmed his brain and he broke out in a cold sweat.

What would he do when he saw Amy? Would he be able to stay cool? How would he greet her? As much as he'd love to just run and embrace her—as the music swelled, like it did in the movies—Jake knew that was probably a little too presumptuous, especially considering that the last time they were together, he had come millimeters away from hitting her. On the other hand, a handshake was obviously too stiff. *Isn't there some sort of middle ground?* Jake agonized.

But even if he made it past the greeting, Jake's problems were only just beginning. What would he say to Amy? Any time he found himself fantasizing over those precious first words to her, he always ended up only wishing like crazy that he could erase those cruel last ones.

Jake thought back to that fateful weekend when he had thoroughly ruined things. After a week of being a disrespectful jerk, he had finally let his pride and selfishness go too far, cutting Amy down and leaving her abandoned. And then, in the stupidest move known to man, he had hooked up with Nicole. *Idiot!* Jake cringed and banged his head against his headrest.

He shuddered just thinking about Nicole. How had he let himself get carried away with her? She couldn't hold a candle to Amy. Amy was gorgeous. She was smart. She cared about others and was passionate about serving God. And she had tried so hard to keep their relationship healthy based on her new-found faith in God. But Jake had taken her for granted and got caught up in his own life at college and blown her off when she was trying to make it work. He had let himself be blinded by Nicole's curves and self-centered advances, and dug himself into a pit that might just be too deep to escape. *That's what I get for letting go of my faith,* he bemoaned.

Of course, God hadn't let him go so easily. After floundering on his own for awhile, Jake was given a reality check when he found Nicole back in bed with Nate Williams several months later. That had been a painful pill to swallow, but had given Jake just enough space to start reevaluating his life. He'd been with Amy since their freshman year of high school, then immediately replaced Amy with Nicole, and was on his way to replacing Nicole with one of the many other girls who threw themselves at college athletes. Having a woman by his side had become an addictive habit, like crack or computer solitaire. And that's when Jake realized that he needed a break from dating.

He'd spent the last eight months as a single man, and although it was hard, he was finding that it definitely had its advantages. He got better grades, spent more time with God, played more ball... and spent less money! Jake was finally growing content with his single status when, out of the blue, Amy had sent him that text the night of his stellar performance in the big game. It had been a harmless ten words, a gracious gesture of congratulations. But it had rocked Jake's world.

Suddenly, there was a glimmer of hope. Suddenly Amy was all he could think about. Suddenly, he wanted more.

Unfortunately, though, it was just one text. Her ensuing replies to his eager messages were brief and vague. Jake felt like such a chick, reading into every nuance of every word that she wrote him and second guessing his own responses for hours after he sent them. But he couldn't help it. He missed Amy.

Even if it was now probably too late.

From what Jake could tell from Facebook, Amy was still "in a relationship" with happy ol' Guitar Boy (as Jake liked to call him based on his holding a guitar in Amy's profile picture). She seemed to be truly happy, and she was finally living out *her* dreams. Jake knew he had no right to intrude. But he couldn't help dreaming.

Jake had talked with Buddy and Chris extensively about his dilemma. He had been honest about his failures, and they had responded with truth and grace. And thanks to their advice, Jake wasn't giving up. They both warned him to tread carefully but to give it his all and let God work behind the scenes.

Jake asked God to be working now, in this moment, opening up Amy's heart to be ready to see him again...and hopefully to give him some sort of second chance. Of course, Jake still had Guitar Boy to contend with, so he talked to God about his competition. Naturally, Jake found himself disliking the guy, but he knew that Guitar Boy was likely an answer to Amy's prayers. So

Jake asked for a generous heart, and if necessary, an acceptance of this guy if he was the one God wanted Amy to be with. Jake hashed out several ideas with God for how to restore at least a friendship with Amy, asking for creativity and wisdom in expressing his heart to her. He rehearsed all the things he wished he could tell her, and begged God for the opportunity. Finally, his mind empty and his emotions spent, he surrendered their future to their Maker and sighed. *I leave her in Your hands, God,* Jake prayed, knowing that was his only real option.

The folksy duet started singing about their ripped jeans again, and Jake glanced down at the clock above his stereo, startled to read one0:57. Where had the last six hours gone? And how many times had he played through this crazy CD without noticing? Jake vaguely remembered stopping for gas several hours ago, but now his fuel gauge was reading near empty again and his bladder was definitely near full. The sign ahead indicated that Springfield, Missouri, was a mere eleven miles ahead and something triggered in his brain.

With one eye on the road and the other scanning his mom's map, Jake found what he was looking for: Springfield, Missouri, home of the Fantastic Caverns, "America's Only Ride Thru Cave." While the thought of *sitting* through an hour long tour inside of a big cave held absolutely no appeal to Jake, he did notice that there was also a Bass Pro Shop nearby. And while the great outdoors had never intrigued him much before, it suddenly seemed like a great place to take a break.

Thirty-seven minutes later, Jake pulled back onto the highway, his gas tank full and a burger in hand. A trout bobble-head now sat on his dashboard, eyeing Jake with a smile as it jiggled to the rhythm of the bumps in the road. The little guy had caught Jake's attention at the register and Jake hadn't been able to resist. With one,400 miles still to go, he could use the company.

Scarfing down his early lunch, Jake steered his truck westward and perused the AM dial in search of some good sports radio. As his mind escaped with the mindless chatter, his speedometer crept past eighty, taking advantage of his lapse of attention to bring him that much closer to home.

SITTING SQUISHED BETWEEN TWO BUSINESSMEN in her tiny airplane seat, Amy updated her Facebook status on her phone and smiled. Finals were done. She had kept her 4.0. And now she was on vacation. *Whew!* There were moments during this last quarter when she thought she'd never make it, but here she was.

Her thumbs scrolled down her phone to scan her friends' updates, and she mindlessly read their meaningless proclamations. It felt good to finally have nothing better to do than waste time on Facebook. And how nice it was to be able to do it from the new phone her dad and stepmom had given her as a congratulations-and-keep-in-touch gift at dinner three nights ago. Her old relic of a cellular device had sufficed for texting and calling, but this one had internet...and she could even Skype on it! She was looking forward to using that feature daily to keep up with her ever changing brother and sister during the next three months she was down in Oceanside.

The guy to her right struggled to take off his suit coat, and his elbow knocked into Amy's shoulder. "Sorry," he grunted, continuing to wrestle with the jacket.

Amy leaned over toward the man on her left as much as she dared and sighed. *The entire summer away from them!* She was going to miss them so much.

Her original plan had been to spend about a month of summer down in Oceanside, soaking up as much time as she could with Cari and Andrea and Melia. But she wanted to spend even more time with her dad and Olivia and Marissa and Ramon in Sunnyvale, her new second home. She had looked forward to taking the kids to the park and weekend trips to the coast and a day at the county fair and a whole list of other things she had missed from her own childhood.

Had it not been for the tragic death of her faithful minivan about a month ago, her plan would have worked perfectly. But when the car expired in a cloud of blue smoke, her mom had quickly bought her a non-refundable round trip ticket whose dates left Amy stranded in Oceanside the whole time. Amy knew the ticket was a huge financial stretch for her mom and she appreciated the effort, but she did not appreciate the obvious ploy to keep her away from her dad and his family.

Amy was actually surprised that her dad hadn't offered to pay the difference to change the flight. She assumed that had something to do with some agreement he must have made with her mom...and the reason Amy had received the phone instead.

Oh well, she huffed. It's not like Oceanside was a horrible place. She had tons of catching up to do with her friends down there, and looked forward to being able to spend time with them at a more leisurely pace.

Her thumb clicked on some new photos posted by Andrea of her high school graduation last week. True to form, she wore gaudy rainbow knee-high socks and yellow sneakers under her white gown, creating quite the fashion statement. *Where does she come up with these outfits?* Amy chuckled. She loved the confidence Andrea exuded. It would definitely be fun to spend more time with her.

After leaving a couple comments on Andrea's pictures, Amy clicked on a recent one she had taken with her brother and sister. They were so adorable! She smiled and even got a little teary as she stared at their beautiful joyful eyes and their chubby little fingers hugging her tight. Spontaneously, Amy clicked on the option to make this her profile picture...and then just as quickly, she wondered what Steven would think. Concerned about hurting his feelings, she started clicking back to her own photos in order to reinstate the picture of her hugging him hugging his guitar.

The phone signal was spotty, and as Amy waited for her photos to load, a bubbly flight attendant began the safety presentation three rows ahead. With more zeal than was warranted, the stewardess explained what to do in an emergency to a packed flight of passengers who couldn't care less. Although it was hard to believe that there was even one person on the plane who didn't already know how to put on a seat belt, Amy found herself empathizing with the ignored performer and intentionally smiled at her. Immediately, the stewardess reciprocated with a bright smile back.

Drawn in by the woman's appreciation, Amy suddenly changed her mind yet again. She turned off her phone without changing the picture of Ramon and Marissa and rested her head against the upright seat back to watch the rest of the lady's spiel. But while her eyes were attentive, her mind quickly traveled elsewhere.

Ah, Steven! She hadn't even talked to him since his parents arrived three days ago. His graduation was tomorrow, and Amy knew they must be busy helping him pack up to move back home to Virginia. But it hurt that they didn't want to see her, even for a quick lunch or something. She assumed they were still mad at her for refusing their son's proposal—in public. And really, she couldn't blame them.

She had relived that dreadful moment in the restaurant countless times. It was one of those awkward scenes sometimes seen in movies, but never supposed to happen in real life. Why hadn't she just said yes, smiled as everyone cheered, and talked to him about it later? That would have been so much easier. It wasn't like she didn't like him...or couldn't see herself married to him *someday*. She just wasn't quite ready to marry him *now* and move to New York *immediately* while he went to music school. But people have long engagements all the time. *Why didn't I just go along with it?*

Amy hadn't meant to reject him, but that is exactly how Steven took it—which was understandable, but so unfair. It had been a long road since then trying to convince him that she still cared about him, still wanted to be with him, still wanted to make things work. But it was as if her caution had triggered a switch in his head, and gone was the adoring charmer, replaced by a wary fretter. And unfortunately, every time things were starting to get comfortable again, something always happened—he would get jealous that she wanted to spend a day with her family or she would get upset when he'd start talking about how great living in New York together would be.

They'd had another one of those conversations the day before his parents came into town. Amy's dad and Olivia wanted to have Steven and his parents over for dinner one night. It seemed like a great opportunity for the two families to meet and get to know each other. But Steven insisted that the timing was just too rushed, too premature. Amy didn't know what else that could mean except that he wasn't sure he wanted to spend his life with her anymore. She just didn't get him. *Why couldn't he have had these second thoughts* before *proposing?*

And that was the last time they had talked.

Her roommate Renee had driven her to the airport before driving home to Oakland—giving Amy an earful of what Renee wished she could tell Steven—and here Amy was without so much as a goodbye from her boyfriend. Chills tingled down Amy's spine. This relationship was reminding her more and more of the end of her relationship with Jake. *Oh, Jake.* Amy cringed at the memory of taking a taxi alone to the airport after her horrible visit to Louisville over a year ago. How was her life repeating itself? *God, I tried to honor you in both relationships! Why are you letting this happen to me?*

As usual, no answer came. *Well, at least I won't have to sit alone at Steven's graduation,* Amy reasoned. *Or with Steven's parents.* Amy shuddered at the thought.

She had been so frustrated when her mom had first sent her the flight information. Besides taking Amy away from her dad and family, she also had thoughtlessly booked it for the day *before* Steven's graduation. What kind of girlfriend misses her boyfriend's big celebration? But in light of this past week, Amy had to concede that her mom's lack of thought had turned out to be a huge rescue.

As uncomfortable as her relationship with Steven had been the past two months, though, Amy still really cared about him. He was an amazing guy who loved God with all his heart and had loved her for better and worse. *And* he had a really great voice and was *so* cute! As Renee liked to say, he was an S-cubed kind of guy—spiritual, smart, *and* sexy. What more could she want?

Him to be excited about my dreams, the pesky voice in the back of her head replied.

Amy felt so selfish when she had thoughts like these, but she couldn't help it. She didn't want to move to New York. Sure, it was a glamorous city, and would definitely be fun to visit... maybe even live in *someday*. But not right now. She was loving her time at Stanford, eating up almost everything the professors could dish up in her counseling classes. Her poor roommate and the other girls on her floor had all been psychoanalyzed nearly to death. Fortunately, they seemed to appreciate the insights into their lives. And next semester, Amy started her counseling practicum at the nearby Palo Alto Child Services clinic. She couldn't wait. *How does Steven not understand this?*

Not to mention, Amy was restoring her relationship with her dad and his family—something that Steven had pushed her to do...in the beginning. Once it started encroaching on her time spent with him, he started to get less supportive. But he had been blessed with a strong family his entire life. *He should know how important this is to me!*

If Amy moved to New York to be with Steven, she would lose two of the best things in her life right now.

But if she didn't, would she lose him?

She'd been through the whole long-distance relationship thing with Jake. It didn't work. So here she was at the impasse. What did she value more: her education and future career and her new family, or the man she could spend the rest of her life with?

How many nights had she kept Renee up anguishing over this decision? How many hours had she rehashed those same conversations with her youth pastor's wife, Cari, on the phone? Amy valued both of their opinions, but neither of them were making it easy on her and just telling her what to do. She almost wished they would. While never saying so in so many words, though, they both seemed to be fans of her sticking to her path at Stanford and letting God do what was best with her relationship with Steven.

After thinking and praying through their lists of pros and cons for each scenario, that's the conclusion Amy came to, too. She'd finally shared that with Steven last week...and it didn't go so well. Steven was trying to be patient and understanding, but he felt like God had told him they were supposed to be together, and he just couldn't fathom why Amy wasn't listening.

Am I ignoring Your will, God? Amy prayed. But no matter how hard she tried to surrender, she just didn't feel a peace about it. *If you want me in New York, God, You're going to have to convince me of it. I'm trying, but I need You to change my heart.*

"Would you like something to drink miss?" the airline stewardess interjected into Amy's prayer.

Amy quickly glanced out the window and realized they were already in the air. How long had she been staring at the seat in front of her? "Could I get some cranberry juice?" she asked timidly.

The cheerful attendant poured the drink and handed her the plastic cup with two bags of peanuts and a wink. "Thanks for paying attention during the safety instructions."

If she only knew! Amy smiled to herself, glad that the woman didn't.

As the stewardess pushed her drink cart to the next row, Amy reclined in her seat and took a sip of her juice. She opened the first bag of peanuts and popped a salted nut into her mouth.

She'd been using that line of thought a lot lately, only not with something as trivial as a safety presentation. In the midst of all the turmoil with her relationship with Steven, she had been letting herself think about Jake more, and she knew it would crush Steven. *If* he *only knew!* This time Amy wasn't smiling.

She had been the one to first open the can of worms with Jake, when she sent him that simple text the night of his big game. She had merely wanted to congratulate him...and let him know she saw him. It had been an innocent impulse, and she assumed that would be the end of it. But Jake's response had thrown her for a loop. He was apologetic, humble, thoughtful, encouraging, everything she had ever wanted from him...and all on the heels of the disastrous proposal from Steven.

Completely unnerved, Amy had tried to make her reply sound as vague and distant as she could. On the surface, she was trying to be the dutiful girlfriend that Steven deserved. But on the inside, she was dying, hoping against hope that Jake wouldn't take the hint.

Again, Jake surpassed her expectations. Since that initial interchange, he had faithfully pursued her with the perfect amount of contact: not enough to be anything more than nonchalant but enough that it was obvious she was on his mind. And Amy had to confess, it thrilled her.

Through his messages, it became quite obvious that her exboyfriend was a dramatically different man than the one who left her stranded in Louisville last year. Jake asked her insightful questions about her life and shared exciting truths he'd been learning in the Bible from his mentorship with some guy named Buddy. He revealed some of his struggles with his roommate and the rest of the team and wrote about how he was managing to honor God in those areas. Most recently, she had been tickled to hear how he was going to work with kids at his church's Vacation Bible School. Bottom line, she liked this new Jake Taylor, and, as much as she tried to avoid it, she was really looking forward to seeing him this summer.

Too bad there's still Steven. Amy sighed. Why couldn't Jake have made this transformation earlier? *Men!*

As if to emphasize her complaint, the guy on Amy's left adjusted his laptop, his elbow jutting greedily into Amy's share of the limited space. His leg, too, sprawled thoughtlessly beyond its invisible boundary. The guy on the right, now jacketless, read the newspaper without regard for conserving space either, inconsiderately unfolding it to its full expanse. Cramped and uncomfortable, Amy twisted the fan above her head to allow more air to her seat. *Lord, seriously. Are you trying to tell me something?*

In the seat pocket in front of her was a teen magazine someone had left behind. Eager for a distraction from her discomfort, Amy pulled it out and leafed through the pages full of ads for fashion and perfume and makeup and cell phones, past an article about some new heartthrob, past ten tips for how to get a bikini body for summer, past the latest celebrity gossip. She had to laugh at the title: "Spring Break-ups and Make-ups." *Sounds like my life.* The very next page was a quiz that caught her attention. "Find Your True Love!" it touted, and Amy couldn't help giving it a second glance. Her eyes skimmed the questions and answer choices, obviously skeptical that a silly quiz could help her figure this out.

God, do I truly love either of these guys? Amy pondered. She refused to let her heart or mind decide but she knew the answer was one she couldn't avoid forever.

AMY PULLED HER MOM'S SEDAN into the familiar New Song Church parking lot the next morning, eager to see all her friends. She'd nearly fallen out of her seat at the kitchen table last night when her mom offered her the car. From the moment Sherry had picked her up from the airport, it was painfully obvious that she was trying to be on her best behavior, bending over backwards to win back some of her daughter's affection that had recently swung over to her father, Sherry's estranged ex-husband. Amy appreciated the effort, but wondered how long it would last. And she wished her mom could understand that it was possible for Amy to love *both* of her parents. There didn't need to be a competition for her love.

Ugh! Amy sighed and shook it off, knowing that a few seconds inside New Song would cure any remaining frustration. *How ironic*, Amy grinned, remembering back to her first visit here, almost two and a half years ago. Newly pregnant and weirded out by her boyfriend's recent changes, she hadn't been able to sit through the entire service without finding an excuse to get offended and walk out early. It was here in the New Song lobby that Jake had chased her down and they had first broken up. *Oh,*

Jake. She couldn't help smiling thinking about how hard he had tried to live for God back then—kind of like he seemed to be doing now. Her heartbeat accelerated inside of her chest, and she caught herself looking around, as if hoping he was here.

Get yourself together, girlfriend! You're here for God, not Jake! Amy lectured herself. Besides, she knew Jake wouldn't be here today. He was still in Louisville finishing up Vacation Bible School. Obviously, a week here without his distraction would be good for her...*and Steven!*

"Welcome to New Song!" A familiar voice rang out, bringing Amy back to the present. Mark-the-greeter stood in front of her with arms stretched wide ready to give her one of his infamous bear hugs. His bowling pin frame was just as stout as ever, his bald head just as shiny, and his gregarious smile just as welcoming.

"Mark." Amy grinned as she was embraced by the friendly old man. She wiped a tiny tear from the corner of her eye. If this was how she responded to the greeter then her mascara had no chance at holding up throughout the rest of the morning.

"Welcome home, Amy." Mark beamed. "I know there are a ton of people in there that can't wait to see you."

Amy nodded and kept walking through the lobby. She noticed that it had received a fresh coat of paint since her last visit over Christmas. It looked good. "Oof," Amy exhaled as a mighty force ran into her left leg, nearly knocking her over.

"Aaaaaaamy!"

She looked down to see an animated Caleb clutching onto her leg like a leech looking for love. Her favorite little kid in the whole world—besides Ramon and Marissa, of course—had grown at least two inches since she'd seen him over Christmas break. She wished he could meet her newfound siblings. They'd get along great.

"Caleb Vaughn!" Amy exclaimed, swooping him off the ground. "Just when I thought you couldn't get any bigger."

"I'm almost as big as Tornado."

"Who's Tornado?" Amy played along.

"He's the dog next-store. Don't tell mommy, but I feed him candy. He likes it."

Amy placed her finger over her mouth to indicate his secret was safe with her. "Speaking of your mommy...do you know where she is?"

Caleb pointed to the youth area. "I'm gonna go to the bathroom now. They got free mints. I already had like seven."

Amy set the feisty six-year-old back on the ground and watched him scurry off. That kid was like the California lottery. She had like a one-in-a-billion chance of ever guessing what would come out of his mouth next. Chris and Cari surely had quite an entertaining life at home with him. Amy turned the corner into the youth lobby looking for those two influential people in her life. Where would she be today without their constant love and wisdom and support?

"Welcome to Souled Out!" a warm but unfamiliar voice interrupted her thoughts.

Amy expected to see Andrea at her usual station behind the welcome table, but realized that now that she was graduated, this must be her replacement.

"I'm Tiffany. What school do you go to?" the perky underclassman asked sounding like Andrea herself. She held out a nametag and a pen.

"Oh, I'm not in high school anymore, but thanks for asking. I'm just looking for Chris or Cari.

"They're right around the corner. What is today, reunion Sunday?" Tiffany smiled back.

Amy looked at her quizzically as she walked through the big brown doors into the high school room. Suddenly, a voice she hadn't heard for over a year stopped her in her tracks.

"Yeah, I pulled in a little after two this morning. I just had to make it home for church!" Jake's voice enthusiastically rang out.

Amy couldn't see his face, but she already felt herself melting just being near him. As she stood glued to the floor, Cari glanced over and saw her.

"Amy!" Cari exclaimed, not so unlike her son, and ran over to give her mentee a hug. Her wide eyes and smirk told Amy she perfectly understood the little predicament Amy had just walked herself into. And her tight mothering embrace assured her everything would be okay. Cari hooked her arm in Amy's and walked her over to her husband and Jake.

"Welcome home, Amy," Chris greeted her with a warm hug, and then stepped aside to leave room for Jake, who up to this point had remained speechless.

Amy knew this moment would come at some point, but not within her first twenty-four hours of being home. *Seriously, God?* She inhaled sharply and fixed her eyes on Jake for the first time. He looked good. His hair was shorter, his shoulders broader, and Amy just couldn't stop her stomach from reeling with attraction toward this man she shared so much history with. *Steven, Steven, Steven,* Amy reminded herself.

Jake stepped forward tentatively, obviously feeling the tension, too. Sweat glistened on his forehead. His hug was brief. "It's really good to see you Amy," he spoke softly.

They'd hugged so many times before, but this one felt different. It reminded Amy of when they'd first started dating as high school freshmen—timid but eager, hesitant but fervent. It was kind of cute. "It's good to see you, too, Jake." Amy released from the hug quickly, repeating *Steven, Steven, Steven* in her mind the entire time. But even that didn't quell the ferocious beating of her heart.

Jake stepped away and a cloud of awkward silence descended.

"Well, I'd love to chat more, but I've got to get this youth service rolling," Chris finally interjected.

"I was just going to grab a seat in the sanctuary; you got anyone to sit with?" Jake offered innocently to Amy.

Amy frantically searched her brain, but no suitable excuses were surfacing. This was not how she envisioned her first Sunday back, and she definitely needed some space and time to sort through everything. Sitting with him would surely not be the worst thing ever, but she really didn't think she should. Besides the very sufficient fact that she had a boyfriend who wouldn't appreciate her getting all gooey over Jake, she also had a list of hurts that Jake needed to rectify before he even deserved getting all "gooey" over.

"You know, Jake, Amy's girls were really looking forward to sitting with her in here now that they're in high school. Can she get a rain check?" Cari came to her rescue.

Amy didn't dare lift her eyes from the floor, but a wave of gratitude for her wing woman swept over her.

"Oh, that's cool. I wouldn't mind sitting in on the youth service..." Jake's sentence trailed off.

Amy glanced up just in time to see some sort of unspoken conversation ending between Chris and Jake.

"...some other Sunday." Jake abruptly finished. "It's really good to see you all." He waved, staring only at Amy, and then turned to walk out the door.

"We're having the college group over for a "Welcome the New Freshmen" barbecue tonight. You guys should come," Cari called out after him.

Amy shot her a quick glance. What was she doing? Cari was supposed to be *saving* her from situations like this! Cari smiled back at her innocently.

Jake, of course, jumped at the offer. "You know I wouldn't miss it! I've been looking forward to kicking the soccer ball around the front yard with Caleb again."

"Actually, he's into martial arts now. But I'm sure he'll love showing you some of his new kung fu moves," Chris encouraged.

All eyes now turned to Amy. Obviously, she would *love* to spend the evening at the Vaughn's. But spending it with Jake was a whole other issue. This was her first day back. Didn't she deserve at least a little more time before delving into the tough stuff? As her brain again searched for the right response, a red-haired bundle of joy ran into the youth room.

"Amyyyyyyyyyy!" Melia's voice squealed as she bounded over to Amy.

"Melia!" Amy ran the final few steps over to her friend and swung her around in a tight hug. As she set Melia down, out of the corner of her eye she saw Jake smiling as he walked out of the youth room toward the sanctuary.

Melia started telling Amy about how great her eighth grade graduation dance had been, and then started babbling about how great the new soft-serve yogurt place was down the street, and how great the Bible passage was that she read yesterday morning, and oh, she couldn't wait for Amy to come hang out with her friends at the mall. Amy just smiled, trying to keep up.

The confident, happy, cute little almost-high-school-freshman standing before her was hardly recognizable from the scared, sarcastic, gangly little girl Amy had first befriended a year and a half ago. Amy had helped Melia finally get rescued from her abusive home just a few months ago, and now she was living with the Vaughns as their foster child. No longer the victim of violence and neglect, she was blossoming into an amazing young woman. They talked on the phone at least once a week, but Amy hadn't seen her since Christmas and she was blown away by Melia's progress.

Amy remembered back to that fateful middle school scavenger hunt for which she had reluctantly agreed to be a driver. Little had Amy known what she was getting herself into. Melia had made Amy's night miserable with her prying questions and tactless remarks. But God wouldn't let Amy get away, and Melia had wormed her way into Amy's heart. Melia became the little sister Amy had always dreamed of, and was the final inspiration to push Amy to become a child psychology major. Taking Melia under her wing had taken Amy on a journey of self-discovery, forcing her to deal with her struggle of giving up her own daughter for adoption and her repressed memories of her own childhood abuse. *Where would I be without this girl?* Amy grinned.

A band jumped on the youth stage and began to play. "Oh crap! I gotta go. I'm in the band," Melia exclaimed.

Cari exchanged a momentary glance with her new "daughter."

"I mean crap*ola.*" The ninth grader smiled as she skipped to the front of the room.

Amy waited at least three seconds before bursting out in laughter. "Wow! Between her and Caleb, you must never have a quiet moment! But she looks likes she's doing *so* well. Thank you so much for taking her in, Cari."

"You know we wouldn't have it any other way. It is so cool to see what a little love and nurturing can do. We are so proud of her."

Chris came over again after talking to a group of boys and put his arm around his wife's shoulders. "So, Amy. Are you coming over tonight or not?"

"You guys are such punks!" Amy looked at both Chris and Cari, shaking her head. "Are you trying to turn my life into a soap opera?"

"I'm not much of a fan of opera," Chris shrugged, "so I have no idea what you're talking about."

"Riiiight. But I gotta say, nice job giving Jake that look, whatever that was. I thought only girls knew how to converse with their eyes. Very impressive."

"Hey, just trying to keep my youth room a drama-free zone." Chris winked and sidestepped to intercept a group of students just walking in. "For what it's worth, though, Jake has changed... a lot. It might not hurt to give him a chance to show you," he called back over his shoulder.

Cari pulled Amy into a side hug. "He has a point, you know. Jake *is* a new man. And if his biceps are any indication—"

Chris cleared his throat over his shoulder. "Babe! Your ruggedly tough husband is standing right here." The students he was talking with laughed and headed to their seats. "What? Don't you have your tickets...to the gun show?" He flexed and tried to look as tough as he could.

"Sorry, honey." Cari grabbed Chris's arm. "You know I love your air-softs."

Chris pecked his wife on the forehead and turned to greet a lone kid standing in the back of the room. Cari hooked her arm in Amy's and pulled her toward two empty seats next to Melia and the rest of the girls from Amy's small group last year. "You know we love both of you, Ames. Just come have dinner with us. It can't hurt just to *talk* to him."

Amy smiled and patted Cari's arm. It was good to be home.

Midway through the third song, Jake grabbed a seat near the back of the auditorium. Suddenly, two hands covered his eyes from behind.

"Guess who?" Andrea's familiar voice cheerfully challenged.

"Wonder Woman!" Jake joked. He turned around to see maybe the friendliest person he knew on the planet.

"Pichew, pichew!" Andrea flaunted her trademark bullet-blocking wristbands and gave Jake a high-five. She hadn't changed a bit. Jake had all but neglected their friendship since he'd left for college, but true to form, Andrea didn't seem to hold any bitter feelings.

"I was hoping I'd see you this morning," Jake confessed with a smile. "Do you have a seat yet?"

"Right next to you, sucka." Andrea moved around to sit next to him. Immediately she was clapping and singing along with the worship band.

Jake joined in the clapping, but didn't know the song. It had been a long time since he'd heard anything other than hymns at church. It was good to be home.

As the worship leader transitioned into the next song, Andrea leaned over and whispered in Jake's ear. "Are you coming to Chris and Cari's tonight?"

Jake nodded.

"Awesome. We're going to grapple in a rousing Catch Phrase competition. Wouldn't want you to miss it," she whispered back without even looking at him as she broke out into singing again.

Jake smiled. Of course he hoped Amy would accept Cari's invitation, but even if she shied away, it would still be good to catch up with some of his old friends. He'd spoken to Billy only briefly this morning, and it would be fun to hear more about how their high school basketball team had fared since Jake had left. Danny Rivers, Pastor Mark's son who had given Jake and Jonny so many problems in high school, would be there. He was actually doing great now, really living for God and, ironically, going to Bible school.

Jake thought back to their fateful encounter in the principal's office after Danny had framed Jonny for calling in a bomb threat. It was crazy how disastrously that one incident could have ended and yet God had used it for so much good. That was what it had taken to finally get through to Danny, and it had also been such a transforming moment for both Jonny and Jake. *Oh, Jonny.* Jake chuckled.

After Roger's tragic suicide, Jonny had been Jake's second chance, his opportunity to redeem the friendship he'd wasted with Roger. Soon after Jake had moved to Louisville, Jonny's mom had been stationed at the military base in Okinawa, Japan, and Jonny had been forced to leave all his new friends to move with her. But now they were back at Camp Pendleton and Jake looked forward to reconnecting with the funny guy. Apparently, he had come to the early service this morning and, since no one expected Jake's surprise visit today, he had gone home before Jake's arrival. He would surely be there tonight, though, and Jake couldn't wait to see his quirky friend again.

Jake's mind drifted back to his present surroundings and he discovered that Pastor Mark was well into his sermon. Jake tried to catch up, but immediately all the exhaustion from his long drive and little sleep crept up on him. No matter how hard he tried, he just couldn't focus on Pastor Rivers' message. The only thing that kept his mind stimulated enough to avoid sinking into the depths of dreamland was thinking about Amy. *I'm sorry, God,* Jake confessed. But since thinking about her was the only thing working, he let his mind wander freely.

He couldn't get their brief conversation out of his head. *It's good to see you, too, Jake.* Did she really mean it? She sounded sincere enough. And it was infinitely better than a slap in the face. But besides those few precious words, she had seemed pretty distant, and definitely hadn't jumped at the chance to talk to him. What was it going to take to get her to at least give him a chance?

The next thing Jake knew, Andrea was nudging him in the ribs as people stood for the closing song. Apparently, not even thinking about Amy was sufficient to overcome his lack of sleep. And now he felt a headache coming on. *Maybe this wasn't such a good idea*, he grimaced.

THE TANTALIZING AROMA OF BARBECUED HOTDOGS

wafted through the air and the din of exuberant conversation filled in the gaps as Jake walked up the driveway of the Vaughn home. Their house wasn't large, but what it was lacking in size it made up for in love. Before Jake had moved off to Louisville, he had been over here all the time.

Jake couldn't help but remember one of his first times walking up this driveway—the nervous walk of shame to tell Chris that Amy was pregnant. At the time, Jake had dreaded a guilt-stained lecture that would kick him out of the youth group. Instead he was met with grace and support. Jake felt similar butterflies today, not because he had to talk *about* Amy, but rather, *to* her.

After the church service, Jake had pleaded with Andrea for advice on Amy. She had encouraged him to simply be casually friendly. He had plenty of time this summer to get down to the nitty gritty and try to resolve things with Amy—and maybe even woo her back. But for today, she advised, less would be more. Jake knew Andrea was right, but he still couldn't stop hoping that he'd get at least a brief moment to talk alone with Amy. Judging by the activity all around, however, he quickly realized that wouldn't be likely.

"Hiiiiya!" Caleb shouted, springing out the front door in his baggy white karate gi and swinging his right leg up and around. He ran over to Jake and karate-chopped his thigh.

"Hey little man!" Jake laughed and turned his attention to the young Karate Kid attacking him. "Watch out! Ninjas!" he yelled, pointing at something beyond Caleb. With six-year-old gullibility, Caleb spun around, giving Jake the opportunity to pick him up, throw him over his shoulder, and start twirling in circles.

"Ahhhhhhh!" Caleb giggled, loving the ride.

"I don't know anything about Karate, Mr. Samurai, but growing up my hero was Jake the Snake Roberts and I'm about to put you, little man, in the sleeper hold."

"Nooooooo!" Caleb squealed, pleading with laughter, "I'm not tired. I don't want to go to sleep."

When Jake could no longer stand straight, he collapsed dizzily to the grass, holding Caleb tightly on top of him.

"You tricked me!" Caleb laughed, trying to wrestle out of Jake's strong grip. A burp escaped his little mouth, and he looked down at Jake peculiarly. "I don't feel so—"

Suddenly, orange-ish, brownish chunky liquid spewed out of Caleb's mouth like a fire hose, drenching Jake's face, hair, and shirt. Without thinking, Jake pushed Caleb off of him and rolled out of the vomit's reach. A four letter word from his wayward days slipped out.

Caleb whispered profoundly, "You said sh—"

Jake clapped his hand over the little boy's mouth before he could finish, his eyes bulging at the significance of what he'd just allowed the pastor's son to hear. "I know, Caleb. I did bad. I'm really sorry; it just kind of slipped out," Jake frantically whispered back, hoping that this part of the conversation could remain just between them."

Caleb laughed and patted Jake on the head. "You have my throw up all over your face."

Covered with regurgitated orange soda and brownies—at least that was his best guess at what the gooey mess that was covering him used to be—Jake was pretty sure that he'd never felt so disgusting in his life. But his little friend's glee was contagious and Jake chuckled with him. "Guess I shouldn't have spun you around so much."

Caleb tried to help Jake to his feet, and Jake looked around, hoping no one had witnessed this little debacle. As if that were possible. Already, a small crowd of students had gathered at the front window, watching the spectacle from a safe distance.

"Caleb?" Cari's voice echoed from inside. Apparently she had heard the news.

"I barfed on Jake," Caleb announced triumphantly when his mom ran out the front door.

"Oh my goodness, Jake, I'm so sorry," Cari gushed, her hands flying to her face in disbelief. "Let me get you a towel." She quickly ran back inside.

By now the secret was out and bemused spectators trickled out of the house, mostly students Jake didn't know. Jake didn't see Amy, and could only hope she wasn't there. *That's all I need!* he groaned, imagining what he must look like. He started unbuttoning his outer shirt, eager to free himself from at least some of the gunk.

"What did you do to my kid, Taylor?" Chris called out as he strolled down the sidewalk, can of soda in hand.

"He started it." Jake smiled.

"He's only six, man!"

"I won, daddy. I won!" Proudly, Caleb started showing off some of his karate moves to anyone who would watch.

"Way to go, champ!" Chris grinned, turning on the hose and spraying down the victor. Caleb laughed gleefully and started running around in circles, getting soaked.

Cari raced out of her house with two towels and frowned at her husband. "Don't encourage him!" she protested, handing Jake one of the towels with a smile. "Welcome back, Jake. Should've warned you that Caleb has been chowing down on Cheetos and root beer ever since he got home from church." She turned to her son. "Caleb, honey, I just washed your karate outfit yesterday.

Yuck! Go change out of it and put it on the washer, please."

Caleb groaned. "Aw, mom!" He continued romping around in the water.

Cari glared at Chris, who immediately released the hose trigger. But this didn't deter Caleb, who still had plenty of puddles to splash around in on the sidewalk, now muddy with run-off. Chris rolled up the hose and prodded his son inside. The remaining curious observers followed them in, and Jake and Cari were now alone.

"Sorry, Cari. It's my bad," Jake apologized, wondering how many other messes he could instigate this afternoon.

"Well, I'll forgive you if you head upstairs and wash all my son's nastiness off of you." She grinned. "Chris will get out a shirt and shorts for you to change into."

"Oh, I can just hose off like Caleb." Jake finished wiping all the puke off his face.

Cari leaned in. "No offense, but you're not walking around my living room—and you're certainly not sitting on my furniture!—smelling like that."

Jake acquiesced with a smile and followed her inside where Caleb was busy flexing for his adoring fans. A swarm of high school girls encircled him, giving him all the attention he could ever desire. Jake couldn't help scanning the cluster for Amy.

"I think she's in Melia's room," Cari whispered.

"Who?"

Cari smiled and winked. "Get yourself cleaned up first, Romeo. You're still in first impression mode. Caleb," she swatted her son playfully on the behind. "Get your heiny out of that uniform now or no karate for a week." Her son didn't need any more motivation than that. He sped up the stairs and wore nothing but his superman undies by the time he reached the top.

Jake waited for the privacy of the bathroom before following Caleb's example, but as soon as that door was locked behind him, he, too, swiftly enjoyed the freedom of getting out of his sticky, stinky clothes. The soap and hot water of the shower felt even better, washing away any stubborn remnants of Caleb's retribution. As Jake stood under the cleansing cascade, his thoughts again turned to Amy. He just *had* to find a way to talk to her.

Once clean and dry, Jake turned to the shorts and T-shirt Chris had left him on the counter. "Got your tickets to the gun show?" the T-shirt flaunted with arrows pointing to each arm. The boasting always seemed comical on Chris' lean arms, but as Jake tried to squeeze into the snug cotton, he wasn't sure he could pull it off without seeming downright conceited. Filling out the shirt to its maximum capacity—and then some—Jake realized that even breathing might push the taut fabric past breaking point. *What was Chris thinking?* Jake had to wonder. Was this his idea of a funny joke, or had he simply innocently grabbed from the top of the pile? Standing there looking at himself in the bathroom mirror, Jake weighed his limited options. *Gun show or vomit?* He stuck with the gun show.

Shrouded with new insecurity, Jake forced himself downstairs. *Maybe this wasn't such a good idea,* he cringed as he neared the mingling throngs. Beckoning with open arms, the front door presented itself as his most inviting option, and Jake slipped towards it, eyes down, determined to escape without any further disturbance. He had all summer to catch up with his old friends. And Amy? Well...he'd figure something out.

"Shirt shrink a little?" the voice he had previously been longing to talk to interrupted his self-conscious brooding.

Jake looked up and there stood the woman of his dreams a mere four steps away—in the opposite direction of the door. "Ahhh, I think Chris and I might not wear the same size anymore," Jake quipped, trying to keep cool.

"I can tell," Amy smirked then studied him silently. "You handled being barfed on pretty well, though," she offered. "And I think orange just might be your color."

"Yeah? I was thinking about dying my hair anyway," Jake joked back. "It's all part of the new and improved Jake Taylor," he added, immediately wishing he could take it back and replace it with something that sounded a little less arrogant.

"Well, I guess we'll see about that," Amy retorted without flinching, although not altogether unkindly.

"I guess so," he smiled back weakly. Awkward silence ensued. *This is your chance, man! Say something,* he prompted himself, but nothing came out. "Uh..." he finally croaked out. "So how's your mom?" *Lame, lame, lame!*

"Not bad, actually," Amy smiled, for some reason choosing this moment to finally engage Jake in consequential conversation. *Maybe she enjoys seeing me so vulnerable!* Jake presumed, forgetting to track with her ongoing chatter. "She's a little jealous of my dad, though—"

"Your dad? Wha—?" In all Jake's years of knowing Amy, she'd never talked about him willingly.

"Yeah, crazy, huh? Thanks to Steven's"—Amy shifted her weight subtly—"prodding, I tracked him down. He has a family near Stanford, and they are *so* amazing, and we've totally reconnected. We have dinner together at least once a week, and, Jake, I have a brother and a sister!"

If the rapid acceleration of her words was any indication, she was ecstatic about this new development in her life, and Jake couldn't help but celebrate with her. "Wow, Amy, that's so great. I'm so happy for you." And then, calmed momentarily by the joy in her voice, he went for it. "I'd love to hear more about them sometime. Maybe later this week we could..." His words trailed off as Amy's attention became riveted behind him and her face drained of color. Jake slowly turned around...and there was Guitar Boy standing in the open doorway with a generous bouquet of lush red roses.

"Steven?" Amy blurted, staring shocked over Jake's shoulder.

So Guitar Boy had a name. *Steven, huh?* Jake practically snarled as he sized up his competition—about six feet tall, carefully trimmed goatee, perfectly groomed hair. He dressed stylishly, and, while Jake would by no means consider himself to be an expert on such matters, he seemed to be a fairly attractive man. In person, he looked a little older, and Jake suddenly found himself wondering who this guy was and how Amy had met him. Instinctively, Jake didn't like him.

"Wow! What are you doing here?" Amy nearly whispered as she ran over to her boyfriend.

Steven enveloped her in a hug and kissed her warmly, unmindful of his audience. "Here, these are for you." He stepped back and handed Amy his extravagant display of affection. *Who else would they be for, moron!* Jake criticized, finding it difficult to be charitable to this suave intruder. "I stopped by your house to surprise you and your mom said you were here."

"Well, yeah, yeah, here I am," Amy stumbled for words, apparently stuck in the puddle of tension thicker than the Oceanside morning marine layer. "You surprised me all right!" She smiled.

At this point, Chris and Cari, always attentive to any newcomer in their home, joined the congregation in the entryway. Andrea followed close behind.

"Uh, here, let me introduce you to some friends." Amy took his hand and pulled him into the house. "This is Cari and Chris, my mentor and youth pastor."

"I've heard so much about you guys," Steven affirmed. "It's so great to finally meet you."

"Welcome to O-side!" Chris shook his hand affably and patted him on the back.

"Any friend of Amy's is a friend of ours," Cari smiled warmly and gave him a hearty hug.

Whose side are they on? Jake complained silently.

Amy conveniently skipped over Jake to Andrea who was standing right next to him. "You remember Andrea, my running buddy?"

"Of course." Steven nodded. "Congratulations on your graduation." His eyes glanced back to Jake momentarily and he looked troubled.

"You, too!" Andrea grinned, regaining his attention. She gave him a high five and chucked him on the shoulder.

A sudden impulse of bravado shot through Jake, and, without thinking, he took the plunge. "Hi Steven, I'm Jake." He offered his hand cordially. "I'm Amy's—"

"I know who you are," Steven cut him off, allowing Jake's hand to hang unwelcomed in the middle.

While not completely unreasonable, Steven's icy response nevertheless squelched the struggling embers of conversation, and everyone just stood there looking at each other awkwardly. Caleb, innately aware that the situation was ripe to give him complete control of the floor, was ready to jump into action.

"Mom." The adorable six-year-old walked into the center of the tight circle and tugged on his mom's shorts. "Did you know that Jake said the sh— word?"

Successful at breaking the original tension, Caleb's interruption only turned up the heat on Jake. Eyes bugged out as stifled chuckles shuffled around the group of six.

"Jake?" Chris's voice sounded disappointed, but his eyes glimmered mirthfully.

"Um, sorry," Jake offered nervously, wishing he could shrink into a hole and never come out. Sweat poured out of his pores and blood thundered in his ears. Amy looked amused but the haughty smirk on Steven's face was more than Jake could bear. *Seriously, God?* How could today get any worse? "Seriously, Chris, Cari. I'm so sorry. It just sort of slipped out when he threw up on me. I feel so—"

Cari touched Jake's shoulder. "Jake, it's okay. Caleb, honey, what do we say when we hear words that aren't nice?"

"It makes Jesus sad," Caleb answered, his face sincere.

"But what makes Jesus happy?" Cari prodded.

"Nice words."

"That's right, buddy," Chris joined in. "So can you help Jake say some nice words?"

Caleb ran over to Jake and looked up. Jake squatted down to his level. "Caleb, I'm sorry for saying that word."

"You should have said, 'uh oh,'" Caleb suggested.

"That's what I meant to say!" Jake smiled.

"I know. Jesus forgives you." Caleb patted his arm. "And I do, too."

"Thanks, man." Jake hugged his little friend and stood.

Caleb scampered off toward the table with all the food on it. "Can I have some more Cheetos, mom?" he called back, off to his next adventure.

"I think it's time for something a little more healthy, buddy," Cari answered, following close behind but not before giving Jake an encouraging pat on the back.

"Okay then," Andrea jumped in. "Want me to grab you a drink, Steven?"

"Uh, yeah, sure. I'll take a Coke," he responded, still staring at Jake.

"Actually, I'd love to put these in your car first." Amy pulled him away, obviously with more than just flowers on her mind.

"Great meeting you, Steven," Chris offered. "Stop by the grill out back and I'll make sure you get a hot burger."

After the two of them walked back out, Andrea took her cue. "Jake, I know this totally sucks for you right now, but give it a chance to play out. If God wants it to happen, it will." With that, she squeezed his arm and left Jake alone to talk to Chris.

"Rough timing, huh?" Chris sympathized. Jake only nodded and stuffed his hands in his pockets. "It's a hard call when the girl you want isn't available."

"I thought God was giving me a second chance. This jerk had all year to work his magic. Why'd he have to come interrupting my game?"

"Maybe this isn't your game to play."

"You're saying I should just move on? You know how much I care about Amy."

"If you truly care, then you'll give her space to make her choice."

"That just sounds like giving up. Whatever happened to working for what's worth it?"

"Absolutely! Do everything in your power to help her see she'd be foolish to pick anyone but you. But do it from a respectful distance as long as Steven's in the picture. No one likes a thief."

An unfamiliar student rushed up. "Chris, we're out of burgers. Do you have any more?"

"Want to join me at the barby?" Chris offered.

"No thanks. I'm still a little queasy," Jake declined.

"We're all pulling for you, Jake."

Chris headed to the back yard and Jake was alone again. He sat on the steps, his head reeling from the last fifteen minutes. He'd love to just go home and sleep it off and maybe wake up tomorrow with all of it just a bad dream. Unfortunately, there at the foot of the driveway, Amy sat next to Steven on the hood of his car. There was no path Jake could take to his own truck that didn't go right past them. Stuck in a situation way beyond his comfort zone, Jake sat watching Amy and prayed.

"Does your ex need me to buy him a new wardrobe?" Steven quipped cynically. "What's he trying to do?"

"You don't even understand, Steven." Amy felt annoyed by the tone of her boyfriend's voice, and she definitely didn't know what to think about his sudden appearance. Sure it was romantic and sweet and should have just swept her off her feet. But no matter how chivalrous his arrival was, it didn't erase the previous week of silence. "What are you doing here?"

"I know I've kind of been a jerk this past week, but—"

"Kind of?" Amy interjected.

"I know, I know, I just had a lot on my mind.

"So that makes it okay for you to totally ignore me, to avoid me, to not even say goodbye?"

"That's why I'm here now, Amy. I know I messed up. But I want to make it right."

He looked so sincere, so desperate. Amy sighed and looked into his eyes. "Steven, I really care about you. And I want to make this work. But what are we going to do about our future? I just can't commit to going to New York with you. It would kill me to leave everything behind. But if I don't come with you, will our relationship survive?"

Steven gazed back at her for a moment before speaking. "The entire graduation ceremony today, that's all I could think about. I didn't hear a word of the commencement address. I'm surprised I even made it across the stage to receive my diploma. I don't remember any of it. All I could think about was you...was us." He grabbed Amy's hand and held it tightly. "I still don't love the thought of being so far from you for the next two years." Steven smiled. "But I realized that if that's what it takes to be with you for the rest of my life...it's worth it. Amy, I'm so sorry for pressuring you to leave Stanford and your family. I love you, and I'm willing to make the sacrifice to keep us together."

All Amy could do was laugh under her breath. Steven looked concerned. "It's not you, Steven," she reassured him, patting his hand gently. "I just never expected today to go anything like the way it's gone so far."

"So...?"

"So...You're sure you're okay with me staying at Stanford?" Amy clarified.

Steven nodded.

"Then what else can I say? Let's see how this goes, right?"

Steven averted his eyes. "I guess I was expecting a little more enthusiasm."

"I'm sorry, Steven. This is all just such a surprise. When I boarded that plane yesterday, I wasn't sure if I'd ever see you again. And now you're here, in the flesh, sitting right next to me. It all just seems so surreal."

"Well let me see if this feels more real." Steven grinned and enveloped her in a tender embrace. He dipped his head in to kiss her and Amy tried to melt into his arms. But all she could think about was if a certain someone might be watching from inside the Vaughn house.

In the past she would have relished the thought of Jake jealously watching her be passionately embraced by another—very worthy—man. But today, that thought made her cringe. *What's wrong with me?* She chided herself. Here was a guy who was everything she could ever want, who had just rushed down here to make things right with her, who was willing to sacrifice his plans so she could accomplish hers. *That's all I ever wanted, right?* Yet there was something in her gut that just didn't feel quite right.

"So are your parents down here, too?" Amy finally pulled away and tried to change the subject.

"Nah." Steven smiled. "The moment the ceremony was over, I had them drive me to the airport. They'll spend the night up there and leave for home with the U-Haul in the morning."

"They must think I'm a real piece of work."

Steven didn't answer right away. "Give them time, Amy. They just want me to be happy."

That definitely wasn't the answer Amy was hoping for, but what else could she do? "So how long are you here for?"

"I don't have to be back for a week. That is if you'll put up with me for that long."

"Are you kidding me? Of course." Amy smiled.

"I've never been to San Diego before. You'll have to show me all around."

"Well...Let's start with the infamous Vaughn house." Amy stood up and pulled Steven with her toward their front door.

Steven held her back and wrapped his arm around her shoulders. "I've just gotta ask you one thing. When I walked in the door just now, the first thing I saw was you and Jake talking. You need to be honest with me Amy. What's going on there?"

Amy's heart started fluttering and she suddenly felt warm. How could she answer that question when she wasn't even totally sure herself? She tried to discreetly wipe the mounting perspiration from her hands onto the back of her skirt as she fought for an honest but delicate way to answer the question. "Nothing," she finally shrugged nonchalantly.

"He sure looked like he wanted more than nothing."

"Well, just because he wants something doesn't mean he's going to get it," Amy retorted, trying to stifle some annoyance.

Steven turned her to look him face to face. He studied her eyes for a moment and then planted another kiss on her lips. "Good." He smiled. "I just wanted to make sure."

He threw his arm around her again and they strolled back up to the house the way they always walked around campus at Stanford. Today, however, Amy just couldn't enjoy the warmth of his touch. Her stomach felt about as settled as a nest of hornets and her mind was a whirl of unintelligible thought. She suddenly really wanted to just go home.

Fighting her inclination to run, Amy led Steven inside, in search of friends who could help contribute to coherent conversation. She saw Cari and Melia out in the back yard and headed in their direction. As they crossed through the living room, Amy also searched for Jake, but he was nowhere to be found.

Jake saw the passionate kiss on the hood of Steven's car and felt like a balloon that had been pricked with a tiny pin. Helplessly watching Amy's intimate conversation with this intruder, Jake deflated into nothingness with every passing second. Over the past few months, he'd envisioned this first face-to-face encounter with Amy in so many wonderful ways. None of them ever ended like this. Jake was in no way ready to concede defeat, but he knew when it was time to take a rest. When Amy and Steven finally stood up and moved toward the house, Jake accepted his opportunity to disappear and regroup. He slipped into the back yard and exited undetected through the side gate. He had known that winning Amy's heart back was going to be tough, but this was turning into a whole new ball game.

JAKE STEPPED INTO HIS HOUSE and breathed in deeply. He was home—for the first time in a year and half, not counting his few brief hours of sleep after rolling into town around two this morning. *What do I do now?* Jake mused, absorbing the vast openness all around him. The Taylor home had always seemed big and somewhat empty to Jake growing up, but now the vacant space felt downright oppressive. Walking into the unoccupied living room, Jake realized how lonely his mom must have felt there. *What kind of a son waits a year and a half before coming home to visit his single mom?* he scolded himself. He made a mental note to apologize and make the most of his time home this summer—and never stay away that long again.

He had seen his mom for only a minute this morning when she ran into his room around eight and swallowed him in tears and hugs. Since she hadn't expected him home so early, she was taken quite by surprise when she saw his truck parked in the driveway. After her emotional greeting, though, she had to rush off to serve at church, and Jake had only seen her across the New Song lobby since then. Jake wondered when she'd be back home again. He was exhausted, but too agitated to sleep, and her company would be soothing.

Jake quickly changed out of Chris's ill-fitting clothes and rummaged through one of his duffle bags to find something more comfortable. *Could things have gone any worse today?* he scowled as he dropped the humiliating gun show shirt into his hamper along with his even more degrading vomit-laden one. What chance did he really stand with Amy? As much as Jake hated to admit it, Steven seemed like a really quality guy. Jake wracked his brain to think of a time he had done anything half as romantic as chasing Amy hundreds of miles because he just couldn't stand to be apart from her. This guy was shaping up to be a pretty formidable opponent.

Which means I need to bring my A-game! Jake tried to lift his spirits. He flopped down on his bed and pulled this morning's church program out of his back pocket. He flipped one of the enclosed flyers over to the blank back side, grabbed a pen, and started to brainstorm.

How to convince Amy I'm ~~worth it~~
better than Steven:

★

Jake's pen hovered over the paper, ready to plunge into action, but his mind remained devoid of any brilliance, so the pen remained motionless. Jake stared at the empty page, willing it to sprout to life. Minutes passed, but still no inspiration came.

"Ugh!" Jake finally erupted and flung his pen against the wall. He rolled over onto his back and dialed Buddy's number. He just needed someone to talk to, and Buddy often surprised him with his keen insights into Jake's personal matters. But just his luck, no one was home. *It figures!* Jake complained, although a nagging thought in the back of his mind questioned where Buddy could be. His wife rarely left home these days due to some recent health complications, and Buddy was usually by her side.

With nothing to do, Jake wandered aimlessly through his house. He looked at some of the family pictures randomly resting on various shelves and walls, finding it weird to see his father staring back at him. Glen hadn't lived in the house for over two years, but apparently Pam hadn't purged him entirely from her life yet. *Maybe that's a good sign,* Jake hoped.

Suddenly struck with a sense of hunger, Jake realized he hadn't eaten anything since a quick breakfast. He promptly headed to the kitchen and searched the cabinets—finding nothing but nutritious foods. That explained why his mom looked so much thinner and healthier; she didn't eat anything that tasted good. After scavenging around, Jake finally found an unopened jar of peanut butter in the back of the pantry. He sliced up an apple and slathered on the peanut butter, creating the tastiest snack he could muster.

Taking his wholesome morsel into the living room, he collapsed on the couch and flipped on the television to watch a second round playoff game between the Celtics and Hawks. But even watching basketball held no joy for Jake. What was wrong with him? His walk with God was going great, and he'd never felt more alive. He was living out his dream of playing basketball for the Louisville Cardinals, and if he kept performing like he had at the end of this season, he might even have a chance at the NBA. His life was going great. Just because he didn't have Amy didn't mean he had to be miserable. There were plenty of fish in the sea, right? Why did he have to have his heart set on the one that he couldn't have?

The sound of the solid oak door creaking open was a welcome relief to his glum thoughts. Pam Taylor walked briskly into the living room carrying a box full of papers. She dropped them on a nearby chair and plopped on the couch next to Jake.

"Jake! I'm so glad you're home. I'm sorry I've been gone all day. I was dying to get back to see you," Pam gushed, giving her son a hug. "Who's playing?"

Jake knew that his mom could care less about any basketball game unless her son was playing. "The Dodgers," he answered with a straight face to see if his mom's professional sports IQ had gone up at all while he was gone.

She looked at him knowingly and patted him on the knee. "Nice try, Jake, but even I know it's not football season yet."

Jake wanted to laugh out loud but he held his tongue. "Celtics and Hawks. So how was your meeting?"

Pam let out a huge sigh. "The two- and three-year-olds are a piece of cake; it's the adult leaders who keep flaking on me at the last minute that are driving me crazy." She had started by simply helping out in the Two's and Threes's classroom at the church every other weekend, but a couple of months ago she was asked to be the preschool coordinator in charge of all the volunteers in that department. Her new role came with a small paycheck each month—and a host of new responsibilities. She had worked tirelessly for Glen's real estate agency for years, but Jake was proud of her for finding a new passion of her own.

Looking at her son's makeshift meal, she turned inquisitively to Jake. "I thought you were going to the Vaughn's for dinner?"

"Yeah..." Jake pressed mute on the television and shrugged. "Let's just say a few things happened that made me lose my appetite."

"Uh oh. Was Amy there?"

"Yeah." Jake chuckled sardonically. "And her boyfriend."

"Oh, honey, I'm sorry." Pam rubbed her son's arm.

"And of course, he just had to show up right after Caleb Vaughn barfed all over me and I changed into some of Chris's clothes which did not fit me at all. It was so humiliating! Seriously mom, it feels like God just keeps on punishing me over and over again."

Pam leaned over and planted a kiss on Jake's forehead. "I don't think these are punishments, honey. Sometimes these things just take some time. But if—"

"If it's God's will that we get back together then everything will just turn out fine in the end," Jake completed her sentence without conviction.

Pam stole a slice of Jake's apple and shook her head. "Well, yes, that's true, but I was going to say if she's really worth it to you, you need to do everything in your power to show her that she'd be an idiot to choose anyone but you—especially some preppy, guitar-playing Stanford graduate." Pam smiled then pulled out a piece of paper and pen from the top of the box she had been carrying. She leaned over Jake and grabbed a magazine from the coffee table to lean on. "So, what's the plan, my man?"

"Plan?"

"Honey, you can't just show up and expect her to want you back. Girls like to be pursued, romanced, swept off their feet."

"Yeah, Steven sure seems to be doing a good job at that."

"So do better. Let's get creative!"

"Mom?" Jake shook his head, confused. "When did you get so—"

"Cool, insightful, fun to be around..."

"Sure."

"What?" She playfully nudged him. "Are you trying to say I wasn't always amazing?"

"Nah," Jake chuckled. "It's just—"

"I'm just teasing you," Pam interrupted, letting Jake off the hook. Her lighthearted tone turned serious and she furrowed her brow and looked intently at her son. "Jake, your father is a fine man with many great qualities. But I allowed him to stifle me. My identity became so wrapped up in him and his successes that I guess I kind of forgot who I was. It took us getting separated for me to find myself again. Now I find my identity in Christ, and I've never felt better."

"I like the new you." Jake said warmly. "Dad's an idiot for letting you go."

She shrugged with a wistful smile. Her eyes glistened with tears.

Jake let his mom's response soak in. Did she still have feelings for his dad? After all he had done to her—his multiple affairs, his workaholism, his anger issues, his taking her for granted? "Mom, be honest. Would you even consider taking dad back now? I mean, how could you ever forgive him?"

"Jake, I've already forgiven him, no matter what happens. And," Pam dabbed at the corner of her eye and grinned, "if he did even half of the things you're going to do to win back Amy's heart, then what girl could resist? Girls just want to know that they matter, Jake. That they're more than just another game for a guy to conquer."

Jake had always vowed to never become like his dad, and yet, in the past year and a half, he had stumbled way too far in his footsteps. Images of his final week with Amy and his ensuing fling with Nicole flickered through Jake's mind. How could he ever share with Amy the extent of his baseness, let alone ask her to forgive him? What was he thinking? And yet, his mom forgave. Jake could only pray that Amy had as much grace as his mom.

"So," Pam interrupted his uncomfortable trip down memory lane. "What's the best idea you got?"

Jake shifted in his seat and delved deep into the creative recesses of his brain. After how many hours he had spent agonizing over ideas on his long drive home, it would seem he should have something good by now. "Okay, well....She's got this big hill down the street from her. She drives by it every day. What if I get a bunch of flowers and write 'I'm sorry, Amy. Love, Jake.'" He spelled out the letters with his finger in the sky and looked to his mom for approval. *Dang, I'm good.* He grinned.

"Okay, that's a start—if you were sixteen years old and asking her to the prom," Pam retorted. "You need something more personal, more irresistible. You want a call to action. This is the woman you want to spend the rest of your life with, right? How are you going to tell her that?"

Jake looked at her oddly. "Mom, this isn't a proposal. I'm nowhere close to being ready to start thinking about marriage yet."

Pam leaned back on the couch and crossed her arms. "You mean you dated this girl for four years, created a child together, then dumped her and acted like a complete jerk, and now you're going to try to convince her to break up with a really great guy who has already made it clear that he wants to marry her. Give me a break, Jake. If you're not already one hundred percent positive that this is the woman you want to marry and grow old with, then quit now and let her be."

Like a little kid in trouble, Jake avoided eye contact with his mother. She was right. He'd already sent Amy on enough of a roller coaster ride. This was far bigger than just outcompeting Steven to get her to like him again. This was about playing for keeps.

As he stared out the window, his mom patted him on the leg. "Think about it, honey. Once you can convince me that you're worth her time, you're ready to try to convince Amy." She stood up and carried her box down the hall to the office. Jake didn't move.

He knew his feelings for Amy were strong, but did he really, truly love her? *Maybe I'm just living in the past,* he contemplated. Or maybe he was simply feeling the pull of attraction because she was hot...and unattainable. Was his fascination with her rooted in anything deeper?

Jake pondered the factors that led to their breakup. Besides the glaring reason of his lack of spiritual leadership, their differing dreams had also become a significant wedge that drove them apart. Jake questioned whether that had changed. Did he care enough about Amy to sacrifice his dreams for her? What if that meant no more Louisville? What if that meant no more basketball? Jake shuddered to think of those possibilities.

God, he prayed, *my mom is right. I have no right to pursue Amy just because I selfishly want her back in my life. But I can't stop thinking about her, God. I think I really love her. But I'm not sure I'm ready to give up basketball for her. It's just starting to go so well, and it sure seems like You're starting to use me to 'glow' back in Louisville. Does that mean I need to let Amy go for good? 'Cause I'm pretty sure if I don't move now, I'll never have another chance. I really do want what You know is best—for both of us.*

FIVE DAYS AND FOURTEEN unanswered text messages, two unreturned voicemails, and one ignored Facebook message later, Jake stood on Amy's doorstep with a single yellow rose and a ferociously beating heart. The feeling of nervousness was not new to Jake—he was used to the butterflies colliding in his stomach before any big basketball game—but the uneasy tension he was currently trying to ignore took nervous to a whole new level. Today's mission could be either a triumphant success or a humiliating defeat. And Jake wasn't sure he could stomach another one of the latter.

He tapped timidly on the door he'd knocked confidently on so many times before and waited patiently a few steps back. He gripped the poor rose stem tighter as he heard footsteps approach, forcing himself to breathe. And then the door opened and there she was. Glowing in a pale blue sun dress, Amy radiated joy... until she registered who was standing before her. The moment her eyes recognized Jake, her smile immediately dropped.

"H-hi, Amy," Jake stammered, already forgetting his opening line.

Amy's eyes opened wide and she snapped a quick look over her shoulder. "Uh, hey." She glanced behind her again and then turned back to Jake. "You know, this really isn't a good time for me. Could I call you later?"

It had taken Jake three hours to psyche himself up for this. He had sat in his truck for forty-five minutes before working up the nerve to drive over here. The last thing he needed was a postponement. "Please, Amy, just give me five minutes."

Amy stepped outside and closed the door behind her, nodding slowly. "I'll give you three."

Her look of annoyance didn't help, but Jake knew he had no time to lose so he immediately launched into his speech. Or at least he opened his mouth to try. Unfortunately, the words he'd practiced over and over again in front of his mom and his bathroom mirror suddenly vanished. "Uhhhh," Jake stalled. He prided himself at being clutch on the basketball court, but here in front of Amy he was throwing air balls. *God, I need Your help!* he pleaded. He stared down at his feet, closed his eyes, and took a deep breath. And suddenly everything clicked.

"Amy, I know I forfeited any claim to your affections a long time ago. I know I don't deserve a second chance. And I know you're even dating a guy who seems to be really great. But I don't want to be one of those pathetic characters in the movies who wait until it's too late to tell someone how they really feel. So that's what I'm doing here today." Jake paused to gather the full impact of his next statement and stared boldly into Amy's eyes. "Amy Briggs, I love you."

Amy shifted uncomfortably, and her face flushed. But she didn't avert her gaze.

"I know those words mean nothing if I don't back them up with actions. So I've spent a lot of time thinking about what that really means to me." Jake fiddled with the rose he had forgotten to hand to Amy and took a deep breath. "Here are the top ten ways I'd love to prove it to you if you'll give me the chance.

"Number ten: I'll treat you like a million bucks. I know I've got a lot of making up to you after being such a jerk for so long.

"Number nine: I'll be interested in your life. I'm sorry I was so self-centered before. You have no idea how much I miss talking with you.

"Number Eight: I'll be a better spiritual leader. Wow! I can't believe how off-track I got with God. You tried to pull me along, but I resisted so hard. I am *so* sorry. Thank you for trying to push me, but you should never have to do that again. One of the things I most miss talking about with you is what we're learning from God. I want to pray together and read our Bibles together and challenge each other.

"Number seven: I'll serve alongside you. I think it's so cool that you've invested your life in your girls. I've just started volunteering with a couple things at my church back in Louisville, and I love it. I don't know what it would look like, but I'd love to get involved in some kind of ministry with you this summer."

Jake couldn't tell what Amy was thinking, but she certainly wasn't frowning anymore. In fact, he almost detected a slight smile when he mentioned her girls. *Keep on going, man,* he encouraged himself. *This is looking good.*

"Number six," he continued. "I'll take a road trip with you this summer to visit your family. I am so excited that you reconnected with your dad. I'd love to hear so much more about it, and if you'd let me, I'd love to meet them."

Again, a faint smile played at the corners of Amy's mouth.

"Number five," Jake rushed on, hoping to keep the momentum rolling. "I'll support your dreams, whatever that takes. Thanks to you, I'm enjoying an amazing experience at Louisville. But I'm sorry that I was so selfish when you tried to have a dream of your own. I want to make that up to you."

At this point, Jake had to pause again. His hands trembled as he prepared to delve into the hardest ones yet. He exhaled sharply. "Number four: When I say whatever that takes, I mean it. Amy, I thought and prayed really hard about this: if being together again and supporting you means that you don't want to do the long distance thing again, I'll transfer from Louisville to some place closer to you. I'm pretty sure I don't have the grades to get into Stanford, but I'll even play at a community college if it means being with you."

Amy's eyes widened and her face blanched. Jake rolled right into his final appeals.

"Number three: I'm *really* serious about doing whatever it takes. I'll even quit playing basketball if you think it would make a difference in our relationship.

"Number two: I'll gladly spend the rest of my life learning to love you better.

"And Numb—"

The door suddenly opened and Steven appeared in the doorway, causing both Amy and Jake to jump like they were caught in the middle of a crime.

"What's going on here, Amy?" Steven accused.

Amy's eyes darted from her boyfriend to Jake and then back to her boyfriend. Feeling the weight of responsibility in this situation, Jake piped up. "Hi, uh, Steve. I was just dropping by real quick to tell Amy—"

"I know why you're here." Steven glared at Jake. "I heard your whole sickening list. You have some nerve coming here like this and—"

"Steven—" Amy interjected.

But Steven cut her off as well. "No. Don't *Steven* me! What were *you* thinking letting him go on and on like that? Did you forget that your *boyfriend,* who came out of his way to visit you, who has treated you with more respect and love than this sad fool ever could, was sitting here waiting for you?"

"Hey, it's not her fault," Jake stepped in. "She just didn't want to be rude. Unlike you, obviously."

"Me, rude? What do you call professing your undying love to a girl who's already taken?"

Catching himself before he said something he'd regret, Jake took a step back and wiped his sweaty palms on his jeans. "Look, I'm sorry, Steve."

"It's Steven," Steven corrected.

"I'm sorry, *Steven*. I'll get out of here and let you enjoy the rest of your afternoon." Jake reached out to shake Steven's hand, but Steven left him hanging. "You're a really lucky guy, man." Neither Steven nor Amy responded and Jake began to walk away. "Oh." He turned back. "This is for your mom, Amy. Can I leave it with you?"

Jake handed Amy the rose as Steven stormed back inside. She took it and just stared at Jake for a moment.

"Sorry, Jake," she said quietly, and then followed her boyfriend into the house.

The door clicked shut behind her and Jake was left standing alone on the sidewalk. *Well, that went poorly,* he attempted to laugh at himself as he gazed at the inhospitable door. But there was nothing humorous about his situation. He had come home this summer a man on a mission, but less than a week in, he was already out of ammunition. His quest for victory had spontaneously combusted into a kamikaze operation and he had crashed and burned as magnificently as it gets. *At least I went down with honor,* he tried to encourage himself.

Jake climbed into his truck and drove sadly away, fighting the despondence rising in his gut with a desperate hope that God had some other...better...plan in store for him.

7

THREE DAYS LATER, Amy sat with Cari in the back corner of their favorite Starbucks. Cari had finished her drink almost an hour ago, but Amy's iced mocha sat untouched on the table in an ever-growing puddle of condensation.

"I just can't believe he was so uptight about it all!" Amy complained, rehashing her frustrations with Steven's response to Jake's visit for the third time. "And the worst part was Steven's final words to me at the airport: 'I love you, Amy, but I'm just not sure I trust you with that guy.' Are you kidding me? How is this *my* fault? It's not like I invited Jake over, or like I wanted Steven to hear it all. What does he want me to do, get a restraining order on Jake?"

Cari smiled and twirled the straw in her empty cup. "Does Steven know you had started keeping in touch again with Jake?"

Amy snorted. "Yeah right. Good thing I never got around to mentioning it! Is that bad, Cari? I know he's my boyfriend. But does that mean I shouldn't be allowed to resolve things with a past relationship?"

Cari shrugged. "I can see why Steven would feel uncomfortable with Jake around. You two have history. It's understandable that he would feel threatened—especially after Jake made his intentions so clear."

Amy rolled her eyes and exhaled. "Seriously."

"I can only imagine what Steven was thinking as Jake recited his list." Cari laughed. "But what about you?"

Amy shook her head and sighed. "It doesn't matter. Steven jumped on a plane to make up with me, and he answered—even surpassed—all of my reservations. I can't entertain any thoughts about Jake."

Cari reached her hand across the table and grabbed Amy's left hand. She studied it and flipped it over several times.

Amy's curiosity won out. "What are you doing?"

"Oh, I was just searching for a wedding ring. Something that showed that you made a lifelong commitment to him," Cari replied nonchalantly.

"He offered me one of those, remember?"

"And you said no," Cari retorted calmly. She let go of Amy's hand and patted it kindly. Then she gave the look that Amy had come to recognize—the look that warned that the next words out of Cari's mouth were probably something to write down. "My daddy gave me some advice when I was about your age." She paused and Amy waited with bated breath. "He said, 'no ring...no thing.'"

Amy ignored those simple words in anticipation for the real insight. But Cari just sat there smiling. "That's it?" Amy finally protested. "I can't believe you're telling me that. You're saying that because I didn't accept Steven's proposal, I can sneak around behind his back and it's okay?"

"No, no, no." Cari shook her head vehemently. "I'm just saying that until you say 'I do' at that altar, you are not required by God nor man to disengage from your feelings and surrender unswervingly to your current option—regardless of how far that option flew to make up with you. Take your time, Amy. Don't just settle for what's convenient."

These were the last words that Amy expected to hear out of Cari's mouth. She and Chris both were always talking about the importance of keeping commitments and following through on one's word. "Cari, this doesn't sound like your usual advice. What about all that talk about let your yes be yes and your no be no? What about following through with our promises?"

"Absolutely. But in our day and age, for better or worse, dating isn't a promise; it's more of an experiment. Sure, we need to be careful to not just start and end relationships carelessly. But we also need to be careful to not stick with relationships carelessly either. You've only committed your present to Steven so far, nothing more."

"I just don't think I could break up with him for no reason. I already shattered his heart when I refused his proposal."

"I don't think you *should* break up with him for no reason. But don't be afraid to consider your options. You're twenty-one, right?" Cari asked out of the blue.

Amy nodded, wondering where Cari was going now.

"Twenty-two...twenty-three...twenty-four...twenty-five... twenty-six...twenty-seven...twenty-eight...twenty-nine...thirty..." Cari counted rhythmically, never breaking eye contact with her young mentee. She continued through the thirties and into the forties. "Forty-five...forty-six...forty-seven...forty-eight... forty-nine...fifty...fifty-one...fifty two...fifty-three...fifty-four... fifty-five...fifty-six...fifty-seven." Cari just kept counting on and on, a slow and steady metronome.

With each passing number, Amy grew more awkward, but she remained glued to Cari's gentle hypnotic voice. *Sixty...sixty-one...*The conversation had taken a strange turn into some kind of staring contest. Whatever point Cari was trying to prove, it was proven. *Sixty-five...sixty-six...*Amy shifted uncomfortably in her seat, wishing the counting would just stop. For the first time, she took a sip of her now room-temperature drink.

"Sixty-nine...seventy...seventy-one...seventy-two...seventy-three...seventy-four...seventy-five...seventy-six...seventy-seven...seventy-eight." Cari finally paused. "Whew, that was awkward wasn't it?"

"Uh, yeah." Amy set her drink down and smiled. "I was starting to think you might have turned into a robot or something."

"The average woman in our country lives until she's seventy-eight years old," Cari explained. "It will probably be even older than that by the time you're that age." She smiled and leaned forward in her seat, closer and closer to Amy. Her motherly hands gently squeezed Amy's. "Let every one of those numbers represent a year of marriage. You think what I just did was awkward, imagine being married to the wrong guy for fifty plus years." Cari leaned back and paused for effect. "Amy, I'm not telling you Steven is the wrong guy. From what you've told me, he seems like a wonderful young man. What I'm telling you is don't get it wrong."

"Do you think he could be the wrong guy?" Amy pressed timidly. Her palms prickled with sweat and she wiped them on her jeans. Cari was prying open the can of worms that Amy had tried to hold closed for a few months now.

"Do you?"

Amy blew her bangs up in the air and leaned back in her chair with her arms crossed. "Cari, how did you know that Chris was the one you wanted to spend the rest of your life with?"

Cari's whole face brightened as she started playing with her empty cup again. "All my dreams of the future included him in it. I knew he wasn't perfect, but he was perfect for me." Cari laughed at herself out loud. "I know, kinda cheesy, but it's true."

Cheesy was the last word Amy would have used to describe Cari's answer. Unfortunately, she was pretty sure that wasn't the same way she felt about Steven. Sure, she sometimes dreamed about their wedding, and making him breakfast in bed, and being serenaded by him as they ate candlelit dinners in the sunset. But none of that was reality. Truthfully, she couldn't figure out how Steven fit into her concrete goals for the future. She thought she loved Steven, but after hearing Jake's mind-blowing confession of sacrificial love, she wasn't sure what to think.

"You know, you never answered that other question," Cari interrupted her thoughts.

"Which question?" Amy feigned innocently, knowing quite well the question to which Cari was alluding. Cari raised her eyebrows and just looked at her knowingly.

Amy smiled and her cheeks flushed. "My heart was racing a thousand beats a minute—partly because I was afraid Steven might hear, but mostly because Jake was owning up to everything I'd ever hoped for and promising more than I'd ever dreamed of. If Steven hadn't been there, who knows what I would have done!" Amy exhaled and laughed nervously. "I can't believe I just admitted that." She glanced down at her cell phone sitting on top of her purse on the seat next to her. She pulled it out and gazed at the picture of her and Steven on the screen. "Oh Cari, what am I going to do?"

Cari took her hand. "Well, I can't say I envy you, girlfriend." Cari smiled. "Just remember, there's no hurry. Take this summer to really figure out how you feel. All these crazy emotions could mean nothing more than you just think Jake is hot."

Amy blushed. She couldn't deny that much was true. Jake had always been cute, but now? Amy couldn't help but wonder what his chiseled body must look like with his shirt off. *Amy!* She scolded herself, knowing Jake's muscles were the last thing she should be thinking about—and the last thing that mattered in considering her future! She shook her head to dislodge the distracting images and tried to catch up with Cari.

"I think this time apart from Steven is going to tell you a lot. Either distance makes the heart grow fonder or—"

"Out of sight, out of mind," Amy finished wryly. "But what do I do with Jake in the meantime?"

"Well," Cari pondered, "when you see him around New Song, I don't see any harm in talking to him. But as long as you have a boyfriend, you probably shouldn't be hanging out with him outside of church events." Cari grinned mischievously. "Which we'll have plenty of, by the way. Steven doesn't want you to quit being involved in church, does he?"

Amy chuckled. "Ugh!" she groaned. "I tried so hard to avoid drama. How did this happen to me?"

"Do you know how many girls would give anything to find an attractive, charming, godly man. Just think how lucky you are that your problem is choosing which one." Cari smiled.

Any chance you could just take one of them out of the picture for me? Amy prayed.

TWO MONTHS AFTER HIS DOORSTEP DEBACLE, Jake stood anxiously waiting outside what Chris liked to call the Disneyland of Oceanside: Costco. Amy would be there any minute now and Jake felt like his head might burst from the pressure.

Since his confession of undying love to Amy, she had been cordial enough at church events, but any contact Jake had tried to initiate beyond that had met with steady rejection. Chris and Cari, Andrea, and even his mom had encouraged him to take it slow, to be patient, to give Amy space while she had a boyfriend. But Jake knew this was his last chance. If he couldn't convince her that he was worth her attention now, then what were the odds that he'd have another opportunity? He was leaving for Louisville in three days, and then who knew when he'd see her again?

It had taken a lot of creative maneuvering to even wrangle Amy into this "necessary" meeting—for the sake of ministry!—today. Amy was helping out with the student leaders' retreat this weekend and Cari had delegated to her the responsibility of grocery shopping for the trip. She timed her request to the precise moment that Jake just so happened to be walking by in the church lobby. On cue, Jake had casually offered to help, since shopping for twenty teenagers would probably be easier with a partner. Besides, Jake had his truck, which would make transporting the groceries back to the church much easier, too. How could Amy turn down this generous offer, right? Amy reluctantly relented and had even agreed to allow Jake to treat her to a hot dog after their shopping was done.

Jake looked at the clock on his phone. *4:03.* Jake swallowed the tension rising in his throat. D-Day was here. He straightened his shirt for the thirty-second time and adjusted his position leaning against the concrete pillar. He tried to look cool, but his stomach was in knots.

When Jake had realized that Amy wasn't going to give him a chance to get close this summer, he had started doing what he could to impress her from a distance. Even if Amy wasn't on board, he could still do his part to live out number seven on his list, so he'd started participating in all the church activities he thought she might be at—which turned out to be a lot. Since Amy was leading a summer girls' small group, Jake volunteered to lead one for freshmen guys. That alone meant that he got to see her every Sunday morning, Tuesday night, and plenty of special event days in between.

The funny thing, though, was that even though contact with Amy had been minimal, Jake was discovering that he really liked youth ministry. His freshmen boys were crazy, but he looked forward to seeing them each week almost as much as seeing Amy. Jake knew from experience how important these years were, and he wished he'd had someone like Chris in his life from the beginning instead of only at the end of his high school experience. Things could have been so much different! Jake knew he was going to miss his guys when he left for Louisville in three days.

Three days! Jake couldn't believe it was already time to return to school—the summer had flown by so fast! Besides his involvement with his freshmen boys, he had also had a ton of fun hanging out with the growing college-aged ministry at New Song. It felt like an extension of the old youth group that Jake had experienced the second half of his senior year. But instead of merely meeting for lunch in the quad, they found plenty of other opportunities to interact in fun and meaningful ways. Sunday afternoons and Wednesday evenings were Ultimate Frisbee, Fridays were bonfires at the beach, and Jake had looked forward to breakfast with Jonny every Thursday morning. While his quirky friend still entertained him with his goofy thoughts, he also provided deep insights as they studied the book of Mark and prayed together. Jonny was maturing, and Jake was grateful to have him as a friend.

Jake had also capitalized on his time at home with his mom. They had lunch together most weekdays, and every Monday night they tried out a new restaurant together. Jake was constantly impressed by his mom's keen observations about life and the amount of grace and patience she displayed. Jake found out that when Glen had served her with the divorce papers, she had gently told him that she refused to give up on their marriage by signing, but that she wouldn't stand in his way once time ran its course. That must have triggered something, because he had halted in his proceedings for the time being. Jake couldn't help thinking of the miracle he had prayed for on his drive out to California. They were still a long way away from reconciliation, but this was at least a start.

Jake glanced at his phone again. *4:one7.* A sinking feeling crept over him. Amy was usually pretty prompt. He knew she wasn't nearly as excited about this meeting as he was, but she wouldn't back out, would she? *God, please don't let her cancel.*

This summer had been good in so many ways, but Jake still couldn't help feeling disappointed. As much as it had seemed too good to be true, he'd just had a feeling in his gut that he'd be able to reunite with Amy. But now, unless God pulled off some miracle this afternoon, he'd be heading back to school with an empty heart. Jake had surrendered his relationship with Amy over to God countless times, and he felt like God had given him the green light to pursue her for the two months he was home. But he knew that once he left, he needed to clear his mind of the past and just move on. Amy was in God's hands, and there was nothing more that he could do. *But Lord, please help me not to screw up today,* Jake begged. He wasn't sure if he could handle another crushing defeat.

4:23. Jake made sure he didn't have any missed calls or texts and shifted his weight. Tired of standing, he finally decided to sit on the concrete bench to his left. The box in his back pocket jabbed into his seat and he pulled it out and studied the carefully wrapped little cube. If all else failed, maybe this little token would remind her of him long after they had parted ways. It wasn't much, but he hoped she would like it. He stuffed it into one of the side pockets of his shorts and leaned back.

At the entrance to his right, a lady checked each person's membership card. Suddenly he wondered how they were going to get in! He didn't have a card. But Amy wouldn't have recommended this place if she wasn't packing. *Right?* Well, worst case scenario, they'd have to go somewhere else, and maybe then Jake could finagle a real dinner into the deal.

"Sorry I'm late," Amy's voice interrupted his new fantasy.

Jake looked up to see Amy in a pair of black leggings and a sweatshirt. Her hair was tied back in a pony tail, and even though she was still beautiful, it was obvious that she hadn't dressed up for the occasion. Jake usually didn't feel self conscious about his clothes, but suddenly the thirty minutes he'd spent agonizing over which shirt to wear seemed a bit unnecessary.

"Andrea and I went for a run on the beach and I guess we just lost track of time."

"No problem. You're worth the wait." Jake chuckled and stood up to give her a hug. Amy lightly patted his back and pulled quickly away. "You've got a membership card, right?" he inquired, nodding toward the Costco bouncer at the door.

Amy flashed a smile and pulled out a black card. "Not just any card; I'm an Executive member. Thanks to my dad adding me to his account." She grabbed a cart and headed toward the entrance.

Jake followed suit. "Ah, you're a high roller." He laughed. "So do they roll out a red carpet for you or something?"

Amy flashed her card and they strolled into the busy warehouse. "They used to, but it got old after awhile so I told them only on special occasions."

ALL or NOTHING

63

"This isn't a special occasion?" Jake playfully remarked.

"Ooh, can you grab two of those cakes?" Amy asked, pointing to a special display table and ignoring his last question like a pro. She pulled out Cari's shopping list and studied it intently.

Jake obediently grabbed two of the lemon cakes and pushed the extra wide cart—ironically large enough to contain more stuff than could comfortably fit into the trunk of any normal car—back to Amy, who was now watching some animated film on a row of televisions. "Which one do you want?" He asked, lightly tapping Amy's hip with the front of the cart.

"You know us high rollers don't even consider anything less than seventy inches." Amy turned to look at Jake and winked. "Ready?"

"Let's do this." Jake smiled back.

Amy led him up and down every aisle, tossing stuff into his cart along the way. Usually, Jake hated shopping, but today, the possibility of some significant conversation with Amy kept him going strong. That, and the hope that at the end of every aisle a sample lady might be waiting for him with some new tasty morsel.

"So are you excited to go back to Stanford?" Jake attempted small talk.

"Yeah, yeah, I really can't wait to get back," Amy replied, grabbing four jugs of grape juice. "How about you?"

"Yeah, I guess I am," Jake responded, relieving her of the juice and loading them into his quickly filling cart. Amy didn't slow down, so as soon as he guaranteed the juice wasn't squishing the bread, he ran to catch up with her. Not wanting to let the conversation die again, he kept talking. "Basketball practice doesn't officially start until October, which will give me time to settle into my classes and all. But once season starts, it's pretty exhausting."

Amy didn't comment but paused to consider the different sizes of tortillas. She chose the soft taco size and tossed Jake three packages.

"Don't get me wrong. I love it," Jake continued after she made her decision. "But that's when I really have to stay focused to keep my grades up. What about you? What's been the hardest part about your classes at Stanford? I mean, it's Stanford after all. Is everybody as brilliant as you?"

"Well, you know." Amy smiled and tossed a big bag of rolls at him. "Sure, the classes are rigorous, but I've really enjoyed them so far. Hold that thought for a sec. Let me run down this aisle real quick to grab the peanut butter."

Amy traipsed away and turned the corner to the aisle next to them. Jake watched her leave, trying to think of some more questions that would get her to talk.

"Jake Taylor?" a familiar voice from his past interrupted loudly.

Jake looked up to see an unkempt Doug Moore at the other end of the aisle. It had been two years since Jake had seen his former-best-friend-turned-enemy, and his best guess was that the college party scene had gone straight to his waistline. Still, Doug's cocky swagger hadn't changed a bit. As he strutted toward Jake, Jake couldn't help but flash back to their last contact with each other. After the whole school found out Amy was pregnant, Doug had called her a slut so Jake had punched him but then somehow ended up on the ground of the school hallway while Doug taunted him. Of course, that was all after Doug had hooked up with her right after she and Jake had broken up. What a great friend.

Are you kidding me, God? Jake groaned. *As if I need another jerk intruder!* "Hey, Doug." Jake pushed his mostly full cart toward his old teammate. The boys awkwardly shook hands and patted each other on the back. "What's it been, like two years?"

"Too long." Doug grinned. Apparently he either had a short memory, or he was willing to keep their grievances in the past. He looked down at the cart. "You here with your mom?"

"No, a-actually," Jake stammered, "I'm actually here with—"

"Doug Moore!" Amy's animated voice interrupted him from behind.

ALL or NOTHING

"Amy Briggs?" Doug shouted back loud enough for the whole store to hear.

A double pack of peanut butter in her hands, she ran up to the guy who had insulted her in front of the whole school and hugged him with significantly more fervor than she had given Jake. A twinge of jealousy pulsated through Jake's veins.

"Wait, are you guys still together?" Doug looked back at Jake with a sly grin, his arm still draped around Amy's shoulders.

"Oh no, we're just friends," Amy corrected almost too quickly.

"Yeah, good times," Jake chirped, trying to sound happy about it.

Doug reached out and pulled Jake into the group embrace. "Man, I've missed you guys."

Jake glanced at Amy, and she gave him a quick knowing smile—which was just enough reassurance to get him through the next forty-five minutes of stories by Doug. According to the big man himself, Doug had started out well at San Diego State on his basketball scholarship, but a combination of the coaches just being real jerks and Doug sleeping through most morning practices with nasty hangovers ultimately cost him the scholarship. After that he didn't see the point in continuing his education. This year he was planning on playing ball for the local community college while he took a few easy classes and worked part time in construction with his dad. That left him plenty of time for partying on the side, which seemed to be all he really cared about.

"Well, it usually doesn't take me this long to pick up my beers!" Doug laughed. "But I'm so glad I ran into you guys! You should totally come on Friday," he invited for at least the fifth time. "It's gonna be a rockin' party at my place."

"Yeah, thanks, but I'll be on my way to Louisville," Jake reminded him.

"And I'll be camping with the youth group." Amy smiled.

"Yeah, yeah, well maybe next time. Definitely look me up next time you're in town, bro." He chucked Jake on the shoulder and gave Amy another warm hug, then turned his alcohol-laden cart toward the cash registers.

"Well, that was interesting timing," Jake grinned to Amy. Ironically, Doug's appearance had actually turned out to be a blessing in disguise. Once he showed up, for some reason Amy loosened up, and while most of the talk had centered around their loudmouthed "friend," Jake was grateful to not have to be the one propelling the dialogue for once.

"Yeah, what a coincidence," she chuckled back.

"So shall we tackle the rest of your list before the hamburger patties completely thaw?"

"Let's do it."

They raced through the rest of the store, laughing and bantering much more freely than before, and before long, both carts were full way beyond capacity. They wrestled them into the nearest line and chuckled at the stares and the comments their ambitious shopping elicited.

"It takes a lot to feed a dozen kids," Jake remarked to one ogling passerby. "I'll start my diet *tomorrow*," he told another.

Amy lightly elbowed him in the side. "Jake, stop." She chuckled then informed the curious shopper in front of them, "We're shopping for our youth group at church."

Several hundred dollars later, they pushed their carts toward the food court, where Jake found an empty table and parked both of their baskets. "How about you wait here with the groceries, and I'll go get our food?" he instructed. Amy agreed and Jake went to the order window.

When he returned a few minutes later, hot dogs, drinks, and almond-covered ice cream bars in hand, he was pleased to catch Amy checking her makeup in a tiny mirror from her purse. The thought that Amy cared even a little about what she looked like for Jake surged a new confidence into his previously insecure hopes for this meeting.

"Here y'go, Diet Coke and a hot dog...*and* Costco's world famous ice cream bar with nuts!" Jake smiled and placed the cheap meal in front of her with a flourish.

"How did you know? I *love* their ice cream bars!" Amy smiled.

"Who doesn't?" Jake grinned.

Amy took a sip of her drink and then began to lift the hot dog to her mouth.

"Ah, do you want to pray, or should I?" Jake interjected, winking at her.

She laughed and placed her hot dog back on the table. "You do the honors."

Eager for the opportunity, Jake grabbed both of Amy's hands. She flinched, but didn't move them. Jake was pretty sure they were as sweaty as his. "Dear God, thanks so much for this chance for Amy and I to hang out. Thanks for our friendship and thanks for these hot dogs and the ice cream. Somehow please make them healthy. In Jesus' name, Amen." Jake squeezed her hands, and to his surprise, she let them linger in his grip a little longer. He would have loved to hold them for the rest of the night, but in a moment of panic, he let go and quickly started unwrapping his hot dog.

The awkwardness descended once again, and they both sat eating in silence. Finally, after finishing her hot dog, Amy folded her hands and looked Jake in the eyes. "Jake, thanks for offering to help me today. I've really had a good time."

Jake faltered in her gaze, and his last bite of hot dog stopped in his throat. He gulped it down and stammered, "I-I did, too. Thanks for letting me tag along." The little wrapped box in his pocket started burning a hole in his leg and Jake knew it was now or never. "Ah, I know this isn't the most romantic place or anything, but I got you a little something."

He fumbled in his pocket and Amy looked at him curiously. "I hope you like it." Jake slowly pulled the small cube out and placed it on the table in front of her.

Instantly Amy's cheeks turned as pale as chalk. She made no motion toward the box but instead started shaking her head. "Are you kidding me, Jake?" she mumbled, her eyebrows furrowed.

"Umm, I—"

"What is wrong with you guys? Can't you give a girl a little time? Jake, I know you love me and you want to spend the rest of your life with me and all that. And yes, I *forgive* you for everything. But that doesn't mean it's that easy to *forget* everything! We've got a lot of work to do before I would ever even *think* about marrying you again."

Jake sat wide-eyed, reeling from the force of Amy's outburst. But as he absorbed the implications of her words, an unavoidable smile crept across his face. "So you're saying there's a chance!" he cheered. "Just kidding, Ames. I didn't even think about what this could look like when I grabbed the box out of my mom's closet. Sorry for the confusion, but it's not an engagement ring." He grinned. "You have a boyfriend for crying out loud."

Amy blushed and looked at the box, puzzled. "Then what is it?"

"Just open it," he prodded.

Amy took a deep breath and tentatively pulled the ribbon loose. She unwrapped the paper and took the lid off of the small box. There inside sat a small greenish bouncy ball. Behind it, Jake had tucked in a slip of paper where he had written, "Glow! Matthew 5:onesix." Amy looked at Jake inquisitively. "Well, it's certainly not a ring!" She fumbled in her purse until she found her pocket Bible and then flipped through the pages. "Matthew 5:onesix. 'In the same way, let your light shine before men, that they may see your good deeds and praise your Father in heaven.'"

"I got this from my mentor Buddy," Jake explained. "It changed my life. See, this ball will glow in the dark for a long time, as long as you expose it to the light first. That's how we're supposed to be. As long as we stay close to our light source, then God will use us to glow wherever we are. Amy, I've been watching you glow all summer. You really are amazing. So, I know you don't really need a reminder to let your light shine, but I thought this could be just a little token of my appreciation for how you've glowed in my life, and inspired me to want to glow to others even more."

Silence fell for a few moments before Amy responded. "Jake," she finally sighed. "This is one of the sweetest gifts I've ever been given. Thank you."

Jake took a long sip of his Coke, relieved at his success. Finally, he had managed to say what he wanted without disaster or interruption.

Amy fiddled with the straw in her drink, obviously wanting to say more. A few more moments passed before she spoke up, though. "I know I've been distant this summer," she finally admitted. "It's not because I didn't want to spend time with you, Jake. It's just...there's Steven, you know, and—"

"I know," Jake stopped her, grabbing her hands once again. "It's okay. I understand." He paused, and with one deep exhale, let go of the stress of holding onto Amy. "You know how I feel about you, Amy. And that's not going to change. You know how to find me if you change your mind about Steven."

He released her hands reluctantly, and instead picked up his now melted ice cream bar. Creamy vanilla oozed everywhere when he bit into the thick chocolate shell, but it didn't matter. He had done what he came here to do. Now the rest was in God's hands.

FALL

UNLIKE IN HIS RACE OUT TO CALIFORNIA, Jake took his time driving back to Louisville. Getting back to school just didn't have quite the same draw as rushing home to see Amy! On his way, Jake stopped in Texas to pick up Grant. Driving the final stretch of the journey with a partner was definitely a welcome change; Jake could only handle so much sports radio and he needed something new to distract him from his endless thoughts about the girl he couldn't stop loving. They arrived at the university a few days before classes started, which was plenty of time to settle into their new on-campus apartment, catch up with their old teammates, and get to know the newbies.

Surprisingly, the guys from last year seemed glad to see Jake and Grant and made no mention of the scandalous news that had caused such sharp division in the team at the end of the season. For whatever reason, it was as if Grant had never even come out of the closet, which was perfectly fine with Jake, and Grant seemed to be okay with it, too. And what the new guys didn't know wouldn't hurt them.

Perhaps one of the biggest contributing factors to the re-newed acceptance of Grant and Jake was the absence of Jamal

Hardaway, who had been picked up by the Minnesota Timberwolves late in the second round of the NBA draft in June. Jamal had been tough on Jake since Jake's arrival at Louisville, and with the help of his attitude, Nate Williams had led his own charge against Jake. Unfortunately, Grant got caught in the crossfire, and when he finally admitted that he was gay to the whole team to protect Jake, Nate and Jamal ensured that both of them were ostracized. But now that Jamal was gone—and after Jake's stellar performance at the Big Dance last year—Nate had no one to support him in his beef against Jake, and it seemed like things might settle back to normal this season.

In spite of making it to the Sweet Sixteen last season—an amazing accomplishment, to be sure—the team was hungry for more and they wouldn't be satisfied unless they made it even further this year. Sure, they had lost Jamal, but the rest of the starters were intact, and Jake obviously hoped that he could slide right into Jamal's spot. It would be interesting to see how the new freshmen and transfer students would play into the mix.

According to NCAA regulations, basketball practice couldn't officially start until mid-October, but the team knew what was expected of them in the meantime. Daily informal strength and conditioning workouts and scrimmages allowed the guys to bond and jockey for position in a more casual atmosphere, without the pressure of coaches watching and critiquing and interfering. For Jake, these times with his teammates were his favorite part of the day. Instead of the constant straining for position he'd felt the past two years, he now enjoyed a camaraderie with the guys he'd be going into battle with in November. Jake couldn't wait to see what the season held.

Nomis had spent his summer playing street ball in a New York summer league again, and he came back scrappier than ever. His jump shot was on fire, he was faster than lightning down the court, and the air he was getting on dunks was ridiculous. Nomis' trash talking skills had also escalated, and Jake couldn't help but laugh at Nomis trying to intimidate the newcomers into submission on the court.

"Better hit the weight room, bro. Your game is weak," Nomis taunted to a redshirt freshman as he flew by him for an uncontested dunk during an afternoon scrimmage. "Forget the circus; I'm the greatest show on earth."

The next possession he flew by the freshman again, but this time Grant was there to clog the lane. His long outstretched arm forced Nomis to change his show just enough for Jake to get a piece of it from behind and the ball fell a full foot short of the rim.

"Even the bearded lady doesn't airball like that," Jake yelled as he patted Nomis on the back and gave him a wink. It was going to be a fun year.

Grant's game was stronger than ever, too. It was clear that he had an axe to grind after most of the guys had turned their back on him last year. He had hit the gym hard all summer and it showed. He came back playing D and banging the glass with a greater fervor than Jake had seen in him before.

Nate Williams had obviously worked hard over the summer, as well, but now that Jamal's position was open, he didn't seem as threatened by Jake. One day in a scrimmage, they both ended up on the same team. The first time down the court, Jake naturally took over the ball and Nate instinctively shifted to number two. And it clicked. There was no rivalry, no contention. They instantly gelled and each performed their roles with ease and grace. Jake's comfort with the ball was unsurpassed and Nate's lethal accuracy from outside was the perfect outlet to Jake's drives. After their third successive score, they caught each other's eye and smiled—as if this was the way it was supposed to be all along.

Jake scoped out the highly recruited young freshmen. They were good, but most were still pretty green. It was amusing to watch them quickly discover that their high school workouts were a joke compared to college ball—and the real practices hadn't even yet begun. Jake remembered back to his own arrival to campus just a year and a half earlier when he'd showed up during the middle of the season. That had been him, thinking he was all ready for what college ball had to throw his way. What a rude awakening he had experienced!

At the same time, Jake remembered the respect and awe he'd felt playing with veterans he'd previously studied and watched on ESPN. Now Jake was one of the experienced ones, and he found himself being looked up to as one of the leaders on the squad. His performance in the NCAA tournament had made him something of a legend to the newcomers who'd watched him take over the game on national television and Jake enjoyed this new state of affairs.

There was one newcomer who wasn't like the rest, however. Tyler Faulk was as blue chip a recruit as they come. He was the first ever two-time winner of the high school player of the year for the state of Kentucky *and* the MVP of the McDonald's All-American game. Jake didn't want to categorize him as arrogant, but Tyler certainly didn't come to sit the bench. It was obvious that the six-foot-nine eighteen-year-old was thinking that Louisville was just a short stop on his way to the NBA.

Interacting with Tyler definitely made Jake start speculating more about his own prospects in the NBA. Thoughts of going pro had always been a fantasy in the back of his brain, and if this season could go as well as last one ended, he definitely had a shot. But lately, the lure of professional sports had been overshadowed by other questions about his future—namely, where would Amy be in that picture?

Jake knew the ball was in her court now, but he couldn't help wondering if there was anything else he could possibly do to influence her in his direction. The only thing that really seemed like it could help was pray. So he did. A lot. He set up a framed picture of her right next to his bed so that she was the first thing he saw every morning and the last thing he looked at every night. Every time he saw her, he talked to God about her for awhile and that seemed to help the longing in his heart...at least a little.

"That girl's like your personal Mona Lisa," Grant would joke. "She's staring at you no matter where you are in the room."

Jake didn't mind. Feeling like Amy was watching him made him want to live each day the best that he could. He already had enough regrets and he didn't intend to add any more. With or without Amy, this was going to be a great year.

10

THE FIRST SUNDAY AFTER CLASSES STARTED, Jake found himself again walking the mile trek from the athletic dorm to Grace Fellowship Church. But contrary to the norm, he wasn't alone. Dressed impeccably in a white sport coat and tie, Grant walked beside him, hesitant about the whole church thing but eager to see Buddy. All summer, Jake had prayed that God would use him to bring Grant to Christ, and Grant's acceptance of his invitation to church was definitely a step in the right direction, even if it was only to see their old friend.

Buddy had written both boys several times over the summer. His eighty-four-year-old scrawl was barely legible, but the thought behind his letters had impressed them. In an age of short texts and quick emails, the time and effort Buddy had taken to keep in touch with them was significant, especially considering what a rough couple of months he'd had.

Yvonne had suffered a stroke three days after Jake had left for home, which is why Jake hadn't been able to get in touch with Buddy that Sunday of Steven's unexpected arrival. Since then, she had never regained full consciousness but simply existed in a nearly vegetative state. Fortunately, all her basic body functions were working, so Buddy had been able to finally bring her home a couple of weeks ago, but now he was homebound taking care of his unresponsive wife twenty-four-seven, except for a couple hours every Sunday morning when a hired home health care worker came in to relieve him so that he could go to church.

Jake had been hit hard by the news. Buddy had made such an impact on his life and he and Yvonne had been so gracious in opening up their home to him. It didn't seem fair that either of them should have to suffer like this.

Not in a million years would Jake have predicted that an elderly former Louisville basketball player would be the reason he was walking with God again. But their spontaneous trip to Chuck E. Cheese had changed his life and their subsequent weekly lunches had quickly become Jake's highlight of last semester. Buddy listened without judgment and his sage responses counseled without sounding preachy. Jake constantly found himself pouring out his deepest problems with complete honesty and heeding Buddy's words with complete acceptance.

Even Grant, who could not have been more disinterested in spiritual things, listened intently whenever Buddy opened his mouth. When Grant had just come out with it that he was gay over dinner last year, Jake had nearly keeled over. After all, Buddy came from a generation where such things weren't discussed. But Buddy had been unfazed and responded with gentleness, love, and common sense. He didn't avoid the truth, but he didn't use it as a weapon either. Jake hoped that more of Buddy would rub off on him this year.

"Remember last time I went to church with you?" Grant reminisced, jabbing Jake playfully with his elbow.

"Oooh." Jake winced, remembering all-too-clearly Grant's wingman role when Nicole had asked to join Jake at church. Jake had actually felt jealous of Grant that morning for the way he had flirted with Nicole. *How ironic!* Jake shook his head and grimaced to think how she had used a fake interest in God to lure him into a relationship. *At least that's one good thing about Amy keeping her distance.* He cringed at the thought of ever having to share the depths of his fall with her.

"So just be warned, this church isn't nearly as, er, polished as that one," Jake warned as they walked up the sidewalk. The usual gray-haired greeter stood at the church entrance. "His name is Harry. He wears that exact suit every Sunday—whether it's snowing outside or over a hundred degrees," Jake whispered under his breath.

"Welcome back, sonny." Harry extended his hand much more warmly than he had on Jake's original visit. "Did you see any Hollywood stars while you were out there in California?" the old man joked.

"Not this time, Harry." Jake smiled, shaking his head. "But I want you to meet a future NBA All-Star. This is my friend and teammate, Grant."

"Pleasure to meet you, sir." Grant nodded.

"'Sir' is what you call people my dad's age…and he died fifteen years ago!" Harry cracked himself up again. "Just call me Harry. It's great to meet you, Grant. I think you just doubled our young adult ministry this morning." Harry patted Jake on the back and the two roommates walked into the church foyer.

Suddenly, the organ burst out into the melody of some hymn that Jake had never heard before. The choir quickly followed, singing along in discordant harmony. The senior pastor doubled as worship leader for the small congregation, and he waved his arms in front of his singers as if they were a world famous chorale. But even though they sounded pretty horrible, the words they sang resonated with Jake's spirit. Day by day he would find the strength to bear his trials. Day by day he would trust in God's infinite wisdom. He had no reason to worry or fear. God was kind beyond all measure, and He'd give Jake what was best for him when the time came—whether that best included Amy or not. Completely taken with the message of the old song, Jake didn't realize he had stopped walking.

Grant leaned in close to him. "If you like it that much, I'll buy you the soundtrack for your birthday."

Jake smiled. "Thanks," he whispered. "I'll burn you a copy."

Grant nodded toward their old friend who was sitting in the front pew on the left. They tried to casually make their way to their mentor, but it was hard to go unnoticed in the scarcely filled room. "Buddy!" they whispered in unison when they reached him.

He turned around and Jake was pretty sure his eyes were glistening with tears. But as soon as he saw his young visitors, his face lit up with joy. "Hey, boys!" Buddy whispered loudly and eagerly hugged them.

Jake couldn't help but notice that his grip seemed significantly weaker than just two months ago. "The choir sounds horrible without your bride," Jake teased him.

Buddy winked. Early on in their relationship, he had confided to Jake that he was well aware that they sounded as bad as a screeching cat. Since then, he had repeatedly apologized for his harsh words. Apparently, he took the command not to slander very seriously, which was just one more cool thing about him. Nevertheless, Jake couldn't help rib him about it.

"I just knew today was going to be a great service. I am so glad you guys are here!" Buddy leaned over and whispered in Jake's ear. Again, his eyes got watery, but he shook his head and regained composure.

Jake patted the feeble man's back and grabbed one of the dilapidated hymnals from the rack in front of him. The choir had moved on to another hymn and Jake glanced at Buddy's to see which page he should turn to. He might not know the lyrics, but it still felt great to be back in a place where he could sing as loud as he wanted and know that his off-pitch voice fit right in.

About an hour and a half and several dozen welcome back hugs later, Jake and Grant finally made their way back out to the front parking lot with Buddy. Jake still wasn't clear what the pastor had taught on, but he counted forty-seven congregational Amen's—not including one from Grant who was just having fun.

"Can we take you out to lunch?" Jake asked. "Our treat."

Buddy grinned from ear to ear and patted both of them on the back. "You boys are way too kind, but I've kind of got a date." Buddy wiggled his eyebrows up and down and then winked at them. "I gotta get back home to the wifey. I told her I'd pick up some lunch on my way home so that we could eat together."

"Oh, then I guess we'll have to take a rain check," Jake quickly responded, not wanting to impose.

"Oh, nonsense!" Buddy exclaimed. "You boys should join me. I'm sure that would make Yvonne's day."

Jake and Grant hitched a ride in Buddy's old station wagon and they picked up burgers along the way. Buddy asked them all about their summers, and once again, Jake marveled at how openly both he and Grant were able to share.

"I don't know why I felt like I had to share with my mom about being gay," Grant confessed as they walked out of the local burger joint. "I guess I was just tired of feeling like my secret could be exposed at any moment."

"What happened?" Buddy asked kindly.

"She laughed at first, thinking I was joking," Grant answered. "But when she realized I was serious, she just walked out of the room, never spoke to me again. She didn't even say goodbye when I left." His voice was barely more than a whisper. "But that wasn't even the worst of it. Even though she never talked to me again, she obviously talked to my brother, 'cause the next night when he came in drunk..." Grant's voice trailed off and he looked away. Jake couldn't be sure, but he thought his six-foot-one0 friend was on the verge of tears. "I'm just glad that I waited 'til my last week. There's no way I could have handled it all summer."

Without saying a word, Buddy stopped in the middle of the sidewalk and gave the much taller Grant a hug. They piled silently into his car and he drove away shaking his head.

"It sounds like in the family lottery, your luck sort of ran out, son," Buddy finally spoke in a soft voice. "But blood relatives aren't all you've got. God's got a family He'd love to have you be a part of, and Jake and I would sure love to be your brothers."

Grant grunted, but still stared off out the window. Jake couldn't be sure what he was thinking, but it seemed like he might actually be considering Buddy's offer. Buddy steered his car slowly into a small driveway in front of a quaint, one-story red brick house. The front yard was small but perfectly manicured with a simple picket fence, some well-trimmed rose bushes, and a tidy hedge. A vegetable garden was tucked into the corner closest to the house.

"Welcome to my humble abode." Buddy gestured with a flourish.

"This place is so you!" Jake grinned, picturing his mentor pushing a lawn mower over the tiny plot of grass while his wife tended to the garden. In his mind, a pitcher of ice cold lemonade awaited them on the tiny front porch. The house just exuded love and contentment.

Buddy turned the key in the lock, but before he opened the front door, he twisted to look at Jake and Grant sadly. "Just be forewarned," he said rather hesitantly. "Sometimes things aren't so...nice."

He opened the door and they entered an equally immaculate living room and then followed him down the hallway to a modest bedroom.

"Look who's home just in time for a diaper change!" a tall blonde woman exclaimed jovially to her patient as she tenderly adjusted Yvonne's motionless body from her side to her back. "And look, sweetie! He brought company. Ooh, it looks like you're gonna have a fun afternoon."

"Hey, Bunny," Buddy greeted warmly.

"Welcome home, Mr. Riha. Did you have a nice morning at church?"

"It was food for the soul." He smiled brightly.

"Well, why don't you take your guests on out to the living room while I get your wife all cleaned up." She grinned and tried to shoo everyone out.

"Thanks, Bunny, but I'll take care of it. I've already kept you here longer than normal this morning."

"Nonsense, Mr. Riha. You have enough on your hands already."

"Really, Bunny, I don't mind," Buddy insisted.

The friendly bickering went back and forth for awhile until the home health care worker finally gave in and gathered her stuff to leave. "Well, I hope the rest of your day is splendid," she said, giving each of the men a grandmotherly hug on her way out the door.

Buddy excitedly walked over to his love and planted a kiss on her forehead. The strong stench of urine and excrement filled the room but Buddy didn't seem to notice. "Look honey, I brought home company. Jake is back for the school year."

Lying motionless in her slightly inclined hospital bed with wide-open eyes staring at nothing, Yvonne looked like a corpse.

"Hi, Mrs. Riha," Jake said warmly, not sure if she could even hear him.

"And this is Grant." Buddy motioned. "You know the power forward that I'm always talking to you about?"

"Nice to meet you, Mrs. Riha." Grant grabbed her hand and gently shook it.

Buddy combed his fingers through his wife's hair and looked up at the boys. "After all this, and she's still a fox." He winked then turned his attention back to his bride, holding her hand and stroking it. "I took lots of notes from the sermon for you, and, of course, I said hi to all the members of the choir. They all miss you."

Buddy stooped down to kiss his wife's cheek and his eyes started getting teary again. Jake marveled at the passion he still had for his sweetheart of sixty-plus years.

Suddenly, Buddy cleared his throat. "No sense in all the fries getting cold. How about you boys start eating out in the kitchen while I clean up in here a bit? I'll join you in a few minutes. There's soda in the fridge."

Jake and Grant nodded and exited the putrid smelling room. For the next twenty-five minutes, they nibbled on their burgers as they overheard Buddy struggling to change his wife's diaper and clothes down the hall.

Jake had never seen such a tangible form of utter devotion and adoration. It wasn't sexy but it was powerful, and it gripped him to his core. *Lord, please give me a chance to learn to love Amy like that!*

AMY STUFFED AT LEAST TWO SUITCASES worth of stuff into her solitary checked baggage and sat on the bulging lid until she managed to force the zipper closed. There was still the risk of explosion in transit, but that was a risk she was willing to take— rather than pay the extra fifty bucks to check a second bag! She lugged it to her mom's car and then returned inside to grab her backpack and her purse.

"Mom! I'm ready," she called out.

"I'll be out in a sec," her mom assured her from the back bathroom, but the sound of the shower still running was unmistakable.

"I'll be waiting in the car," Amy mumbled, knowing that it would be at least fifteen minutes until her mom would appear. At least she'd added thirty minutes of wiggle room into their departure time. Hopefully they wouldn't hit any traffic on the way down.

Amy settled into the passenger seat and pulled out her journal. What a summer it had been! As much as she had originally resented her mom's power move to keep her in Oceanside the entire three months of vacation, Amy had to admit that it had actually been good for her. Her mom was right; she would have the next eight months to see her dad's family as much as she wanted. This summer was about investing in relationships down here. And that had been so worthwhile.

Amy's relationship with her mom still wasn't perfect, but for the first time in her life, Amy felt like they actually had a relationship. For the first time since Amy could remember, Sherry started coming home immediately after work and actually wanted to spend time with her daughter. For the first time, Sherry listened like she actually cared. Countless nights had passed this summer with them just sitting and talking at the old kitchen table until the wee hours of the morning. And for the first time, Amy actually became comfortable talking with her mom about virtually anything. They talked about school, and boys, and work, and boys, and friends, and boys...and even a little religion.

God was such a huge part of Amy's life now that any conversation inevitably touched on the subject. Previously, her mom would either ignore her comments or change the subject completely. But this summer, for the first time, Sherry finally opened up about her own religious past.

Amy had been shocked to hear that her mom had actually grown up going to church, and had even been a student leader in her youth group. But then when she was in eighth grade, the church secretary turned up pregnant, and come to find out, the pastor turned out to be the father. In the ensuing scandal, Sherry's family left the church and never looked back. Who needed all those rules when everyone just turned out to be hypocrites anyway? Sherry loved the new freedom she entered high school with, and totally lived it up...until she got knocked up her senior year, and Amy knew the rest of that story.

Her mom wanted to let it rest at that but Amy pushed her to talk about it more. Amy's entire childhood had been one giant knot of secrets and regrets and guilt and misunderstandings. No wonder she had grown up feeling so conflicted about who she was and where she fit in the world. But building the bridge to her dad had started releasing her from that sticky web, and she wanted her mom to experience that real freedom, too. One conversation at a time, the tangle of their past slowly unraveled, and the more it straightened out, the more whole Amy felt. It was amazing!

Sherry initially resisted hearing anything about Amy's dad and how he had changed and how he deeply regretted the way he'd treated them. The fact that he was now super involved with God and church only added fuel to the fires of bitterness raging inside of her. But sometime during the summer, she finally broke down. She released her grudges and accepted the truth and started asking Amy more and more questions about her dad and her faith and her contagious joy and peace. By the end of the summer, they were actually praying together before meals and, for the first time, Amy had hope that her mom would one day fall in love with Jesus, too. *Jesus, please keep working in her life, even after I'm gone*, Amy prayed silently.

In addition to her personal growth and her budding relationship with her mom, spending the summer in Oceanside had also afforded Amy plenty of positive bonding times with her girlfriends. Regularly running with Andrea and going out for coffee with Cari had been mutually encouraging, and Amy felt blessed that God had brought such godly women into her life. And then there were the countless days spent at the mall or the beach with Melia and the other girls in her small group. In spite of their immaturity, Amy found herself learning from them every time, and she was more excited than ever to be studying adolescent psychology this next quarter at school. The teenage mind was so fascinating, and Amy knew she wanted to spend her life investing in this age group.

And then there was Jake. How many pages had she filled in this journal thinking and praying about her situation with him? He had changed—there was no denying it. And this new Jake was more than she could have ever dreamed of. He loved God passionately, his spiritual insights were deep, and his joy in life was infectious. He enjoyed serving, he was amazing with his freshmen boys, and his smile lit up the room. He was living out his dreams, but intent on using them for God's glory...and he was willing to give them up for her! And, to top it all off, he was so dang hot! Yes, Steven was attractive, but Jake took attractive to a whole new level. It's not for nothing that certain clothing companies flaunted muscular shirtless guys in their ads. *There's just something irresistible about muscles!* And Amy had to confess that she had certainly enjoyed the view at the youth group beach days.

But, ah, Steven. What was she going to do with him? He loved God, too, and he was wise and generally happy and he served as a worship leader—and was really good at it—and his smile, oh, his smile. *And* he was willing to let her stay at Stanford so that she could follow her dreams while he followed his in New York. That's what she wanted, right? He hadn't done anything wrong, anything to deserve a break up. If Jake had never come along, Amy would have been perfectly content with him...*Right?*

A feeling of dissatisfaction gnawed at her mind. *Lord, am I just being fickle, here? You obviously brought Steven into my life for a reason. I don't want to take your gift for granted...But I just can't get Jake out of my mind. Please help me, God.*

Steven truly had been so amazing. But compared to the new Jake, his passion for life was just a little dull. Of course, Jake had lost that zest before, too, so what was to say this wouldn't fade with time? *Maybe I just need to wait it out,* Amy pondered, but she wasn't sure how much more of this indecision she could take. It was only a matter of time until Steven would figure it out, and who knew what he would do then.

Ever since Jake's unexpected visit and his profession of undying love, Steven had become a different boyfriend. He'd become ultra-sensitive about everything Amy said and did and super-obsessive about knowing every little detail of her day. Their nightly conversations over Skype usually felt more like an interrogation now than a conversation between two people who loved each other.

Amy understood where he was coming from after Jake's little stunt, and she had respected him and steered clear of her ex-boyfriend all summer. But she couldn't help but be secretly ecstatic whenever Jake turned up at church events she attended. And when Jake had volunteered to help her shop for the retreat last month...Amy still didn't know how she'd been able to hold herself together. If Steven ever caught wind of who her Costco partner had been, he would have flipped out—but what he didn't know wouldn't kill him. Jake had been a perfect gentleman, and even his little gift had been so sweet and innocent.

"So are you *finally* ready?" Amy's mom asked with a smile as she slid into the driver's seat.

Amy jumped and quickly flipped her journal closed.

"What?" Sherry prodded. "You writing something about me that you don't want me to see?"

"No, mom. Just talking to God about Jake and Steven."

"Oh, them again." Sherry rolled her eyes. "Well, you know what I think. Jake had his chance. And Steven comes from money. Seems like an easy enough choice to me."

Now it was Amy's turn to roll her eyes. "Mom."

The conversation lulled and Amy absorbed the sights of her hometown as her mom navigated the side roads to the freeway. Sherry accelerated onto Interstate 5 and they headed south toward the San Diego Airport.

"Not that you really care what I think," Sherry broke the silence. "But for what it's worth, you do have a special spark in your eyes whenever you talk about Jake...And he did bring me that rose." She ran her fingers through her daughter's hair and then fixed her eyes on the road ahead. "So, when does that internship start again?"

"October," Amy answered, but her mind was still mulling over her mom's observation. What did her mom see? Did it mean anything? Her thoughts started to race down that road again, but she cut them short. She looked over at her mom and smiled. "I still can't believe they selected me. Only two Stanford students are selected each—"

"Year," Amy's mom finished her sentence and smiled back. "You've only told me a few dozen times. But why are you so surprised? You have your dad's smarts and, well, my determination." Her mom grinned. "Anyone would be foolish not to pick you."

It was so weird to hear her mom talk so lovingly and encouragingly—and to mention her dad in normal conversation like it was no big deal. But Amy would take it while it lasted. "Thanks, mom."

They drove on in silence for a few miles and passed the Del Mar fairgrounds on their right. Jake had taken her there every summer back in high school. Amy flashed back to some of their fun times there, but then caught herself. *Why does everything have to remind me of him?* She groaned inwardly.

"Who's picking you up in San Francisco?" her mom broke into her thoughts once again.

"My roommate, Renee. Her family lives in Oakland and we're going to hang out for the day. Then she'll bring me to dad's house and he'll bring me back to school."

"Sounds fun."

Amy glanced over and noticed that her mom was gripping the steering wheel with both hands and her cheeks were moist. "Mom? Are you okay?"

Sherry sniffled. "I'm fine, sweetie. I've just had such a great summer with you home, and I'm really going to miss you." She brushed away the tears and fanned air into her eyes. "I know I haven't always done the best job of showing it, but I love you, honey."

Amy rested her head against the seat and absorbed her mom's uncharacteristic words. "I love you, too, mom. Thanks for making me spend the summer down here." And she meant it.

12

WALKING THROUGH THE SAN FRANCISCO AIRPORT
terminal to the baggage claim, Amy could hear her loud roommate long before she saw her. As Amy rounded the corner, there she was yapping it up with a white-haired couple. Looking like a young Oprah Winfrey, the enthusiastic girl could have easily held her own on a talk show.

"Amy Briggs!" Renee's boisterous voice echoed through the airport while Amy was still a good twenty yards away. The couple she was talking to smiled politely and quickly walked away.

Renee's exuberant welcome momentarily transported Amy back to Jake's dramatic greeting at her arrival in Louisville the year before. He had been so romantic...at first! Amy quickly reminded herself of his less-than-loving disappearance when it was time to take her back to the airport at the end of the week. *Watch it, Amy!* She warned herself and quickly dashed all thoughts of Jake out of her brain. Scooting by some slower walkers in front of her, she sped over to her dancing roommate.

"What's up girlfriend?" Amy threw her neck and shoulders into it for her best Renee impersonation.

Renee pulled back and gave Amy a once over. "You are *so* skinny girl," she practically shouted. "Do people eat in Southern California?"

Amy put her arm around her friend's neck and walked her towards the luggage carousel. "It's called exercise...I'll teach it to you." Amy laughed.

"Oooooooh. Do you know what that would do to my luscious boo-tay?" Renee intoned, fingers snapping. A few bystanders looked at her curiously.

Amy just shook her head and grinned. If Renee wasn't proof that God cared about even the little details in life, then Amy didn't know what was. After hearing tons of roommate horror stories, she had worried about who she'd get stuck with and had asked God to match her up with someone good. Renee was more than just good. She was an amazing soul sister who daily challenged Amy in her faith. Together they studied the Bible, prayed for the people and issues in their lives...and, of course, talked about boys.

"So, tell me about this Brian character I keep seeing pictures of on Facebook," Amy prodded Renee when they were loaded up in the car.

"Girl, he is my kind of awesome!" Renee beamed. "He loves Jesus with all his heart, and, ooh, that boy can preach the Word. And he fine. Ooh, don't you think he fine?"

Amy smiled. "He is pretty fine. So what's up with you two?"

"Well, we met at this inter-church outreach this summer, and started talkin' and seein' each other at more church events. Amy, seriously, I've never met a guy like him before. Even my daddy like him!" They both chuckled. "He goes to Berkeley; he's real smart and mathematical...but guess what he wants to do with that?"

"What?"

"He wants to be a middle school math teacher. Isn't that so sweet? He wants to stay in the ghettos of Oakland and make a difference in the kids' lives who don't have good male role models."

"Wow, that's really cool," Amy responded, and she couldn't help thinking about how good Jake was with the boys in his small group. Steven was great on stage, but she never saw him getting down and dirty in interpersonal ministry. In fact, the more she thought about it, he really stayed pretty aloof from investing in people's lives. It was nice while all his attention was focused on her, but was that really how she wanted to spend the rest of her life? "So is there anything wrong with him?" she suddenly found herself blurting.

"Absolutely nothing," Renee crooned. "At least, nothing that I've found yet. After hanging out as friends all summer, he took me out to dinner last weekend and told me that he knew we'd only just started getting to know each other, but from what he saw so far, he could see himself spending the rest of his life with me. He'd already got my parents' blessing and wanted to know if I'd be interested in being *courted* by him. Isn't that just the most romantic thing you've ever heard? We both have two more years until we graduate, and then he'll have an extra year to get his teaching credential and I'll have to get my master's in social work, so we're looking at three more years at least until we would get married, but, Amy, I really think he's the one."

"Wow!" was all Amy could say as she stared wide-eyed straight ahead. How was it so easy for Renee to just know? Steven's proposal had freaked Amy out. Was she just less mature than Renee? Was she too independent? *God, why can't I just be content with spending my life with Steven? Why do I have to make things so tough on myself?* Renee had continued babbling on about Brian, and Amy raced to catch up. As she finished describing some community improvement project they had served at this summer, Amy backtracked to her previous comment. "Renee, how do you know he's the one?"

Renee's eyes danced and her whole face looked lit up. "You just know, Amy. You know that he's everything you've ever wanted, that nothing better could ever come along. You know that when you're around him, your dreams become reality, and you become the best version of yourself. You know that God is his number one priority, and because of that he treats you like the treasure God created you to be. You know that all you want to do is follow him, and the more you follow him, the more in love with God you get. Amy, it's amazing. I've never felt anything like this before!" Renee was giddy with excitement, and Amy couldn't help but catch her enthusiasm. "But enough about me, give me the update on your love life. You still got both fish on the line?"

"Ugh," Amy groaned and banged her head against the window.

"Hey, it could be worse," Renee comforted. "Imagine if your line was empty...So, which one you gonna cut loose and which one you gonna deep fry?"

Amy chuckled at Renee's cavalier analogy. "I don't know, Renee. I wish it was as easy as it was for you."

"Hey, if neither of them hit the mark, then cut 'em both loose."

Amy silently pondered this new option that she'd never considered before. But that didn't comfort her either. The truth was she had two very quality guys that any other girl would be thrilled about. She just couldn't decide which one thrilled her more...Or to be more truthful, she knew which one thrilled her more, but she just wasn't sure how long that thrill would last and she was afraid to open her heart up to him again. Steven was the steady one, and she didn't want to cut him loose unless she was confident that Jake was the real thing. Unfortunately, she wasn't quite sure how to ascertain that while Steven was still on the line. Amy rolled down her window and yelled into the thunderous wind. "Ahhhhhhhhhhhhhhhh!"

"Sounds like we'll be talking about this topic a lot this semester." Renee giggled. "Now roll up that window, girl; the air conditioning's on."

Amy rolled the window back up and grinned at her roommate. There was plenty of time for boy talk this year. For now, they had plenty of other summer details to catch up on. They sped down the freeway in Renee's old green Saturn, and for the moment, Amy forgot about her boy woes and enjoyed the company at hand.

After a lively dinner at Renee's family's home, Renee graciously chauffeured Amy out to her dad's house, where they both would spend the night. As they pulled onto her dad's street around one pm, Amy reminisced about her first visit there the year before. She had been so nervous—how else was she supposed to feel about seeing a dad who had been absent for the past decade and a step mom and siblings whom she hadn't even known existed? But meeting them had turned out to be one of the best surprises of her life.

She was hardly more prepared for the surprise that awaited her tonight. Sitting in the driveway with a giant red bow on the hood was a cute white Honda CR-V. On the windshield was a huge sign that read, "To, Amy. With Love, Dad, Olivia, Ramon, and Marissa."

"Is that yours?" Renee gasped before Amy could fully comprehend what her eyes were seeing.

She'd already mentally resigned herself to the fact that her first big purchase this year would be a bike that she could ride around to her classes and her internship. If it rained, well, she'd just have to wear a raincoat, or borrow Renee's car if it was too bad. But this? This was amazing!

As Renee slowed the car to a stop directly in front of the house, the front door burst open and Marissa and Ramon sprinted toward their big sister.

"Amy's here! Amy's here!" Marissa's high shriek alerted the neighbors. If any of them were sleeping, they probably weren't anymore.

Amy jumped out of the car just in time to get attacked by her six-year-old twin siblings. During Amy's first visit, Marissa had hung back, but now she clung on to Amy's leg like a tick in the desert.

"Why aren't you guys in bed?" Amy laughed, scooping both of them up into her arms.

"Did you see your present?" Marissa asked excitedly while pointing wildly back to the driveway.

"Is that really for me?" Amy asked, still in awe.

"Duh!" Ramon looked at her incredulously. He wiggled out of her arms and ran over to the car, pointing to the sign. "It says your name right there, see? A-M-Y, Amy."

"Nice spelling, dude," Amy encouraged and tousled his hair. "Well, I got you a little something, too." Amy grinned.

"Really? What is it?" Marissa gasped, eyes wide.

"Well it's tucked away in my suitcase, so I'll have to find it for you tomorrow, but I'll give you a hint...it rhymes with ship and shide."

Marissa looked at her big sister, puzzled, until a huge smile suddenly exploded onto her face. "Did you get me a barbie?"

"No," Ramon corrected sarcastically. "She got us a slip n' slide."

"Ohhhhh. Can you take us for a ride in your new car?"

"How about tomorrow, honey?" Amy's dad's voice intervened from the walkway. "I'll bet your sister is pretty tired and—"

"Dad! You're amazing!" Amy interrupted. She set Marissa down and ran to her father. "Thank you *so* much!"

Ray chuckled softly. "It's nothing fancy. Our neighbor a few houses down was selling it and gave me a deal I couldn't resist. I'm sorry you didn't get to pick it out yourself."

"Oh, dad, it's perfect! I would have been happy with a bicycle. This has *four* wheels! And it's really nice. I absolutely love it." Filled beyond capacity with gratitude, Amy felt a wave of tears threatening to spill over. She quickly inhaled, shook her head, and squeezed her dad tightly. "I love you, dad."

"I love you, too, Ames," he whispered tenderly in her ear as he stroked her hair.

How far her perception of this man had come in the last nine months! *What if I had never read those letters?* She shuddered, grateful to Steven for pushing her to forgive her father. Tiny hands wrapped around her waist as Ramon and Marissa flanked her on either side. Then Olivia's arm's reached around and hugged her from the other side.

"Aw, man. I just can't help myself." Renee laughed and joined in on the ever growing group hug.

Amy was truly surrounded by love. *Thank you Jesus...for everything!*

＊ ＊ ＊

The next morning, Amy waved goodbye to Renee after a breakfast of waffles with all the fixings. She spent the rest of the day just hanging out with her family. It was one of those days that to an outsider might seem rather dull, but for Amy, it ranked among the best in her first twenty years of life. They set up the race track slip n' slide in the back yard, and the whole family got into the races. In the end, her dad came out the overall speed champion, but Ramon definitely took the prize for most creative landing maneuvers.

After a couple hours of soggy fun, they took the twins to the nearby park and sat on a bench catching up while the kids played. On the way back home, they stopped for ice cream at the neighborhood quickie mart and then worked on a family puzzle at the dining room table. After a delicious dinner of Olivia's chicken enchiladas, they set up a fort in the living room and told stories over a flashlight campfire. Eventually, the twins had to go to bed, and Amy relished their pudgy embraces. This was the life she had always dreamed of!

Skyping all summer had kept her abreast of the details of their lives, but she couldn't get hugs like those over the airwaves. It had been good for her to spend the summer in Oceanside, but she was so glad she got to spend the school year here. Surrounded by her new family, things fell into perspective. The stress of figuring out who she wanted to spend the rest of her life with paled in light of the joy she got from spending time with her family now. God had given her this gift, and she wanted to appreciate it to the fullest.

WITH TWO WEEKS STILL TO GO BEFORE PRACTICE officially started, basketball hype was already in full swing around Louisville and Jake was already feeling like a celebrity. Billboards around town plastered his face larger than life next to his teammates. Front page articles in the local newspapers heralded high hopes for him and the team. And everywhere he went, people greeted him like an old friend. Sometimes it really seemed as if the entire Louisville population knew him on a first name basis, especially the girls.

Jake had to admit, he enjoyed the popularity, but he worked hard not to let it go to his head. "Pride cometh before the fall," Buddy had warned him—right after he had asked for Jake's autograph to give to one of his neighbor's grandkids. His tone was humorous, but Jake understood the legitimacy of the admonition. He'd fallen hard enough last year and had no interest in coming even close to that again.

After saying hi to an eighth stranger on the short walk from his apartment to his Kinesiology class, Jake ducked into the glass doors of the two-story building, relieved to be near his destination.

"Jake!" a familiar voice chirped in front of him.

Jake looked up, and there was Nicole, dressed for weather at least thirty degrees warmer than what he'd just left outside. Immediately, a flood of unhealthy memories of their times together crowded into the front of his mind, and it was all he could do to push them back out. It had been a year since they broke up, and Jake could probably count the times he'd talked to her since then on one hand, yet still, those unwanted and unwholesome thoughts of her haunted him whenever he saw her. "Uh, hi, Nicole," he stammered.

"It has been so long since I've seen you! What, are you like trying to avoid me or something?" She smiled and tried to give him one of her tight hugs.

Jake patted her back weakly. "I guess our paths just don't cross much this year, huh?"

"Well, then, we should just make some new paths then." Nicole playfully tugged on the arm of Jake's sweatshirt. "I've got a major test to study for tonight. Want to be my study buddy in the library?"

Are you serious? You're still playing this game? Jake recoiled inside. He had zero interest in succumbing to her charms now and wondered how he had been so dumb last time. "You know, I actually have other plans tonight. Sorry."

"Awww," she pouted seductively. "You've been hanging out with Nate too much."

"Yeah," Jake smiled. "We've actually become pretty good friends this year. You've got a great guy in him." Nicole gaped at Jake, speechless. "Well, hey, I'm late for my class, but I'm sure I'll see you around." Jake patted her shoulder and walked away feeling surprisingly lighter. This was the girl who'd made him weak in the knees ever since he arrived at Louisville, but today, he'd withstood her allure without hesitation. *Thanks, God.* He grinned.

Jake slipped into a seat in the back of the auditorium just as his professor was beginning the lecture. The girl next to him smiled warmly, and he politely smiled back—and couldn't help noticing how attractive she was. But as he turned back to the front, her pretty face merely melted into Amy's, and once again, Jake was lost.

No matter how hard he tried, Jake couldn't stop thinking about Amy. Of course, it probably didn't help that he scouted out her Facebook page several times a day. That feeble connection served as a desert mirage for a thirsty man, and as fleeting and unsatisfying as mirages were, they nevertheless provided the hope necessary to carry on.

Of course, Amy's mirage was a pretty desolate one. She always looked so happy in her profile picture with Steven, and her status updates always sounded like her life was just perfect the way it was—without Jake. It had been over a month since Jake had tossed the ball—literally!—into her court at Costco, and while that conversation had left him with a glimmer of hope, since then, Amy had done nothing to keep it alive. It seemed pretty clear now that she had let that ball just roll into the corner and was fully engaged in the action in Steven's court.

God, is it time for me now to just move on? Jake struggled as his professor droned on about ligaments and their functions. Usually Jake enjoyed the class, but today he just couldn't connect. *I mean, am I waiting for something that isn't meant to happen? If Steven wasn't the guy for Amy, wouldn't she have figured that out already?* Jake sighed at the logic of that. It was true. Amy had had plenty of time to make her choice. Obviously she was choosing Steven over Jake. And maybe it was time for Jake to accept that. He sighed again. *Okay, Lord, I get it. But I need your help here. If You're not going to change her heart, then I really need You to change mine.*

With fresh resolve, Jake tuned back in to the professor's lecture...and turned to the girl next to him for the notes he had missed.

A WEEK INTO THE FALL QUARTER, Amy was busier than she'd ever been in her life, but loving every minute of it. On top of all of her activities at school, she'd made it her goal to spend nearly every weekend with her family. Hearing about her brother and sister's new experiences in kindergarten was always a highlight, as was going to church—as a family!—on Sunday mornings. She wondered how her life might be different if she had grown up doing so, and prayed that her mom would someday come back to her faith.

Finally done with her general education courses, Amy carried a full load of upper division Psychology classes that kept her up late studying nearly every single night. But as hard as they were, she was thrilled to be learning so much and couldn't wait to put her knowledge to work at her internship.

She was still super involved with Intersect—InterVarsity Christian Fellowship's club on campus—and looked forward to their weekly meetings and social activities. She also was leading a dorm Bible study with Renee again, and was elated to see several new girls joining them. One of them still wasn't a Christian—yet—but she had tons of questions that kept Amy talking to Cari for advice at least once a week and poring over her Bible on her own every day.

Intersect was definitely a different experience without Steven there. He had been the first person she had met there, and his graduation left a pretty big void. But if anything, Amy found herself far less distracted—she was able to concentrate on God much better when her boyfriend wasn't standing behind the microphone! She missed him—kind of—but the longer they were apart, the less Amy thought about him. They had tried to Skype every day over the summer, but once both of them started classes again, their busy schedules and the three hour time difference between New York and California left them speaking at best every three to four days. And even when they did talk, there just didn't seem to be as much to say.

Making an effort to keep the relationship alive, Amy tried to do what she could. She intentionally thought of details in her day that Steven might be interested in and attempted to ask him thoughtful questions about the things he shared with her. She sent him cute text messages throughout the day and posted little love notes to his Facebook wall. She even baked him cookies at her dad's house and sent him a care package. But a girl can only do so much, and she was getting tired.

"Steven," she pleaded during her lunch break. "You never feel like talking anymore. Are you mad at me, or what?"

"Amy, I've told you," he answered wearily. "I've just been real busy."

She had interrupted his piano practice, and he only had a thirty minute slot today and needed to prepare for a performance exam tomorrow. "Well, when are you going to have more time?"

"Not today."

"How about tomorrow?"

"I don't know. I'll call you when I can."

"Steven."

"Amy, why do you have to turn everything into drama? I warned you things would be like this. Why do you think I wanted you to come to New York with me?"

"Right. Because things would be *so* much better if I had moved out there. If you can't even carve out a few minutes to talk with me on the phone, I can only imagine how much time you'd be finding to *hang out* with me."

"Whatever. I don't have time for this. I'll call you later." And with that, he hung up.

Amy dropped her phone in her lap and picked at the salad on her plate. The nagging reminders of the end of her relationship with Jake crept to the forefront of her brain once more. "Ahh!" She exhaled sharply and flicked her fork onto the other side of her cafeteria tray. Her appetite gone, she looked at the time on her phone. Today was the first day of her internship. It wouldn't hurt to show up early. She dumped her lunch in the garbage and headed out to the parking lot where she jumped into her car and drove off.

Every time she drove her new car, she was reminded of just how good her life really was. In spite of her relationship with Steven going poorly, there were plenty of other really good things she should be thankful for, not the least of which was this car, and her family that gave it to her, and the internship she was driving to. She'd never known that a car could drive so quietly and shift so smoothly. It made her mom's old mini-van feel like a dump truck. *Thank you, God. You really have blessed me.* She turned up the worship song playing on her stereo and regrouped.

Working with a non-profit clinic that helped children and families dealing with abuse was the last thing Amy would have ever considered doing going into her senior year of high school—which, although it seemed like an eternity, was really only three years ago. She had always wanted to do something glamorous, something high-powered...like being a courtroom attorney or a politician or a business executive. But those high-status positions held zero interest to her now.

Amy was such a different person than that insecure cheerleader whose biggest concern was how to get everyone to like her. Her unexpected pregnancy and the ensuing adoption process, her tumultuous breakup with Jake and the correlating heartbreak, her redeeming relationship with Jesus and the newfound purpose He awakened, and all the friendships God brought into her life since then had all played a role in shaping her new hopes and dreams for the future.

Ironically, though, she was in the very early stages of this development when her interest in psychology was first piqued. Weeks after giving birth, the sting of giving her baby away still excruciatingly tender, and days after watching her boyfriend drive away to live out his dreams, Amy had entered Mr. Sullivan's Psychology one0one class at Mira Costa Community College. When all around her was unstable, the lively old man had unwittingly thrown her a lifeline, and she had grabbed on and enjoyed every moment of the ride. Psychology explained things she had always wondered about, and hinted at solutions to her troubles. It was a scientific grid to help her track the very unscientific glitches in life. She loved it.

When Amy had first shared with Cari that she was going to declare psychology as her major, Cari had said something like "God never wastes a hurt." Amy had applied the pithy comment to her pregnancy woes and recent split with Jake. But meanwhile, God was peeling back a whole new layer of past hurt for Amy to deal with, thanks to her unlikely relationship with Melia. The process of helping Melia escape her abusive home not only forced Amy to unwrap her own childhood trauma, but also grew in her an inescapable compassion for other hurting kids. She couldn't wait to spend the rest of her life helping children heal from wounds that had silently hurt her for too long.

"Can I help you?" an Asian woman in her late forties asked from the reception desk as Amy entered the waiting room of Palo Alto Child Services.

The clinic was one of many medical offices radiating off of a lush central courtyard, and filtered sunlight streamed through the large front windows. Muted earth tones, oversized couches, and Tuscan décor created a calming environment, and Amy immediately felt at ease.

"My name's Amy Briggs." She smiled as she walked toward the lady. I'm one of the new interns from Stanford. Today's my first day."

"Welcome to PACS," the woman greeted warmly. "Please take a seat and Dr. Wyatt will be with you shortly."

Amy sank into the nearest sofa and observed her surroundings. In the corner to her right, a man and woman sat rigidly as a small girl put a puzzle together at their feet. All three of them were unnaturally silent. Amy tried not to stare, but her mind was already speculating about their situation. Were they married? Was the father abusive? Or was he even the father? Or had someone else hurt their little girl? How long had it taken for them to believe her? Or did they even believe her now? And how would she ever be sure of the truth if she were the doctor?

Her head reeled with the possibilities—and the magnitude of this new step toward her future. Suddenly all the scenarios and terms and diagnoses she'd studied in classes exploded into the reality that each one was inexorably tied to myriad real people, real stories, real faces. Sure, she'd known that all along. That was the reason she wanted to enter this field after all. But seeing three new real faces in front of her suddenly sent her heart racing. Were her own hurts still too fresh for her to be able to help others? And she was still so new to the program. Had she learned enough? *God, this is heartbreaking work here. Can I really help?*

Relax, a new voice spoke into her apprehension. *I am in control. I placed you here. And I want to use you to let Me help them.*

Amy closed her eyes and absorbed these truths. This was an opportunity of a lifetime, and God knew what He was doing.

"Miss Briggs," a deep male voice boomed into her thoughts.

Amy looked up to see one of the largest and most intimidating men she had ever met in her life. "Uh, yes?"

"Hi. My name's Dr. Wyatt, but my friends call me Teddy." He extended his large hand to Amy who stood up and shook it back.

If it weren't for the stethoscope around his neck and the "Dr. Wyatt" embroidered on his jacket, Amy was pretty sure she would have pegged him for a professional wrestler. "Teddy" was at least six foot five with a round inviting face that was mostly covered by a dark brown beard. The extra large white lab jacket did little to hide his robust figure and even the generous sleeves barely fit around the circumference of his enormously large biceps. Immediately, Amy's thoughts transported her back to Chris and Cari's house when Jake had come downstairs looking similarly ill-fitted. She started to smirk, but then caught herself and focused on the moment at hand.

"It's really nice to meet you, Dr. Wyatt." Amy smiled. She looked him in the eyes and did her best to give him a firm handshake even though her fingers barely curved around his palm.

"You come very highly recommended." He grinned. "Mrs. Mozon is a family friend and her letter of recommendation was one of the best I've ever read."

So that's how I got this job, Amy thought to herself. Amy had written a thank you note to last year's child psychology professor immediately after completing the application for the internship, but she made a mental note to stop by Mrs. Mozon's office sometime and thank her again in person. Amy had learned so much in that class, and now this incredible opportunity was just the icing on the cake.

Amy followed Dr. Wyatt through the door next to the front desk. In spite of her experiences as a child, this was her first experience in an official counseling center, and she couldn't help but wonder how her life might have been different if she had been given a safe place like this to talk during those younger years of her life. Amy gave her mom the benefit of the doubt that she must have been unaware of places like this while Amy was suffering in the aftermath of her uncle's abuse and her dad's abandonment.

Dr. Wyatt opened the door to his office and Amy was surprised by the tidiness of the small space. Something about his eccentric appearance triggered images of those absent-minded professors whose desks lie buried beneath stacks of files and journals and books. But this man's workspace was impeccably orderly and clutter free. He sat down behind his bare mahogany desk and motioned for Amy to take a seat in the plush chair in front of it.

"So I've read your application and know all about your qualifications, but I was particularly interested in your own experiences with abuse. If you don't mind me asking, would you tell me a little more about yourself and your past?" the doctor requested, his deep voice surprisingly soft.

Whereas a year ago, Amy would have been immediately alarmed by a question like that, today, she was eager to share. She told him about her relationship with Melia and how Melia's abuse had triggered memories she had suppressed for years. She explained how hard it had been to help Melia while avoiding her own hurts, but that with the support of friends and the grace of God she had faced her past and experienced deep healing and even restored her relationship with her dad. "And now I just feel like I need to pass it on," she concluded.

The whole time the bearded doctor smiled warmly and nodded along as he listened.

"Thank you for sharing your story with me, Amy," he responded when Amy was finished. His eyes reflected genuine compassion. "You'll have a lot to offer these kids."

Dr. Wyatt pulled a manila folder out of the top drawer of his desk. "As you discovered with your young friend Melia, many of the children we encounter here at PACS come from homes which from the outside seem to have it all together. Their parents are successful doctors or lawyers or computer engineers. They live in opulent houses in prestigious communities. They go to the best schools and wear the best clothes and participate in plenty of extracurricular activities. And often, their parents are even there watching. But behind closed doors, life is a different story. Take this young man, for example."

He pulled a picture of a small boy out of the folder. The face was blurred out, but the dark bruises covering his body from his neck to his knees were all too visible.

Amy had to look away. She'd seen Melia's bruises but those were nothing compared to what this boy had gone through. What kind of monster would do something like this? A righteous anger began to boil inside of her.

Dr. Wyatt leaned forward and put his elbows on his desk. "Amy, I understand completely what you are feeling right now, but in order to make a difference, you need to learn how to control those feelings and keep them off of your face." He said it kindly, but his tone was serious.

Amy inhaled sharply and shook her head. "I'm sorry."

"Don't be sorry for the feelings. If you didn't feel anger at a picture like this, there would be something wrong with you. But that's not what these kids need." Dr. Wyatt's compassionate gaze pierced into the depths of her soul. "What these kids long for is someone to just give them a voice, to listen, and to give them hope that it's all going to be okay." He paused to let that sink in. "And one more thing: We're not here to judge."

Amy immediately thought back to the couple with the little girl sitting in the waiting area. She knew nothing about their situation but had immediately let her brain assume the worst.

"You will probably see some absolutely atrocious things here. But we're not investigators. We're not the law. Our county has an excellent Child Protective Services department, and we trust them to do their jobs. Our role here is just to help the kids...and their parents. No matter what we think the truth might be, we're here to help anyone who comes through our doors asking for it."

Amy slowly nodded her head, thinking about her own Uncle Harold. Long before he had brutalized her, he had desperately needed the services of a place like this when he was being abused as a child. "Whew!" she sighed, contemplating the enormity of the task ahead of her. She hadn't even seen one child yet and already she was learning. More than just becoming a better child psychologist, she could see that this was going to be starting a lifelong exercise in overflowing grace, love and compassion. "I can do this, Dr. Wyatt," she finally asserted in the strongest voice she could muster.

"I know you can, Amy." A big smile crossed Dr. Wyatt's hairy face. Amy could see why his friends called him Teddy. Beneath his grizzly exterior, he was one of the warmest, most kindhearted people she had ever met.

"So, when do I get to start seeing real kids?"

"Next week. Today you get to fill out a mountain of paper work." He grinned and led Amy back out to the front waiting room and passed her off to Terri, the woman at the front desk. "Welcome to the team, Amy Briggs." Dr. Wyatt extended his hand again and walked back through the swinging door.

"**HEY, DAD**," Amy said nonchalantly as she raced back from PACS to an afternoon study session with some of her Psych 302 buddies.

"Hey, Ames. What's up?" her father's voice resonated out of her car speakers. One of her favorite features of her new car was the built in Bluetooth.

"Sooooo, I just had my first day at the internship," she began.

"That's right! How was it?"

Amy just couldn't get Dr. Wyatt's words out of her mind about not judging and helping even the perpetrators of abuse at their clinic. And every time they replayed, they were accompanied by the sullen face of her Uncle Harold. "Well…" she faltered. She just wasn't sure how to get this out. "Um…When was the last time you talked to Uncle Harold?"

Silence ricocheted around the cabin of her car.

"Dad? You there?" Amy confirmed.

"Yeah, yeah," her father's voice whispered hoarsely. "Uh…" He paused again. "About two weeks ago."

The silence came from Amy this time. *What?* She had expected an answer more in the *years* category. How had her dad not told her?

"I'm sorry, Amy," Ray responded as if reading her mind. "I just didn't think it would ever come up in a conversation, and I didn't want to hurt you."

Amy tried to say something, but no words came to mind.

"Amy, really, I'm really sorry."

"No, no, Dad, it's okay," she finally mumbled, her head still reeling. "Um, he's still in jail, right?"

"Yes, of course. He has another three years before he even comes up for parole."

Amy felt the hairs on the back of her neck prickle. Three years really wasn't that long. "Oh." She turned into the parking lot nearest the library and pulled into a space, then just sat there staring straight ahead. Her study group had started seven minutes ago, but she felt paralyzed.

"Amy, are you okay? Why did you even ask about my brother?"

Amy hesitated then pushed herself to continue. "How often do you guys talk?"

"Well, I try to visit him once a month, and call him two or three times in between," her dad admitted slowly.

"So his prison is nearby?"

"It's about an hour and a half away, up in Vacaville. Why do you ask? You know you're safe, now, right?"

"No, no, I know, Dad. It's just..." Amy searched for the right words. "I guess I've never been able to get your story about your own childhood out of my mind, and the doctor I'll be working with said something today that made me think of your brother. Dad, he needs God's love, too."

Silence came from the other side again, until Ray whispered, "I know."

"Well," Amy hesitated, afraid of her next words. "I'm not sure if I'm anywhere near ready to face him, but I can't escape the thought that maybe it would mean more if it came from me."

More silence. "You have no idea."

Amy looked at the time. "Dad, I really gotta go, I'm late for a study group. I'll let you know when I'm ready to talk about this more, 'kay?"

"Amy, you're amazing. You know that, right?"

Amy smiled. "Thanks, Dad. I love you." She stepped out of her car, slung her backpack over her shoulder, and speed-walked to the library. What a can of worms this internship was opening!

Amy breezed through the doors and spotted her study group at their usual table, books open and heads down, intently focused. Their professor believed in the power of the pop quiz. "Anyone can give the right answer when they know what questions are coming; but the best psychologists are ready for anything at anytime," he had stated during their first class—and he had backed it up with six surprise tests already.

"Where do you want me?" Amy whispered to a friendly girl named Christy as she slid into the empty chair next to her.

"Page fifty-seven to sixty-three in Rosenberg and Chapter 5.1 in Grotzky. By the way, you're late," Phil, a senior from Japan, interjected in his thick accent without ever looking up from his books.

"Sorry. No excuse." The rest of the group gave Amy a quick smile as she settled in and opened up the first huge textbook. Every thirty minutes each group member was responsible for reporting the key concepts from the pages assigned to them. Amy was already twelve minutes behind and her head was still a million miles away.

Her eyes bored into the pages as she skimmed them for pertinent information, but before she could even highlight her first noteworthy tidbit, her phone buzzed inside her pocket. Her hand shot to her hip to grab it, but she caught herself just in time and resisted the urge to check it. Whoever had texted her would be able to survive the next hour without her response, and she would surely survive without knowing who it was. She focused again on the words below and skimmed a few more pages. Just as she highlighted another term, her phone buzzed again, causing her to jump and streak an errant line of yellow across the page.

Phil looked up at her and scowled, so Amy kept her head down and kept reading. She polished off the last few pages in the first book and quickly flipped to her assigned spot in the second book. She just might be able to catch up in time. But the annoying buzz of her phone disturbed her once more. Concerned that this might be an emergency, Amy slyly pulled the phone out of her pocket and looked down at the texts.

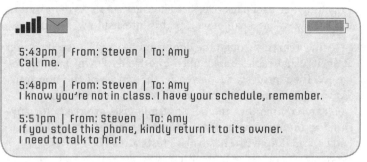

5:43pm | From: Steven | To: Amy
Call me.

5:48pm | From: Steven | To: Amy
I know you're not in class. I have your schedule, remember.

5:51pm | From: Steven | To: Amy
If you stole this phone, kindly return it to its owner.
I need to talk to her!

Amy shook her head and sighed. What could be so important that Steven needed to talk to her so suddenly? *He sure didn't see the need to cut* his *studying short today!* He would just have to wait. She shoved the phone back in her pocket and tried to focus...but to no avail—no sooner had she turned her eyes back to the page than the phone resumed its annoying intrusion, but this time the buzzing continued in an incessant pulsing vibration.

"Are you going to answer that or what?" Phil glared at her.

Amy shrugged apologetically. "I'll be back in like two minutes." She walked briskly out of the library and answered the call. "Look Steven, I really don't have time to talk—"

"I can't do this anymore, Amy," Steven's voice interrupted her on the other end. "It's just not working out."

Amy stood motionless for a moment. Was this what she thought it was? "Um...Are you breaking up with me, Steven?"

"I think we both knew this was coming."

"Uh, wow," Amy stammered. "I...I guess I don't know what to say." She sank to the curb and stared out at the sea of cars in the parking lot in front of her.

"And that's just the problem."

"Excuse me?"

"You've lost the will to fight for our relationship. You're not crying, you're not listing all the reasons why you still want to be with me, you're not even asking me why. It's just as I suspected: you don't even care."

"Okay, wait a minute. That's hardly fair. You just interrupted me in the middle of a study group and blindsided me before you even said hello, and somehow this is *my* fault? I have done nothing *but* care about our relationship. I'm the one who's been trying!"

"But Amy, your heart isn't in it. I can tell. I love you, Amy, but I need someone who's going to love me back even more."

Amy really didn't know what to say. Steven had a point. A good relationship did need both parties to love each other entirely, and the truth was she had always had a slight reservation in her heart when it came to him. But she had always assumed that would change with time. He was the one who wanted to move so fast. And she had sure gone out of her way to *act out* love toward him, and isn't that what true love was all about. "So this is the way you show someone you love them?" she finally blurted quietly.

Steven was silent on the other line for a moment. "I wish it could have worked out between us, but I don't want to do this anymore. Goodbye, Amy."

With that, the connection went dead—Steven had hung up. Amy dropped her head into her hands and watched a tiny ant scrambling around. *God? I sure didn't see that one coming.* A certain sense of disappointment crashed down on her, and she waited for the tears to come. But her eyes remained surprisingly dry. And as she contemplated what had just happened, the burden she had been carrying all summer slowly evaporated. She lifted her head and breathed in deep. Steven was a great guy and she definitely needed to give herself time to mourn this loss. But a sense of peace washed over her, and she knew God was in control of her future. Amy turned her cell phone completely off and walked back into the library to join her study group.

✚ ✚ ✚

Three hours later, after studying for Psych 302 and two other classes, Amy flopped on her bed and divulged the latest twist in her soap opera life to Renee.

"So you're saying he's back on the market?" her roommate joked. "You still got his number?"

"What? I'm pretty sure Brian wouldn't appreciate you callin' up some new guy."

"Oh, it's not for me. I got a friend who might be interested. You gotta admit that boy was fi-ine...Mmmhmm."

Amy threw her pillow across the room. "Shut up. You wouldn't dare."

Renee laughed. "Nah. But he was a catch."

Amy sighed and got up from her bed. She walked over to the collage of photos she had hung up by her desk. "Well, I guess I won't be needing these anymore." She started peeling off all the pictures that included her now ex-boyfriend—which was most of them. Of the few remaining, her eyes lingered on a group shot of the Souled Out lunch group she had joined at the end of her senior year of high school. In the photo, she was visibly pregnant... and standing next to Jake.

"So you gonna call him, or should I?" Renee's voice a foot back startled her.

"Who?" Amy tried to respond naïvely.

"He was cute in high school but I want to see what he looks like now." Renee spun around and flipped open her laptop on her desk.

"What are you doing?"

"Oh, I'm just googling University of Louisville basketball." Renee yawned. "No reason in particular."

"Renee!" Amy walked over to join her. "I'm pretty sure I shouldn't be looking at that yet," Amy said halfheartedly.

"Who said anything about you lookin'? Get over to your side of the room."

But Amy remained glued to her spot peering over Renee's shoulder. The University of Louisville Men's Basketball page loaded and there at the top of the screen was Jake practically staring right at her.

Renee whistled through her teeth. "He's pretty cut for a white guy. You sure those muscles aren't airbrushed?"

"They're real," Amy assured her with a grin.

"Dang, girl. And you said he loves Jesus, too?"

Amy nodded.

"So what are you waiting for?" Renee jabbed her playfully with her elbow and gave her a wink.

Amy shook her head and squeezed into the desk chair next to her roommate. "It can't hurt just to look, right?" She scooted Renee's hand off the mouse pad and clicked on the player profile.

"Hey now!" Renee protested, bumping Amy right back out of the seat.

"I just want to see what it says about him and—"

"Sorry, Amy, but this computer is for doing homework, which I've got plenty of. So why don't you scurry on over to your own laptop and send that boy an email."

Amy shook her head again and laughed. "I think I'm going to go to the gym." Running always helped her clear her head.

As much as her heart longed to immediately contact Jake, she knew she needed time to process and make sure this was the next step God wanted her to take. If things were going to work out between them, she needed to be in a stable state of mind, not rebounding from a broken relationship. Once she opened that door to Jake, she knew she was crossing a line that would be permanent—for better or worse.

Message	
From:	Amy Briggs **x**
Subject:	Brace yourself.

JAKE STARED AT THE CRYPTIC MESSAGE TITLE, frozen to his seat.

In spite of his best intentions, he still hadn't been able to stop thinking about Amy. After his Kinesiology class last week, Jake had promptly returned to his room and took Amy's picture down from next to his bed. He hadn't checked her Facebook even once since then, and he had even made efforts to engage some of the girls in conversation at Campus Christian Fellowship on Tuesday night. But so far, it had been to no avail. Amy was still the first thought in his head every morning and her face was still the last thing he saw as he dropped to sleep each night. He'd given up on the hope that he'd someday hear from her, but his heart still refused to move on. And as if he wasn't struggling enough as it was, now this unexpected message from her in his Facebook inbox stopped him in his tracks.

Jake rarely got online before his early morning workouts—it was hard enough to get up in time to read his Bible and talk to God for a while before heading out to the weight room. But for some strange reason his eyes had popped open early this morning, and after spending an hour reading through the book of James in the Bible and journaling about how he could live out his faith more to his teammates, he felt pumped up and ready to "glow." Then he'd had the sudden urge to check his Facebook messages, and Amy's line was the first thing he'd seen.

"Brace yourself," Jake whispered. *What's that supposed to mean?* Images of what Amy's horrible news could possibly be raced through his mind. Someone was sick? Someone was dead? Someone was....

Suddenly he pictured Amy in a wedding dress next to Steven, and all his fears tightened in a knot like a punch to his stomach. He knew what she was going to say before even reading it: Steven had proposed, and, this time, she had accepted.

God? Jake questioned as he sat at his desk, now quivering in his boxers and t-shirt. *You had to wake me up for this?* He swallowed the lump in his throat and pulled the picture of Amy out of his top desk drawer. A verse the pastor had read last Sunday immediately came to mind. He had read it again this morning in James, perhaps as a foreshadowing of what God knew was coming. *Consider it pure joy, my brothers, whenever you face trials of many kinds, because you know that the testing of your faith produces perseverance.*

Jake and Buddy had talked about that one for awhile. Buddy knew how much Jake was struggling to get over Amy and offered an always-listening ear and occasional advice. But for Jake, Buddy's best counsel came from his life. Jake had learned so much from watching the humble way his mentor dealt with the pain of watching his beloved wife slowly slip away in her stroke-induced cocoon. Jake knew that Buddy's trials far surpassed his own, and yet Buddy was the most joyful person he knew.

Newly inspired just by thinking about the old man, Jake shook his head. *Lord, I'm not sure if I'm ready for this trial, but let Your joy be my strength.* He took a deep breath and finally clicked on the message.

Between **You** and **Amy Briggs**

> Brace yourself.
>
> I'm not quite sure how else to say this, so I guess I'll just come right out with it: Steven and I broke up. It happened last week, but I didn't write you right away because I didn't want to act on impulse. I wanted to give God time to reveal His plan in this and not just rush to my own conclusions. And just so you know, for whatever it's worth, Steven is the one who broke up with me.

Wait...What? Jake puzzled and rapidly reread the paragraph. *So she's not engaged?* Jake sat back in his chair for a moment to let the significance of that good news sink in. A smile spread over his face and he quickly returned to his position hunched over his computer.

> Jake, I can tell you've grown up a lot since we were last together. Just seeing how you've respected me and given me space is proof of that, and I want you to know how much I appreciate it. I'm sure it hasn't been easy for you, and I really do thank you.
>
> I witnessed plenty more confirmation of how much you've changed while watching you this summer. Yes, I confess, I was watching you. At Costco, you said I inspired you, which was so sweet, but Jake, the truth is, you inspired me. You were great with those crazy boys in your small group! So many times, watching you reminded me to have more patience—and more fun—with my own girls. They looked up to you, Jake, and you did a great job of showing them what a godly man should look like.
>
> I imagine you had loftier goals for this past summer regarding the two of us. But I noticed how you maintained your joy and servant's attitude in spite of my inapproachability. That says a lot. I want you to know that your efforts were not in vain. Not only did I notice them, but I haven't been able to get them out of my mind. While completely unappreciated by Steven, your stunt at the beginning of summer hasn't gone a day without replaying in my memory. That was the best description of love I've ever heard.

Jake looked up from the screen and shook his head. The knot that had knocked the wind out of him had gradually dissolved and now settled in his stomach as a severe case of jitters. This was going better than he could have ever imagined. But what was the punch line?

But here's my problem: I'm afraid. I love everything about the Jake I saw this summer. But you've lost that glow before, and how do I know that this isn't just a phase that will wear off once you get what you want?

I'm still not ready to plunge into something new, but I've been thinking about what it would take to get us back to a starting point. I'm not going to make this easy on you, Jake, but if it's worth it to you, this is what I'm looking for. Are you ready? Again, I warn you: brace yourself.

Wait. I never actually got to hear what the number one thing on your list was, but the number one thing I need from you is time. I don't want to just rush into another relationship. God uses everything for a reason and I think I need to take some time to reflect on my relationship with Steven and grow in some areas. So I know you've already given me a lot of space, but I need just a little more. Please don't even think of contacting me for at least two months, and even then, only if you've taken the rest of this list seriously.

Pray. The only way this is going to work is if God wants it to. I need you to pray every day about whether this is meant to be and for wisdom about how to proceed.

Lead me spiritually. You already mentioned this in your list, which I loved. But it bears repeating. I want to spend my life with a man who is always one step ahead of me in his walk with God. I am so ready to be inspired and encouraged and challenged in my faith. (BTW, I loved the glow ball.)

Take initiative. You certainly attempted to this summer, and even though I didn't feel free to respond, I appreciated your persistence. Please don't stop. Towards the end of our last relationship, I felt like I was the one scrambling to keep us together, whether

ALL or NOTHING

it was talking about God, talking about life, or even coming for a visit. I'm not going to do that again. Your job as the leader is to pursue me. You've started out great, but I'm just warning you: if you start slacking, I'm out.

Marry me. I know you mentioned this in your list and I know I kind of freaked out when I misunderstood your gift at Costco. (Sorry about that, BTW J) So I just want us to be on the same page on this one. Yes, if we do this again, I want to be playing for keeps; nothing immediate, but let's figure out a general timeline to make sure this really could work.

1. Dream with me. If we're going to spend the rest of our lives together, then it really can't just be about you supporting my dreams. I totally appreciate your offer to sacrifice your life in Louisville to come along side me—that was so sweet and so humble and says so much about you! From the bottom of my heart, thank you. But ultimately, if we are meant to be together, then we need to be able to dream together. It can't be my dreams and your dreams; it has to be our dreams. And I've realized that I have no idea what your dreams for the future are anymore. Are you still gunning for the NBA? Do have any other plans for after college? As for me, in the past year or so, God has ignited my passion for helping kids, especially those coming from abusive experiences. There's a lot about my past I've never told you, but thanks to Steven and Melia and Cari and a bunch of my Psychology classes, God has healed me and given me a vision for how he wants to use my hurts for His glory in the future.

2. Visit me. So, I really don't want you to give up Louisville, much less basketball, for me. It seems like God is using you there, and I would never want to interfere with that. But that doesn't mean you can't come visit me. If you want to make this long distance thing work, then figure out how to make me a priority.

3. No secrets. I can still picture you looking like a deer caught in headlights when you introduced me to Nicole. I don't know if anything was going on but it was clear you didn't want me to know about her. If we go forward in this relationship, we've got a lot of air to clear. Then we can start with a clean slate and move forward with all honesty from here on out.

4. No sex. I hope this one is a no-brainer considering our past, but Jake, I don't want to get anywhere even close. I have enough regrets from my past, and I don't intend to add any more. In fact, I think those stories of couples who don't even kiss until their wedding day are pretty romantic. I'm not sure if I have the strength to go that far, but I need you to lead the way in keeping us pure—especially if it's a long road.

5. Get my dad's blessing. That meant a lot that you mentioned visiting my new family in your list. A lot has happened in the past year, and my dad and I are very close now. He is an amazing godly man and I value his perspective so much. So if you still want to move forward in this, talk to him first. His name is Ray.

Jake, I know I'm setting the bar pretty high. But I don't want to get hurt again. Think about it, and if this is still what you want, maybe we can talk about it over Christmas break or something.

Love, Amy

Attach: ▬ ◄ ▮ ▼   Reply

Jake reread the lengthy message two more times before he finally stood up from his chair. His heart pounded inside of his chest, but he couldn't wipe the smile off his face. *Is this all you got, Amy?* He grinned. Sure, the list was demanding, but he had offered half of those things already in what he liked to call the "Doorstep Debacle." The best things in life don't come free and he was willing to give up much more than this. He quickly dressed to work out and bounded across the hall to pound on Grant's door.

"Steven's gone! Amy's free! And she's willing to give me a second chance!" he shouted.

The soft thud of what was probably a pillow hit the door and Jake heard Grant grunt inside. They still had twenty minutes before practice, and Grant was obviously trying to squeeze every minute of sleep out of the clock that he could. But Jake was so excited he could hardly contain himself.

ALL or NOTHING

Thank you, Jesus! Thank you, God! he repeated as he walked back into his bedroom. He pulled out his calendar and counted two months from today. Sure, Amy had said they could talk at Christmas, but Jake didn't see what good the extra two weeks would do. He did a quick check of his basketball schedule to see if the date conflicted and what he saw made him look up and smile to the heavens above. If this wasn't a sign then what was? Louisville would be making their farthest trip west all year to play in a new tournament the University of Nevada at Las Vegas was hosting...on Friday, December 12, through Sunday, December 14. If Jake asked Coach this far in advance, maybe he would let him stay behind and miss a day of classes and practice to go visit Stanford after they were done playing.

The more Jake thought about it, he got so excited he could barely breathe. He circled that weekend in his calendar, printed up Amy's list and pinned it up next to his bed—right above Amy's picture, which was promptly replaced on his nightstand. With a few more minutes to spare, Jake clicked online to check out plane tickets. If things went according to plan, two months and three days from now on December 15, Jake would be at Stanford University giving Amy the surprise of her life.

17

STILL FLOATING ON A CLOUD OF GIDDINESS from Amy's message, Jake glided into his apartment after his evening class.

"Whip-p-chow!" Grant greeted him with a whipping sound from the couch. "Your neck sore from that leash she's got you on, lover boy?" he asked, laughing.

Jake just smiled and shrugged.

"Well, do you remember what today is?"

"Uh..." Jake wracked his brain but came up blank. "Happy birthday?"

"Jake! The preseason poll came out today."

"Oh! Wow! I totally forgot. How'd we do?" Jake asked, quickly sinking onto the sofa next to Grant and pulling out his laptop.

"I don't know! I waited for you."

"Seriously?" Jake typed in the web address, and then looked over at his roommate in surprise. "Thanks, man."

Grant just shrugged as the two of them waited for the page to load. "Do you think we cracked the top twenty-five?"

"I call seventeenth."

"What? Why?"

"No reason. It just sounds good. How 'bout you?"

"I don't know. I guess I'd be happy even with twenty-fifth. We lost Jamal, you know."

"Yeah, but we got Tyler, and—"

Suddenly, the anticipated chart appeared, and both boys fell silent as their eyes raced down it in search of Louisville's spot.

AP Top 25			
RK	TEAM	RECORD	PTS
1	Duke (22)	0-0	773
2	Butler (4)	0-0	704
3	Kentucky (2)	0-0	676
4	Kansas (12)	0-0	659
5	Ohio State (1)	0-0	630
6	Georgetown	0-0	555
7	Connecticut	0-0	554
8	North Carolina	0-0	532
9	Arizona	0-0	531
10	Louisville	0-0	503

"Wahoo!" They both erupted in unison as they spotted their team at number ten. Whooping and hollering like they had just won the lottery, they jumped around and exchanged high fives. A top ten ranking was no small feat! There was still an entire season to play to back the position up, but starting out tenth in the nation was an accomplishment that deserved celebrating. Apart from Georgetown, they were ahead of every other team in the Big East, the conference most basketball fans believed was the most difficult in the nation. As if Jake's day hadn't been great enough already, now he was soaring even higher.

He rolled his finger over the mouse pad to read the rest of the rankings.

11	San Diego State	0-0	479
12	Pittsburgh	0-0	448
13	Brigham Young	0-0	376
14	Notre Dame	0-0	336
15	Wisconsin	0-0	311
16	Texas	0-0	290
17	Purdue	0-0	276
18	Syracuse	0-0	250
19	Florida State	0-0	197
20	Marquette	0-0	159
21	Richmond	0-0	152
22	Florida	0-0	147
23	Washington	0-0	108
24	Kansas State	0-0	73
25	Utah State	0-0	71

Jake found San Diego State's ranking slightly ironic. In high school, he had privately scoffed at their recruiter, but now they were merely one spot below Louisville. Jake couldn't help but silently wonder how his life might be different had he stayed close to home and played for the Aztecs. Obviously, his basketball career wouldn't have suffered too much!

In the midst of his brief contemplations, Grant prodded him back to reality. "Hey, click on our school name. Let's see what they have to say about us."

Jake yielded and their eyes scanned the team preview.

"The Louisville Cardinals are coming off a rebound season in which they won ten more games than the previous year. Their

Sweet Sixteen loss to eventual National Champion Duke in the NCAA playoffs showed the nation what they are capable of. Losing only one player from last year's squad and gaining McDonald's MVP Tyler Faulk, this team looks stronger than ever. Look for surprise star Jake Taylor to take the reins as this year's leader with help from a solid supporting cast of Faulk, Nate Williams, Grant MacIntire, and Aaron Simon."

Jake and Grant exchanged looks. A year ago, they had been elated just to make the team; now here they were being touted by sports writers around the nation as leaders of the tenth-ranked Louisville Cardinals. The feeling was unbelievable.

Of course, none of this would matter at all if they weren't the ones cutting down the net after winning the national championship next April—or at least coming close. Preseason rankings meant nothing; they were mere predictions of what could be. A top-ten ranking signified that a team had the potential of winning it all—but there were plenty of other teams along that journey who would do their best to keep that from happening.

"Let's go for a run." Jake abruptly set his computer on the coffee table and jumped up and down. He and Grant had gotten into the habit of going for a short three mile run each night to wind down before bed and Jake definitely needed to burn some energy tonight. Tomorrow, practice officially started—with ESPN3 there to cover their opening scrimmage—but today, it was just them, backing up their pact that no one on the team would work harder.

Grant looked up at him and grinned. "Yeah, baby! Let's do it," he yelled.

After quickly changing clothes, they started out on their usual loop. But after a day like he'd just had, Jake felt a bit more adventurous and without explanation veered down an unfamiliar road. As they jogged further and further into this uncharted territory, they noticed a distinct decline in their surroundings. Bars on windows, graffiti on walls, and an overall unkempt appearance made it clear they were definitely on the "other side" of town.

"Look at that," Grant breathed, nodding ahead to their right.

There in the distance was a rundown partial sports complex. In the darkness, Jake couldn't see how far it extended, but set on the street side of a field of patchy grass, a couple of faded asphalt basketball courts were dimly lit by an adjoining street light. The court nearest to them currently played host to a rigorous game of two-on-two between young boys. Deftly dodging cracks and weeds, the kids handled the ball with ease, and their trash-talking filled the air louder than the clanging of the metal backboard.

"So which bus you want me to take you kids to school in?" A skinny kid with a big fro taunted as he dribbled the ball through his legs at the top of the key. He juked right and then raced by his opponent on the left, taking it all the way to the basket where he tossed a sweet finger roll lightly through the net-less hoop. "Ha ha! Let me see your finger roll," he sang as he did a little victory dance. He knocked knuckles with his teammate, who had done nothing but stand out at the three-point line. "You're game's like moldy Swiss cheese," he laughed in the face of the kid who was guarding him. "It stinks, and it's full of holes."

"Shut up and just play ball," the boy guarding him retorted with a scowl. He checked the ball with a hard chest pass just below the cocky kid's face.

"Is that what you call what you're doing?" He jeered. "'Cuz I think yo momma could play better than that." He laughed again, faked left, and this time just stepped back and drained a three pointer. He winked. "Just call me area code, fool, cuz I dial long distance."

Before the mouthy kid could say any more, his larger rival heaved the ball into his face. Instantly blood gushed from his nose, and he doubled over. "Yo, bro," he growled from his bent-over position. "That's a foul." He stood up and shoved the other kid hard.

But the other kid was ready and dished out a quick uppercut to his mouth. "See if that'll shut you up for a sec," he sneered.

"Fight, fight, fight!" the teammate of the puncher began to chant.

Bloody but bold, the sassy kid lunged at his antagonist and the two fell hard onto the rough pavement, swinging, kicking, and rolling all around. Immediately, the other two boys jumped in—both on the bigger kid's side, making the fight three against one.

Exchanging a quick glance, Jake and Grant sprinted over to the escalating brawl.

"Hey! Stop it," Jake yelled, knowing even as the words came out of his mouth that he sounded no more threatening than the noon duty aide at his elementary school.

Sure enough, the four pre-teenagers didn't even glance in his direction. Instinctively, Jake grabbed the top kid and pulled him off of the heap. Grant pulled the next one away, and they both struggled with flailing arms on the sideline. They still had two to go, but at least now it was a fair fight. The mouthy kid took full advantage of this turn of events and elbowed his attacker hard in the side of the head.

As soon as his kid stopped struggling as much, Jake let go and raced back to break up the final pair. But as soon as he stepped in to work like a crow bar and pry them apart, the kid he'd just let go of raced back into the action. Now at the center of their vicious skirmish, Jake looked to Grant for help, but he was doing all he could just to hold his own kid out of the fray. The math was simple: they were outnumbered. It didn't matter how strong they were—there was no physical way possible to separate the four boys.

"GUYS!" Jake finally yelled at the top of his lungs, which provided just enough of a distraction to get all involved parties to look at him momentarily. Taking advantage of this millisecond of peace, Jake quickly asked, "Why are you fighting?"

"What's it to you?" The biggest kid who threw the first punch shot back with a scowl on his face.

"'Cause fighting is stupid," Grant responded matter-of-factly.

"And three-on-one is definitely not fair," Jake chimed in.

"Yeah, they would need at least four or five to make it fair against me," the kid with the fro jeered from behind the safety of Jake.

This kid doesn't know when to shut up! Jake marveled as the three others lunged at him once more. "Hey!" Jake yelled with a new idea. "If you walk away, we'll get you all tickets to Louisville's first basketball game."

Immediately, he had their full attention.

"For real?" The trash-talking kid looked in disbelief.

"The game's sold out. How you figure getting us tickets?" the biggest kid snarled.

Jake smiled. "Weeeeell…" he tantalized them. "My friend and I here just happen to be on the team. Aaaaand we just so happen to get free tickets to all the games." Jake stealthily glanced to Grant for approval, and he just shrugged back with a grin.

"How do we know that you're not just messing with us?" a third kid asked.

"Come on! Haven't you seen us on the billboard coming into town?" Jake and Grant struck poses to mimic their gigantic likenesses on the sign.

"Or just check out the Louisville men's basketball website," Grant added. "We're all over it."

The boys still looked dubious.

"Or how about we challenge you to a quick game to ten and you can test us yourselves?" Jake offered.

"Yeah!" The boys cheered in unison and high-fived each other, suddenly unconcerned by their recent rivalry.

The impertinent kid ran after the basketball and took it to the top of the key where he enticed Jake to guard him. "Just call me Vegas, baby, cuz, man, I'm feeling lucky today." He faked right and dribbled left, but not fast enough to clear Jake's left hand which stripped him of the ball.

"Wait. Don't you need this?" Jake smiled as he dribbled the ball in the kid's face. The boy scrambled to steal it back, but Jake easily stayed out of reach. After messing with the kid for a while, he took a quick dribble to the right and sprung into a jump shot. The ball fell cleanly through the old rusty rim. "Looks like I just hit the jackpot, Vegas." Jake shrugged.

The rest of the boys whooped and hollered.

"What's your name, man?" Jake asked, tapping the kid warmly on the shoulder.

"Debron. Like Lebron, but I play D." He laughed.

Jake liked this kid.

SITTING IN THE PARKING LOT of Palo Alto Child Services with fifteen minutes to kill before she was scheduled to report, Amy perused Facebook on her phone. It didn't take long before she found herself just staring at Jake's picture yet again. It had been a week since she sent him her demanding list, and a day hadn't gone by without her checking in on him multiple times... and chastising herself for the idiotic move of telling him not to contact her until Christmas. How was she supposed to know whether or not he was willing to rise to the challenge? *I mean, I gave him a pretty tall order.* She shook her head. *If he was smart, he'd turn and run*, she lamented. *That's what Steven did!* And she'd never even given him a list.

Sure, the ultimatum she'd sent Jake encompassed what she really wanted in the next guy she dated, which hopefully would be her husband. But she was in a funk—probably instigated by lack of sleep and too much studying—and it was easy to second guess herself. *Maybe I should have started a little easier.*

Nothing new was posted on Jake's wall, so, for the first time since their breakup, Amy spontaneously searched for Steven. What she saw landed like a brick in her stomach: Steven's profile picture popped up and next to his beautiful smiling face was an equally adorable brunette. Amy quickly scrolled down and, sure enough, his new relationship status declared for all the world to see that he was most definitely "in a relationship."

What did you expect, Amy? She scolded herself as she brushed away a few tears that spilled over onto her cheeks. Up until now, she had buried all suspicions that Steven's unexpected breakup call had something to do with someone new he had met. But the proof was in the picture—obviously he'd had help in moving on. *Am I that easy to get over?* Amy lamented.

But Amy couldn't really fault him. In all honesty, she'd moved on pretty easily, too. She'd pushed herself to focus on Steven while they were still together, but once the relationship was over, she suddenly found herself far less interested in what was going on in New York and far more intrigued by what could be happening in Louisville. *Lord,* Amy sighed, *I want what you know is best for me...but it sure would be nice if that included Jake.*

She checked the time and was startled to realize that she should be inside already. She hurriedly locked her car and raced into the reception area.

"Hi, Amy!" Terri-the-receptionist greeted her brightly.

"Good morning!" Amy reciprocated, doing her best to put on her cheerful face. She knew that no matter what kind of drama she was feeling personally, while she was here at PACS it wasn't about her, it was about the patient.

"Dr. Wyatt will see you in the Forest Room."

Amy loved how each counseling room was aptly named according to its own soothing décor. The Forest Room reminded her of a refreshing walk through the woods, complete with subtle chirping birds and a faint pine scent. But her favorite space was definitely the Cabana Room. Distant crashing waves rumbled in the background and real palm fronds created a relaxing canopy over a plush swinging hammock. The walls were covered by a calming tropical mural of white sandy beaches met by clear azure waters met by vibrant blue skies. Just walking into the room felt like going on vacation, and Amy imagined the peaceful atmosphere provided amazing therapy for patients before Dr. Wyatt even opened his mouth.

But the ocean was not the order for today, and Amy walked past that door to join Dr. Wyatt in the forest. After a quick explanation of their case for this session, he welcomed in a teenager named Rosalynn.

The record may have indicated that Rosalynn was fourteen, but, based on the way she was dressed and dolled up, Amy would have guessed she was closer to twenty. Apparently, she had been molested repeatedly by a neighbor from the age of eight to twelve. At that point, her parents divorced and she moved to California with her mom. She never told anyone what had happened, but became more and more rebellious and angry at the world. Her mom had attributed her daughter's attitude to the nasty divorce, but when she took her in for a physical last year, it was discovered that Rosalynn had a latent case of Chlamydia. The mom, of course, initially blamed her, but in a moment of frustration, Rosalynn came out with the truth about her abuse, and eventually her mom believed her. She was immediately referred to PACS for treatment, and had been coming to counseling for the past year. Unfortunately, the neighbor had moved, and what with the difficulty in tracking him down as well as the elapsed time since the abuse, the case against him was still pending.

Rosalynn had made much improvement throughout the year under Dr. Wyatt's care, but due to the lack of resolution with her abuser as well as the continued strife between her parents, she was still dealing with a lot of anger issues. Amy felt an immediate connection with this girl in so many ways, and hoped that her fresh perspective would be able to steer Rosalynn straight before she did anything to hurt herself even worse.

"Hi, Rosalynn," Dr. Wyatt began warmly. "Today, we have the new counselor I was telling you about who's going to start meeting with us."

"Hey." Rosalynn was obviously not excited. She averted her eyes and slouched in her recliner.

"Hi! I love your heels!" Amy attempted to crack through her tough shell. She was pretty sure she detected a faint smile flit across Rosalynn's face.

"So, do you remember what we talked about last week?" Dr. Wyatt jumped right in.

Rosalynn huffed audibly and her body tried to squeeze deeper into the thick chair pillows. Silence.

"Do you remember I told you it was time for us to move to the next step?" Dr. Wyatt prodded in a gentle voice that definitely didn't match his sturdy frame.

Silence. And then a nearly imperceptible nod.

"Do you remember what that next step is?"

A long pause and then a faint whisper: "Forgiveness."

"You're right!" Dr. Wyatt praised softly. "You're never going to be free of the pain he caused you unless you're free of the anger toward him. And you're never going to be free of that anger unless you forgive him."

A lone tear trickled down Rosalynn's cheek.

Amy sat nearly mesmerized by Dr. Wyatt's gentle persuasion. If she hadn't experienced her own process of forgiveness last year, she was sure she would be the one in tears right now.

"I can't do this, Dr. Wyatt," Rosalynn broke the silence with her first complete sentence.

Dr. Wyatt looked directly at her and smiled warmly. "You *can* do this, Rosalynn. I know you can. Remember, forgiving doesn't mean you're saying what he did was okay. It means you're saying you're not going to let it hurt you anymore. It allows you to begin leaving your pain in the past. If you work with me here, I think you'll go home today feeling a little less angry than when you came in. And whether you realize it or not, that's going to feel really good."

Rosalynn sniffled and then gave him eye contact for the first time. "Okay."

"Okay." Dr. Wyatt nodded. He pulled up a chair and placed it in front of her. "Pretend he is sitting here, under the weighty judgment of the law, powerless to hurt you anymore. I want you to remind him of what he did to you, in as much or as little detail as you'd like. And after each thing you share, we'll stop and talk about what it looks like for you to stop holding on to that pain and to forgive him."

Rosalynn nodded and then stared down at her fidgeting fingers in her lap. The only sound in the room was the quiet chirp of birds for at least a minute. Finally, Rosalynn looked up at the chair and began her story, faltering and hesitant at first, but picking up steam as she continued. Amy found it interesting that she started out almost blaming herself—she was the one who let her neighbor in when her parents weren't home, she was the one who accepted his offer to play with dolls in his basement. Dr. Wyatt didn't try to correct her irrational thinking, but instead guided her to forgive herself each time, and then turned each instance to show how the neighbor was even more at fault and helped her extend her forgiveness to him.

"You were wrong for what you did to me," Dr. Wyatt prompted her to say to the chair. "But I refuse to bear the weight of your guilt. May you suffer from your own conscience and the consequences of your actions. You hold no power over me anymore. I am free."

Amy was struck by the growing erectness of Rosalynn's posture with each statement of forgiveness. The relief she obviously felt was tangible, was immediate, was huge. She was still clearly in a lot of pain, and Amy's heart still wrenched with every example Rosalynn shared. But instead of letting her sympathetic emotions creep into her facial expressions, Amy turned her compassion upward and prayed for the girl to have the strength to let go.

Rosalynn's process of forgiveness inevitably triggered Amy's recollections of her own process last year. But strangely, the memories of her childhood nightmare were muffled and dim and disassociated from the bitterness and anger that used to plague her. *Forgiveness really works!* she marveled, fully comprehending the significance of the milestone she had passed with Steven's help. Her mind recalled her recent conversation with her dad about contacting her Uncle Harold—something which she had conveniently never gotten around to pursuing. A sudden burning in her soul insisted that now was the time, and she resolved to work on writing him a letter this evening.

After almost thirty minutes of sharing, Rosalynn leaned back in her chair and let out a huge sigh. She hadn't made it much past the first year of the abuse, but she evidently needed a time out. In spite of barely moving in her chair, she glistened with perspiration and was clearly exhausted.

"Rosalynn," Dr. Wyatt said kindly, leaning forward in his chair. "I am *so* proud of you."

Rosalynn smiled weakly but her eyes still filled with tears. Soon the tears turned into sobs and she buried her face in her hands. Amy couldn't take it anymore. Impulsively, she jumped up from her seat and threw her arms around the hurting teenager in a gentle hug.

"It's going to be okay," Amy whispered in her ear then quickly returned her seat without looking at Dr. Wyatt. She had obviously crossed over the unspoken counselor-patient boundary and she hoped that wouldn't jeopardize the rest of her internship.

Rosalynn took a deep breath, grabbed a tissue from the side table, and dabbed at her mascara streaked eyes and cheeks. She pulled a compact mirror out of her purse and wiped away all evidence of her breakdown. Without makeup, Amy observed, she looked so much more fragile and young. After gathering herself, she glanced over at Dr. Wyatt. "I know there's more time left, but I think I'm done for today."

"You did an amazing job, Rosalynn. I think you've definitely earned a break. How about we wait until next week to do any more?" Dr. Wyatt stood up in his chair.

Rosalynn nodded and quickly exited the room. As soon as the door clicked shut behind her, Amy gushed, "Oh my gosh, Dr. Wyatt. I am so sorry. I know I overstepped my role. I don't know what I was thinking."

Dr. Wyatt just smiled. "Let me guess, Mrs. Lowe lectured on the power of touch this week."

"Yeah..." Amy trailed off. She hadn't made the connection before, but it was true. In her Psychology in Modern Life class yesterday, her professor spent the entire hour and a half describing the power—and uses—of appropriate touch. Amy had noted that kids who are physically or sexually abused often become resistant to all kinds of touch as a defense mechanism. But humans are wired to need touch, so that form of protection ends up turning into a detrimental downward spiral.

Amy could sure relate to that in her personal life. She'd always felt awkward around touchy-feely people, and had only been physical with the guys she'd dated because she'd assumed that was what they expected of her. She didn't enjoy it, but since it got them to like her, she learned to tolerate it. Jake had been different when she started going out with him their freshman year of high school, but—no thanks to her own warped perceptions of what a good relationship should look like—that didn't last. What a downward spiral that had turned out to be!

But, as her professor explained yesterday, touch could always be redeemed. Already, Amy could see that in her own life as she healed from her past abuse, regained a healthy relationship with her dad, and even more so, acquired a whole new perspective on her self-worth through her relationship with Jesus Christ. And, Amy had to admit, hopefully that redemption would also extend to her relationship with Jake.

Her professor had also extended this concept of touch to counseling individuals with a history of abuse. She described how if a therapist could get an abused child to simply feel comfortable with giving a high-five or receiving a tender pat on the shoulder, this held the potential for gigantic breakthroughs. *No wonder I felt compelled to hug her!* Amy chuckled to herself. That's what she loved about her psychology program. Nearly every day she learned something new she could instantly apply to either herself or the internship...or both. It was so cool!

"Don't ever apologize for caring about people," Dr. Wyatt broke into her thoughts. "Heartfelt empathy trumps psychological protocol any day. Besides, this case is a doozy. A little basic humanity was definitely in order."

"Thanks," Amy replied with a bit of relief. "I just couldn't resist. She just looked like she was hurting so much."

Dr. Wyatt smiled. "You know, last year, a group from my church went on a two week mission trip to an orphanage in Romania where some kids hadn't been really touched by an adult for years. But by the end of our stay there, these previously withdrawn and emaciated kids had started to come alive. They were smiling and talking and climbing all over us like we were human jungle gyms."

"Wow. That sounds amazing. What church do you go to?"

"Menlo Park Pres." Dr. Wyatt looked at her for a second. "Do you have any spiritual beliefs?"

Amy smiled brightly. "Yes! I'm a Christian, too."

"I thought so." He grinned. "Well, I don't know if you'd have any interest, but we're sending another team there this December."

"Really?" Amy asked, suddenly breathless. "I would love to go!"

"I think I have a brochure in my office. It's not a cheap plane ticket, but that's what friends are for, right?" The doctor joked.

"Great idea." Amy smiled. She'd heard bits and pieces in the past about how deplorable many of the orphanages were around the world, but she'd never considered ever visiting one. But suddenly, her heart beat fast and she couldn't imagine doing anything else over her Christmas vacation.

Later that night, after writing a brief letter expressing forgiveness to her uncle, she still couldn't stop thinking about the trip. Perhaps that was her mind trying to cope with the enormous feat she had just attempted.

No matter how much she thought she had forgiven her abuser in her heart, actually communicating God's grace and love to him had been a lot more difficult than she'd anticipated. It was as if the "fair" side of her wanted him to remain miserable in his guilt forever, in spite of the undeserved second chances God had freely given her. But after strenuously working through those old feelings of justice and revenge, Amy managed to craft a succinct note that offered mercy through the saving blood of Christ. After several hours of writing and rewriting each thought, Amy folded up her final draft and sealed it in an envelope before she could second guess herself.

Desperately needing a positive distraction, she read through the pamphlet Dr. Wyatt had given her, staring at the smiling faces of the orphans in the arms of last year's team members. Their stares bore into her soul. *But where am I ever going to find $2,800?* she tried to reason with herself. She absentmindedly twirled her index finger in circles on the mouse pad of her laptop, and the screen came to life. Half a dozen of her friends' latest updates greeted her from her Facebook page, and she suddenly had an idea.

 Amy Briggs

I'm going to Romania for two weeks at Christmas to work at an orphanage! Anyone wanna help me raise $2,800 dollars? Check out www.h2hint.org

Cari Vaughn

That is so awesome, Amy! Count us in for $100.

Andrea Stephens

Me too! $50 here comin' your way. Pichew!

JanandFrank

Amy, you are incredible. Give those orphans a hug from us. We'll send you $100.

Raymund Briggs

Where did this come from? But of course we'll support you. $500.

Doug Moore

Nice idea, Amy. If you raise extra, let me know. I'm going on a trip, too—to Tijuana!

Sherry Briggs

I thought you were coming home for Christmas break. *dislike*

LESS THAN TWELVE HOURS LATER, Amy jumped on Facebook before running to drop off her letter to her uncle at the mail center and then dashing over to her morning class. She had to get her morning fix of Jake, of course, especially in light of the emotionally draining note she held in her hands. But the overwhelming response to her spontaneous status update kept her from ever making it over to his page. She was shocked by everyone's generosity. Dr. Wyatt was right; friends were amazing!

Seeing her parents' responses, though, reminded her that she probably could have informed them about her sudden desire to jump on a plane to Europe in better ways. She made a mental note to call them in between classes today. *Help mom not to freak out too much, God,* she asked as she grabbed her bag and headed out the door. *And thanks for putting such great people in my life. Seriously.*

20

"DUDE, YOU WERE A'IGHT OUT THERE TONIGHT," a familiar young voice spoke up to Jake's right as he walked out of the locker room toward the parking lot after their season opener against Northern Kentucky.

Jake turned his head to see Debron leaning against a pole ten feet away in a Louisville t-shirt and blue jeans. Jake and Grant had met Debron and the other three boys before the game to give them their tickets, but the game had ended over an hour ago. *What's he still doing here?* Jake wondered. It was almost eleven o'clock at night. "Hey, man. Thanks," he responded as he walked over to the small kid with the big mouth. "Where are your friends?"

"Those guys? They ain't my friends; they just like hanging around 'cuz I make 'em look good."

"Right," Jake grinned. "Well, are they around here, too?"

"Nah, they took off. I coulda gone with 'em, but I wanted to wait for you. Wanted to give you some pointers and all."

"Yeah? You took notes on my game?"

"Fo' sho'! Man, you pretty good an' all, but you gotta learn to break some serious ankles out there." Debron showed off some fast-feet crossover moves.

Jake laughed. "Those are some pretty tight moves." He grinned, too tired to exchange any more trash talking with this kid. "So, is your mom on her way to come get you?"

Debron just shrugged.

"She knows you're here, right?"

"Sure," Debron shrugged again. "But she's real busy."

"So you need a ride home?" Jake offered with as much enthusiasm as he could muster.

"Yeah, that'd be coo'." For a kid that always seemed to have something to say, Debron was suddenly silent. But not for long. "You know those kids that got to sit behind the basket?"

"The ball boys?"

"Yeah. Any chance you could hook a brother up? They got to shoot hoops during half time in front of everybody. They mostly just threw up bricks, but I'd give the people something to cheer about."

"Hm, I don't know," Jake answered honestly. "But I'll find out for you, okay?"

"Coo'." Debron smiled. "So what kind of ride you got, man? It better be nice."

Jake just shook his head. "How does a truck sound to you?"

Debron pondered the question. "Hm...Two door or four?"

Jake wearily raised up two fingers. This kid was starting to get annoying.

"Just two? So what do you do when you got like five ladies that want to hang wich'u?"

Again, Jake could only shake his head. "How old are you, man?"

"Almost eleven. I've got two girlfriends, but they don't know about each other."

"Do they even know they're your girlfriends?" Jake laughed back.

"That's just plain cold, man."

After finally making it to his truck, it was about a ten minute drive over to Debron's neighborhood, which Debron filled up with more than enough banter. Among other things, Debron leaked that he already had NBA scouts talking to him, he was practically a black belt in Karate, and he would have had straight A's except that his punk teacher didn't like him. Finally, they made it to his apartment complex, across the street from the court where Jake had met him last week. Even though Debron repeatedly insisted that Jake didn't need to, Jake parked his truck in the street and walked him up to his door. Jake felt like his mom might want some sort of explanation for why he was out so late with her son.

Debron fished a key out of his pocket and flashed a nervous smile at Jake. "Wait here a sec, 'kay?" He opened the door a crack and slipped through the narrow opening.

"Where you been?" a loud male voice interrogated immediately.

"At the game," Debron shot back aggressively. "What's it to you?"

"Don't smart mouth me, foo'. I'll beat you."

"Don't you lie to us," a gruffer male voice piped up. "Ain't nobody playin' out there all night."

"Nah! We weren't playing. We were *at* the game. Front row center, baby," Debron boasted.

While the escalating situation inside sounded anything but amusing, Jake couldn't help but find Debron's enhancement of his seat funny. *From the nosebleeds to front row center, huh?* Apparently the guys inside found it humorous, too, because a cacophony of voices erupted in laughter.

"Ha! How does a runt like you get tickets to the Louisville opener?" what sounded like a third voice asked.

"My friend, Jake. He's on the team."

Again, a round of laughter.

"I'm serious, man. If you don't believe me, just open up that door."

"Who's out there? Santa Claus?" More laughter.

Jake heard an angry growl emit from Debron and next thing he knew the door was open and he was staring into a smoky room full of three older Debron-look-alikes. Suddenly, their laughter turned to stony silence.

"Who are you?" the nearest one asked coldly.

"I'm Jake." Jake tried to play it cool. "I met your brother when I was running through the neighborhood last week, and I invited him to our game."

A brother lounging on the couch narrowed his eyes and sized Jake up. Jake wondered if he was carrying a gun. Suddenly, he gave Jake a slight nod of approval. "Yo, D," he spoke toward the brother sitting at the kitchen table. "I think I remember seeing him on TV in the game against Duke last year."

"Hey, that's right," "D" smiled. "You weren't so bad out there."

Jake smiled weakly, hoping the awkwardness had been averted.

"See, I told you!" Debron pushed the brother nearest him.

"Don't push me!" the brother snarled and shoved him to the floor.

Jake's eyes opened wide. "Uh, I just wanted to meet your mom, apologize for bringing him home so late," he stammered, trying to quell the escalating tension.

"She ain't home. But you want to keep him?" the brother on the couch quipped as the others laughed along.

"Shut up foo'," Debron shot back. "I'll kick you're a—"

"Anyway, I just wanted to make sure he got home safely," Jake interrupted.

"Unfortunately," the brother at the table responded. Debron just scowled at him.

Jake looked at his new friend with a new understanding of why he acted the way he did. "Well, I guess I'll see you later, Debron." Jake tried to encourage him with a smile.

Debron nodded his head without saying a word. Taking his cue, Jake shut the front door and left.

As annoying as the too-cool ten-year-old was, Jake felt sorry for him. Walking back to his truck, Jake wondered where Debron's mom was at this time of night. Was she working...or doing things that were less helpful for the family? As Jake thought about Debron's struggle to impress everyone—and the trouble that got him into—he knew he got it from his home life. But how could he teach him that there was a better way? He wished he could pick Amy's brain on this one, and he even contemplated breaking her two month rule to do so—for the sake of ministry, right? *God, why did you bring this kid into my life?* He asked as he drove back to his dorm apartment. *How am I supposed to help him?*

As Jake drifted off to sleep that night, for the first time in a long while, Amy's face was not the last thing he saw. Instead, thoughts of Debron kept flitting through his head.

NOW THAT OCTOBER WAS COMING TO A CLOSE, the Louisville weather was turning significantly cooler and less pleasant. Today, however, had turned out to be surprisingly warm. So, during a break between his morning classes, Jake parked himself on a bench and enjoyed the heat of the sunlight radiating down on him as he finished journaling some thoughts from his earlier Bible reading. As usual, he had woken up early to spend time with God, but today's Scripture passage had given him a lot to chew on—especially in light of last night's troubling interaction with Debron and his brothers—and he'd had to run to practice before he'd been able to fully digest it.

Today's reading was Deuteronomy 21-24—definitely not normal devotional material for a young guy. But at the end of summer, Jake had been inspired to tackle reading through the Bible in a year after Chris had challenged in one of his messages, "If you say that your whole life is based off this book, don't you think you should know what's in it?" After consulting with both Chris and Buddy, Jake had developed an informal plan to try to cover four or five chapters a day. Since then, he had been pretty good at spending time with God most mornings. And now that Amy's list was posted right by the head of his bed, he never missed a day. How was he supposed to be a spiritual leader if he didn't know God's Word?

Plowing through the chapters with fervor, for the most part Jake found himself glued to the pages...and often in shock at some of the stories. Sometimes, he'd try to lure Grant into studying the Bible with him by sharing some of the crazier tales. Grant always had some excuse for not joining, but he joked that it sounded like the Bible should be rated R.

The book of Genesis had been a fascinating story that taught Jake a ton about the roots of God's people. Exodus had started out pretty interesting, but Jake found himself getting frustrated with the rebellious Israelites. Of course, each time he thought about how lame they were, God was quick to remind him of his own disobedient days, which gave Jake a new appreciation for God's grace. Reading through parts of Leviticus and Numbers had been a bit cumbersome—so he'd skimmed them like he did with some of his textbooks. And now he was plodding through Deuteronomy.

He'd gotten into the habit of underlining parts that were interesting to him and this morning he found himself fixated on three words: foreigner, fatherless, and widow. Four different times God commanded his people to take care of these groups. And each time Jake read it, that command turned into a question that wouldn't stop pounding in his head. *What does that look like for me?* Now basking in the rays of the sun, Jake wrote that question at the top of his journal and then made three columns underneath it, labeling them for each of the groups God wanted him to be concerned about.

The foreigner one had him stuck. He immediately thought about Amy giving up her Christmas break to work with fatherless foreigners in Romania. He was so proud of her and couldn't wait until December so that he could ask her all about it. She was so inspiring! But again, the question plagued him. *What does that look like for me?* Obviously, he couldn't just hop on a plane and go with her. Besides the obvious fact that they weren't in a do-things-together place yet, the trip fell right in the middle of basketball season, and even though Coach had agreed to give him the extra day to visit Amy in December, taking two weeks off just as league play was gearing up was out of the question.

Jake's pen hovered above the page, waiting for inspiration, but none came. He didn't even know any foreigners here in Louisville. Maybe that should change, but he had no idea how to go about meeting them. After a minute of blankness, Jake gave up and moved to the next column: Fatherless.

This one was easy; Debron's little face raced immediately into Jake's mind. While Jake didn't actually know for certain that Debron's dad was out of the picture, it sure seemed from their spurts of conversation between basketball and trash talk that it was just him and his mom and three older brothers. Jake quickly scribbled on his list to look for an opportunity to ask Debron about his dad...and the rest of his family, for that matter. Whatever men Debron did have in his life, it was evident that he needed more positive male role models. *I could try to be one,* Jake thought, and wrote down several more ideas of how he could care for Debron: Jog by his park more often in order to see him, play some pick-up games with him, take him out for dinner some time, invite him to watch another Louisville game, look for things to praise him for and avoid cutting him down—even in trash talk; be willing to give him rides home, bring him to church.

The ideas for how to reach out to Debron just kept flowing, but Jake figured he had plenty to attempt for now. He could always add more later, depending on how these unfolded. Jake glanced at the next column: Widow.

Again, Jake wasn't positive about Debron's situation, but he wrote down Debron's mom anyway. He never got to meet her last night, but he scribbled that down as his first goal. As he sat on the warm bench, Jake tried to step into her shoes. Taking care of four boys without their father had to be a huge challenge, both to raise them carefully as well as to even just feed them. He wondered if buying some groceries would help...or if that could be insulting. He put a question mark by that idea, and then pondered how maybe just showing concern for her youngest son would be a big blessing to her.

Lord, show me the best ways to show her Your love, Jake prayed as he set his pen down and closed his eyes. He asked God for an opportunity to meet her soon, as well as for opportunities to pour into Debron's life. He prayed over each idea on his list, inviting God to move him and work through him every step of the way. As he talked to God, he had the sudden realization that maybe he and Grant's decision to take a different route on their run that night a couple weeks ago hadn't been an accident. *Haha, God! You're pretty awesome!* He laughed, and asked God to work in Grant's life, too, through their relationship with Debron. Jake opened his eyes and looked at his blank Foreigner column. *And Lord,* he added, *help me figure out how to take care of foreigners.*

Jake spent awhile talking to God about Amy. He prayed for her as she prepared for her trip, and asked God to use her in awesome ways as she cared for those orphans and that He would bless her like crazy. Suddenly, a crazy idea popped into his head. *No way! That's awesome, God!* he cheered, eager to get back to his room and onto his computer.

An abrupt buzzing of his phone in his pocket begged him for attention. Since he was pretty much done with praying, he pulled it out and saw a new text from Andrea.

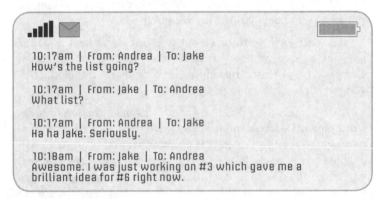

10:17am | From: Andrea | To: Jake
How's the list going?

10:17am | From: Jake | To: Andrea
What list?

10:17am | From: Andrea | To: Jake
Ha ha Jake. Seriously.

10:18am | From: Jake | To: Andrea
Awesome. I was just working on #3 which gave me a brilliant idea for #6 right now.

22

AMY'S MOM STILL WASN'T CRAZY ABOUT the idea of her flying halfway around the world the day after Christmas, but since Amy had promised to spend the holiday with her instead of her dad, she couldn't complain too much. Everyone else had been nothing but supportive.

Once she got the green light from her parents, Amy had eagerly completed the application and turned it in to Dr. Wyatt. Since then, she was officially welcomed to the team and was looking forward to the first meeting next weekend. Yesterday, she had scheduled her passport appointment, gone to the university clinic to get any needed vaccination boosters, and bought her required reading book *The Hole in Our Gospel*, by Richard Stearns. The only area she was far from ready in was the minor detail of raising $2,800.

But even in that matter, God was providing. As of last count, Amy had $one,one40 in her account, thanks to the generosity of so many loved ones in her life. Renee was definitely not well-off, but she had gladly contributed $50 to the fund, telling Amy that she was going without fast food for the month in order to help the orphans. Melia had begged Chris and Cari to give her extra chores so she could send Amy some of her own money. Even Amy's mom had eventually committed to donate $25, which was a huge step for her. Tons of other friends from New Song and Intersect sent her what they could, and it was all adding up. Amy was more than grateful for every little gift, but unfortunately, her list of givers already far exceeded her expectations and she had no idea where she was going to find the second half of the money.

She also had to admit she was slightly irked by one glaring non-giver: Jake. She was convinced he knew about her trip, thanks to insights provided by Cari and Andrea. And thanks to their hints, too, she had been encouraged that Jake was definitely working on "the list." *So why hasn't he helped out with my trip?* she wondered in frustration. Obviously, it wasn't that he was obligated to support her, but it sure seemed like if he was truly interested in restoring a relationship with her, he could muster up even a few bucks to show he cared. This was definitely a red flag for their future.

Filled with disappointment in spite of herself, Amy sat down in front of her laptop and logged in to her trip account. Instead of moping about Jake, she figured she might as well focus on the positives and write some thank you notes to her most recent donors.

What popped up on her screen next made her gasp. Her new trip total was now $2,six40! Amy quickly did the math. Where had that last fifteen hundred dollars come from? Humbled yet again by God's goodness and others' generosity, she burst out in tears...just as her roommate burst into their room singing at the top of her lungs.

"What's wrong with you, girl?" Renee abruptly stopped and rushed over to give Amy a hug.

"Nothing!" Amy sobbed, trying to control herself, but all she could do was smile and point to the new total on the screen.

"Sweet Jesus!" Renee exclaimed and started raising the roof in praise. "Either you've got a huge stack of new thank-you notes to get busy on...or one very, very appreciative one. Who's it from?"

"I don't know. I just saw it right before you walked in."

"Well, let's find out!" Renee prodded and scooted Amy half out of her desk chair.

Amy clicked on the details of her account and, sure enough, the money had come in one lump sum; but much to her chagrin, the donor was listed as anonymous.

"What?" Renee yelped. "That's just not fair! So who do you know that's that rich?"

Amy wracked her brain but absolutely no one came to mind.

"What about that doctor you work for? He's probably pretty well off."

Amy shrugged. "Maybe." But no matter how compassionate her hearty boss was, that just seemed like a ridiculous amount of support. "I don't know. Doesn't that seem...almost too much?"

"Maybe it's his way of paying you for all your work at the clinic," Renee suggested. "Hey, click on the actual donation. Maybe there are more details hidden."

Amy followed her advice, and a new screen opened but all fields on the form were blank...except for one lone five-digit number at the very bottom.

"Hey, it's your donor's zip code," Renee observed. "Let's Google it so we at least know where they're from." She quickly typed the number into the search field, but the familiar digits registered in Amy's brain and she gasped...just as Renee breathlessly read out the search results. "Louisville, Kentucky."

"I think I'm in love again," Amy whispered.

WINTER

Jake Taylor

Vegas, baby, Vegas!

IN THE MIDDLE OF DECEMBER, even a desert gets

cold and Jake and his teammates experienced this first hand
as they exited the Las Vegas airport into the dry Nevada chill.
Jake, however, felt anything but cold. In fact, ever since they'd
boarded the plane, he'd felt like he might explode in anticipation. Sure, he was excited about the tournament. Louisville was
the number two seed, behind North Carolina, and they had their
undefeated 9-0 season record to uphold. But obviously, Jake had
even more significant things on his mind. More than a tournament win, Jake hoped to return to Louisville with a girlfriend.

Tomorrow would be two months to the day since Amy had
sent him the email—two months of blissful expectation as he
did everything he possibly could to win her back—and Jake just
couldn't wait to talk to her. All he had to get through was three

days of games, an evening with her dad to ask for his blessing, and then he'd be on her doorstep to ask for her heart. He was so close, but he wasn't sure how he was going to make it until then.

"Here's your bag." A hand lightly slapped his shoulder causing him to jump. "Whoah, someone's edgy," Nomis smirked.

"He thought you were *Amy!*" Tyler joked, pretending to flip his hair over his shoulder.

"I think Amy's a little cuter than *that,*" Grant ribbed Nomis.

Jake could only grin. All the guys knew about his little side trip after the tournament, and no matter how he tried to downplay it, they loved to tease him. They just couldn't understand why Jake would go so far to pursue a girl when there were plenty throwing themselves at him wherever he went. Fortunately, no one but Grant knew about the list—or "Amy's Ultimatum" as Grant liked to call it—or else Jake would have never heard the end of it. Grant thought Jake was totally whipped, but he was trustworthy and kept mum about Jake's little secret.

After everyone grabbed their bags, they boarded a bus to the hotel, which was noticeably far from The Strip—presumably in hopes of keeping the guys out of trouble and focused on their primary task at hand: winning basketball games. But in Vegas, "fun" is never far away, and they kept plenty busy in their own little compound. Jake, however, excused himself early and went to bed. He knew sleep would probably elude him for hours, but he craved the time alone, if for no other reason than to prepare for his upcoming rendezvous with Amy. He'd rehearsed his speech countless times, but he still stumbled on how to begin. Nothing sounded quite right.

Amy? Whoah, you live here?...What are the odds?

Hey Amy, long time no see.

Hi, Ms. Briggs. Will you be my girlfriend?

Lying in bed in the dark of his room, Jake sighed, wishing he could just close his eyes and be with her already. He imagined the warmth of her arms around him, the softness of her fingers interlaced in his as they sat talking. They had so much to catch up on.

Of course, Jake had to get through her list first, but that part was easy...except for number eight. That was the only one that caused him to falter. *No secrets. Start with a clean slate and move forward with all honesty from here on out.* Jake fully understood why this one was so important, and he totally agreed. If they didn't have trust in their relationship then they really had nothing. But did he really have to tell Amy *everything*?

Sure, Jake supposed she should know about Nicole, even though he knew it would hurt her. But what good could possibly come from confessing *the timeline* of his relationship with Nicole? Did Amy really need to know that, long before they'd broken up, he'd shared a passionate kiss with Nicole, within minutes of talking to Amy on the phone? Or even worse, that after they'd broken up, he'd been in bed with Nicole before Amy had probably even made it home from her visit to Louisville? Regret still plagued Jake over how he'd handled that whole situation, and he was pretty sure that telling Amy would only make it worse—for both of them.

His soul in anguish, Jake kicked off his covers and sat up in bed. *God, do I really have to tell her all of that?*

The darkness of the room started closing in on him so Jake flipped on the bedside lamp. He noticed the hotel pen and pad of paper lying next to it and immediately thought of his dad. He may have learned more from his dad of what *not* to do in life, but there was one useful tool that he found helpful with most major decisions: a pros and cons list. Jake sat back in bed and started to write.

To Tell Amy or Not to Tell...

PROS
*Amy specifically asked for honesty
*No secrets
*Clear conscience

CONS
*Amy could freak out
*Amy could decide to not get back together.
*Amy will be hurt.
*Amy could freak out more.
*What I did doesn't really show who I am now
*I've repented for my stupidity

Jake looked at his growing list of cons and started elaborating on its case inside his brain. Amy was a junior...at Stanford University. She was carrying a full load of difficult classes, plus that internship. Wasn't it selfish of him to give her another burden to carry around? And really, on that note, it was also pretty selfish of him to do this just so he could have a clear conscience. Amy's mind would obviously be a lot clearer if he didn't tell her *all* the details. Jake knew that God had already forgiven him for all of it, and he remembered hearing a verse about God forgetting our sins once we confessed them, something about as far as the east was from the west. Well, if God forgot his sins, didn't that mean that he should, too? But if he told Amy, then neither she nor he would probably ever be able to forget after that.

The more Jake thought about it, the more he leaned toward a selective telling of his involvement with Nicole. And the more he leaned in that direction, the better he felt...kind of. Amy's wish for "no secrets" still nagged at the back of his brain but Jake quickly squelched it with more rationalization. Around and around in circles he went until eventually, his arguments ran out and truth's nagging refused to be silenced.

So he did what any desperate guy would do: he changed the subject. Sports were always a good distraction, so he turned his thoughts to tomorrow's game. He lay back down, turned off the light, and willed himself to envision executing various plays against his competition. Unfortunately, the harder he tried to focus, the more he saw Amy's disappointed face. And the more he fought to ignore her face, the more he lost sight of the ball. Eventually he drifted off to a fitful sleep, but nightmares of failure plagued him the entire night.

When he finally opened his eyes to see sunlight streaming through a crack in the drapes, he felt exhausted, but he welcomed the relief that daylight brought. He still felt uneasy about his upcoming conversation with Amy, but that wouldn't take place until Monday. Right now, it was game time.

24

SPORTING THEIR CRIMSON AWAY JERSEYS, Jake and his teammates stepped onto the UNLV court a few hours later to warm up for their first game of the tournament against the University of Southern California. While the Trojans weren't currently ranked in the top twenty-five, Coach warned the guys that this was not a team to take lightly. Jake went through his usual routine to gear up for the competition, but despite all his efforts, he just couldn't get into his groove during warm-up drills.

"You better get your head in the game," Grant warned him after Jake sent another poor pass his way.

Jake tried, but the harder he focused, the more he felt distracted. Arena speakers pumped techno music so loud he couldn't think and he couldn't find his zone. But ready or not, the game had to begin, and Jake lined up in the backcourt hoping that maybe he'd find it once the clock started.

The moment the referee tossed the ball up in the air, the Trojans started fighting as if their lives depended on it. They grappled for the opening tip, and quickly scored the first bucket.

Nomis inbounded the ball to Jake who called a play for his teammates to set up. Coach had harped on them to get the ball down low to establish an inside game and Jake went straight to work. He lobbed the ball in to Grant who spun around his defender and banked the ball off the glass from six feet away for Louisville's first score. *Okay, that'll work,* Jake encouraged himself as he rushed back on defense.

His assignment, Tyreke Miller, was a high school All-American recruit who would probably only spend a year or two in college before heading to the pros. Jake picked up the eighteen year old as he crossed the midcourt line, barely giving him an inch. The freshman passed across the court to a teammate in the corner and, before Jake realized what was happening, sprinted to the basket and received the ball back for an easy layup. *Crap!* Jake felt immediately deflated. Out of the corner of his eye, he saw his coach shaking his head vehemently. Not a good start.

The game seesawed back and forth for the first twenty minutes of play. Jake tried to get his teammates involved as he repeatedly drove towards the basket and then either kicked the ball back out to Nate for open threes or dumped it off to the big men underneath. Although he himself couldn't buy a basket tonight, like any good point guard, Jake was holding his own at spreading the ball around. He fed plenty of scoring opportunities to his teammates, which racked up a solid eight assists for his record, but Jake couldn't remember the last time he'd been held scoreless for an entire half.

At half time, the Cardinals were behind by seven and Coach wasn't happy. As the team exited the locker room after their mid-game talk, he pulled Jake aside. "Jake, I'm not sure what's going on with you tonight, but don't make me regret my choice to let you stay an extra day out here. It's none of my business, but if your choices off the court start affecting your play on the court, we're going to have a problem. I'm starting Williams this second half. We really need a scorer at the point and that's not you today."

Jake nodded along stoically, but his insides felt like they were being torn apart. Losing his starting role to a new guy? *This can't be happening,* Jake groaned. A local freshman, Jadon Williams was a decent player, but Jake wasn't ready to lose his position. He'd fought so hard to get here. *Get a hold of yourself, man!* Jake berated himself as he brooded at the end of the bench. But he couldn't stop feeling distracted.

By the time Coach signaled to Jake to enter the game there were only twelve minutes to go and Louisville held a comfortable nine-point lead. Jadon had done a more-than-adequate job as Jake's replacement, collecting eight points and two assists. As he crouched by the scorer's table, Jake felt a tinge of jealousy. *If Coach wants a point guard who can score then I'll show him one.*

Jake entered the game and dribbled the ball up the court. He quickly faked a pass to Nomis while he blew by Tyreke at the top of the key. As the USC big men converged on him, Jake stopped on a dime to put up a fifteen footer. But just as he released the ball, Tyreke's finger tips barely grazed it from behind and it fell well short of the hoop. *No!* Jake cringed and tried to shake it off as he raced back to play defense, but before he made it to half court the USC center flung the ball like a quarterback over Jake's head to a streaking Tyreke who elevated high for a two-handed slam. *Are you serious?*

The next four minutes progressed just as dismally, and Jake was swiftly taken back out of the game. Coach didn't even look at him as he jogged off the court. Wallowing in misery, Jake slunk down in his seat at the end of the bench and watched his teammates carry the Cardinals back into the lead. By the time the final buzzer sounded, they had willed the team to a three-point victory and their ensuing good spirits were certainly justified. But Jake felt numb, his head a million miles away.

As he crossed the court behind his celebrating teammates, for some reason Jake lifted up his eyes and scanned the crowd… and suddenly, time stood still. Was he seeing things? He shook his head to clear his troubled mind, but no, she was still there, her eyes locked on him. Had she been there all along, watching his humiliating performance? It didn't seem to matter; her smile greeted him brightly. "Hi, Jake," she mouthed, and Jake's heart started beating fast. The roar of the crowd and the blaring music faded into nothing as he raced over to her section. He slithered his sweaty body past rows of oblivious fans until they stood face to face.

"What are you doing here?" Jake asked breathlessly.

"I'm mostly here to gamble, but figured I might as well catch a game." Amy laughed. "You didn't play so well."

"I've, uh, had a few other things on my mind."

Amy smiled and looked away.

"Amy," Jake faltered, overcome with emotion. "You have no idea how much it means to me that you're here. But I've got to get to our team meeting. Coach is already mad enough at me—"

"Go." She held her hand up to stop Jake from saying any more. "I'll wait for you in the coffee shop in your hotel lobby. Meet me there when you're ready."

"Wait. How'd you...?" Jake just stared at her, unable to take his eyes off of her beautiful face.

"Go." She giggled, pushing Jake toward the stairs.

Her touch sent quivers through his body, and he remained glued in place.

"Jake!" she prodded. "You don't want to be late."

Reluctantly, he turned to leave, but he kept looking back every few steps to make sure this wasn't all a dream. He made it into the locker room just as everyone was settling down for Coach to speak. Grant and Nomis both nudged him and gave him a knowing smile. Jake tried to stifle his own grin, but it was impossible. He stared straight ahead at Coach, hoping he wouldn't think Jake was taking his poor play lightly, but while his eyes looked like they were focused intently on the post-game debriefing, his thoughts were everywhere else.

With his carefully laid plans now tossed out the window, Jake felt the exhilarating thrill of a free fall. But in the back of his mind lurked a quiet fear of the stiff landing that might await him.

About two hours later, Jake entered the relatively empty coffee shop and immediately found Amy studiously reading a textbook in the back corner. *Dang, she looks good.* He hated to get stuck on the superficial, but it was true. About a bazillion new butterflies joined the ones already racing around in his gut. *Stay cool, man. Stay cool!*

"Whatcha reading? Jake interrupted as he grabbed the seat across from her.

"Oh, you know, a little pleasure reading about cognitive brain development. Fascinating stuff." Amy smiled back, seemingly as calm as could be.

"So, how are the slot machines treating you?" Jake joked, afraid to turn the conversation to what he really needed to say.

Amy grinned and pulled out a piece of paper and placed it on the table between them. "I've actually had better luck with PayPal."

The paper was a printout of his anonymous donation to her Romania fund. How'd she figure out that it was him? "Wow, it looks like someone really believes in you," Jake responded vaguely. "I'd love to hear all about your trip. But first..." Jake pulled out his own piece of paper and covered the receipt up with Amy's email. "I'd love to talk about this. The fact that you're sitting here in front of me makes me think that you know what today is."

"The fact that you have that list gives me hope that I didn't come here for nothing."

"Two months ago today I read the best email of my life." Jake smiled. "I posted it on the wall by my bed and studied it every day."

Amy shook her head. "You didn't think I was like a psycho girl or something?"

Jake chuckled. "I thought you were writing to tell me you'd decided to marry Steven. Your list was the best news of my life."

Amy stared at Jake thoughtfully. "You didn't think it was even a little bit over-demanding?"

"Amy, you deserve nothing less. And I want to spend the rest of my life proving that to you. Which I guess brings me to the conversation I was planning on having with you on Monday after the tournament...but more on that later." Jake picked up the piece of paper and cleared his throat. "Number one: wait. I think I've done pretty well on that one." He smiled. "And believe me, I've definitely taken this list seriously."

"Thank you," Amy responded softly.

Jake nodded and continued, "Number two: Pray. I've never prayed so much in my life for something, even before these last two months. When your list came, that was just confirmation that God was smiling down on my deepest desires. Amy, after all we've been through, God must have some pretty special plans for us—together—and I look forward to seeing them unfold. In the meantime, I am still far from perfect, but I am going to do my best to lead us down the path that will best prepare us for those plans. Which brings me to number three: lead you spiritually."

Jake inhaled deeply. "Man, that is a humbling one, especially considering how much you've grown over the past two years. Amy, you are an amazing woman, and just being around you challenges me to do better." Jake looked up from the sheet and smiled at Amy. "But I have been working my butt off to try to catch up with you, and as iron sharpens iron, I will do what I can to spur you on in your faith.

"It's hard to really quantify a relationship with God, but let me just say that I've never felt closer to Him than I do now. At the beginning of the school year, I started this reading plan to go through the Bible in a year, and I am learning so much! I never knew how many crazy stories there are in the Old Testament, and some are really kicking my butt. To help me with all that I'm learning, I have an eighty-four-year-old mentor named Buddy who is teaching me more than I could have ever imagined."

"You mentioned Buddy this summer," Amy interrupted. "He sounds really cool."

"You have no idea. He's prayed for you...for us...so much."

"Well, I hope I get to meet him some day."

"I hope so, too...but you're breaking my momentum." Jake grinned, turning his attention back to the page. "Number four: take initiative." Jake chuckled and fished in his back pocket for another folded piece of paper. "Man, you're making it hard for me to get started on the right foot here...but I sure tried. If you don't mind, I'm going to lump number seven and number ten in with this one."

Instead of saying anything more, Jake simply dropped the computer printout of his Las Vegas to San Francisco flight confirmation on the table in front of them.

Amy picked it up and gasped. "Is this what I think it is?"

"I got permission from my coach to fly back a day late and thought I might kill three birds with one stone. I've already talked to your dad, and we made plans to hang out on Sunday night before I drove over to pay you a surprise visit on Monday morning. But you kind of beat me to the punch on this one."

"Sorry." Amy wrinkled her nose cutely. Her eyes looked like they were getting a little teary.

"It's cool. I like your plan better." Jake leaned forward and for the first time dared to rub Amy's hand. A thrill coursed through his body. And since she didn't move, he maintained contact as he looked back at the list. "Number five: marry you. I've already told you how much I want to spend the rest of my life with you. But obviously, your input is kind of important on this one, too. I'd marry you in a second if that's what you wanted. Otherwise, I'm thinking maybe we should wait until we both finish college. I'll still have two years of eligibility left after this one, but I know you'll probably finish school a year ahead of that. We'll obviously have a ton of details to figure out, but if it would help, I don't have to play that final year. I'd give up almost anything to wake up every morning next to you. And to make sure I can get my degree in time, I took a full load of classes this semester, and I'll take summer school and whatever else I need to do to get ahead."

Amy just shook her head, and the tears spilled freely onto her cheeks. Jake wanted nothing more than to pull her into a tender embrace, but he restrained himself and moved on to the next item on her list.

"Number six: Dream with you. Again, Amy, you blow me away. I can't wait to hear all about your dreams for the future. But to be honest, I'm still figuring mine out. Sure, I'd love to play in the NBA, and some days that seems like a real possibility. But then there are days like today..." Jake paused and they both laughed. "I know God is using me right now, but maybe we can figure out together how He wants to use me after all this."

Jake glanced at Amy and tried to absorb her radiance. Although she hadn't said a word in a few minutes, he was pretty sure this was going well. She seemed genuinely touched by his efforts to be not only the man that she desired but the one that she deserved. *Only a few more,* he urged himself as he looked back down at the list. Suddenly, he felt like throwing up. "Uh, I guess I already covered number seven about visiting you, so that brings me to number eight: no secrets." Sweat gushed out of his pores and his fingers trembled as he held the list. "Um, I'd really like to leave this one for last if that's okay with you," his voice trembled.

A look of concern flitted across Amy's face, but she nodded her head in agreement.

"Okay, number nine," Jake hurried on. "No sex." He placed the still quivering paper down and looked sincerely into Amy's eyes. "Amy, I am so, so sorry for pushing our physical relationship too far. Back in high school, I didn't really know any better, but I am so sorry for all the pain that caused. And I'm even more sorry for how I pushed you when I should have known better. I was completely inappropriate when you came out to visit me, and I am so ashamed. You were trying to be honorable, and, while I didn't respect that then, I am so proud of you now. With God as our witness, I will never, *ever* push you to have sex again—or come anywhere close. Until our wedding night, of course, which I will be waiting for with eager anticipation...but I probably shouldn't have said that last part out loud," Jake blushed with a goofy grin.

Amy gave him a mock scowl, but she was obviously trying to cover up a smile, too.

"Seriously, Amy, I think that's really cool about the no kissing part, too. I mean, you have no idea how much I want to just kiss you all night long right now." Jake quickly looked away, unable to maintain eye contact. He traced his finger along the edge of the table. "But I can see the value of delayed gratification. We've already done it all, so what if this time, we start fresh, and our wedding day can be the big celebration of a relationship done right?" With this proposition, he finally looked questioningly back up at Amy, who simply nodded.

"I love it, Jake," she said softly.

"Of course, this *is* Vegas, and I heard there's a wedding chapel at the back of our hotel." Jake wiggled his eyebrows and grabbed Amy's hand. "If you want to make number nine a little easier on us, that is."

"Tempting," Amy grinned. "But who said I want to make this easy for you?"

"Oh yes, I forgot," Jake smirked. Then he took a deep breath and rubbed his hands down his jeans. Ready or not, number eight was here. In spite of all his reasons from last night to avoid disclosing all details, staring into Amy's deep blue eyes now convinced him that full truth was his only option. "Which is perfect, because I think this last one just might be the hardest thing I've ever done in my life.

Amy looked at him curiously, but Jake forced himself to plow ahead. It was now or never.

"It's not that I want to keep any secrets from you, Amy; it's just that during my year and a half of backsliding, I did some things that I am really, really embarrassed of...and I think some of them might really, really hurt you."

Amy leaned back in her chair and bit her lip. Jake stared down at the table so that he wouldn't chicken out.

"You were right about Nicole. I promised myself that there was nothing there, but I have to confess, we kissed once that spring before your visit." Jake winced at his words and glanced up at Amy. Her eyes stared stoically back at him, giving him no clue to her thoughts. "I could easily pin the blame on her, but I knew what I was doing and should have avoided the situation." Jake took a quick deep breath. "But it gets even worse. After we broke up, I rebounded to Nicole pretty quickly. It was not a good time for me and—" Jake closed his eyes to finish the last part. "—we had sex a lot." Jake looked back into Amy's eyes, willing her not to shut him out of her heart. "I could give you tons of excuses, but the bottom line is I screwed up. Really, really bad. And I am so, so sorry."

Utterly exhausted, Jake sank into silence and waited for Amy to respond with his fate.

"How quickly did you guys hook up?" she asked quietly after a few tense moments.

Jake inhaled and sat on his hands. "The next day," he cringed.

Amy sucked in her breath, obviously taken aback. "Wow... And how long were you together?"

"We broke up last fall. I still see her around campus occasionally, but we rarely talk. She's back with another guy on the team, a guy that I've surprisingly become friends with this year. But believe me, any time I see her, she reminds me of a terrible time in my life to which I never want to return."

Amy tapped her empty cup on the table, her eyes fastened down. Jake watched her in silence, wretched in his guilt. After what seemed like an eternity, she placed the cup to the side and looked up at Jake.

"Jake, thank you for taking my list so seriously. You have surpassed my expectations and even my hopes in so many ways. And thank you for being so honest with me. That really reveals a lot about your character, because I know how easy it would have been to tell me only what was safe." A long sigh escaped her lips and her eyes focused on something above Jake's head before she continued on. "But wow, the truth sure hurts. To be honest, Jake, I kind of expected some of this. I mean, the pictures of you two were all over Facebook last year. But I guess I just wanted to believe it wasn't as bad as it looked. And I definitely never considered that she was in the mix before I was even out. Man, I am thinking some very unchristian thoughts about that...girl."

Amy shook her head and gazed out the window while Jake sat awaiting her verdict.

"Jake, I'm not sure what to tell you right now. Would you mind giving me some time to think? I know this isn't the response you hoped for, but I...I just can't give you anything else."

"Take as much time as you need," Jake croaked, wondering if it was too late to get a refund on his plane ticket.

25

"CARI! I REALLY NEED TO TALK TO YOU!" Amy cried into her phone as she left a third desperate message for her mentor. It had been three hours since she'd left Jake in the coffee shop, and she knew that Cari would be going to bed any time now. In frustration, she flopped onto the bed of her cheap hotel room and buried her face in the pillows. *God, why?* she implored. *What am I even doing here?*

Long before she'd heard Jake's response to her list, Amy had all but made up her mind that he was the one God wanted her to spend the rest of her life with—and that she was more than okay with that. His fifteen hundred dollar donation had sealed the deal for her, and she couldn't wait to thank him in person—which is why she'd spontaneously decided this morning to make the surprise visit to Las Vegas.

But even her confidence had been barraged with hesitation. On the drive out, she had pulled off the freeway no less than four times, overcome by the conflicting emotions swirling around in her mind. She knew Jake was a changed man, but their past was a tall hurdle for her to climb over. And now adding his accelerated involvement with Nicole into the mess was almost more than she could bear. *The next day!* She seethed. *How insulting.*

And yet, Jake's thorough attention to her list had been nothing short of amazing. His responses to nine out the ten items had swept her off her feet, and even that irksome final confession had been merely his attempt to give her what she asked for. *But why did he have to get with Nicole in the first place? Lord, why couldn't you have stopped him?*

Her ringing phone interrupted that line of thought, and Amy eagerly answered. "Cari!"

"Amy, what's wrong?"

"Well...I'm in Las Vegas—"

"What?" Cari interrupted.

"Jake's here for a tournament, and I thought I'd surprise him," Amy explained.

"Amy! You're not going to do anything crazy, are you?"

"Crazier than driving nine hours to surprise a guy who I've barely talked to in two years?"

"Well...yeah. So...did you find him? Did you guys talk yet? He's been working so hard on that list. I can't believe you're in Vegas!" Cari gushed.

Amy recounted the first ninety-seven percent of their conversation, but had to pause to keep her voice from breaking before she shared the coup d'état.

"Wow," Cari responded in the silence. "That boy isn't playing around. So what's the problem?"

"He cheated on me." Amy's voice cracked as she unloaded the burden she'd been struggling to carry alone. "With the girl I stayed with when I visited out there. They had already made out before, and then—" Amy's voice faltered again. "Then they had sex right after I left."

"Ohhh."

Amy lay back on her bed. "Wait, what do you mean, 'ohhh'? Did you know about this? Why didn't you warn me?"

"Oh, man. I knew Jake had shared with Chris about some regrets he had, but I had no idea *when* he'd made those mistakes. Amy, I'm so sorry."

"I don't need an apology. I need some advice. What should I do, Cari?"

"Well...You asked Jake to be honest, right?" Cari's voice spoke back softly.

"Yeah."

"And he was. He took a huge risk letting you know about his mistake."

"I know! But it's a *huge* mistake," Amy cried.

"True. But that's what grace is for. And you know we're called to forgive."

"I know," Amy groaned. "But I'm just not sure I could ever really forget."

"It will definitely be hard," Cari agreed. "But you pretty much have only two options here." Her voice turned suddenly serious. "You can either forgive him and allow this grievous mistake of his to lie buried in the past, or you can hold on to it and watch bitterness eat up the rest of your life."

"So you're saying I should take him back?"

"Well, throw out the whole cheating thing. Would you take him back then?"

"Duh."

Cari chuckled on the other side of the phone. "Are you afraid that he'll be unfaithful again?"

Amy thought back to the look of total repentance on his face. "No."

"Then I'll let you answer that question for yourself."

Amy sighed and sat up. "Thanks, Cari."

"I'll be praying for you, girl. You know we have been all along." She paused, and then exclaimed, "I am *so* excited for you guys! I can't wait to tell Chris where you both are!"

Amy hung up and paced the room cradling her phone in trembling fingers. She knew what she needed to do, but it was such a big step. *Jesus, you gave me a great example of forgiveness, but I sure need your help to forget.* She chased the haunting images of Jake with another girl out of her mind and quickly sent him a simple three word text.

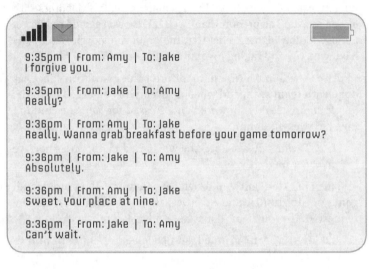

9:35pm | From: Amy | To: Jake
I forgive you.

9:35pm | From: Jake | To: Amy
Really?

9:36pm | From: Amy | To: Jake
Really. Wanna grab breakfast before your game tomorrow?

9:36pm | From: Jake | To: Amy
Absolutely.

9:36pm | From: Amy | To: Jake
Sweet. Your place at nine.

9:36pm | From: Jake | To: Amy
Can't wait.

After a marvelous conversation over some mediocre pancakes at Jake's hotel café, Amy settled in to watch her new *boyfriend* play his next game later that afternoon. She'd watched enough of his games in high school to know when he was in the zone, and today he was definitely in it. From the opening minute, Jake played like a man on fire. Host team UNLV collected the tipoff, but Jake easily stripped their point guard of the ball and raced down the court for an uncontested layup within the first fifteen seconds. And he never let up. By the time his coach pulled him out to take a breather with three minutes to go in the half, he led his team with twelve points, five assists, and three steals. Whereas yesterday he played as if in a lethargic fog, today he had an extra spring in his step, and Amy grinned to realize the reason why.

The second half was more of the same. Louisville went into it with a comfortable double-digit lead, so the UNLV Running Rebels attempted to set up a full court trap defense. But it was useless against Jake. Every time, he instinctively found the weak spot and either made the perfect pass to his open man down the court or charged through the hole himself. By the time he was finally taken out of the game again, he had accumulated twenty-five points with eleven assists. The predominantly UNLV crowd seemed to give an almost audible sigh of relief that the Louisville coach was finally having mercy and taking his star point guard out.

After the game, Amy hung around the gym until Jake was done with team stuff, and when he eventually emerged from the locker room, freshly showered and dressed for fun, she couldn't take her eyes off of him.

"Jake Taylor, you are hot!" she whispered in his ear as he gave her an eager hug.

Jake chuckled softly and held her tighter. "The guys are all going out to dinner, and I'd love it if you'd come with us," he requested. "I promise, it'll just be good, clean fun."

"I'd love to," Amy grinned, and Jake led her out with him to join the rest of his team.

As they approached the exit doors, Jake tentatively grabbed her hand and a million tiny fireworks went off inside of her. She laced her fingers through his, and he squeezed them firmly, and Amy wasn't sure if she'd ever felt so wonderful in her entire life.

After a terrific night of getting to know Jake's teammates over karaoke and sushi, Amy returned to the UNLV gym the following day to cheer them all on in their final game against the also undefeated North Carolina Tar Heels. With the game being nationally televised on ESPN, both teams played like they had something to prove; but ultimately, the Cardinals prevailed in overtime.

Diving for loose balls every chance he got, passing laser crisp bullets to his teammates whenever they were open, and shooting with lights-out accuracy from three-point-land, Jake led his team the entire time, so it was no surprise to Amy that the house announcer awarded the MVP trophy to him at the end of the tournament.

"I am so proud of you," she told him as they walked to her car after the rest of the team left for the airport.

Jake still had the appointment with her dad that he wasn't about to stand up, but Amy had convinced him to accompany her on the drive back instead of flying—and had talked the airline into giving him a voucher for another flight.

"I can't believe all of this is really happening," Amy murmured as she wrapped her arm around his waist.

"Believe it," Jake said with a smile as he rested his arm around her shoulders.

His cell phone buzzed with a new text from Debron.

"Who's Debron?" Amy asked curiously.

"I think he might be the reason I'm at Louisville."

AFTER ACING HIS FIFTH AND LAST FINAL,

Jake went back to his apartment and flopped on the couch. The past week had flown by in an absolute blur and he needed a moment to recover. Spending the weekend with Amy had surpassed anything he'd ever imagined, yet since stepping off the plane back in Louisville four days ago, he hadn't stopped running.

"Hey, babe! I love you so much, and I'm praying for you," Jake left a message on Amy's voice mail knowing she was in the middle of her final exam. "I can't wait to talk to you tonight." He hung up and sighed. Life was good. God was good.

Jake picked up the copy of the local newspaper sitting on the coffee table and reread the article about him being named the Big East Player of the Week. *As if I needed anything to make my week even better!* He grinned. When Coach had announced the honor at practice the other day, Jake had been stunned. Apparently, his complete collapse in the first game of the tournament had been overlooked in light of his more inspiring performances in the last two games. "I was just having fun on the court," he had told the reporter who stopped by during practice.

"That is so wonderful!" Buddy had exclaimed when Jake had given him an autographed copy of the paper during their brief lunch together yesterday.

Grant hadn't been able to join them, but Jake just couldn't wait any longer to tell Buddy about his time with Amy. He knew Buddy had been praying for the encounter and would be thrilled to hear how well it had gone.

"Jake, I am so happy for you," Buddy had responded merrily. "'To whom much is given, much will be required.' I can't wait to see what God's got in store for you this year."

Jake couldn't get that verse out of his mind since then. God had definitely poured on the blessings lately, and Jake was ready to give back. He wasn't exactly sure what all God wanted him to do, but the easiest place for him to start had been with a certain fifth grader who couldn't keep his mouth shut for longer than five seconds if his life depended on it.

Later that night after practice, Jake and Grant embarked on their regular run. In spite of their busy schedules, they had started rerouting their regular course on Fridays to include a twenty-minute pick-up game with a growing group of kids in the park by Debron's house.

"Yo, yo, my boys are here!" Debron called out as the joggers approached. "I think the coaches sent them out here to scout out my game for college," he boasted to the gathering swarm of kids. "I don't know, though. I'll probably go play in Europe instead; I'm not really down with more school."

"Europe's a pretty big continent. Almost as big as your head," Grant grabbed the kid from behind and put him in a playful headlock.

"Whoah! Respect the 'fro!" Debron looked serious as he wriggled free and carefully felt his puffy hair to make sure it hadn't been disturbed.

Grant laughed and started passing the ball around the mob. Jake pulled Debron aside.

"Dude, I got you a Christmas present."

Debron quickly perked up and peered around to see where Jake was hiding his package.

"No, no, not like that. I got you a job. You're now an official Louisville ball boy."

"Sweet! Do I get like a uniform and a locker?"

"How about a T-shirt?"

"Okay, coo'. Yo, yo, listen up," Debron immediately started bragging to anyone who would listen. "My boys here hooked me up with courtside seats for the rest of the season." He ran off to boast to some of the younger kids and Jake just chuckled as he joined the game with Grant. This kid had a long ways to go.

Forty minutes later, what started as a simple half-court game had morphed into an absolutely ridiculous free-for-all with ten to fifteen kids on each side all wanting Jake and Grant to throw them on their shoulders for the easy dunk. By the end of the night, a few curious parents had even showed up to watch from the sidelines. When the game dissolved into irreparable chaos, Jake and Grant slipped away from the mayhem to talk to them. Jake hoped that one of them might be Debron's mom but she wasn't part of the group. They did, however, learn from one mom that there used to be city league for these kids, but budget cuts had stripped it away two years ago. And since none of them had the money to join a club team, all they had were these pick-up games in the park.

"Wouldn't it be cool to be able to do something more for them?" Jake dreamed aloud to Grant as they jogged away later.

"Maybe. But if coach ever finds out that two of his starters are playing ball with a ton of kids on a court that's a sprained ankle waiting to happen, do you realize how much trouble we'd be in?"

"I guess. But you got to admit, it sure is fun."

"True," Grant agreed. "Did you see when..."

He recounted the tricky dribbling skills of one little girl who couldn't have been much older than five. Singlehandedly, she had driven the ball down the court past defenders twice her size. Some of the older boys sure hadn't appreciated that!

The rest of Jake and Grant's jog home was filled with laughter and stories as they rehashed the crazy antics of the different kids out there tonight. Jake wasn't sure what God was doing, but these kids were digging out a place deep inside his heart.

FOUR DAYS LATER, Debron made his debut as ball boy during Louisville's game against Bellarmine. Despite his big mouth on the neighborhood court, he'd been respectfully quiet throughout the competition and had hustled to retrieve balls and wipe up the players sweat with zeal. The Cardinals walked away with an easy sixteen-point victory, giving Jake and Grant plenty to celebrate as they gave Debron a ride home.

"Dude, I dominated like Dwight Howard out there on the court tonight," Grant boasted good-naturedly.

"Whatever," Debron retorted as he spun a ball in his hands. "He ain't half the player that Dwayne Wade is!"

Jake usually hated meaningless debates like that, but he was feeling good and took the bait. "What are you talking about? Dwight Howard leads the league in rebounds and blocked shots almost every year," he shot back confidently.

"Rebounds and blocked shots! Come on, is that all you got?" Debron mocked.

"What are you talking about? Rebounding is huge!" Grant represented his position.

"Okay, you and I play one on one and you get a hundred rebounds but I score just one point. Who wins?"

They all rode in silence for a moment, Jake and Grant unwilling to concede the victory.

"Dumb question," Jake finally responded. "'Cause there's no way you're scoring a point off of me." Jake stripped the ball out of Debron's hands onto the floor of his truck.

"Hey!" Debron protested. "At least I didn't get escuela'd by that Bellarmine guy on that play at the end of the first half."

"Escuela'd?" Jake repeated.

Debron leaned forward to pick up his basketball and rolled his eyes at Jake. "Escuela means school in espanol. So you got—"

"Schooled. I get it." Jake smiled and reached over to knock knuckles with the wordsmith. It was good to have a kid like Debron in his life, just to keep him grounded.

In spite of getting schooled by his man that one time, Jake had played another monster game today. Seeing every pick and cut as if in slow motion, he had carved up Bellarmine's defense like room-temperature butter. When the final buzzer sounded, Jake led the team with nineteen points and eight assists—in spite of Coach giving Jadon Williams the last twelve minutes as the lead kept growing.

Jake didn't like to talk about it much out loud, but he couldn't help wondering if this kind of play would be enough to give him a real shot at the NBA draft in the next year or two. What athlete didn't dream about the chance to go pro? *Shoot, I'd even play for a lousy team like Golden State or Sacramento,* he grinned to himself as Debron chattered on. The Warriors or Kings might not give him a shot at a championship, but he'd still be getting paid to play the game he loved...and he'd be awfully close to Amy.

"So Christmas is in two days. You asking for anything big?" Jake heard Grant ask Debron.

"Nah. I don't believe in Santa anymore."

"What? Then who's going to bring you presents?"

"Presents? It's not like I'm in Kindergarten, man."

Grant fell silent and Jake caught his eye over Debron's hair. *Is Debron saying what I think he is?* Jake speculated. Based on the look that Grant gave him, they were thinking the same thing: Debron's family was too poor to celebrate Christmas.

Immediately, the wheels in Jake's head started spinning. Coach was giving them Christmas Day off, but with a game the following day, it wasn't like Jake—or Grant, for that matter—could really go home. Buddy had been kind enough to welcome the two of them over to his house for the day, but since his wife was still completely bedridden, it wasn't like they were going to enjoy a home-cooked meal or anything. Jake and Grant had offered to pick up some DiGiorno's and dessert, and Buddy had assured them he'd take care of the snacks and drinks. It probably wasn't much different than the way Debron would spend the day...but at least there would be joy. Jake made a mental note to ask Buddy if he could invite a guest.

"So I was shooting hoops today, and these three punks started harassing me." Debron continued to babble on.

"Why?" Jake and Grant asked almost in unison.

Debron looked at Jake with a cocky smirk. "I escuela'd them in a game of horse and they were embarrassed."

"And let me guess, you didn't just play ball, you kept your mouth running, too." Jake prodded.

"I was just messing. They had no sense of humor."

"So what happened?" Grant asked.

"Well, I was about to go all Jaden Smith on 'em..." Debron karate-chopped the air in front of him. "But then Mrs. Williams called me over so I told 'em I had to dip."

"And they let you just dip like that?" Jake asked as he pulled up to Debron's now familiar apartment complex.

"Hel—I mean heck, yeah. You think they wanted a piece of this?" Debron scowled and flexed his skinny arms.

Both Grant and Jake stifled a laugh. "You know," Jake looked at his little friend seriously. "A coach once told me that only losers talk trash, only the ones who can't deliver."

"That's stupid," Debron snapped. "I always win."

"Then act like a winner," Jake countered looking him square in the eye. "A winner doesn't need to make a big deal about it to everyone. Just smile and move on and let your actions do the talking for you."

Debron looked at Jake seriously but didn't respond as Grant got out of the truck to let him out. It was cold outside, and he ran toward his apartment without a second glance as soon as he exited the cab. Jake sighed, wondering what it would take to get through to this kid, when suddenly Debron stopped. Jake quickly rolled down his window to see what was the matter, and Debron turned and jogged back to the truck.

"That's tight, bro. I might try it sometime," Debron smiled sincerely. "And thanks for the ride." With that, he hurried back around the corner and disappeared from sight.

1:22pm | From: Amy | To: Jake
Ni se imbarca in avionul. I think that means we boarded the
plane in Romanian.

1:22pm | From: Jake | To: Amy
Duh. Who doesn't speak fluent Romanian?

1:23pm | From: Amy | To: Jake
Jake, I'm so excited.

1:23pm | From: Jake | To: Amy
Just promise me you won't stay there long.

1:23pm | From: Amy | To: Jake
Haha. And what if I do.

1:24pm | From: Jake | To: Amy
You think I could make one of the Romanian basketball teams?

1:24pm | From: Amy | To: Jake
Yes.

1:24pm | From: Jake | To: Amy
Then I guess we could negotiate.

1:24pm | From: Amy | To: Jake
Negotiate what?

1:25pm | From: Jake | To: Amy
You get Romania, and I get you. Such a deal.

1:25pm | From: Amy | To: Jake
Seems like a win-win for me

1:25pm | From: Jake | To: Amy
Me too :] I love you, Amy Briggs, and I am praying for you
like crazy.

1:26pm | From: Amy | To: Jake
I love you, too, Jake. Good luck in your game. Talk to you
in two weeks.

JAKE HAD USED THE "L-WORD" FLUENTLY WITH AMY

long before they ever got back together, but this was the first time Amy had reciprocated. As her fingers hovered over the screen of her phone, the significance of her message sunk in. She loved Jake. She really, really loved him. She cared about her dad and her mom and Olivia and her brother and sister, and, of course, Melia and Cari and Andrea and Renee and her other friends. And she had really, really cared about Steven. But she hadn't felt this thrill of all-consuming, soul-aching love for a long, long time. *Since, well, the last time I was with Jake,* she realized.

It felt really, really good...and suddenly Amy had a desperate longing to see Jake face to face so that she could tell him in person—and see his beautiful face, feel his strong embrace, hear his reassuring voice. She had been counting down the days to this trip to Romania from the moment she had turned in her application, but now that she was buckled into the squished airplane seat, she was overcome with the realization of how much she was going to miss her boyfriend.

It had barely been two weeks since they'd reunited in Las Vegas, but all of the emotions towards Jake that Amy had denied and stifled and ignored and repressed for the past two years had immediately returned with fervor. Amy had no idea how she'd made it through finals successfully—all she could do was think about Jake! This past week, though, had been pure bliss. With both of them done with school, they'd been able to spend hours talking over Skype, and Amy was learning more and more that she loved about this new man. His humility was endearing, his integrity inspiring, his simple faith challenging, his passion to make a difference with every opportunity rousing.

God, thank you for bringing him back into my life, Amy prayed for probably the millionth time. *You know how much I miss him already. But I know You want me on this trip to Romania. Help me to be fully present there, and to make the most of every opportunity.* She heard the plane start to accelerate down the runway and opened her eyes to watch the takeoff. There was no turning back now. And that was a good thing.

Apart from missing Jake, Amy was still ecstatic to be going on this trip. For one thing, this would be her first real excursion out of the country, not counting a couple of afternoon shopping trips across the border into Tijuana with her mom. Although getting a passport had been more expensive than she'd anticipated, Amy was elated to get her first stamp. And far more than the adventure, Amy could not wait to love on the kids.

Besides "stalking" Jake on Facebook, the other online addiction Amy had discovered this past quarter was perusing websites about Romanian orphanages. Many an hour that she should have spent studying had flown by while she was reading about the horrendous conditions some of these children lived in. She was devastated by their stories, but eager to play a part in helping some of them.

Part of this drive to do whatever she could to help the innocent definitely came from her internship at PACS the past few months. It was like she had become both harder and softer through working with the abuse victims: harder in that she was no longer surprised to hear what people were capable of doing to defenseless kids, but at the same time softer as her compassion grew more and more unbearable. So many pages in her journal were smudged with tears from her conversations with God about the suffering she was witnessing. Amy had become wrecked this fall—fabulously wrecked by God's heart for the distressed.

A guest speaker at Intersect one week had hit the nail on the head for her. He shared on the topic of "holy discontent"—that personal state of restlessness when some issue of injustice sparks a righteous indignation until something is done about it. For Amy, the cries of hurting children were calling out to her more and more loudly and this trip was another step in her quest to lend a hand.

Now soaring somewhere over America, Amy leaned her head back against the rigid head rest. As she mused over what her experiences might be like in Romania, her eyelids grew increasingly heavy. Between studying for finals, talking with Jake as much as she could, preparing for this trip, and celebrating Christmas with both families, she hadn't found much time to sleep the past few days. With nothing better to do than watch an on-board movie that held no interest for her, she pushed the button to recline her seat back and closed her eyes. Before she knew it, she had sunk into la-la land, where dreams of Jake and malnourished infants competed for attention in her subconscious mind.

Amy had no idea what time it was, but it was dark when she and her other seven team members disembarked from the plane into the frosty Romanian air. Palo Alto winter had seemed cold enough for a girl who had grown up in sunny San Diego, but that was nothing compared to these arctic conditions. Amy pulled the beanie Jake had given her for Christmas lower over her ears and wrapped her wool scarf once more around her face and neck.

On the other side of immigration, the team was met by a smiling couple named Jim and Jodi—who were ironically from Southern California. They actually still owned a home there, but now spent most of their year helping mission teams from all over the world love on the Romanian orphans. Amy marveled at how normal they seemed. If she were to run into them on the street back home, she'd have no idea they were missionaries changing the world one orphaned kid at a time. But here they were, greeting each team member with a warm hug and a genuine expression of gratitude for being there.

After retrieving the luggage, everyone packed into a fifteen-passenger van and Jim drove them about an hour to a house in a residential area where they would be staying. Amy was paired up with a woman in her mid-forties named Kelley. She was a mother of two teenagers but, like Amy, had never been on a trip like this before. This was the biggest step of faith she had ever taken in her life and her nervous excitement oozed out of everything she said.

Over dinner, Jim and Jodi shared how their journey had begun just like everyone on the team: with a short-term trip. On that trip, God had grabbed hold of their hearts and they were permanently changed. Now fourteen years later, they thought they had the best jobs in the world getting to spend their days loving on God's precious children while giving others the chance to do the same.

As the team devoured a typical Romanian meal of a sour but tasty soup called *cibora* with *chiftele*, a type of large meatball covered with a breadcrumb crust, they explained what the next twelve days were going to look like.

"We work with a bunch of different orphanages all within an hour of the Bucharest area," Jodi explained to the team. "During this holiday ministry trip, we'll be spending time at all of them, delivering Christmas packages and celebrating the birth of our Lord with the kids. We'll start tomorrow with one of our newer projects, a baby hospital about forty-five minutes away. This will probably be one of the toughest days, because the kids are still unfamiliar with loving attention and the conditions are pretty appalling."

"There are over sixty kids between the ages of zero to four who live there," Jim stepped in. "More than anything, these kids just need your touch. Many of them are in their cribs twenty-three hours a day, more like a solitary confinement situation than a comforting place to sleep. But thanks to the donations from your team and several others, we were able to purchase fifty new cribs that you can help assemble while you're here."

"Wait. Why don't the hospital workers pick up the kids?" Amy blurted after swallowing her mouthful of meatball.

"Unfortunately, many of the care-workers resent giving the orphans attention because they feel like the orphans are getting a free ride while they are working long hours trying to feed their own children," Jim replied. "Especially the orphans with special needs. Even kids who are simply born with crossed eyes are deemed mentally retarded and a waste of time—and are subsequently left to pretty much fend for themselves."

Upon seeing the look of horror on many of the team's faces, Jodi reminded them, "You are definitely going to see some things that frustrate you here, but it's not our job to judge; it's our joy to love."

"How will we communicate with the older kids if we don't know Romanian?" Kelley asked.

"We do have several translators, but I think you'll find you won't need them much. Love is a universal language...especially with young children," Jodi assured her as she stood up to start clearing the table. Jim immediately joined to help her.

Amy watched them exchange a smile as they walked toward the kitchen and she was struck by how much they loved their life...and each other. They practically glowed with contentment, and delight leaked out of everything they did. Amy was particularly fascinated by the way their passions lined up and supported each other. *Could Jake and I ever be this amazing?* she wondered.

THE NEXT MORNING after a plate full of *mămăligă*, a
corn meal mush that Amy was surprised to enjoy, the team drove
to a whitewashed brick building that really looked more like a
prison than a place where over sixty young children lived. There
was no playground or grass to play on, no sign at all that kids
were present. As the team piled out of the van into the vacant
crumbling parking lot, Amy glanced up to a second floor window where she spotted three very young faces staring at them.

Jim and Jodi led the way through the large front doors as they
gave instructions. "Today is transition day. All we want you to
do is love on kids. Give them their presents and then give them
your love. If you do, I promise you'll have a few new best friends
by the time we drive home tonight."

The team walked upstairs and down a long corridor with
peeling paint only partially covering the cracks in the walls.
Cobwebs hung from every corner of the ceiling and dust bunnies
flurried along the dirty floors. An overwhelming musty odor
hung thick in the air, momentarily triggering Amy's gag reflex.
This is the most depressing place I've ever been in, she thought as
she braced herself for what was next.

Jim and Jodi looked back at the team just before pushing through two wide steel doors. "Remember, your smile may be the first one they've seen in a while," Jodi prompted.

Amy quickly readjusted her lips into a forced grin as she followed them into the first room. But immediately her heart sank and her eyes brimmed over with tears. In front of her were five rows of dilapidated cribs, each housing one or two toddlers who, surprisingly, were completely quiet. In fact, the entire room was shrouded in a deathly silence. *How can this many kids be in one room without any noise?* Amy marveled sadly.

As if he was reading her mind, Jim addressed the group. "When a baby discovers that crying does no good, they learn to just keep to themselves," he explained solemnly.

"But this isn't a morgue; it's party time," Jodi's voice sang out jubilantly. She pulled an iPod with speakers out from her backpack, and pumped lively children's Christmas music quietly into the gloomy silence. Jodi turned to the nearest baby and scooped the little girl up in her arms. Initially, the child seemed to stiffen, but Jodi held on tight, caressing her cheek and arm with a light touch and cradling her like a newborn. Within minutes, the girl visibly relaxed, and eventually she even cracked a smile. Temporarily propping this child on her hip, Jodi pulled a teddy bear out of her bag and turned to the next crib. Setting its occupant on the floor with the stuffed animal, she proceeded to the next crib and encouraged the rest of the team to get involved.

"Come on, you guys, let's set them loose!" she cheered.

Amy tentatively followed suit. Ignoring the foul stench of stale urine, she approached the nearest crib, which housed two tow-headed little boys, both of whom very visibly had Down's Syndrome.

"Hi!" she tried to greet them jovially. "Salut!"

Their empty eyes looked back at her without response.

"Uh, do you want to play?" Amy stuck to English while holding out a bright red ball in hopes that they might understand.

A flicker of interest seemed to spark in one of the boy's eyes and Amy took that as a yes. She hoisted both of them from behind their dingy bars and sat on the floor with them on her lap near where Kelley was sitting with her own little girl.

"Watch this," Amy said as she lightly bounced the ball to Kelley.

"Ooh!" Kelley exclaimed as she caught the ball and handed it to the girl. The girl touched it but quickly withdrew her hand, so Kelley bounced the ball back.

Amy put the ball into the hands of the boy on her left leg and guided his arms in a throwing motion. The ball barely rolled to Kelley, but he smiled at his accomplishment. They continued this little cycle of taking turns and, within fifteen minutes all three kids were in on the action. In between turns, Amy and Kelley gave lots of hugs, and before long, the ball had disappeared across the room and their little game had dissolved into a tickle fest.

Eventually, Amy and Kelley carried their new friends into the room downstairs where other kids were waiting. As Jodi entertained the older kids with a retelling of the Christmas story using big felt pictures, the rest of the team grabbed whatever babies seemed most in need of attention. Amy found herself cradling a little girl who looked to be about two years old. She had tangled blonde curls and grayish-blue eyes and had been lying listlessly on a torn mattress. Amy gazed into her dirty but precious face and suddenly started thinking about the little girl she had given birth to two years ago. A lump formed in her throat, and she fought to swallow it.

Over the summer, Amy had seen Emily most Sundays at church, and while she always felt a sort of maternal longing for the child who looked so much like her, Amy was still assuming she'd marry Steven back then, and she'd felt confident in her decision to let Frank and Jan adopt her baby. Their family was so adorable, and it was beautiful to see the way they loved their daughter as if she was their own flesh and blood. But now that Jake was back in her life, Amy had a new realization: no matter how great their future together might be, they'd always be missing a tiny bit of their past.

With this sad thought, Amy gazed down at the lethargic orphan in her arms, conflicting emotions battling within. Before long, negative voices started to drown out her empathetic ones.

Who was she to care about these kids whose parents had given them up? After all, she'd done the same thing. She'd been part of the problem! She was the last person in the world who had a right to try to help them. She gave up her rights when she signed her daughter away. What kind of a parent does that?

No! Amy caught herself and pushed the damaging messages back. She had dealt with all of these worries already, thanks to Cari's reassuring wisdom. God is a God of second chances, and He had used her mistake of getting pregnant to give an amazing couple a child. *He never wastes a hurt,* she reminded herself. These orphans were close to His heart, and He had given her this passion to help them. If He thought she was worthy, then who was she to argue?

The girl stirred in Amy's arms and Amy brushed her hair out of her eyes and gave her a hug. Emily might always be a missing piece of Amy's past with Jake, but there were plenty of other pieces that were gone, too—things that needed to stay out of the picture. God had given them a fresh new start and there was no room to hold on to regrets. Besides, Emily was in a much better place than she would have been had Amy tried to raise her alone these past two years.

Mentally clutching to this inner pep talk, Amy lavished her attention on the little girl in her arms. She might be here for only a day, but she was going to make the most of her time. She cuddled the girl and tried to get her to smile. She cleaned her face with a baby wipe and tenderly tried to untangle her hair. When she'd done the best that she could, she fastened a little pink bow clip in the curls and showed the girl what she looked like in a handheld mirror. The girl, who had probably never seen a mirror in her life, stared at the image in front of her in astonishment, her amazement growing as the reflection imitated every move she made. Before long, she started pointing at herself and giggling. Amy made faces in the mirror, and the girl giggled even more.

By this time, story time was over, and a horde of kids crowded around Amy to see their reflections in this novel contraption—and try their hand at making their own funny faces. Fortunately, the team had brought a dozen of the brush and mirror sets, and they distributed them now and tried to help the kids share them. It was astounding how easy it was to bring joy to these kids who had nothing, and as Amy sat on the floor surrounded by all the jostling children, her heart felt like it might burst with happiness.

But in the midst of all the joy, another gloomy though struck Amy: no matter how much love she was able to shower on these children today, it was only a drop in the bucket compared to the loneliness and abandonment they would face the rest of their lives. Again, tears pricked at Amy's eyes. *God, what am I doing here?* she cried silently.

She wanted to make a difference, to change lives. But what was one day really going to do? *Whatever you've done to the least of these, you've done unto Me.* Jesus' words rushed to the front of her mind. *Yeah, but is this enough? I want to do more, God!*

How much more? The question rang out loud and clear in her mind, so clearly that she looked behind her to see if someone else had said—or heard—something.

That question stumped her. There was so much to do! She could always drop her life in California and move here to Romania like Jim and Jodi. That would sure be doing a lot. And Jake had joked that he'd come here with her. But even then, she wouldn't be able to solve all the hurt and loneliness for every child. And there were still a ton of hurting kids back home, not to mention all over the rest of the world. It was all so overwhelming!

Amy looked around her. A few kids still sat scattered around her making faces at themselves in the mirrors, but most of the toddlers had crawled off to play with some of the other new toys. The three men on the team worked on assembling the new cribs and taking apart the old ones while the women each did their best to love on the kids closest to them. But there was no way humanly possible to spend "enough" time with each child. Amy looked down at the little blonde girl still lying in her lap staring at herself in the mirror. The girl caught her eyes and smiled, and fresh tears stung Amy's eyes. Sure, she was happy right now, but Amy shuddered to think about the unfriendly existence this child would go back to tomorrow...and the next day, and the next day, and the rest of her life.

Cold and stiff and her mind far from settled, Amy maneuvered herself into a standing position without agitating the girl too much and found herself instinctively swaying back and forth to an inaudible rhythm. Immediately the little girl's eyelids began to droop, and within minutes she curled up into Amy's embrace and dropped off to sleep, her tiny fingers wrapped tightly around Amy's shirt. Amy knew she should probably set the child down in her crib so that she could interact with some of the others, but she just couldn't resist snuggling with her a little longer.

Darkness fell and it was time to say their goodbyes. They placed each child back in their cribs, and it was all Amy could do to hold back the tears. The delight in the kids' eyes immediately turned to fear and loneliness. At least they had their new toys to clutch onto, but an inanimate object was obviously not even close to what they needed. On the drive home, Amy sat silently staring out the window.

"You're awfully quiet," Kelley prodded her softly.

Amy turned to look at the sweet woman next to her. "It's all just so overwhelming. I want to do so much more."

"I know," Kelley agreed and patted Amy's knee.

Amy pictured the little girl she had held all afternoon and murmured, "I just wish I could take her home with me." The moment she spoke it, an idea bloomed in her mind. Maybe that was how she could give more. Maybe she could adopt one...or more...of these kids! *Is that weird, after giving up my own child for adoption and all?* she wondered, but quickly pushed that hesitation aside. *I wonder what Jake would think.* Amy ignored that thought as well and tapped their leader on the shoulder. "Jodi, what would it take to adopt these kids?" she asked breathlessly.

Jodi turned around and smiled at Amy, but her smile was almost sad. "Unfortunately, Romania closed its doors to international adoption several years ago," she replied. "In order to gain entrance into the European Union, that was one of the areas that they were required to rectify. There was a lot of corruption going on, and so, over a period of several years, they completely shut that option down."

"What!" Amy exclaimed, her impromptu plan dashed to pieces. "Do they want these kids to be messed up for life?"

"Well, part of the system overhaul has placed a greater emphasis on finding Romanian families to adopt these kids, and there is significant financial incentive for foster parents, too...which has opened up its own can of corruption, but that's a whole other story. The goal is actually to eliminate all institutional orphanages like the ones we work with by the year 2020. I'm not sure if that is possible, but they are making great improvements."

"Well, it doesn't seem like it's enough."

"True, without the power of Jesus' love, it will never be enough. But that's why we're here, to bring in that missing ingredient. Remember we told you that today's baby hospital is one of our newer projects. The rest of the week you'll see how visits from teams like yours are really making a difference in these kids' lives, kids like Bogdana, who you'll meet tomorrow. When we first started coming to her orphanage about eight years ago, she seemed like a lost cause. She was eleven years old and the angriest child I've ever seen. She was emaciated and dirty and refused to give anyone eye contact. She spent her days alone in her bed, pulling out her hair and gouging herself with her fingernails."

"Poor thing," Kelley responded under her breath.

"I won't tell you any more, but I can't wait for you to meet her." Jodi's eyes sparkled and Amy's curiosity was definitely piqued. "God is using you, ladies, even if you never get to see the results. There's always more to do, but God doesn't ask us to do everything. He just wants us to do what we can...in His strength."

Amy pondered those words the rest of the drive home, knowing that they related to her current struggle but still unsure about the specifics. After dinner, they had team devotions, and one of the guys shared from 2 Corinthians Chapter one. Verse three and four jumped out to Amy: "Praise be to the God and Father of our Lord Jesus Christ, the Father of compassion and the God of all comfort, who comforts us in all our troubles, *so that* we can comfort those in any trouble with the comfort we ourselves have received from God." Again, these words resonated with Amy, but her mind remained unsettled.

After briefly hanging out with her teammates, she escaped into bed still wading in a paradoxical pool of emotions. Her heart overflowed with compassion yet ached to be able to do more. Amy suddenly wondered how God must feel looking down on all this pain and suffering, especially when He knew He could solve all of it if people would just turn to Him instead of doing their own thing. *I don't know how you stand it, God,* Amy sighed. But she knew that He must love when people like Jim and Jodi dedicated their lives to pushing others toward His healing love. *That's what I want to do, God. I want You to use me.*

Again, the question rang out almost audibly. *How much?*

Again, Amy didn't have an answer. How much did God need from her? Hypothetically, she knew He wanted everything, but what exactly did that mean? Did that mean she needed to give up Stanford...America...Jake? *Ouch.* That last one especially hurt. She'd already had to relinquish her plans for her future with Jake once, and she wasn't too keen on doing it again. *We just got back together, God. I mean, I thought You brought us back together. You don't really want me to give him up again, do You?*

Her head remained silent. Amy knew God wanted her to live with open hands and that her plans should always be open to His direction, but she didn't want to do anything without Jake. She was so excited about this new chapter of their relationship and how it was going to help both of them grow. And she was sure they could find a way to make both of their plans fit what God wanted for their life. *Isn't that enough, God?*

Still, no answer.

Amy huffed and tried to think of ways she could fit her plans to be a counselor and Jake's basketball plans together. Nothing specifically came to mind, but that didn't mean the two couldn't coexist. Of course, none of that did anything to help these kids here. *Okay, maybe Jake and I could come back on trips here like once a year. Would that be enough?* But even as she thought it, the idea felt unfulfilling. That didn't even seem to be enough right now. *Lord, just tell me what you want me to do.* But instead of waiting quietly, her mind raced to all the potential solutions she could think of.

Obstacles loomed large in front of every single one. She could move here...but how would she finish school? She could wait until she was done with school...but what would she do in the meantime? She could spend her summers here...but what about Jake and the rest of her family? And just like she had realized earlier, as sad as the situation was here in Romania, devoting her time here didn't quell the burning in her heart for other hurting kids. *Lord, what do you want from me?*

Before God's still, small voice had any chance to respond, however, Amy's brain sped on ahead again, racing round and round in restless circles. She wanted to serve God, but if she were honest, she was afraid to do it on His terms. For some reason, for the first time in her life, she felt strangely protective of the plans that seemed best in her mind. Her heart wouldn't rest until she figured out how to help these kids, but her mind refused to give God *carte blanche* with His ideas. As a result, Amy wrestled with the repercussions of her questions without answer until long after Kelley had come to bed and fallen asleep.

Finally exhausted and frustrated, Amy glanced at the clock. It was one:one3 a.m. *God, why is this so difficult? You know I just want to help!*

How much? came the pesky recurring reply.

How much do you want? she finally complained in exasperation.

I want it all.

The answer was so simple...yet at the same time, so terrifying. But she had no strength left to fight. *Fine,* Amy relented. *It's all yours. Take Jake, take Stanford, take my family. Take my hopes and dreams and plans and goals and use them for Your glory.*

As soon as the words formed in her mind, an immediate wave of peace and joy washed over her. The burdensome desire to do so much more was replaced by a refreshing sense of purpose. Amy still had no clue what God wanted her to do, but somehow that didn't bother her. An image of her sitting on her Heavenly Father's lap popped into her head, and she could tell He was so excited to show her what all those things looked like in

His plans. Excited to see what He was so excited to show her, she drifted off to the most refreshing sleep she'd had in a long time.

The next day, the team delivered presents to another orphanage. This one housed about fifty kids from age five to fifteen. Heart to Heart ministries had been working here for several years, and the difference was immediately noticeable. The conditions were still fairly run down, but the kids were markedly more social and happy. They enjoyed playing with their new toys and brushing their teeth with their new toothbrushes and eating their fresh oranges. But even more than the presents, they loved the attention. They swarmed the eight Americans, tickling them and playing with their hair and hanging from their legs and arms and backs. Again, Amy's heart overflowed with compassion, and she had the time of her life learning to sing Romanian Christmas carols with them and building snowmen outside and dancing and coloring pictures and playing games and just cuddling with them.

Shortly before lunch, Amy sat on the floor surrounded by almost a dozen little girls. They each colored their own pictures from a brand new coloring book. Out of the corner of her eye, Amy noticed a smiling girl who looked to be in her teens walk into the room. Immediately, all the little girls jumped up and greeted her with hugs and kisses. She lovingly responded to each one individually and they chattered away in Romanian for awhile before the girls all returned to their coloring projects. While the atmosphere had been generally cheerful before, once this new young woman entered, the joy was almost tangible. Amy wondered who she was. Before she had too much time to be curious, though, the girl came and sat down with them, propping her back against the wall and pulling a sewing project out of a bag as she sat and watched.

"Hi! My name's Bogdana," she told Amy in a heavy accent. Her English may not have been the best, but she didn't let that hinder her from being friendly.

"*You're* Bogdana?" Amy gasped, totally not expecting this happy young woman to be the orphan Jodi had told them about last night.

"Yes. What's your name?" she asked.

"I'm Amy," Amy reciprocated, still stunned.

"These girls think you are very pretty, Amy." Bogdana smiled generously.

"Oh, uh, well thank you." Amy blushed. "What are you working on there?

Bogdana took awhile to figure out what she wanted to say in her non-native tongue, but eventually conveyed the message. "I'm fashioning dolls to give to each child. If they have something to love, then they will feel better about themselves."

"Wow." Amy was genuinely impressed. "Where did you get an idea like that?"

"That's what helped me." She pulled a raggedy little doll out of the bag and showed it to Amy. Attached to it was a worn little card with faded Romanian script inside.

"What does this say?"

"It's a Bible verse from Ephesians. It says God sees us as perfect and has lovingly adopted us as his children through Jesus Christ. This verse changed my life," Bogdana smiled.

Amy nodded, struck by the simplicity—and yet profundity—of the message Bogdana had just shared. Could it have been any more perfect for these kids? "So, how many dolls have you made so far?" she asked.

"Only seventeen," Bogdana answered and dropped her head. "I have so many more to go, but I'm not sure how I'll get enough supplies."

Undertaking a project like this would be no easy feat for anyone, but when there was no Wal-Mart or craft store down the street...Amy couldn't even imagine. She couldn't wait to get more information from Jodi about this resilient girl.

"Bogdana is amazing!" Amy gushed later over dinner.

"I know, right?" Jodi chuckled. "Her orphanage was one of the first ones we started working with, and while her progress wasn't immediate, Jesus' love radically touched her, and I don't know if we've seen another child transform as much as she."

"How old is she?"

"Nineteen. Last year, she aged out of the system, but we were able to transfer her into our girls' transition program. It's tough because there just aren't as many jobs out there for young women—which is why so many of the orphan girls turn to prostitution when they're turned out into the street. It's so sad."

"What will Bogdana do?"

"Well, in the transition program, she's able to continue her education, so maybe she can become a teacher or something. But her passion is really to pour back into the orphans. She comes alive when she is able to tell them about Jesus' love. You've seen her dolls, right?"

"Yeah, that is so sweet."

"Totally! It's such a good idea. These kids have nothing, and so to be given something to love and care for on their own...it's almost miraculous."

"She was telling me about the Bible verse that went with it, something in Ephesians?"

"Yes, Ephesians one:4-5. It's an amazing verse for any of us, but for kids like her it really resonates. No matter how unloved and unwanted they feel from their own families and caretakers, God loves them...and wants them to be adopted into His family. When you don't have a family, that's the best news you can hear."

Amy ate for a while in silence, thinking about Bogdana's difficult past and yet the ways she was trying to give back. This girl who was only a few years younger than her was changing lives. *She is so inspiring!* "What would it take for her to accomplish her dream of giving every child a doll of their own?" Amy blurted.

Jodi thought for awhile. "There will probably never be an end to the orphans in Romania," she sighed. "There are thousands right now. That's a lot of sewing. A lot of fabric. A lot of materials...Bottom line, a lot of money."

Unfortunately, Amy didn't have much to give in any of those areas. She bit her lip and stared out the window. "I just wish I could do something," she murmured, mostly to herself.

"Bogdana is a special girl and God definitely has His hand all over her life," Jodi assured her. "Do you know what her name means?"

Amy shook her head.

"Gift from God. How perfect is that? I know God is going to use her in special ways, and He'll figure out how to make that happen."

Amy went to sleep that night once again with her head spinning, but this time in a really good way. Something about that girl struck a chord in her heart, and she really, really wanted to be able to enable her to pursue her dreams. *God, any chance You could help me figure out how to help her?*

30

Amy Briggs

I am "gloriously ruined"!

AMY CLICKED THE BUTTON to update her Facebook status on the archaic computer of the shabby internet café in downtown Bucharest where Jim had worked out a special deal for the team. Thirty minutes of online time wasn't much, but it was obviously way better than nothing and Amy was determined to squeeze the most out of every minute. Knowing there was no time to write a personal note to everyone she wanted, she decided to upload some pictures and use the captions to tell her story.

As she clicked on the photos that seemed to best capture her experiences so far, she was flooded with fresh memories. One week into the trip and her brain already felt like it was on overload. Every day, her heart broke for even more kids, and every night, she went to bed with her head reeling with emotions. But God was molding her and growing her in good ways. She still had no clue how God wanted to use this experience in the long run, no clue how all her plans with Jake and Stanford and everything else would fit into His plans, but rather than feeling stressed about it, she still felt excited to see how it all would work out.

She and Kelley had talked late into one night about this. As a wife and mother, Kelley had her life plans set even more than Amy. Unless God made some major changes in her husband's and kids' hearts, she certainly couldn't just up and move to Romania. But she knew she wanted to do something more. As they struggled together with what full surrender in their lives might look like, Kelley shared a quote she had read by Kay Warren. As the famous pastor's wife struggled to surrender her plans for the future to God's desire that she get more involved in the AIDS movement, she said she became "gloriously ruined" by God's grace. Amy could totally relate.

Amy waited for the pictures to upload and thought about Bogdana. Since that first day Amy had met her, Bogdana had joined the team at their different orphanage sites every day. She was an incredible help, always working hard and going out of her way to be friendly, and her English skills made interacting with the kids so much easier. Every moment that Amy was near this girl who was barely younger than her motivated her to want to make more of a difference in the world, and Amy still wracked her brain for ways to be able to help her make her dolls. Nothing big had come to mind yet, but Amy knew there were small sacrifices she could easily make—like Starbucks or other treats—to help her at least a little.

The final picture Amy uploaded to her Facebook album was of her and Bogdana surrounded by a crowd of smiling kids. Amy thought that it perfectly summed up her entire trip so far. For the caption she wrote: "I know God still has plenty to teach me the rest of my stay here, and I'm not sure of all the ramifications of the changes He is making in me. But I'll keep on seeking Him, keep my heart open to His promptings, and then keep on walking the path He's already set before me until He reveals the next step."

Amy clicked save and glanced down at her watch. She had four minutes left, just enough time to shoot over to the Louisville Basketball page to see how her stud boyfriend had fared in his game against Georgetown earlier in the week. The headline said all she needed to know: "Taylor Records Triple-Double in Hoya Rout." Amy laughed out loud as she pictured Jake—at six foot one—battling in the paint against the much taller guys for ten rebounds. That boy was crazy. She raced over to his Facebook page and posted a quick message to his wall.

Jake Taylor's Wall

Amy Briggs

I just realized that I don't have your autograph Mr. Triple-Double...Can't wait to talk. God is amazing! I love you.

Trace Adams

Great game, dude!

31

JAKE YANKED OPEN THE GLASS DOOR of the campus health clinic and hustled into the warm waiting room. He felt horrible. After several days of a scratchy throat, he woke up this morning with a full-blown cold that met every symptom on the side of the cold medicine box: fever, chills, body aches, runny nose, congestion, sinus pressure, and a throat so sore he could hardly swallow. This was his first time being really sick since he'd been away at college—which meant this was his first time without his mom there to take care of him. Fortunately, the campus clinic was there to help.

This year, the athletics department had taken a more aggressive role in keeping athletes healthier, and mandated several exams throughout the season to ensure competitors were drug-free, injury-free, and otherwise in good health. Only last week, Jake had come in for his mid-season check-up, complete with a nutritional evaluation, blood and urine samples, and even a flu shot. Too bad the flu shot hadn't helped him from getting this bug! Hopefully, the doctor would be able to give him something to get him feeling better before their next game in four days.

Jake signed himself in and then turned to collapse into one of the waiting room chairs. As he sluggishly spun around, he came face to face with Nate Williams who was entering the reception area from the back.

"Hey, man," Jake groggily greeted his teammate, but Nate just gave him a weird look and walked right by him out the door. *Do I look that bad?* Jake bemoaned. But he couldn't blame Nate for staying away. He wouldn't want to get his germs either.

Jake crumpled into the chair and leaned his head back against the wall. His head was so stuffy he couldn't focus on anything... except, of course, Amy. He had just seen her pictures and note on Facebook and he was so proud of her. He couldn't wait to talk to her again, and he was even more excited to give her the surprise he had just figured out. *Only five more days!* he mulled, wondering how he'd make it that long. Since classes didn't start back up until next week, all he had was practice and one game to distract him during this wait...and his current misery sure didn't help.

"Jake Taylor?" a nurse called out to the empty room as she held the door open.

Jake pushed himself up and followed her into the hallway. She directed him to the scale and Jake stepped on it. one84 pounds. She pulled up the measuring stick and measured his height. six-foot-one. Jake was pretty sure none of this had changed since last week, but he was in no mood to argue. She led Jake to one of the little examination rooms where she checked his blood pressure, eyes, and reflexes, and then scribbled some notes on a page in Jake's folder.

"The doctor will be with you shortly," she said curtly and then bustled out of the room, clicking the door shut behind her.

Jake wondered what she was in such a hurry for. Since most students were still away for the holidays, it wasn't like there was a long line of people waiting to be seen. *People are always in such a hurry nowadays,* he mused, thinking about his lunch at Buddy's house yesterday after church.

Yvonne was still non-responsive and spent her days lying in her bed either staring at the ceiling or out the window if Buddy propped her up. Buddy still had Bunny the nurse coming in on Sunday mornings so that he could get out and go to church, but his finances were tight and he hated to leave his beloved wife for any longer than he had to, so he spent the rest of his days sitting by her bedside, reading her Scripture and other books, praying "with" her, and singing songs.

Jake had started bringing him groceries once a week and looked forward to just hanging out with his old friend. Sometimes Grant would join them, but lately, he'd been spending more time with a friend named Rafael. Jake was a little perturbed by his roommate's priorities—and seemingly backwards progress—but Buddy stayed as loving and full of grace as ever, welcoming Grant with open arms whenever he did come.

Yesterday, Jake had asked Buddy if he ever got tired of just sitting at home all the time now, especially since he used to be so active, to which Buddy had readily replied, "People are always in such a hurry nowadays. I'm lucky to have an excuse to spend my days just sitting and being with the two people I love most in this world, God and Yvonne."

Jake loved the simplicity of that perspective, but he wasn't sure how he could manage to apply it to his life, especially once classes started back up. Even during this current vacation, his days were governed by whatever was the next thing he had to do. He tried to spend quality time with God every morning, but there was always a tiny bit of pressure to get through it so he could move on to practice...or clean his room, check Facebook, play video games with Grant, or a variety of other important things. Sitting here in the health clinic right now, however, he had nothing else to do, so he tried to bask in the slowness of the moment and talk to God about Buddy, and Yvonne's recovery, and of course, Amy.

Just as Jake was about to move on to pray for Grant, a slight knock on the door startled him back into the present. Dr. Witherspoon, a gray-haired man whom Jake had seen far too often with all these athletic checkups, walked in. Dr. Witherspoon was a diehard Louisville basketball fan and usually shot the breeze about the season for a few minutes before he gave Jake a clean bill of health to keep on playing. But this time, Dr. Witherspoon sat on his stool at eye level with Jake and got right to it.

"Not feeling so well, huh, Jake?" the usually friendly doctor asked without a smile.

"Pretty miserable," Jake admitted.

The doctor felt the swollen glands in Jake's neck, checked his tonsils, and listened to his heartbeat. "Well, the good news is it hasn't settled into your chest," he said. "But the bad news is there's not much we can do for the common cold. I'll have Patricia give you some cold medicine on the way out, but the best thing you can do is just stay in bed and rest. And drink lots of water to flush your system out, and you might as well be taking your vitamins while you're at it. I'll write you a pass to give to Coach. You probably shouldn't be practicing for at least the next two days."

"Ugh, that's what I was afraid of," Jake sighed. "I haven't been this sick in years."

"You athletes run yourselves down pretty ragged. Your body's just trying to tell you it needs a break."

"Too bad it's the middle of season," Jake groused. "Sorry to bother you for nothing, Dr. Witherspoon."

"That's what I get paid for," he winked. "But actually, I'm glad you came in. We were going to call you in for a follow up appointment anyway."

"A follow up?"

"Yeah. I need to talk to you about the drug tests we gave you last week."

Something about his tone of voice warned Jake that this was not one of their friendly little chats. But that didn't make sense. Jake had been completely clean for over a year, and he'd never taken any type of steroid his entire life. There was no way that he could have failed the test. "Drug tests?" Jake responded cautiously.

"Don't worry. You passed," Dr. Witherspoon reassured him. "But there is one thing that I wanted to bring to your attention."

"Okay?"

"Per your consent on the paperwork you signed at the beginning of the season, we tested your blood for a variety of STDs. I don't know if you are aware, but you carry the Herpes Simplex 2 Virus."

Jake jerked back on the table feeling as if he'd just been hit by a football lineman. "What? But I haven't had sex...in over a year," he stammered. "And, ahhhh, I wore a condom with her." Jake's voice had dropped to a whisper; he was mortified to be having this conversation, especially now that he was trying to live a life that glorified God as an example to others.

"Unfortunately, Herpes is an incurable virus that doesn't go away. You will carry it for the rest of your life. And Herpes is spread through skin-to-skin contact. There's a lot of skin that condoms don't cover," Dr. Witherspoon responded matter-of-factly.

"But I've never had any symptoms," Jake fought back feebly, still struggling with denial. Yet even as those words left his mouth, he suddenly recalled some discomfort he had experienced soon after breaking up with Nicole. Since it had been awhile since they'd slept together, Jake had never even considered the possibility of it being an STD. It had made more sense to attribute the soreness to chafing during practice or something like that. But that had been the longest lasting, most uncomfortable, weirdest location of chafing he had ever experienced.

"Some people go a long time before noticing an outbreak of warts or sores, since they usually occur in places we don't tend to look at very often." Dr. Witherspoon smiled wryly. "But if indeed you've had no noticeable outbreaks, then hopefully it will continue to be tame for you. Mind you, even if you don't have symptoms, you are still contagious to any future sexual partners."

Amy's face floated into Jake's mind. *Oh no!* He'd had a tough enough time telling her about Nicole in the first place. The thought of telling her about this new development mortified him. Suddenly, he wasn't nearly as excited about her return.

"And you might want to talk to past partners as well, just to make sure they're aware. Yours is not an isolated case on this campus recently."

Immediately, Nate's disturbed face flashed to the front of Jake's brain. *Ewww!* He winced, realizing that they now shared something more personal than just a love for basketball. No wonder Nate had rushed past him so abruptly. He'd probably just found out, too. Nicole was the only other girl Jake had ever slept with, and she had been on-again, off-again with Nate the whole time. For the first time, the grossness of casual sex with multiple partners really hit Jake. He'd already known it was wrong and really regretted it, but now he was just disgusted by it. No wonder God designed the intimate sharing of sex to be constrained within the boundaries of a committed marriage relationship! People didn't willingly share each other's toothbrush, so why was everyone so obsessed with sharing each other's bodies? It was repulsive.

"If there's good news in all of this," the doctor interrupted Jake's thoughts, "this doesn't affect your eligibility to play basketball. Just try to play a little more carefully *off* the court."

Jake cringed at the crude pun. Dr. Witherspoon had no idea. Once Amy found out, Jake wasn't sure if he'd ever have sex again.

JAKE TRUDGED TOWARD THE LOCKER ROOM

minutes after the final buzzer feeling like he was sloshing around in wet cement. He'd strained to give his all to the game tonight but it had taken everything out of him. His body still weak from being sick and his mind still burdened by Dr. Witherspoon's unpleasant news, he'd struggled to keep up on defense and his offense was so inconsistent that he had no idea how he'd still managed to score a few baskets…or why Coach had persisted in letting him stink up the court for thirty-two of the forty minutes.

"Good game, Taylor!" a fan shouted from the nearby bleachers.

Jake nodded and forced a smile. He appreciated the man's generosity, but he knew full well how pathetic he must have looked tonight. The rest of his team played pretty well as they pulled off another win, but Jake felt like he had been sputtering on fumes the entire game.

"You looked great out there, Jake," a female voice chirped to his right.

Jake looked up to see Nicole and jumped, then rolled his eyes and kept on walking. Even if she was just waiting for Nate, Nicole was the last person he wanted to talk to right now. Out of the corner of his eye, Jake spotted Nate walk up and give his girlfriend a big sweaty hug. Jake's stomach lurched and he quickened his pace off the court.

Ever since their abrupt bump-in at the clinic a few days ago, Jake and Nate had yet to talk. At practice, Jake had steered as clear of his teammate as possible, and Nate sure hadn't tried to come his way. So it was no wonder that their usually well-oiled game had been glaringly out of sync tonight. Every pass from Nate reminded Jake of so much more than just a basketball and he found himself cringing with every contact they had. Jake started wondering where their common contamination had originated. Had Nate been the initial contributor, or had Nicole infected both of them off of someone else? Either option was thoroughly repulsive and Jake couldn't escape the reminder of his newly discovered disease fast enough.

As Jake sped toward his retreat, a local newspaper reporter intercepted him, notepad ready to record Jake's humiliation. "Getting a lot of rest on this break from school?" the journalist asked good-naturedly.

Jake shrugged, confused.

"Well, what do you have to say about all the speculation about you entering the draft this year?"

Jake furrowed his eyebrows, even more confused. *What speculation?* he wondered. The only speculation he was aware of was the fantasizing in his own head. And clearly after a game like tonight, those fantasies were a waste. "Uh, I don't know," Jake mumbled as he stumbled toward the door leaving the reporter with nothing but a blank page underneath his eagerly poised pen.

Jake bumped into the crash bar of the door with as much strength as he could muster, hobbled to the benches where the team would congregate for their post-game debrief, and collapsed with his head between his knees. The thundering behind his eyes was almost unbearable and he winced at every whoop and holler of his teammates as they trickled in from the court. He felt a few thumps on his back but remained hunched over with his eyes closed until he heard Coach's voice enter the room.

"It looks like Taylor should get sick more often," Coach joked as all the guys huddled around the center of their locker room. "Twenty points, nine assists, eight rebounds. You almost had your second triple-double in a row." He grinned and Grant, Nomis, and some of the other guys knocked knuckles with Jake.

Coach kept talking, but his voice faded into nothing more than a distant buzz as Jake struggled to wrap his head around his stats. He didn't remember doing all of that, but Coach had the record book. No wonder he wouldn't take him out of the game, no matter how often Jake tried to get his attention. *Wow, God. Thanks,* Jake breathed, grateful that he hadn't stunk it up as much as he thought. But that didn't change the way he felt; and it sure didn't diminish the consequences of his disease. Amy was flying home tomorrow, and Jake was mortified at the thought of confessing this new shame to her.

Things had been going so well, so hopeful. And he was so excited about his surprise for her return from Romania. But all that was overshadowed by the incredibly painful conversation he now had to have with her. She was going to come back with so many exciting things to share with him, and all he had to share was a lifelong disease. He felt like such a failure.

Coach wound up his talk and Jake went through the motions of showering and changing into his street clothes while the rest of the guys celebrated their victory. He bundled up into his warm parka and exited to the parking lot without even saying goodbye. Once seated in his truck, a wave of nausea hit him and he rapidly rolled down the window and gulped the crisp night air down. He felt like he was hurdling off of a cliff. Who cared if basketball was somehow still going well if he lost Amy thanks to a past mistake he thought he had already dealt with. He'd come clean, he'd accepted his guilt, and he'd done as good a job as he could at moving on. But here the past came to haunt him and he wasn't sure if he had the strength to fight it anymore.

Desperate for advice, Jake pulled out his phone. It was after ten, which meant that Buddy was probably already asleep, but it was still early enough in California so Jake called Chris, embarrassed to admit his new struggle but needing his youth pastor's wisdom.

"What's up Jake?" Chris' familiar but tired sounding voice replied after only one ring.

Jake was pretty sure that he had never caught Chris in a bad mood. He was one of those guys who didn't just see the glass half full. For Chris, that glass always seemed to be overflowing all over the place. "Uh, you okay?"

"I'm in the middle of an extreme yoga workout with Cari," Chris panted. "This stuff is kicking my butt! But she said I can have a five-minute break to talk to you. What's shak'n?"

Jake pictured Chris awkwardly balancing himself in the Vaughn living room and had to chuckle. "Um, I got some really bad news at the health clinic this week," he began.

"Okay?"

"The doctor said I have Herpes."

A heavy silence settled with only the sound of the Yoga instructor's faint voice in the background until Chris finally spoke up. "Wow."

"I know," Jake moaned. "What do I do?"

"Well, you obviously have to tell her," Chris responded slowly, obviously understanding that Jake's dilemma lay with Amy more than the disease itself. "And sooner is definitely better than later." The message was blunt, but Chris's voice was filled with sympathy.

"That's what I was afraid of," Jake lamented. "But how do I break news like this to her? I mean, I can't just buy her roses and chocolate and say, 'I hope you like this gift, 'cause I've got something else I'm gonna give you, too.'"

Chris chuckled softly. "Yeah, I'm pretty sure that's not going to help." They both remained silent for awhile before Chris spoke up again. "Man, this really stinks, Jake!" he exclaimed softly. "I am so sorry you are having to deal with this." He sighed. "I guess you're getting to learn firsthand about the sucky side of sin. It's too bad the front side seems so appealing, huh?"

"Seriously. Why don't we ever think about the problems *before* screwing up?"

"If we did, Satan would be having a whole lot less fun."

"This wasn't the way I wanted to greet her back from Romania."

"Maybe she'll be so pumped up it won't faze her as much?"

"Yeah, maybe." But Jake didn't feel very hopeful.

"Jake, we will be praying for you. I know this is such a bummer, especially since you thought you'd already dealt with all of your bad choices. But Amy has forgiven you of everything else. I'm sure this will be no different."

Jake let the words sink into his brain for a few moments, knowing Chris was right but wishing there was some other way. Soothing Asian-inspired music played softly in the background and Jake remembered that he was interrupting Chris's workout. "Thanks, man. I know yoga beckons."

"Don't tell Cari," Chris whispered, "but I've enjoyed the break. By the way, how'd your game go tonight?"

"Apparently, pretty good." Jake shook his head. "I don't remember most of it, but Coach was happy."

"That's awesome, Jake." Jake could hear the encouragement in Chris's voice. "God's doing something. And your new problem is no surprise to Him. The truth will set you free, man."

Jake sighed. "I know," he answered softly.

After hanging up, Jake slumped against his steering wheel trying to formulate the words with which he could break the news to Amy. There was no easy way to do it, but he knew he just needed to get it done and over with. This wasn't the way he'd seen his surprise unfolding, but he knew what he needed to do. He still felt sick, but a new surge of strength and hope welled up within him. *Lord, please help me,* he prayed.

AMY'S PLANE TOUCHED DOWN on the busy O'Hare International Airport tarmac, and as soon as the stewardess gave permission for passengers to power on their electronic devices, Amy took her up on it. Everyone who knew her knew she was out of the country, so there was no reason for anyone to call or text. But she couldn't help hoping for something to show that she was missed.

It was nice to be back on American soil, but she really, really wished she was landing in San Francisco right now instead spending the next five hours in Chicago on a layover. She'd heard Chicago was a fun city, but the most she'd be seeing of it would be the food court nearest to their next departure gate, and she was pretty sure she could do without. She had spent the last fifteen hours traveling from Bucharest to London and now to Chi-town and she was exhausted and just wanted to be home. Her final flight was scheduled to arrive in San Francisco a little before seven tonight, which meant she'd probably get to Stanford by nine, just in time to crash before her winter quarter classes started less than twelve hours later. *Whose brilliant idea was this?* she complained to herself.

And of course, once she finally made it home tonight, she'd probably still be up for hours catching up with Renee—which maybe wouldn't be so bad since her body would still be on Bucharest time, which meant she'd be just waking up for their 7 a.m. breakfast call. *Ugh,* she groaned, dreading the next few days. Everybody told her the best way to fight jet lag was to drink lots of water and to stay awake until her normal bedtime tonight. The water part should be easy enough, but how was she supposed to keep herself stimulated enough to stay awake for the next few hours?

Amy's phone interrupted her whining as it started buzzing to indicate its retrieval of her messages. She looked down, surprised at its incessant rattling in her hand. By the time it stopped, she had seventy-three texts and sixteen voicemails waiting—all from Jake. Immediately, a smile spread across her face. Suddenly this layover didn't seem so dreadful. *At least I can talk to Jake.* She grinned.

As passengers way in front of her started jostling to get their carry-on luggage ready for disembarking, Amy hugged her backpack and started listening to her boyfriend's voice. Every night that she had been away, he had called at their usual time before he went to bed and prayed for her. Amy couldn't help getting a little misty-eyed as she got to hear Jake's conversations to God about her. *God, I have the most amazing boyfriend in the world!* she sighed. She saved each message to listen to later and then started reading Jake's texts. Just as endearing as his prayers, each one expressed his encouragement or something that he loved about her. Amy wondered if she could figure out a way to print all these out. They were amazing!

People started moving two rows in front of her, so Amy paused reading long enough to follow her teammates down the narrow aisle and out of the plane. Once they made it through the gate, they were welcomed by a teeming maze of lines for customs and immigration. Her teammates chattered around her as they moved at a snail's pace, but Amy engrossed herself again in Jake's loving texts. Each one made her grin wider and wider, and finally Kelley nudged her in the side.

"Looks like someone got some good news."

"Just some texts from my boyfriend." Amy blushed.

"He sounds like a great guy," Kelley smiled. They'd had plenty of late night talks sharing their stories during the past two weeks of being roommates. "I hope I get to meet him some day."

Amy grinned and finished reading the six remaining messages. Finally she came to the last one, sent last night.

10:32pm | From: Jake | To: Amy
Guess what? You're coming home tomorrow. I love you so much.
I need to talk to you about something.

Amy sighed with contentment, eager to call her boyfriend. She was excited to find out what he wanted to talk to her about, but she figured she should wait until they had all made it safely to the waiting area for their next flight. She wanted to enjoy her conversation with him with as few distractions as possible. She tried to tune in to the conversations of her teammates around her, but suddenly she was filled with antsy impatience.

After what seemed like an eternity, she finally made it to the immigration officer, and he quickly scanned her passport before sending her on her way. She was the last one of her team to be cleared, and they made their way through the airport to the baggage claim where they had to pick up their luggage before checking it back in for the final leg of their flight. Amy, however, had given all of her clothes away to the girls in the transition program, so the only luggage she had was her carry-on backpack. As they headed toward the carousel that would soon be spitting out their suitcases, Amy's phone buzzed. Startled, Amy jumped and checked the new text.

11:47am | From: Jake | To: Amy
Welcome to Chicago. I have a surprise for you.

Amy glanced up from the screen, puzzled. He must have remembered she had a stop in Chicago from the flight itinerary she had sent him and her parents. *Man, he's got good timing!* she smiled. Curious about his surprise, she slowed down to text him back.

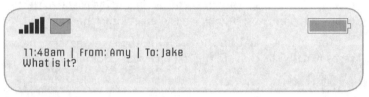

11:48am | From: Amy | To: Jake
What is it?

Before Amy could catch up with her teammates, her phone buzzed again.

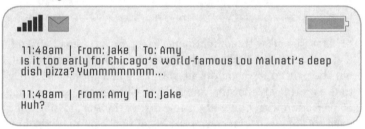

11:48am | From: Jake | To: Amy
Is it too early for Chicago's world-famous Lou Malnati's deep dish pizza? Yummmmmmm...

11:48am | From: Amy | To: Jake
Huh?

Yes, the pizza sounded good, but it wasn't even noon yet—and who knew what time her stomach thought it was. And what did pizza have to do with Jake's surprise anyway? Amy sauntered toward the baggage claim, eyes still on her phone, waiting for Jake to make sense of all this.

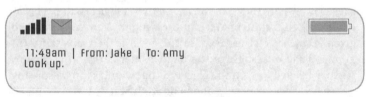

11:49am | From: Jake | To: Amy
Look up.

Amy shook her head, sure she was missing something in her overtiredness. She had no idea what Jake was talking about, but instinctively she followed directions and looked up to where her team was gathered ahead. Out of the corner of her eye she spotted a guy sitting on a bench with a huge pizza box on his lap and she chuckled. *Wouldn't it be cool if that were Ja—Wait!* "Are you kidding me?" she yelped and ran over to the man. "You're here?"

Her shriek had alerted everyone in the vicinity that something special was going on, and dozens of onlookers observed her jump into Jake's arms as he spun her around. Soon her teammates gathered around and she gleefully made the introductions. "Guys," she gushed. "This is my boyfriend Jake, from Louisville. Jake...this is everyone."

Everyone shook his hand and exchanged witty banter as Amy just tucked herself in underneath his arm and basked in the warmth of being so near to him.

"I'd say you got yourself a keeper here." Kelley motioned approvingly toward Jake. "I'm sure you guys have a lot of catching up to do. Since you don't have any bags to check in, why don't you just meet us at the gate before boarding, Amy?"

Amy smiled and nodded.

"It was such a pleasure to meet you, Jake," Kelley enthused. "I've heard so much about you."

"I can't wait to hear all about you and your trip." Jake smiled back.

Kelley and the others grabbed their bags and headed toward check-in while Jake grabbed the pizza with one arm and Amy with his other.

"Jake, what are you doing here? I just can't believe it!"

"Well, pizza sounded good for lunch, and I heard someone might have a layover here, so I thought I'd just stop by on my way home."

"Your way home! How long did it take you to get here?"

"Eh, it was nothing."

"Jake."

"A mere five hours. Which went by *so* fast because I was thinking about you the whole time."

"Jake! You're driving ten hours today, just to see me for a tiny bit?"

"It was shorter than driving to California. Why? Do you have something better to do on your layover here?"

"No!" Amy grinned. "It's just...this is so sweet. Why are you so wonderful?" She leaned her head against his shoulder and wrapped her arms as tight around him as she could. "I love you so much," she whispered. "I'm the luckiest girl in the world."

Jake knew this could be his perfect opportunity to break his unfortunate news about his disease and his heart started pounding in his chest. "Uhhhh," he stammered, trying to muster up the strength to just come out with it. But Amy just got there. He didn't want to ruin the rest of their time together already. So he chickened out. "Uh, I spotted a little snack shop around the corner. I'd love to hear everything about your trip." *After she's done talking, then she'll ask me about my two weeks, and then I'll come clean,* he rationalized.

"Well, do you want the two minute, twenty minute or two hour answer?" Amy smiled.

Jake looked down at his watch and did the math, "I'm all yours for the next three hours and forty-eight minutes...If you're willing to run to your gate."

They settled into a booth at the hopping little café, and Jake slid in right next to Amy. Couples who sat on the same side of the booth together when it was just the two of them was normally a pet peeve of Amy's, but today, she wanted to be as close to Jake as possible so this arrangement suited her just fine. Amy looked around and had to chuckle. It was no wonder Jake had picked this spot—televisions broadcasting sports were visible from every angle. But as her eyes rested back on Jake after her brief survey of their surroundings, she realized that it was quite clear Jake could care less. His eyes were completely glued on her, even in her silence. And they stayed that way for the next three and a half hours as she shared about her experiences in Romania.

He smiled when she described the joy of bringing Christmas to each different orphanage. He listened intently as she recounted her struggle with surrendering her future—including Jake—to God. He studied each picture she showed him on her camera as she explained the story behind it. And Amy could have sworn that Jake even had tears in his eyes as she told him all about Bogdana and her dream to help other orphans.

Long after their pizza had been polished off and their drinks had turned watery, Amy finally shrugged and said, "I think that's about it. It was amazing."

Jake smiled and grabbed her hands gently. "I've been praying for the past month that you'd come home a new person. It seems pretty obvious that God answered that prayer."

"What? I thought you liked the old me," Amy joked.

"No, no. I love the old you!" Jake corrected without skipping a beat.

"I know," Amy reassured him. "And yes, this was an absolutely life-changing experience."

"So how are you going to be different now that you're home?"

"You sound just like Chris!" Amy playfully punched his shoulder.

"Sorry?" Jake looked cautious.

"No, no. That's a good thing. You'd make a great youth pastor." Amy grinned as she pulled a magazine page out of her backpack. "So, I think I have an idea."

"Did you rip that out of a magazine from the plane?"

"Yeah."

"Isn't that kind of like stealing?" Jake's face was completely deadpan.

"It's not like I took the whole magazine. Besides, they had like five hundred copies."

"And the bank has hundreds of dollar bills but I'm pretty sure it's not okay to just rip one in half and take it."

"What?" Amy looked at him in confusion, wondering where this sudden lesson in ethics was coming from.

"Just kidding." Jake broke into a huge grin. "I think those magazines are there for you to take anyways. But I love to see you have a bit of a wild side. So what's your idea?"

Amy shoved a colorful magazine ad with lots of smiling children doing fun things in front of Jake's face. "It's for Make-a-Wish, the organization that grants wishes to children who have serious diseases."

"Okay?" Jake responded, sounding a little confused. "So do you want to volunteer to help sick kids now?"

"No—although I'm sure that's a good thing." Amy sighed. "Kids like Bogdana have wishes that they need help with, too. What if I could figure out a way to raise money to empower them to achieve their dreams? That would be...amazing."

"You could call it Make-a-Dream," Jake joked.

Amy chuckled. "Maybe. Do you think it's a dumb idea?"

"No! I am so proud of you. And I'm excited to see what you come up with."

"That's the hard part. The idea part was easy. But how do I raise enough mon—" Suddenly, Amy's phone began to buzz on the table. "Crap!" she exclaimed, noticing the time above Kelley's name. "Hello?"

"Hey, Amy. You almost here?" Kelley asked.

"Uh, yeah...Actually, I still have to go through the security line."

"Well, we'll try to stall for you, but kiss that little dreamboat of yours goodbye and get over here in a hurry, because they're just getting ready to board the plane."

"Got it. Thanks, Kel." Amy hung up, and turned to Jake, who had already cleared the table and was standing there waiting with her backpack. "Man! I had been dreading this layover, and now I don't want it to end," she groaned as she fell into Jake's arms.

Seventeen hugs later—it took everything inside of her not to break down and just kiss him like there was no tomorrow!—

Amy separated from Jake at the security checkpoint. He stood watching her until she finally ran around the corner to her waiting plane. She scooted into line behind the last few people and was buckled into her seat in between Kelley and an unknown middle-aged man within the next few minutes.

As Amy settled in and tried to catch her breath, she noticed that the guy next to her was reading a Sports Illustrated article about the hottest college basketball teams mid-season. Curiosity piqued, she tried to subtly crane her neck to see if Louisville was mentioned. Sure enough, after scanning the entire article in reverse, she noticed a beautiful picture of the man of her dreams on the far side of the page and underneath it was a few paragraphs about the Cardinals. It was difficult to read the fine print, but in the midst of all the team jargon, Amy made out something about Jake being the assist leader of the Big East conference and potentially a dark horse in the NBA draft.

Wow. Amy relaxed her head against the seat and tried to wrap her head around her boyfriend's success as her plane lifted off the runway into open air. *It sounds like he's had an amazing two weeks, too! And yet all he did was listen to me yap the whole time!* This new Jake was getting more and more attractive—and she was feeling more and more undeserving. Suddenly she remembered Jake's text from the night before, about needing to talk to her about something. *Shoot! I never even asked him about that!* she cringed. She knew she'd get in too late to talk to him about it tonight so she made a mental note to remember to ask him first thing tomorrow.

34

THE FIVE-HOUR DRIVE BACK HOME from the airport was nowhere near as exciting as the trip up to Chicago, but Jake did enjoy a certain sense of relief. As much as he had been *ready* to share his devastating news with Amy, it certainly wasn't something he *wanted* to do. He had been only too happy to let her fill up their entire time together with her own stories. Sure, there was still a nagging sense of dread that lurked in the dark recesses of his mind, but it was fairly easy to ignore that subconscious naysayer as he rehashed Amy's excitement about the kids she helped in Romania.

She was so inspiring! It was almost like she was a volcano erupting when she told him about her idea to help underprivileged kids around the world achieve their dreams.

"Who thinks that way?" Jake said out loud to the cars racing by him on the other side of the six-lane freeway. *Oh yeah, my girlfriend does,* Jake smiled.

As usual, Amy's rousing example prompted Jake to want to do more with his own life. He was living out his dreams at Louisville and, considering his past mistakes, things couldn't be going much better. *But...*

Jake shook his head. How many people in his position—full-ride scholarship playing ball for a nationally-ranked college, possible future career in the NBA even, and above all else a smoking hot girlfriend who had character to match—would ever even think about a "but"? But Jake couldn't help it. *But...what if God wants more from my life than all this?*

He thought about Amy who was determined to change the world one mistreated kid at a time—whether here or in Romania or anywhere else God showed her. But what was he doing to help other people? Sure, he served in a few different ministries at church, and he and Grant still played basketball with Debron and the other kids from the neighborhood once a week. But was he really leaving a lasting impact? Was he really doing everything he could to honor God with all the blessings God had given him? *To whom much is given much is required,* Jake remembered Chris saying one time. *God, what else do You want me to do?*

Jake drove along for a few more miles, his mind reeling with unformed possibilities. Then, somewhere around Indianapolis, an idea finally burst into full bloom that actually seemed like something Jake could handle. As he drove closer and closer to home, he grew more and more excited about revealing his plan to Debron and the gang. Of course, first he'd have to get Coach's approval, and bring Grant and the other guys in on it, and obviously he'd talk to Amy and Buddy about it and get their input on how to make it even better. But by the time Jake rolled into the parking space in front of his apartment, he could barely wipe the grin off his face. *Thanks God! This is going to be awesome.*

Three days later, Jake knocked on Coach's office door with sweaty palms and eager jitters. He had a good relationship with Coach, and everyone including the guys on the team thought this was a nice idea, but Jake was making a big ask here and he couldn't help but feel a little nervous.

"Come in," a hoarse voice instructed from within.

Jake opened the door to the familiar carpeted corner office that looked like a cross between a lawyer's and a PE teacher's space and waited until Coach looked up from the notes he was reading intently.

"Hello, Jake!" Coach greeted him enthusiastically as he slid his reading glasses off of his face. "Great practice yesterday. Everything okay?" He waved for Jake to take a seat on the couch across from his large mahogany desk.

"Yeah, yeah." Jake took a deep breath, still not sure how coach was going to respond to his idea. On the one hand, ever since his idea had sprung to life inside of his brain a few days ago, his heart had been burning with the impulse to do something about it. But on the other hand, Jake knew that the only thing Coach really wanted him to be thinking about this time of year was basketball and school—and only enough about school to get by and stay eligible to play basketball. Everything else was an unwelcome distraction. So, tiptoeing carefully out onto the thin ice, Jake gingerly began. "Coach, you know that kid Debron that I got to be a ball boy for our team?"

"Uh huh," Coach nodded.

"Well, um, Grant and I have started getting to know a lot more of his friends lately."

"I don't think we need any more ball boys this late in the season, Jake," Coach interrupted.

"I know. It's just, well, they all live on the other side of town, you know, and they really don't have much. They're the kind of kids that society has mostly given up on, and, if things keep going the way they are, most of them will probably live up to everyone's negative assumptions about them." Jake paused to try to read Coach's expression, but his face was blank.

"But they love basketball," Jake continued, "and they really love their Cardinals. And I was thinking it would be really cool to show them that people do care about them by bringing them to one of our home games."

Coach folded his hands on his desk and studied Jake. "How many tickets are we talking about here?"

Since the weather had turned colder, Jake and Grant's usual throng of basketball fans had diminished somewhat, but there was still a crowd of fifteen to twenty regulars who came out each week to play with them. "I was thinking about twenty?"

Coach nodded thoughtfully as a small smirk appeared on the left corner of his mouth. "These kids where you and Grant picked up some of those scrapes and bruises I've noticed?"

Jake nodded sheepishly, hoping the consequences for his extracurricular injuries wouldn't affect the kids. "Sometimes we have just a little too much fun out there with them," Jake admitted reluctantly then quickly added, "but they're really good kids."

Coach leaned back in his chair placing his hands behind his head. "I'll make you a deal. You and Grant slow down on your late night pick-up games until the end of season and I'll see what I can do. Non-contact games of Horse can be fun, too, you know."

Jake immediately broke into a gigantic smile. "Deal! Thank you so much, Coach."

"You're a good kid, Jake," Coach said with a wink.

Jake stood to leave, and then remembered one more part of his plan that needed Coach's approval. "Uh, I was wondering, too, could the kids come to the locker room after the game to meet the guys?" he blurted before he could chicken out.

Coach smiled and shook his head. "I'll tell you what. You get a triple-double in a victory against Marquette this week and you can invite your mom's uncle's dog into the locker room."

That Saturday, Jake terrorized the Marquette Golden Eagles on both ends of the court. He was already averaging seventeen points and eight assists a game, but his six-foot-one frame made him a midget on the court and usually didn't help much with bringing down rebounds. Tonight, however, it seemed like every loose ball flew in his direction.

With thirty-two seconds left on the overhead scoreboard and Louisville comfortably ahead with a double-digit lead, Jake still defended his man with fervor. He had a glowing twenty-three points and eleven assists...but only nine rebounds—one short of his coveted triple-double. As the clock ticked down, he eased up on his man a little, almost willing him to take the open three. The guy took the bait and heaved up a shot. With too much gusto and not enough precision, the ball careened off the glass right into Jake's hands near the foul line. A smile broke out on his face as he dribbled the ball slowly up court until time ran out. He glanced over at Coach who gave him a little smirk.

A MONTH AND A HALF LATER, Jake's idea finally saw its fulfillment at the final home game of the season. Coach had given him tickets for twenty of the neighborhood kids to attend—plus two more for parent chaperones. Jake found it sadly ironic how the usually uninvolved parents had shown sudden interest in what he and Grant were doing with their kids once they found out free tickets were involved. In the end, they asked the only two fathers who had ever stopped by *before* the free tickets to accompany the group to the game.

After the Cardinal's comfortable victory, Jake and Grant paraded the wide-eyed kids around the locker room where not even reporters were allowed to go. To make the night even more special, Jake had talked to Sid, the equipment manager, about donating old basketballs to the kids. One by one, each of the players on the squad greeted each of their young fans by name and added their autograph to the worn balls. Star struck, the usually too-cool youngsters were rendered speechless as they admired their new prized possessions and the superstars in front of them. Every teammate performed admirably, giving each child their utmost attention. Jake was so proud of them...and his kids.

When all was said and done, Jake found himself in his truck driving Debron home for the last time this season. The rest of the kids had left an hour before on the city bus, but Debron conveniently missed that ride while Jake was showering and dressing. As the now twelve-year-old chattered incessantly about the game and all the things he would have done differently if he had been playing, he mindlessly twirled his "new" basketball full of signatures from every guy on the Louisville squad. Debron had grown accustomed to hanging out with the team on the court during his stint as ball boy this season, but tonight had been special even for him.

"I think this was the best day of my life," Debron concluded as Jake's truck pulled to a stop in front of his unkempt apartment. "Thanks dude...for everything." The now twelve-year-old reached over and gave Jake an unexpected hug before opening the door.

As the cool winter air gushed in and Debron rushed out, Jake let his little buddy's words sink in for a second. *The best day of his life. And this was so easy, God!* Jake followed Debron's fluffy fro as it bounced around the front of his truck and then spontaneously raced to Jake's window. Jake rolled the window down to see what Debron wanted.

"You know, you probably could have had another triple-double tonight if you would have used some of those moves I taught you last week."

"I know, man, but I just can't do them as good as you."

"Sure 'nough. That's why I keep telling you, they oughtta let us young folk play. I could have had that triple-double, no doubt."

"I don't know," Jake said with a laugh. "I've seen you on the court. You're fast man. You probably would have had ten steals too...I think that's called a quadruple-double."

Debron smiled and knocked knuckles with Jake, then ran off around the corner to his apartment. Jake knew it didn't make sense, but for some reason, tonight definitely ranked up there as one of the best nights of his life, too.

✚ ✚ ✚

Later that night, Jake lay wide awake for hours, unable to stifle the joy still bubbling up inside of him. Finally, around one a.m., he switched on his bedside lamp and started jotting down his thoughts in his prayer journal.

Dear God,

Here I am at Louisville, living out my dreams. It's been so much fun ... and I've been playing so well. I mean, what's a couple of three point-ers compared to creating the universe? But You know what I'm talking about. But here's the cra-zy thing, after it's all said and done, the smiles on those kids' faces is what I can't get out of my mind. And I'm far more excited about the hug Debron gave me than being highlighted on Sports Center tonight. It feels so good to be making a difference in their lives. I'm not sure what this all means. Am I crazy? Show me what You want me to do God. And thanks for tonight. Everything was awesome.

Love, Jake

"SO HAVE YOU TOLD HER YET?" Buddy asked bluntly as soon as he, Grant, and Jake sat down with their plates piled high with take-out Chinese food.

The bite of roll in Jake's mouth quickly turned to cotton and stuck in his throat. It was weird enough that his eighty-five year old mentor was one of the first ones he told about his STD, but sometimes it was even more awkward that he was so frank about it. It was such a personal thing and a constant reminder of his past mistakes. Yet Buddy never focused on the past or came anywhere close to laying on the guilt. He simply wanted to help Jake keep his future clear—something Jake hadn't quite accomplished yet.

Grant stared at Jake and shook his head. He knew Jake still didn't have a satisfactory answer to this weekly question.

"There just hasn't been a good opportunity yet," Jake mumbled. "I'm trying." Grant snorted by his elbow. "Seriously! I really am."

"Jake, you had the perfect opportunity when you met her at the airport," Grant chided. "I'm sure she was like putty in your hands after you drove all the way up there to surprise her. You could have told her you killed her cat and she would have still thought you were the greatest thing since sliced bread!"

"She doesn't own a cat," Jake corrected sullenly. "I know. I blew it. But she was so excited to tell me all about her trip, and I didn't want to ruin it. It wasn't like I avoided it. She just had a lot to talk about."

"And since then?" Buddy piped up for the first time since instigating this conversation.

"There's always some excuse," Grant answered for Jake.

Jake couldn't argue; it was true. And he knew that the longer he waited, the harder it was getting. There would never be a perfect time to drop this bomb.

"When it comes to love, Jake, it's all or nothing," Buddy said calmly. "Do you love her?"

"You know I do."

"I'm almost afraid he loves her too much," Grant joked.

Buddy smiled and rested his fork on his plate. "That's impossible. Real love is one hundred percent or it's not the real thing. I know our culture has tried to make love into just a nice feeling you get when a pretty little lady who's got your fancy walks into a room. But that's not love...that's lust. And any thirteen-year-old, pimple-faced boy can do that. It takes a man to love."

Jake stared at Buddy and mulled over his words. "So," he began carefully. "What does that have to do with my current dilemma?"

"Okay, quick grammar lesson." Buddy quickly grew animated. "When you say you love someone, what part of speech is love?"

"Verb?" Grant answered promptly.

"Bingo!" Buddy exclaimed. "That just about says it all, huh?" He picked his fork back up and resumed eating his fried rice.

Jake shook his head, confused. "Wait, I don't get it."

"If love is a verb then it's an action not a feeling," Grant interjected.

"Thank you." Buddy slapped Grant's shoulder with his free hand. "If I just did nice things for my wife when I felt like it then I would be a horrible husband. But it's those times I love her through my actions when I *don't* feel like it that shows my real love for her."

"But Buddy, you're like the most loving person in the world. It's easy for you," Grant said.

The old man let out a loud belly laugh. "That's a good one. You really think I get a thrill out of changing my wife's diapers? You think I enjoy spending hours talking to her every day knowing she might never be able to talk back to me? Yvonne and I have had our rough patches in the past, but these past seven months have been the hardest thing I've ever gone through."

Jake's and Grant's forks both hung suspended in mid-air. This was a new side to Buddy that they'd never seen before. Usually he was so positive, always looking at the bright side of things. It made sense that he was struggling through his wife's deterioration, but he'd never let them into that truth before. Jake searched for words to say to encourage his older friend, but nothing came to mind.

"But here's the crazy thing, boys: It's when I love my wife through my actions that I actually find my feelings start to grow again. I can tell you honestly that I am more in love with Yvonne today, after all I've been through with her stroke, than I've ever been before." Buddy swiped at the corner of his eye where a tear was beginning to glisten. Jake reached out and gave his hand a squeeze. Buddy patted Jake's hand and then pulled two pens out from his front shirt pocket. Throwing them across the table to Jake and Grant, he said, "Write this down on a napkin, boys." Buddy paused as they got ready for the nugget. "Real men learn how to lead their hearts."

"So I guess that means I need to tell Amy right away, huh?" Jake said as he looked up from scribbling down the quote.

"You tell us, Jake. How much do you love her? Put your money where your mouth is."

"Dang, you know how to hit it where it hurts," Jake replied with a slight smile.

Buddy winked at Jake and focused back on the last few bites on his plate. "You know I'm going to keep asking you about it."

"I know." He bit into a crunchy piece of orange chicken, wondering how he was going to follow through on this.

"Good, because there is something else I've been wanting to talk to you boys about that's much more enjoyable."

"Yeah?" Jake and Grant asked almost in unison.

"Tell me about this little basketball ministry you've got going on with the kids."

"You mean taking them to the basketball game and all that?" Jake clarified.

"I'm not sure I'd call it a ministry," Grant corrected. "Remember, I'm not like you guys. I'm still unsure about all this Jesus stuff."

Buddy reached across the table and patted Grant's arm. "A year ago you were pretty sure you wanted nothing to do with Jesus. I love the progress." He turned to Jake. "Yeah, how did the game go last week?"

Jake turned to Grant and grinned. "It was pretty epic," he beamed, and recounted all of his highlights of the evening, especially Debron's hug at the end. Grant piped in with his own favorite parts, and Buddy grinned the entire time.

"That sounds so great," Buddy affirmed when they were done. "I don't care what you call it, you are bringing God's light to these kids' lives, and that's what ministry is."

Jake mulled it over for a few moments before answering. "I guess so. I wish we could do something more than just bring them to a single game and stop by to play with them once a week."

"Like what?" Buddy prodded, leaning forward in his seat.

"I don't know." Jake twirled some chow mein noodles around and around on his fork. "They really liked being around the team. I wonder if we could get some of the other guys and host a free camp for the kids after the season."

"Love it!" Buddy exclaimed without hesitation.

"Me, too," Grant agreed.

Buddy leaned back in his seat and patted his belly contentedly. "Something like that would take more than just a few basketball players. You would definitely need some volunteers to bring the food and drinks and help set up and—"

"Whoa, Buddy," Jake interrupted "Aren't you getting a little ahead of yourself? I don't know that many people!"

Buddy smiled. "Oh, *I* know some people. This is going to be great."

37

TWO EXTREMELY BUSY WEEKS LATER, Jake sat waiting for his name to be announced in Louisville's first game in the NCAA tournament. Their hard-fought loss to Georgetown in the final game of the Big East tournament had knocked them down in their rankings, but they still easily qualified for a first-round bye. Now they faced fourteen-seed Santa Barbara, a University of California campus that had recruited Jake but to which he never even gave a second glance in spite of its much closer location to his home in Oceanside. UCSB looked like it would be an easy opponent, but Coach had made it perfectly clear in the pregame speech that they should never take any competition lightly.

Jake glanced around at the packed stands of thousands of cheering fans all around him and marveled that he was sitting here in this spot. This was his dream come true. His mind raced over the past year that had brought him here. Was it really just a year ago that Nate had injured his ankle in this game, giving Jake the opportunity finally to step up and shine? So much had changed in the last twelve months. Feeling the added pressure that came with his new role as leader of the team, Jake noticed the perspiration collecting on his palms.

"And starting at point guard, standing six-foot-two, Jake Taylor," the announcer yelled, breaking Jake out of his contemplations.

Jake wasn't sure when he had grown that extra inch. Last time he'd checked, he'd still been six-foot-one. But that was the least of his worries this evening. Jake sprung from his seat to join the rest of his teammates near the free throw line.

The Cardinals burst out of the gates running, and by the time the first half came to a close, it was evident that Santa Barbara was no match for everything Louisville had to offer. While Jake was far from shy of throwing up the rock himself, he was even better at delivering the ball to whoever had the hot hand. Today, that happened to be his roommate. Grant was like a basket-scoring machine, converting every pass into points no matter where he was on the court. Assists had never come so easy for Jake.

Grant had started most of the year but late into the season his jump shot had grown cold, causing Coach to send him back to the bench. Jake had rebounded countless hours of jump shots with him trying to fan his touch back to flame, which made today's performance even sweeter. Coach pulled both of them out for the last six minutes when it was clear that victory was in hand. They would need to be well rested for their round-three opponent.

Two days later on the same court, Jake and his teammates faced eleventh-seeded Virginia Commonwealth University. The Rams had been one of the surprise stories of the last round, trouncing Louisville's nemesis Kentucky. Coach made it abundantly clear that this would not be the case with his team tonight. His team was faster, stronger, more talented...and better coached. And they needed to go out there and take care of business like they had all season.

While the pep talk sounded nice in the locker room, four minutes into the game, it certainly wasn't doing any good. Maybe on paper VCU was a lesser team, but in reality, they were outscoring, outrebounding, and outplaying everything Jake and his teammates were throwing at them.

Jake's matchup was sticking to him like a pesky mosquito who wouldn't stop buzzing inches away from his face. To make matters worse, his breath reeked like rotten eggs. Jake tried not to hold it against him, but the guy's mouth also streamed a never-ending flow of trash talk that would have put Debron to shame and Jake was getting sick of it.

Unfortunately, with this kid in his way, Jake couldn't seem to buy a decent pass and a good shot had been even harder to find. At halftime, Jake's stats included a pathetic four points and three assists. Louisville only trailed by six, but Jake knew that if things didn't change, he'd be watching the rest of the tournament from home.

The Cardinals sulked back to the locker room looking deflated. They needed Coach to pump them back up, but apparently he didn't have anything to say, because he didn't join them. So there they all sat stewing in silence with nothing but the sound of a dripping faucet to keep them company.

"These guys are fast," Nate finally spoke up from the corner, a towel draped over his head.

And then, as if his complaint gave everyone else permission to air their own grievances, the circle started buzzing with grumblings.

"It's like they're playing in the last game of their lives while we're trying to pace ourselves for the Sweet Sixteen," Nomis fumed, flinging his headband against his locker.

"We just gotta slow this thing down," Tyler seethed. "We can't let them make us play their game."

"They're just shooting so well," Jadon whined.

"And we can't grab a rebound to save our lives!" Grant added.

Jake listened to all this, too annoyed to speak. He couldn't believe he was letting some eighteen-year-old get into his dome. He slammed his locker door open and searched through his gym bag for the tin of mints he knew was in there. All that polluted air he'd been breathing had given him a bad taste. Finally finding what he was looking for, he popped a candy into his mouth... which popped an idea into his head that suddenly made him smile. Holding one of the small but potent little tablets of cinnamon freshness in his right palm, he finally spoke up.

"Maybe we need to stop making excuses and start stepping up." Jake paused. "Maybe we need to take control of this game and not let them keep playing us." He let his gaze fall on each of the guys around him. "If they want to run, let's show them how to run. Let's shift this baby into sixth gear and see how fast we can go. I'm sick and tired of letting some punk kid think he owns me. And I don't know about you guys, but I'm gonna do something about it."

Throughout Jake's little speech, as simple as it was, heads lifted, bodies raised, and the general atmosphere grew lighter. A chorus of agreement rippled around the room and a couple of the guys started to slowly applaud Jake's proposition. Their steady rhythm gathered steam and snowballed into a thunderous round of clapping and stomping. Coach walked into the center of the new huddle with a slight smirk on his face and merely held his hand up for the team yell.

"One, two, three—"

"Cardinals!" they all shouted and ran back out to the court looking like a completely different squad.

As Jake ran by, Coach grabbed his shoulder and whispered in his ear, "You're going to make a great coach someday."

Jake nodded at the compliment, but his mind was elsewhere. He couldn't wait to show good ol' number eleven how he really played this sport.

"I got you something," Jake whispered to the freshman just before the ball was inbounded to him to start the second half.

"What's that, old timer?" he replied with a scowl.

Jake opened his hand to reveal the mint. "No offense, but your breath stinks."

Number eleven angrily knocked the white tablet out of Jake's hand and blew a deep breath right at Jake.

"Suit yourself," Jake said with a smile as he took the inbound pass from Grant and raced up the floor faster than he had the whole first half.

The freshman guarded him tight but Jake pushed even harder. At the top of the key, Jake faked a three-point shot and threw a no-look pass to a streaking Nate on the baseline who put up a reverse layup for an almost uncontested basket.

Not to be outdone, number eleven tried to race back up the court for his own quick play, but he never saw Grant step out to seal the double team. Stinky-breath lost control of the ball and Grant quickly scooped it up and flung it down to Jake who had instinctively streaked back toward the other hoop. Jake leapt high off the floor for his first slam dunk of the season to the approving roar of his teammates and the Louisville fans in the arena. Normally, Jake liked to conserve his energy and leave the high-flying moves for the taller guys on the team but he wasn't holding anything back today.

"I can't believe I'm watching Sports Center reruns just to see you again," Amy laughed on the phone that night.

"You sure you're not just into the hockey highlights? Some of those guys are pretty studly, too," Jake joked from his seat on the team bus later that night. At least three of the guys were snoring nearby but Jake didn't care how tired he was, he always looked forward to talking with Amy.

"True, true, but they're not Jake Taylor. Hey, after the game that announcer Burnt Mushbooger—"

"Brent Musburger?"

"Yeah, whatever. He made a comment about Jake Taylor's possible future in the pros next year."

Jake waited for Amy to convey her thoughts about the offhand remark, but she remained silent as if expecting him to explain it. Jake's eyes darted around to the guys within earshot. Besides late night conversations with Grant littered with exaggerated dreaming, Jake hadn't told anyone about his secret consideration of leaving school two years early to enter the draft. And he sure didn't want raise any suspicions now, two games into the NCAA tournament. He figured he had plenty of time to worry about his options at the end of the season—which hopefully was still two more weekends away. "Huh, that's funny," Jake finally responded. "I guess we'll just have to see. Doesn't Jesus say, 'Don't worry about tomorrow, because today has enough worry of its own'?"

"Touché, Mr. Spiritual," Amy retorted good-naturedly. "Just promise that you'll never make me one of those Real Housewives of the NBA.

"Deal." Jake laughed. This was definitely a serious conversation they needed to have at some point, but tonight was not that point. Besides, he had another even more serious chat he needed to have with Amy first...and he definitely didn't want to do that right now in the middle of all his teammates. The weight of that burden settled on his shoulders and he yawned.

"I'm sorry, babe, I should let you fall asleep."

"I love you, Amy Briggs."

"I love you, too, Jake Taylor."

The four days in between the third and fourth rounds seemed like the longest week of Jake's life. Sitting through his classes listening to lectures on physiological responses and biomechanics and standard units of measurements made it even worse. Jake tried to pay attention and take good notes, but all he could really concentrate on was the big game at the end of the week.

On top of his own struggle to stay focused on his classes, everyone else made it nearly impossible. Jake knew if he could spend as much time on homework as he did in conversations with random strangers and radio interviews and signing autographs, then he'd probably be able to pull a 4.0 no problem. He thought he'd learned to strike a healthy balance in dealing with his crazy popularity on campus, but during March Madness the previously intense attention soared even higher. And his monstrous dunk in the last game did anything but squelch it. It seemed like everyone felt some compulsion to relive it with him.

When the team finally boarded the plane to fly to Texas for the Southern Regional semi- final, Jake was ecstatic to finally be able to focus only on basketball again. Ironically, their opponent was San Diego State, the number two seed from their corner of the tournament draw. The Aztecs had been ranked in the top ten all year and had finished the season with only two losses.

Once again, Jake couldn't help but wonder if he'd be in a better spot had he gone there instead of Louisville. Not that he was unhappy with his choice of Louisville, but if he'd stayed close to home, he probably would have never stopped going to church which meant he probably would have never made the mistakes he was still reaping the consequences of. *Wouldn't that be nice!* Jake grimaced, still feeling the weight of his need to come clean with Amy.

The past is past. Live in the present, Jake told himself, trying to shake it off. In spite of all his mistakes, he knew God was using him in Louisville, and that's what really mattered anyway.

Jake leaned back in his seat and redirected his thoughts by replaying the game tape they'd spent hours watching this week. His task would be guarding the Aztec team captain and certain NBA lottery pick, Demetrius Nichols. Another San Diego County local, Demetrius had played for a school Jake's Pirates usually met up with in playoffs each year, and the matchup between the two of them had always attracted a lot of press. Jake knew Demetrius could waste him if he wasn't careful, but he had to admit he was looking forward to the duel, like old times.

The nationally-televised Sweet Sixteen game held up to its billing and more. With high-flying action and breath-taking speed, the game raced back and forth the entire forty minutes, with neither team able to pull ahead to a comfortable lead.

Jake remembered Demetrius being fast in high school, but that seemed like the slow lane compared to now. Over and over again, the twenty-one-year-old raced Jake down the court, pushing so hard it seemed like a collision was inevitable, but it was like the guy had eyes not only in the back of his head but somewhere near his ears as well, because no matter how heavily guarded he was, he always seemed to find an open teammate somewhere. And that was what Jake started hoping for, because it was when Demetrius would stop on a dime to shoot a perfect jumper that he became really dangerous. It seemed like he couldn't miss, no matter where he shot from. It was no wonder there was so much hype about which NBA team would swoop the star up in the draft.

Fortunately for Jake and the rest of Louisville nation, though, Demetrius' supporting cast was struggling. If they got hot the Cardinals would be in serious trouble, but as the minutes ticked away, their shots kept missing and the game stayed close.

Jake was exhausted trying to keep a body in front of his extremely talented counterpart, but he held his own. What he lacked in speed he made up for in persistence. Like the Energizer Bunny, he just kept going and going, no doubt thanks to his consistent nightly runs with Grant. Usually, his hustle would eventually prevail in games like these, but the jury was still out over whether he would be able to wear Nichols down. They both seemed to be playing on another level tonight, willing their teammates to victory with every ounce of effort they could muster.

With forty-five seconds left to play, the score was all knotted up at sixty-three. Demetrius dribbled the ball up the court, eyes on Jake, the basket, the clock, and his streaking teammates seemingly all at once. Jake picked him up at the half court line holding both hands out like he'd been taught since he was five. His legs felt like wet noodles from racing up and down the court for thirty-seven of the thirty-nine minutes of the game thus far, but he knew that he had to push through it.

Demetrius held up two fingers to call out the play and instantly streaked to Jake's right. Nate's warning that a screen was coming was drowned out by 19,000 yelling fans and Jake ran face first into a broad-chested power forward whose sweat-filled jersey drenched Jake's nose and eyes. Jake clamored to get back to his man, but the split second it took was all that Demetrius needed and all Jake saw was the swish of the ball through the net. SDSU's fans in the packed house erupted but Jake wasn't giving up.

Jake glanced up at the clock as he raced to get open to receive the inbound pass from Nate. *Fourteen seconds.* As soon as the ball was in his hands, he heard Coach hollering for him to push it up the court. The San Diego State defense immediately double-teamed him, and Jake tried to see past them to find his open man.

Ten seconds. For all their streaking to the basket, none of his teammates were open.

Seven seconds. Time was running out. Jake had to find someone. Suddenly, he jerked his head back as if looking to heave the ball over his defenders' outstretched arms. Taking the bait, they both leaped high to block him, giving Jake just the space he needed to duck under and break free. Jake raced toward the three-point line, but still no open man.

Three—two—one. Jake hurled the ball toward the open hoop from five feet behind the three-point line. Jake, Demetrius, their teammates, and millions of television viewers watched the ball soar through the air with bated breath. It hit the backboard hard...and banked right in for the winning shot. Louisville had made it to the Elite Eight!

They say in sports that the highest highs are never as intense as the lowest lows. That could not have been truer for Jake and his teammates the following day. Matched up against the number-one-seeded Florida Gators, Louisville trailed from the beginning tipoff.

Florida had a pair of seven footers that clogged the lane like Los Angeles rush hour traffic. The only way around them was to shoot from outside, but unfortunately their perimeter was locked pretty tight, too. Jake and his team hustled with everything they had until the very end, but it was never enough to gain the upper hand and their ultimate seven-point loss made the game sound closer than it really was.

Feeling like he'd just been run over by a Mack truck, Jake hobbled into the locker room with his teammates. The joy and elation they'd basked in a mere twenty-four hours earlier was nothing compared to this sinking sensation of defeat. Normal aches and pains throbbed worse, minor irritations flared greater, and Jake couldn't help but wonder if it was even worth it. He plopped a big bag of ice on his aching right knee and leaned his head back against the cool locker as he listened to Coach give his expected end-of-season speech—he loved them all like sons, he was proud of them for taking Louisville to its first Elite Eight in over a decade, blah, blah, blah.

And then it was all over. Gone was the anticipation, gone was the confident excitement. All they had to look forward to now was catching up on all the classes they'd grown dismally behind in. They'd had a good run this season, but it had to end some-time. Too bad that end came before the championship game.

Long after Coach had finished speaking, Jake continued to sit motionless on his bench, wishing the ice could numb his crushed emotions in addition to his tender knee. He didn't feel like talking to anyone so he grabbed his phone out of his bag to look occupied. In the avalanche of messages from friends and family, only three made his heart beat faster.

7:27pm | From: Amy | To: Jake
So proud of you. Wish I could be there to hug away your sadness.

7:32pm | From: Debron | To: Jake
Yo man, even the best of us lose sometimes. Does this mean you get to start playing ball with us again?

7:33pm | From: 646-555-3111 | To: Jake
My name is Jordan Spiro, and I'd love to help you get drafted this summer. Let me buy you breakfast next week and we'll talk about you going pro next year.

SPRING

IF THERE WAS ANYTHING POSITIVE about Louisville's loss yesterday, it was that the team didn't have to stay at school during spring break. Season was over; the players were free. As soon as Jake realized this, a new sense of acceptance washed over him and he immediately got online and found the cheapest flight to San Francisco. Six hundred fifty dollars was far from a steal, but it was more than worth it to be able to spend a week with Amy.

Fifteen hours after their devastating defeat, Jake zipped his Cardinal duffle bag closed and he couldn't wipe the smile off of his face. In eight more hours he would be face to face with his girlfriend and he couldn't wait. Amy would still have classes while he was visiting, so he stuffed a few books into his backpack so that he could work on getting caught up on his own classes. He shoved his dirty laundry into his closet, made a neat stack out of all the papers on his desk, and quickly made his bed. Any other cleaning could wait until his return to school. In eleven minutes he was leaving for the airport.

Jake crossed the hall and thumped on Grant's door. "Ten more minutes, bro," he prompted. Ten thirty in the morning wasn't ridiculously early, but for the first day of vacation after getting in late last night, Jake acknowledged the sacrifice his roommate was making by driving him to the airport.

Dumping his bag by the front door, Jake paced the living room as he waited. His exhaustion from the night before had miraculously dissipated and now he was an eager bundle of energy. Jake looked at the clock. *Six more minutes.* He contemplated knocking on Grant's door again, just to make sure he was up, when suddenly, a knock on the door stopped him in his tracks.

Jake flung the door open to find Nicole standing there in all her glory. In spite of himself, his heart skipped a beat, but once he put his normal masculinity in check, a wave of disgust crashed over him.

"Jake!" Nicole exclaimed coyly. "You're looking good for this early in the morning. I wasn't sure if you'd even be up yet." She reached over and flirtatiously touched his arm.

Jake lightly jerked his arm back. "What's up?"

Nicole pulled a copy of the local newspaper from behind her back that sported a front-page picture of Jake shooting over a defender in yesterday's game. "I know it's a bummer you lost last night, but according to this article, some NBA scouts have their eye on you. Have you been keeping that a secret from all of us?" she asked playfully.

Just the way she said "all of us" rubbed Jake the wrong way. Since when did he owe her an explanation for anything he did? This was a private matter, one that he hadn't even talked to Amy about yet, and he sure wasn't about to let Nicole in on his thoughts. "Hm, yeah. I guess I'm not in on that secret either." He grabbed the paper and put his other hand on the door to move the conversation toward the finish line. "But thanks for bringing this over. Amy will love to see it."

"You guys still together, huh?"

Again, the way she said it got under Jake's skin. He wanted to answer that it was none of her business, but figured he might as well keep it cordial. "Yep. I'm actually leaving for the airport in five minutes to go visit her."

"Oh, that's so sweet." Nicole looked genuinely happy for him, but Jake knew it was just a façade. Then her smile dropped a little and she adopted an air of concern. "Does Amy, uh, know about...us?"

Jake couldn't believe he was having this conversation right before leaving to see Amy. Talk about timing. "Yes, Nicole. And she took me back anyway. Go figure."

"Wow, even with your, uh, little problem?"

Something about his look must have given Jake away, because Nicole immediately pounced on his hesitation.

"Oh. You haven't told her about *that* yet. I guess I shouldn't be surprised."

"What's that supposed to mean?"

"I guess Nate's fine with it now, but he was pretty peeved at you for spreading it around without telling either of us."

"What? You're the one that gave it to me!"

Nicole scowled. "How do you know it wasn't the other way around? Men. You always want to blame the girl."

"Whatever, Nicole. You know Amy's the only other girl I've ever slept with, and she's clean. They tested her when she got pregnant."

"Whatever. Believe what you want. It's not like it's going to make any difference when Amy finds out." Nicole spun around and walked away, calling sarcastically back over her shoulder, "Enjoy your trip."

Jake watched her leave, puzzling over her ridiculous logic. What did he ever see in her? But she had brought up an important point: Jake needed to tell Amy about his Herpes. And this trip was his perfect opportunity. He dreaded it, but he knew he had to do it.

"Was that Nicole?" Grant's groggy voice sounded behind him, startling him back to the present.

Jake just rolled his eyes and shook his head. "Yeah. You ready?"

39

AMY WAITED WITH ANTICIPATION at the San Francisco Airport baggage claim for Jake's arrival. Ever since he'd called her last night with his impromptu idea, she'd been antsy with impatience and studying was out of the question. An entire week with her boyfriend? This would be the longest they'd be together in person since they got back together, and she had so many exciting ideas of things they could do. Fisherman's Wharf in San Francisco, jogs in the park, a double date with Renee and Brian...Amy was thrilled.

Of course, in the midst of her eagerness, she couldn't help but think back to her disastrous spring break visit out to Louisville two years ago. But there was no way this trip could go that poorly. Jake had been the perfect gentleman over the past three months of their new relationship. In their brief times together, he hadn't even attempted to kiss her, something she'd been impressed by especially since every time he looked into her eyes she was pretty much like putty in his hands.

Amy unscrewed the lid to her water bottle and took a swig while she paced the airport terminal. Unfortunately, no water came out. During this mindless waiting, she had downed the entire thing...and now all that liquid was suddenly screaming to exit her body. Amy glanced down at her watch. Jake's plane should have landed ten minutes ago, which meant that Jake should be walking down that escalator any moment now.

Weighing her options frantically in her mind, Amy quickly came to the conclusion that unless she found a bathroom soon, she'd be too miserable to enjoy Jake's arrival anyway. She made a calm bolt for the restroom and hoped she'd be back in time to greet her boyfriend.

She couldn't have been gone for much longer than a minute or two, but by the time she returned, the baggage claim area had changed drastically. People swarmed everywhere waiting for their luggage and Amy realized that Jake must be somewhere in the midst of them. Her eyes scanned the throngs desperately. And then she saw him. Standing by carousel number three with his cell phone to his ear. She could only see the back of his head, but that was enough. She quickened her pace, a smile plastered to her face, and when her phone rang, she answered it without even checking who it was.

"Sorry, Jake. I knew I should have waited! I had to run to the bathroom."

"Uh, Amy, this isn't Jake," a somewhat familiar female voice spoke into her ear.

Amy jerked the phone down to check the number. She didn't recognize it. "Who is this?" she asked, a little annoyed.

"This is Nicole."

Amy stopped in her tracks. Who did this girl think she was? And why was she calling this second, of all times? "Uh, what do you want? This isn't really a good time."

"Look, I know you must hate me. And I guess I don't really blame you. Jake's a great guy and I feel fortunate that I got to get to know that side of him," Nicole prattled on without regard.

Amy could feel her blood beginning to boil at Nicole's flippant discussion of their past. "Nicole," Amy interjected. "I'm actually picking Jake up at the airport right now. Can this wait?"

"Oh, sorry!" Nicole gushed. "I didn't know he was leaving for spring break. It's just that I recently became aware of a darker side of Jake, and I thought you might want to know, too, you know, before things got too..." Her voice trailed off.

Twenty feet in front of her, Jake turned around and spotted Amy. With all the commotion swirling around her, she couldn't hear anything, but she read his lips call out her name as they erupted into a beautiful smile. But all her excitement to see him was distracted by her attempt to wrap her head around what Nicole was saying. "What? I don't—"

"Just ask him what he knows about Herpes," Nicole interrupted and then hung up, just as Jake's arms wrapped tightly around Amy's waist.

"Hey, babe, how's it going?" he spoke into her ear.

Amy tried to absorb the warmth of his hug, but Nicole's odd request triggered a sudden reservation. Was Nicole insinuating what Amy thought she was? Did Jake know? And why was Nicole the one telling her? How often did Jake talk to this girl? What was going on here? All these questions collided in her mind while her body attempted to greet her boyfriend.

"Did you just get in?" Amy mumbled, trying to pull herself back together.

"Yeah, I was looking all over for you."

"Sorry, I had to go to the bathroom."

"Who were you on the phone with?" Jake questioned nonchalantly, taking her hand as they walked outside toward parking.

"Uh, just an old friend. Sorry, she was making it really difficult to get off." Amy decided to leave the details for another time. If Nicole was being truthful, then Jake had a lot of explaining to do and Amy would rather him initiate that conversation. She decided to give him plenty of opportunity tonight at dinner. "So, I was thinking while we're here in Frisco we could spend the afternoon seeing the sights and then do dinner at Fisherman's Wharf. They have some killer clam chowder in bread bowls."

"Anywhere you're at sounds perfect to me," Jake said as he draped his arm around her shoulder.

Eight hours later, Amy tiptoed into her dark room so as not to wake Renee.

"So? How was it? Are your lips still pure?" Renee flipped on a light and sat up in bed.

"Didn't even come close to kissing," Amy grinned. "And I've got an eight a.m. class, so I'm heading to bed."

"What? That's all I get? Where are the juicy details, girl?"

"We had ice cream at Ghirardelli Square, chowder at Fisherman's Wharf, and we walked it all off in between. What more do you want to know?"

"Hmph!" Renee huffed playfully. "I guess that's enough. Did you have fun? You just don't sound near as excited as I'd be if I was seeing my boyfriend for the first time in two and a half months."

"I'm just tired," Amy shrugged as she picked up her cosmetics bag and walked out to the bathroom.

The truth, however, was that Amy couldn't get Nicole's warning out of her head, and no matter how much she had let Jake talk tonight, he hadn't come anywhere near the subject. Amy was starting to get more than just annoyed. And tomorrow they wouldn't have any time to talk seriously. Amy had classes most of the day, and then they were going to spend the evening with Renee and Brian. Maybe a double date would help to get her mind off the matter, but Amy wasn't sure how much longer she could go without getting to the bottom of this.

After a fitful night of sleep, Amy suffered through her classes feeling more and more miserable. She met Jake for a quick lunch in her cafeteria and was able to maintain small talk decently well, but Jake must have known that something was off. *Good! Maybe that will get him to start talking!* Amy thought as she rushed off to her next class.

Around 4:30, Renee hitched a ride with the two of them into Oakland, where they met up with Brian at the middle school where he supervised an afterschool program. He was just helping a kid finish up a math assignment when they walked in.

"Hey, honey!" Renee bubbled as she ran over and gave her boyfriend a hug.

"Hey, babe. Perfect timing! Javier here is just about done."

"Thanks, Brian," Javier said as he slammed his book closed and knocked knuckles with his tutor. "See you tomorrow."

"Honey, this is Jake. Jake, this is Brian," Renee made the introductions.

"Great to meet you, Jake. Been watching a lot of you on ESPN lately. Sorry about Florida, man."

Jake chuckled. "Hey, if they didn't take us down, I wouldn't be standing here right now."

Brian slapped him on the shoulder. "Good way to look at it, man. Well, hey, if you're missing the court at all, tomorrow we got afterschool practice. The kids would be thrilled to have a visit from a superstar like you."

Jake rolled his eyes but looked at Amy for approval.

"Yeah, sure, I've got a late afternoon class anyway. You can take my car." Amy knew it would be good for Jake to experience what Brian was doing with his kids, especially in light of Jake's involvement with Debron and his friends, but she could feel the tension rising within her the longer she avoided the topic Nicole had instigated. *God, help me out here,* she prayed under her breath. *I don't even know if this is anything I should worry about, but we need to get this out in the open. Ugh! This is so annoying!*

Jake drove back from Oakland, totally pumped up by what he saw there. Brian's afterschool program gave him so many ideas for his little activities with Debron and his friends. Every day of the week, the kids had something to do in a positive environment. Homework and basketball were the two primary concerns, but they also made trips to museums and parks and businesses and factories, and enjoyed music, art, cooking, and exercise classes in between. Brian made this all happen with the help of tons of volunteers he mobilized from different churches and some of the concerned parents of the neighborhood.

Jake knew he was limited by his basketball schedule, but now that he was in the off-season, he could do so much more. All afternoon, he picked Brian's brain, and by the time he finally left, he was overflowing with inspiration. He had already talked a little with Buddy and Grant about his thoughts for a summer basketball clinic, but now those sketchy suggestions were sprouting wings.

Amy had showed Jake how to connect his phone to her car's internal Bluetooth, so Jake spontaneously ordered it to call Buddy. He just had to share some of his new brainstorming immediately.

"Hello?" Buddy answered, sounding a little hoarse.

"Hey! It's Jake. You know that idea we had for the basketball camp for the kids in Debron's neighborhood? Well, I just got a bunch of new ideas for it.

"Oh, Jake. That's great."

Jake suddenly realized that Buddy didn't sound very good at all. "Buddy, are you okay?" A long pause ensued, and then Jake thought he heard sniffling. "Buddy? What's going on?"

Some more muffled sobs came from Buddy's side of the phone, until he finally choked out, "Yvonne's gone."

Those two words hit Jake like a ton of bricks to the chest. Jake knew from his weekly visits that Yvonne hadn't progressed—at all—in the past nine months since her stroke. But she'd made it so long in her unresponsive state that Jake just assumed she'd be like that for the long haul. "Buddy! Wha—? Why? When?"

"I don't know," Buddy sniffled. "Yesterday morning she just seemed...different, so I called the home nurse. Bunny was with us all day, and only went home at night. I slept by Yvonne's side last night, and this morning, when I woke up, she was just... gone." At this point, Buddy broke down into full weeping, and Jake couldn't help getting a little choked up himself.

"Oh, Buddy. I'm so sorry," Jake finally said softly as the tears quieted down. He knew their only son had passed away in his twenties, which meant that now Buddy was completely alone in this world. "I-I can change my flight and come back tomorrow."

"Nonsense!" Buddy exclaimed with sudden strength. "You stay there with that pretty lady of yours and make the most of the time you have with her. You never know when it'll be cut short."

Jake found it sweetly amusing that Buddy considered his time with Yvonne cut "short," considering that they spent over sixty years of their life together. He hoped he was fortunate enough to enjoy that much time with Amy. "I just don't want you to be alone, Buddy. You've been there so much for me. That would be the least I could do."

"Alone?" Buddy questioned. "Do you realize how many blue-haired old women have come by to bring me dinner in the last ten hours? Once they stop coming by, I'll have casserole company for years. Which means I'd be pleased to have you over for dinner sometime next week."

Jake marveled at the positive spin Buddy was able to see. "All right. It's a date. But now that season's over, I might want to come over more than once a week."

"I guess that might be nice. And then we could iron out all these new details for your basketball camp."

"Sounds good."

"But Jake?"

"Yeah?"

"Have you told her yet?"

Was he serious? He'd just suffered the devastating loss of his wife. He was the one who should be receiving comfort and encouragement right now. Yet he still found a way to prod Jake with the accountability question he'd been asking for the last few months. "Uh...no," Jake confessed with shame.

"Jake," Buddy chided in his loving, gentle way.

"Okay, seriously. I've been trying to. But there just hasn't been the right opportunity. It wasn't like I was going to greet her at the airport with a, 'Hi! It's so good to see you. I have Herpes.' And then she planned this really special day in San Francisco, and I didn't want to ruin it for her. And then we haven't really been alone since then, except for like fifteen minutes at lunch before she rushed off to class."

"Hm," Buddy acknowledged Jake's predicament. "So, when are you going to do it then?"

"Well, we don't have anything planned tonight...that I know of."

"So..."

"So, I guess tonight's the night."

"Alrighty then. I'll be praying for you."

"Buddy, you have enough on your mind. You don't have to be worrying about me."

"Jake, you think I want to just sit here moping about my loss? Yvonne's gone, and I'm going to miss her like crazy. But I know she's in a better place, running and leaping and probably even flying. Which is a whole lot better than just lying in this old bed here. I'm sad for me, but I'm happy for her. And you'll make me a whole lot happier if you'll just tell that girl of yours the truth."

"Okay, Buddy. I hear you." Jake paused, trying to put words to his next thought. "Thank you...for everything. You're like the grandpa I never had...and I...I love you."

In the silence that followed, Jake started to think he must have lost reception. But finally Buddy responded, his voice gravelly once more. "I love you, too, Jake."

That night, Jake offered to take Amy out to a little Italian restaurant in town. They both engaged in pleasantries cordially enough, but any deeper conversation struggled. Jake, in addition to carrying the burden of telling Amy about his disease tonight, was still shaken up by Yvonne's death. But something was up with Amy, too, and he couldn't figure out why. So, now worried that she was already upset with him for something else, Jake started backpedaling in his resolve to come clean tonight, wondering if it might be better to save such detrimental news for a time when she might be more receptive.

"So, uh, how's your lasagna?" he asked, probably for the third time.

"The lasagna's still great, Jake. Look, I know you're sad about Yvonne and all, so I feel bad bringing this up now, but I just can't hold it in any more. Nicole called me the day you flew in. She said something about Herpes? Jake, is there something you need to tell me?"

Jake's face blanched and he felt like he'd suddenly been tossed into a furnace. *Nicole! That little—* Jake cut himself short, knowing full well this was his fault as much as Nicole's. If he'd come clean from the beginning, then Nicole would have had no power over him now. Still, what was she thinking? "Uh...yeah."

The look Amy gave him could have boiled water, but it was too late to retreat now, so Jake inhaled and dove headfirst into his confession.

"Amy, when you were in Romania—"

"Romania!"

"—I went in for one of my routine physicals, where they did a test and discovered that I..." Jake paused, inhaling another gulp of air. "I have Herpes."

Amy looked like she was being stabbed in the back and her eyes filled with tears. Jake wished that he could just enfold her in his arms and promise her that everything would be okay, but he knew that wasn't in his power, so instead he just kept explaining.

"Nicole is the only other person I...I ever did anything with, and Nate has it too," Jake winced. "So I must have gotten it from her. I never realized I had the symptoms, until I went in to see the doctor. Unfortunately," Jake paused again, "it's something that will never go away. There are things to treat the symptoms, but not to cure the disease. Which means..." Jake faltered, willing himself to share the worst part. "Which means that I will forever be contagious to my future partner. I'm sorry, Amy. I'm so, so sorry. I have done everything possible to atone for my year of bad behavior, but sin has a way sinking its claws deep, making us pay long after the wrong was committed. I would willingly bear my share of this burden alone, knowing that I brought it on myself, but bringing you into this punishment kills me. Which is why it has taken me so long to tell you. I'm really, really sorry. Because I know that it's only fair that..." Jake looked away, unable to bear Amy's hurting gaze any longer. "...I understand if this is a burden you do not wish to share with me. You deserve so much better, and I know you will find it if you choose."

Jake couldn't bring himself to meet Amy's eyes, so he stared into his plate of now cold gnocchi.

Well, there was the truth, plain and simple. It's what Amy had asked for. But now that she had it, she almost wished that she didn't.

Truth was such a complex thing. Just like when she had asked Jake to come clean with her about Nicole, there were some things that she would rather not know. Then again, being ignorant of the truth didn't change the facts—in this case, that Jake had Herpes, thanks to his relationship with Nicole, and that was never going to change. The issue now was what Amy was going to do with that truth.

Amy sat watching her boyfriend. He looked so cute, so sweet in his agony. A small part of her was frustrated by this new consequence of his past, but an even bigger part wanted to just reach out to him and kiss all his worries away. He sure had messed up that year when they broke up, but since then, he had grown into a guy who surpassed her wildest dreams.

During one of her less scintillating lectures this morning, Amy had let her thoughts roam free in response to Nicole's warning. Using her phone, she had read up a little on the details of the disease. What she discovered was disgusting and depressing, but it wasn't quite as bad as she'd feared. As with any sexually transmitted disease, Herpes was definitely not something God intended when He created sex as a gift for husbands and wives. Warts and sores spread by others did not belong in the intimate pleasure God designed. And the thought that Jake—and, eventually, Amy, too—would always have a tangible reminder of his relationship with Nicole saddened Amy to the depths of her soul.

But as she sought God for wisdom, she knew that this didn't have to ruin their relationship. It was one more obstacle to overcome, but they had already dealt with giving their own child away for adoption. They could handle this. As she continued to pray about it, her annoyance at Jake's seeming avoidance of the issue also dissipated. She knew how tough it must be for him to tell her, and she asked God to give him the strength to do it.

Hearing Jake's heartfelt confession tonight was the heartbreaking answer to her prayers. She never even considered that he'd be agonizing over the possibility of her dumping him. The poor guy. She suddenly remembered back to his text the night before her return from Romania—and how she had been the one to hog up that entire conversation. She replayed what she remembered of conversations since then and realized that he had tried to tell her on multiple occasions, but there had always been some distraction to cut him short. So, finally, he flew out here to reveal his shame. Jake had tried to own up honorably, and now it was up to Amy to respond with equivalent grace.

A few minutes passed in tense silence until Jake felt a tender touch grab his hand. He glanced up at Amy and the look of love emanating from her eyes caught him by surprise.

"Jake. We've been through so much together," she began softly. "And while the thought of sharing this virus with that...girl, Nicole, completely grosses me out, I know you've already paid your penance several times over. You are already more of a man than I could ever dream of. You are perfect for me, and I love you. For better or worse. In sickness or in health. I know we still have some time before we commit to those vows, but when that day comes, I will gladly become one flesh with you, Herpes or not."

The little smirk on Amy's face offered Jake more hope than he ever imagined was possible after this conversation, and it was everything he could do to restrain himself from pulling her into a long, passionate kiss.

40

JAKE CAME BACK FROM HIS TRIP out to Stanford flying sky high. The few days remaining after he'd finally bared his soul to Amy had been pretty close to the best days of his life. They laughed and had fun every second they were together, and Jake couldn't wait until they could live in the same town again. So when that agent guy called to follow up his text, Jake was more interested than ever to talk about his potential in the draft. They decided to meet this morning for breakfast, and Jake was as excited as he was nervous. For moral support and an extra set of discerning ears, Jake had asked Buddy to come along and Buddy of course said there was no way he'd pass up a free meal.

They walked into an elegant country club on the outskirts of Louisville, and Buddy was already ooh'ing and ah'ing. Rich wood paneling and molding ensconced the walls of the lobby, adorned by elegantly framed black and white photos of famous celebrities who had visited the swanky establishment over the past several decades. Luxuriously upholstered couches provided ample lounging space for guests, and an opulent chandelier dangled from the towering vaulted ceiling.

The place was nice, but Jake's dad had been a member of a country club back in California, and Jake had spent many summers as a kid enjoying the pool and tennis courts and other fun amenities. Since then, one of the perks of being a top college athlete had been various invitations of different sorts to dinner at places like these. Nevertheless, Jake hadn't become too snobby to recognize a special treat, and he glanced around at his surroundings in appreciation. He was also suddenly grateful for Amy's last second fashion tips that persuaded him to exchange his jeans and polo shirt for slacks and a button up.

A young, attractive hostess greeted them at the entrance of the restaurant. "You must be Mr. Taylor. Your party is waiting for you at their table. I will escort you there."

Jake and Buddy exchanged smiles and followed her to the other side of the restaurant. Massive windows opened up to a perfect view of the first few holes of the lush private golf course, but what really caught Jake's attention was a face he recognized at the table in front of the window. Jamal Taylor, his former teammate who he'd certainly never considered a friend, sat next to a well-dressed stranger Jake presumed to be Jordan Spiro. The two of them rose from their seats to greet the newcomers.

"Jake, my main man. It's good to see you," Jamal said with a grin as he hugged his former teammate.

"Good to see you too, Jamal. Aren't you in the middle of your season?"

"As luck would have it, we're playing the Grizzlies tomorrow and when Jordan told me who he was having breakfast with I hopped on over."

"It's nice to finally meet you in person, Jake. My name is Jordan Spiro. Believe me, I'm a big fan." The Italian man in his early forties with salt-and-pepper slicked-back hair extended his hand.

In the few days since receiving Spiro's follow-up call, Jake had dug up as much information on the man and his sports agency as he could. From what he could tell, this guy was the real deal, representing a number of athletes currently playing in the NBA.

Apparently, he was also the guy that helped Jamal get picked up by Minnesota during the draft this past summer.

"Nice to meet you, too, Mr. Spiro. This is my friend and mentor, Buddy Riha," Jake introduced.

"Oh, call me Jordan. And how do the two of you know each other?"

Jake glanced at Buddy and smiled. "Oh, we're both ushers at Grace Fellowship Church here in Louisville. And he also happens to be a former Cardinal hoopster himself."

"Well, I'm glad you could join us today," Jordan smiled, but Jake definitely noticed his tone wasn't quite as warm. Jordan motioned to them to take their seats around the circular table.

After a few minutes of chitchat, a server took their order, and then they continued to shoot the breeze until their meals came. Jordan kept reminiscing about Jake's various highlights and heroics, which was kind of fun at first, but after awhile, Jake wished they could talk about something—or *someone!*—else. Their omelets and pancakes came, and still all dialogue revolved around Jake and his success this season. Finally, as their plates were cleared from the table and the conversation waned, Jordan finally cleared his throat and pulled a piece of paper out of his briefcase.

"Well, Jake. You know we didn't just come here to talk about the past. I think we all know that you've got quite a future ahead of you."

Jake felt his knees go weak. This was it. The secret fantasies of his heart that he'd tried to squelch all season were now about to come to light.

Jordan slid his paper across the table to Jake. "This is a projected report of the top prospects from colleges and overseas for this year's draft. It is nothing more than a prediction of what is likely, but the analysts who compile it get paid a pretty penny to be accurate."

Jake's eyes quickly scanned down the list of familiar names until they stopped cold at number thirty-eight. *Jake Taylor, University of Louisville.* There he was, at the beginning of the second round. Was this for real? Jake almost pinched himself to make sure he wasn't dreaming.

"Now, you could go slightly higher or lower based on who actually enters the draft, how you perform at the combines this spring, and of course, how the NBA teams fare throughout the rest of the season. But as of now," Jordan looked up at Jake's still awestruck face and smiled, "you're looking pretty good."

Jamal reached his hand across the table to knock knuckles with Jake. "I knew this California white boy was gonna be a star the moment he walked into practice."

Jake smiled back but couldn't help grimacing inside. He remembered all too clearly his first introduction to Jamal and the rest of the Louisville squad. Fresh in from California, Jake had been taunted by Jamal and Nate and Tony Anderson to pound down three shots of vodka and prove himself on a rough school-yard basketball court in the freezing cold. The not-so-subtle ultimatum had been risky: Sink a three pointer or else. Jake had often wondered what that "or else" entailed. Fortunately, his ball had swished through that weathered net with reckless abandon. But what if it hadn't? Would it have really made a difference that year he was redshirted on the sidelines? Would he have ever been able to regain their respect? Would he even be sitting here right now? Jake tried to shove those what-ifs away and glanced back to Jordan Spiro.

Jordan pulled out another piece of paper with a similar list, but this one had different names and next to each name was a team and a dollar amount. "This is last year's draft. As you can see, next to each name is the amount each player signed for with their respective team. I can tell you from doing this for a while that the numbers for this year will be comparable."

Jake dropped his eyes down to the thirty-eighth player drafted last year, Brandon Westbrook from the University of Washington. Jake's eyes bulged as he looked at what the Orlando Magic was paying him this year to occasionally come off the bench. *$799,000!* Jake thought about his dad who had worked over eighty hours a week for the past two decades and only brought in a fraction of that. *And I could make that much playing ball!* This was a deal that seemed almost too good to be true.

Jake glanced over to Buddy. The eighty-five-year-old raised his eyebrows with a sly grin and gently elbowed him back in the side. His subsequent whistle expressed exactly what Jake was thinking. After being quiet almost the entire meal, Buddy finally spoke up. "That's a lot of money! And I notice that the higher the draft pick, the bigger the number."

Jordan smiled condescendingly. "Yeah, that's normally how it works."

"Hm," Buddy grunted and resumed his silence.

Jordan spoke up. "Obviously, we'd try to get you to go as high as possible, and there's always room for negotiation of course. If we played our cards right, who knows, we could maybe even push close to a mil. How does that number sound?"

His grin was infectious and Jake couldn't help but be swept away. He could do a lot with a million dollars. But then Buddy spoke up again.

"Mr. Spiro, I'm noticing dashes next to some players' names. Look, even number thirty-two and thirty-five. What do those mean?"

"Well, sometimes a team picks up a player and then they realize he isn't the right fit. Or sometimes the player just doesn't perform well enough to make the cut. It's not—"

"So what do they make?" Buddy interjected.

"Uh...nothing." It almost came out as a mumble.

"Wow," Buddy gasped. "That doesn't seem fair. But I'm noticing none of the guys picked up in the first round get zeroed out."

"Well, yes, that's true. First-round picks are guaranteed a spot, but second-round picks don't get that benefit."

"So do these guys that get cut get to go back to their college teams?" Buddy asked.

"Uh...no," Jordan huffed.

"Whew!" Buddy whistled. "That sounds like quite a gamble. Jake here could take his chances this year working with you and risk losing everything to gain a second-round slot, or he could wait it out a year or two and have much better prospects."

"It's a gamble either way, Mr. Riha," Jordan responded curtly. "Sure, Jake, you could have another stellar season next year and move into the first round with all its perks. But nothing is guaranteed in this world, my friend. You could also flounder, you could get injured, your team could stink it up. And then your options could disappear like smoke on a windy day. The choice is yours. I'm just here to let you know your options and make my services available to you like I did for your friend Jamal here."

"Best decision I ever made," Jamal piped up. "I got picked up number forty-seven and now I'm rolling in so much money I don't even know what to do with it all." He laughed. "The pros are so much better than college. No classes, no homework. Just ball. And I get paid to play. Can't beat that."

Jake exchanged glances with Buddy, hoping for some more wise counsel. His questions and observations had been good, better than Jake would have ever thought of on his own, and Jake wanted him to ask some more. But his mentor remained silent, his face like a locked box.

"Wow!" Jake finally filled in the silence. "Well, you sure have given me a lot to think about. I never realized my options looked so good."

"Jake, they look great. And if I were you, I wouldn't waste them. Don't be one of the ones left dreaming about what could have been. Claim your stake in your future right now. I'll be here to make sure you don't regret it." Jordan handed Jake his business card and a folder. "Take a look through these and feel free to give me a call if you have any questions whatsoever. I'll call you in a few days to check in."

"Thanks," Jake murmured as he leafed through the pages of facts and figures.

"There's a lot of info there. Take your time, but remember you must declare your eligibility before the NBA deadline in three weeks."

Three weeks wasn't exactly a ton of time to decide the course of his future. Jake gulped at the rising anxiety in his throat. "Okay, thanks."

After a few more minutes of small talk, Jake said his good-byes to Jamal and Jordan, and Buddy followed suit. They walked in silence out of the sumptuous country club, and didn't say a word until they were safely in Jake's truck.

"Wow!" Jake finally exhaled as soon as his door was shut. "That's a lot of money. And Jamal sure looked happy." Buddy remained silent as they drove through the gigantic wrought-iron gates of the country club. "But that Spiro guy was a little pushy. I don't know. What do you think I should do?" Jake asked.

"I think it's what God thinks that matters."

"So what do you think He thinks?" Jake sighed.

"I don't know. You'll have to ask Him."

"I will, I will," Jake grinned. He loved that Buddy always brought him back to the spiritual side of things. "But sometimes God speaks through fellow believers. I was hoping that could be you."

Buddy smiled back. "Well, I'll spend some time talking to God about it, too, but I've got a gut feeling that He is cool either way. My dad used to always tell me, 'God's far more concerned with your conduct and character than your vocation and location.'"

Jake chuckled. "That's a good one."

"So, what do you *want* to do?" Buddy questioned.

"All I've ever dreamed of was playing for Louisville. Playing in the pros was always a distant fantasy, but I could never think much past college."

"And you're fulfilling that dream."

"Yeah, but in the background of that dream was winning a championship with my Cardinals."

"Well, you made it to the Elite Eight this year. That's pretty close."

"Sort of," Jake agreed halfheartedly while his mind sped ahead to wondering what next year could be like if he stuck with the team. Tyler was the only one who had dreams of leaving early to go pro. Jake was pretty sure none of their other starters were going anywhere. If ever they were going to win it, next year they had a great shot.

At the same time, it sure would be nice to move on to the next phase of his life. If he was out of college and making money then he'd be able to support Amy, and that meant they could get married. *Shoot, if everything worked out just right, maybe we could even get married this year!* Jake thought about how much fun it would be to spend every day—and every night!—with her. Just the thought of that got his heart to racing.

Of course, Amy wanted to finish up at Stanford, which would take her through the end of next season. But if God was in this, maybe He'd let Jake get picked up by one of California's two northern teams. *That would be awesome!* Jake grinned.

Then Jake started thinking about the money. He'd always grown up with more than enough, but this was more than he could imagine. "I sure could do a lot of good with that kind of money," he thought aloud.

"True. But money doesn't make someone generous; it merely reveals generosity."

"Ooh, another good one. Was that from your dad, too?"

"Nah, just made that one up. Think about it. What could money help you do that you aren't already doing?"

Jake leaned back in his seat and drove in silence for a moment. "I don't know. I guess it could help with our basketball camp."

"Jake, we're already doing it."

"Yeah, but money could make it easier."

"Sure, sure. But it would also take you away from your kids. How are you going to play ball with Debron and his friends if you're traveling the country with the NBA?"

Jake bit his lip. He never thought about that. Of course he was going to have to leave Debron someday. He just never planned on it being so soon. "Man, there are a lot of factors to consider in this decision."

"If it were easy, then everybody would do it." Buddy patted Jake on the knee as they zipped along the windy country road.

God, help me do the right thing, Jake begged.

AMY GOT OFF THE PHONE WITH JAKE and fell back onto her bed. She couldn't wipe the giddy smile off of her face. *My boyfriend is going pro!* she giggled. As much as she loathed the idea of becoming one of those snobby, drama-ridden superstar wives, the thought of walking alongside a guy like Jake into the lifestyle of the rich and famous definitely set her fantasies spinning. Without meaning to, her mind raced ahead of her, dreaming of the fancy dinners, trendy fashions, and stylish home she'd be able to enjoy. What an amazing life they'd live, full of fun and adventure!

But then the pendulum swung back to the side of reality, and like a wrecking ball, it shattered her swiftly built castles in the sky. The glorified vision of stardom might sound fun, but Amy knew the everyday version would be far less glamorous. It was already hard enough to maintain a long distance relationship with Jake; what would it be like with him traipsing all over the country for most of the year, never spending more than a few days in any one spot, surrounded by beautiful women whose sole goal was to make a celebrity conquest?

Jake had excitedly mentioned the possibility of them getting married sooner rather than later...like maybe even this summer. Again, the pendulum soared to Amy's fantasies. Her mind raced to images of a fairytale wedding and riding off into the sunset of perfect wedded bliss. But as much as she longed to spend her happily ever after with Jake, unless he got picked up by Sacramento or Golden State, that meant she'd have to give up her education at Stanford. And while that idea didn't seem nearly as appalling as it had only a year ago when Steven had asked her to consider it, she now had only a year left to go before she was done, and she had some exciting prospects for next year.

One of her professors had just talked to her about applying for the senior honors research program. It was a prestigious distinction to be selected, and would give her freedom to tailor her final year of undergraduate studies to her interests. Thanks to her work with Melia and in Romania, she had been toying with the idea of studying how others-centered behavior and activities can aid resiliency and recovery in victims of abuse. If she was chosen, this experience could be unmatchable.

And what about Jake's education? Amy guessed that if he made it to the pros, he didn't really need a degree. But it wasn't like he'd be there forever. A free college education was a terrible thing to waste.

Ah! Amy yelled inside of her mind. This was such a tough decision—and the decision wasn't really even hers to make. Poor Jake. He was carrying the full brunt of this burden. In their conversation, Amy had tried to make it very clear that she would support him no matter what, but the more she thought about it, the more she hoped he would decide against entering the draft...at least for this year. They'd made an extensive list of pros and cons, and each side had been very convincing in its own right. But if Jake could hold off for even one more season, it sure seemed like they got the best of both worlds.

One of Jake's reasons for staying that most caught Amy's attention was Debron and the ministry in his neighborhood. Amy was so impressed by Jake's concern and compassion for those kids. It was so touching...and convicting. Jake had already been touching their lives weekly, and then he had organized the big event where he brought them to the Louisville game and got them to meet all the players, and now he was gung-ho in planning the summer basketball clinic. He claimed that Amy had been the one to inspire him with all her stories from Romania, but the truth was she had done nothing with all her impassioned plans to help Bogdana. Three and a half months had come and gone since her trip, and she hadn't done a single thing to move her plan forward.

Chris used to frequently say in youth group that he was an expert at getting challenged and then doing nothing about it. Those words rang alarmingly true for Amy right now. With a full load of upper division classes that took turns kicking her butt around campus, her internship at PACS, her involvement in Intersect and church on Sundays, and her growing relationship with her new family, her schedule was pretty much void of any margin. Oh, and then there was her boyfriend who lived on the other side of the country. In some ways, the long distance was a blessing in disguise. But Skype—and Jake's appearance on television several hours a week for the past few months—cost her almost more time than she saved. Not that she didn't enjoy chatting with him or cheering for him! But every minute she spent watching Jake were precious minutes that could be used for studying...or figuring out how to help kids in Romania.

Of course, the hefty paycheck that would accompany Jake in the NBA could sure go a long way toward meeting her biggest obstacle: how to raise money to fund Bogdana's dream. Jake had told her Buddy's comment about money merely revealing generosity that was already within the heart, and that sounded well and good, but she didn't know how that applied in her situation. She had more than generous aspirations; she just had no idea how to turn them into reality.

Maybe that's because you haven't taken the time to think about it, a small voice nagged within her mind.

When have I had the time? she pushed back.

How about right now?

Amy snorted and sat up in bed. The voice was right. Maybe instead of letting her mind wander off in la-la-land, daydreaming about all the perks of being married to a superstar, her time could be better used developing a plan to help Romanian orphans. It wasn't like she could focus on any other homework right now anyway.

She went to her desk and flipped open her laptop. Whether Jake made millions playing professional basketball or not, God had ignited the passion to help Bogdana right now. She had to do this. Her fingers hovered over her keyboard, waiting for input from her brain. Nothing came. *God,* Amy begged, *if this is from You, You're gonna have to speak up here.*

Slowly, her fingers started tapping the keys in a tentative rhythm. Amy doubted that any of this was any good, but she just kept plodding, steadily dumping every random thought into the document.

Bogdana's Dream

Purpose: To empower kids from difficult family backgrounds to be part of the solution in making their community a better place. When a child learns that he or she can not only rise above their abusive situation but actually help others do the same, they are being set up to literally change the world.

Background: I met nineteen-year-old Bogdana on my recent trip to Romania. A victim herself of the horrible conditions of Romanian orphanages, she was transformed by Christ's love and is doing all she can to share that love with others. Her vehicle of choice is sewing dolls with cards that have Ephesians one:4-5 written on them. She would like to sew dolls for every orphan in the system. Unfortunately, she doesn't have sufficient materials or the finances to obtain them. I want to empower and finance Bogdana and those like her to live out their dreams.

Solution: First, raise money to buy supplies for Bogdana.

Eventually, find other young people who have similar noble goals to help the hurting and needy, and raise money to fund their dreams, too.

Amy had a sudden thought that inspired her even more. Bogdana was the one with the dream, but there were a couple dozen other young ladies living in the transition house who could help her accomplish her goal. If Amy could raise enough money, they could all be paid an hourly wage for their doll making, kind of like a regular job. In that way, not only would they make providing every child with their own doll a very real possibility, but the girls would also gain tangible sewing skills, *and* they all would be growing in their heart for others. It was perfect.

Amy did a quick search online. Current estimates showed about twenty thousand children were currently in Romanian orphanages. *Whew!* That number was definitely daunting, but if the task was divided by twenty girls, that would be "only" a thousand dolls per person. That was still a lot, but if they gave themselves a year to reach their goal, it was definitely doable.

Amy found a piece of scratch paper. Let's say they could make each doll for a buck. That sounded reasonable. She did a little more searching online and discovered that unskilled workers in Romania earn the equivalent of about a dollar an hour. Once the girls got into a routine, Amy figured they could complete a doll in an hour, maybe two at the most. So if they were paid a normal wage for their work, that would bump up the cost of the dolls to maybe three dollars apiece. *Three dollars times twenty thousand equals...Eek! That's a lot of money.* Amy leaned back in her chair, definitely daunted. She typed the numbers onto her screen and they screamed out in ridicule. Where in the world did she think she could find $60,000?

Suddenly, Jake's NBA salary sounded a whole lot more attractive. But that would be Jake raising money for them, and God had called *her* to do something. What was *she* going to do? *But there's no way I can raise that much, God!* Amy cried out inside.

God doesn't ask us to do everything. He just wants us to do what we can...in His strength. Jodi's voice rang out in her mind from her first day in Romania. Amy sighed and looked at the picture of her and Bogdana on her desk. She envisioned handing Bogdana a huge box with all the supplies she needed, and then she pictured sitting down at a long table with all the girls and sewing the dolls together. Cheerful laughter filled the air and smiles lit up the room. Girls who would otherwise likely be walking the streets as prostitutes were alive with hope as they worked with purpose to bring joy to others.

A sudden knock on her door jolted Amy back to her dorm room, but that momentary image was just the glimpse she needed to keep on dreaming for those girls. She looked at the time—it was already noon! It had taken her over an hour to just type out these few short paragraphs. And now she had to rush off to a study session with some of her Psych buddies.

"Come on in," Amy shouted through the closed door, assuming it was Katarina, one of the girls in her Cultural Psych class. She quickly copied and pasted her work from the past hour into an email to Jake, Cari, and her dad. Maybe they could help her flesh out her ideas even more.

"I don't know how to go about raising $60,000," she wrote at the bottom, "but I sure want to try. Jim and Jodi work directly with about a thousand orphans. Maybe that should be my goal. I just want to do something. Any ideas you have are welcome. I love you guys."

She pressed send and grabbed her books. *Lord, these plans are yours,* she prayed. *Show me what You've got.*

Eight hours and a big headache later, Amy wearily staggered back into her room. Her Cultural Psych group project was well under way, and her Personality and Affective Science paper was done. She felt exhausted but accomplished, and now she was excited for her Skype date with Jake. Seeing his gorgeous face, hearing his beautiful voice, just being in his presence was the perfect reward for a grueling afternoon.

Amy flipped open her laptop, and as usual, her awesome boyfriend was already waiting online. She loved that he made it a point to be early every day. She was also pretty sure he made it a point to dress up for their nightly dates. His hair was always combed, his face always clean shaven, and his shirt always fresh and unwrinkled. Even though it was ten p.m. in Louisville and Jake was definitely more of a morning person than a night owl, it was clear that he tried to look his best for her. Amy clicked the button to call him and waited for him to answer.

"Hey, babe! You have no idea how excited I am about Cari's idea," Jake gushed within seconds. Sure enough, everything about him was perfectly in place as usual.

"Hi!" Amy asked in confusion. "What are you talking about?"

"Don't you checked your email, girl? I was all ready to jump right into that draft, which, you know, maybe I still will, 'cause that kind of money could really make a lot of dolls, but then I read Cari's idea, and that's pretty good, too. It might not pay for all of them, but it would get more people here involved, which is really cool. Amy, your heart is so infectious. I love it."

"Whoah, slow down," Amy said with a laugh. "I've been studying all day and have no idea what you are talking about. But you are so cute!"

"You really need to start using your phone for more than just texting and looking at pictures of me," Jake laughed. He was obviously in a good mood. "You'll have to read it for yourself, but Cari has a great idea for how you could raise some money."

"Really?" Amy's heart started beating fast.

"And I talked to my mom. She's totally on board and thinks we should move the event from the venue room to the main auditorium at New Song. She's got some connections with a bunch of different businesses from working with my dad and thinks she can get them to pitch in. Get an article in the Times, some interviews on local radio morning shows...this thing could go viral and get really big. And then your dad had some good ideas, too. Who knows? Maybe we really could raise enough for dolls for every kid. Amy, this is so exciting!"

Amy loved that Jake was getting so passionate about her idea, and that he automatically considered himself part of the solution. And she loved that he had already started planning out details with his mom. But she started feeling really out of the loop, and it must have showed on her face.

"Babe? Are you okay?" Jake asked.

"Yeah, yeah," Amy tried to recover. She hated to throw a damper on the conversation when it was her idea he was so excited about. After all, given his morning with the agent, Jake had plenty of his own to celebrate and focus on.

"I'm sorry. I'm getting ahead of myself," Jake interjected. "I tell you what. Check your emails, call Cari, and then call me back after that." Jake grinned. "I love you so much, babe. I love being part of your amazing life. You're my inspiration." And with that, he was gone.

Amy shook her head and smiled. *How did I get such an amazing man, God? You are too generous.*

Amy clicked onto her email and skimmed the replies from Cari and her dad, but her heart started beating too fast for her mind to fully absorb what they were saying. She looked at the time. If she were going to talk to Cari tonight, she needed to call now, so without hesitation she dialed Cari's number.

Cari answered the phone in a hushed voice after only one ring, which could mean only one thing: Caleb had just been put to bed. Amy knew from experience that the little man couldn't stand people having fun without him and the slightest disturbance was enough to keep him wide awake for hours.

"Sorry!" Amy whispered into the phone, forgetting that it wasn't her voice that Caleb could hear. "I wasn't sure if he'd be in bed yet."

"No problem! I was looking forward to your call," Cari responded with quiet exuberance. "Let me move into the other room." Amy heard the sound of muffled footsteps and the clicking of a door, and then Cari's voice came back more loudly. "I told Melia I'd be in her room to do her hair, so I can't talk long, but what do you think?"

"So I just barely skimmed your email, but wow! Tell me more."

"Well, one of the joys of being a pastor's wife is getting asked to be involved with various events...many of which I have about as much excitement over as a root canal."

"Lucky you," Amy joked.

Cari chuckled. "This year I was asked to head up the annual Women's Christmas Tea. I don't even like tea! And I definitely felt like there were better uses of my time. Just this morning I was griping about it to God, and He got on my case. He convicted me of my bad attitude and told me to turn it into something that I would be excited to go to that would bring Him glory.

ALL or NOTHING

Well, that sounds all nice, but I had no idea what that would look like. I was thinking about it all day, and then I finally checked my email and read your notes about Bogdana's Dream, and immediately something clicked. What if we turned the Tea into an event where we raised money for a worthy cause, like yours?"

"I like it," Amy grinned.

"But wait, it gets even better. Just as I was scheming up some feeble ideas, Jake's mom called me after he had talked to her. Amy, that woman is a gold mine! I was thinking maybe a simple potluck and five-dollar tickets or something, but she was already way beyond that. She started scheming about a raffle and gourmet foods and live entertainment and a craft fair and all sorts of outlets to bring in money. Amy, if we succeed at only a fraction of what Pam was envisioning, we'll bring in thousands of dollars."

"Wow," Amy exhaled breathlessly.

"Now the only place we ran into a problem was finding a keynote speaker who might spread the vision...for free."

"Uh," Amy stammered, still catching up with all of Cari's ideas.

"Just kidding, girl! Obviously that would have to be you! I know the end of the quarter is a busy time for you and all, but do you think you could maybe squeeze out a weekend in early December to come down here?"

"Uh, yeah! Cari, you guys are amazing. I feel like such a slacker. I merely come up with a problem I think needs fixing, and before I know it, everyone else does all the hard work to solve it. Am I useless or what?"

"Amy, your heart is infectious. And I think God wants this to be bigger than just you."

Amy pondered those words long after she ended her conversation with Cari, and they still resonated inside of her as her head finally hit the pillow after talking with Jake for another hour. As she drifted off to sleep, the image that kept replaying in her mind was the smiles on Bogdana's and the other girls' faces as they opened up the box of materials for the dolls.

SUMMER

42

JAKE WALKED OUT OF HIS LAST FINAL and breathed deeply of the warm, summery Louisville air. He'd made it. With so many weighty considerations bouncing around in his mind for the past month, he had no idea how, but if that last exam was as easy as it seemed then he'd passed every class this semester with at least a B minus and now he was done. It felt good.

"Have a nice summer, Taylor," a tan brunette in a miniskirt interrupted his satisfaction as she passed by him and waved.

Jake smiled and forced himself to maintain contact with her eyes. He used to look forward to this time of year when warmer weather left less to the imagination in females' clothing. But now that he was trying to glorify God in everything—including his thoughts—he found himself frequently singing "The First Noel." Obviously, it was the wrong time of year for Christmas songs, but Chris had taught him the valuable tactic back in high school. Any time he saw a girl who caused his thoughts to wander lustfully, he merely had to start humming, "No-L, No-L, No-L, No-L!" and his mind promptly returned to the straight and narrow.

Taking another deep breath, he headed back to his apartment and enjoyed the light feeling of freedom.

"So glad you're coming back, Jake," a beauty in a low-cut tank top greeted with a cute southern drawl. She squeezed his arm as she passed by him closely on the sidewalk.

Holiday tune blaring inside, Jake kept his gaze level and smiled. "Thanks," he replied and kept on walking.

He had tried to keep pretty tight-lipped about his NBA options for next year, but his contemplations about going pro somehow leaked eventually, and the past couple weeks had been an eruption of public opinion about his decision. More than ever before, Jake found fans and foes everywhere he went—between classes, in the cafeteria, during workouts, and around town. Some pushed him to go, some said he'd be selfish if he left, some looked forward to his professional career with anticipation, while others rudely predicted his demise. Some wished him luck, some begged him to stay, and many simply followed him with their eyes, their gaze filled either with admiration or scorn.

It had been tough juggling all the notoriety, especially when his own friends and teammates were some of his biggest critics. He tried to explain to them that he was just keeping his options open, but he understood why they didn't like the possibility of him leaving. Next year was their year. The rest of the team was remaining intact. Even Tyler had decided to stick around. If Jake stayed, they'd really have a shot at winning the championship. If not, who knew?

Jake carried that burden heavily and the whole decision-making process became an unpleasant drain on his soul. He had been quick to gather the wisdom of his closest family and friends and spent hours asking God for guidance in the matter. But nothing left him completely at peace.

Besides Buddy's open-ended food for thought and Amy's supportive-no-matter-what preference that he stay in college, Jake had received a resounding take-the-money-and-run from his dad and a just as decisive don't-do-anything-until-you-finish-school from his mom. Chris had responded similarly to Buddy, asking him guiding questions to help him come to his own conclusion. Coach had been surprisingly understanding, but he definitely encouraged Jake to stick around for at least another year to hone his skills—and, of course, hopefully win it all next March. Grant had been silent for an entire minute before he had ultimately encouraged Jake to go for it and save him a spot wherever he landed. With everyone telling him something different, Jake's head had been a mess.

As the draft pool widened, however, it became painfully clear that Jake would be far from the choicest fish in the pond. As many as forty-three other players who focused their talents at the point guard position were looking for spots in the NBA this year, and while few of them had better numbers than Jake, most of them had more size. No matter how much hustle and heart Jake demonstrated, being six-foot-one limited his prospects at least a little. Since he was done growing, he wasn't sure if his draft stock could improve much by next year, but he figured if he could put even more time in at the gym getting stronger and improving his outside shot, in addition to boosting his assist stats and his play-making skills on the court next season, it definitely couldn't hurt.

Since he had redshirted his first season after staying behind a semester to help Amy through her pregnancy, Jake still had two more seasons of eligibility left, so feasibly he had two more seasons to build up his profile for NBA scouts. With Amy graduating next year, however, he was pretty sure he had no interest in sticking around Louisville for a fifth year. Amy could always come out here while he finished up, but since there was no way he could support her financially, it didn't make sense for them to get married, and waiting a whole extra year for that didn't sound appealing to Jake at all. So in the end, it all came down to what Jake wanted for next year. Did he want to forgo his dream of Louisville to take his chances at a limited taste of professional basketball? Or was another year of NBA uncertainty worth enjoying his final stint at college?

After three weeks of grueling deliberation, Jake finally made a public decision via Twitter the day of the NBA deadline. Amidst all the speculation and suggestions swirling around him, he ultimately decided to keep his college eligibility intact and forgo entering this year's draft. Upon making his decision formal, his own relief had been immediate and support from his fans had rushed in like a flood.

"Good call, bro! See you next year," a fellow athlete—Jake thought he played baseball—said as he passed by right outside their apartment building, reminding Jake once again that most people agreed with his decision.

Jake had to admit, that was nice. Every so often, however, he still felt a tiny seed of curiosity within him that wondered how things would have turned out had he thrown his name in the pot after all. *Oh well,* he sighed as he looked at his clock. *11:42!* That last final had taken longer than he realized. Scheduled to meet Buddy at noon for a celebratory lunch, he decided to head on over a few minutes early and veered out to the parking lot to find his truck. Now that draft decisions and finals were over, it was time to get to work in planning out the details of the summer basketball clinic. They had a lot to talk about.

"So, thirty-two more volunteers signed up to help," Buddy announced excitedly as he greeted Jake at his door ten minutes later.

"No way, that's awesome!" Jake hugged the old man.

At church last Sunday, Buddy had given a special announcement for the camp. Far from the traditional polite request for help, Buddy had called out the congregation of senior citizens, reproaching them that if they didn't bother to step up and do their part then they might as well just lock the church doors and shrivel up and die. Jake had been impressed by his guff, but wondered if it had been too harsh for the white-haired flock. Apparently not. Out of a church of less than one hundred regular members, they now had over sixty of them serving at the week-long event in some way.

"Are we going to have enough for them all to do?" Jake asked.

"You betcha!" Buddy motioned Jake over to his kitchen table where sandwiches, a bag of chips, and a pitcher of lemonade were waiting next to a pad of paper already filled with notes.

Jake followed him over and couldn't help getting a little misty eyed when he saw Yvonne's portrait at its new place on the table. It had been less than a month since Yvonne had passed away, and while Buddy was as jolly and encouraging as ever, he clearly missed her. He kept a framed picture of his beloved wife near her chair as his way of keeping her close to him. After over sixty years of marriage, moving on was obviously not on Buddy's radar and Jake couldn't blame him.

"Boy oh boy, do we have a lot to talk about!" Buddy enthused as he poured Jake a glass of lemonade and handed him a plate. "So what did you find out about your summer classes?"

All the considerations about the draft had forced Jake to think more concretely about his future than ever before. Once he decided to stick around for one more year, he realized he needed to step it up if he was going to get anywhere close to finishing all his units. So when he discovered he could get three classes out of the way by staying for Louisville's summer sessions, he signed up as soon as he cleared it with Amy. Both she and his mom were big fans of him earning his degree before moving on, so she'd been hugely supportive. And it didn't hurt that she had been offered a paid position for the summer at the counseling center she'd been interning at. Neither of them was excited about spending another few months apart, but they knew it was best for their long-term goals and willingly accepted their plight.

Jake figured it was probably best for their purity goals, too, since even seeing Amy on Skype excited his hormones almost more than he could bear. Long-distance relationships were tough, but he could only imagine how much tougher it would be to restrain his passion if they were together every day.

Since they couldn't touch, they were forced to talk, and everybody said communication was one of the most important parts of a relationship. Not meaning to be overconfident, Jake felt like they had communication in the bag. They hadn't argued since...well, he couldn't remember ever quarreling with Amy since they'd started talking again. There had been tense moments, of course, centered around his own previous mistakes, but even those they'd managed to talk through in a healthy way.

"So, I'll be done every day by 11:30 that week of camp." Jake shook his thoughts away from Amy and forced himself to focus on Buddy's question. "I know the morning is the best time of day, before it gets too hot and all, but do you think it will kill us to do it in the afternoon?"

"Nah, we'll make it work." Buddy waved his hand and started making a new list in his notebook. "I'm sure we can find some pop-up shade tents, and there are plenty of old gals who would love to supply their best lemonade."

Jake took a sip of his own icy drink. "Grant and I got four other guys to help out: Nomis and Tyler, and two local freshmen named Travis and Jadon. I can't believe they're all willing to stick around for a month."

"They're good guys," Buddy agreed. "And I think your passion is contagious."

Jake shrugged bashfully. He liked to think he was making a difference, glowing in his teammates' lives, but it was hard to tell. "I was talking to Debron," Jake changed the subject. "You know how he is always talking big. But he thought we'd easily be able to get fifty kids if we really got the word out. Do you think we could get the women to sew more scrimmage jerseys, just in case?"

"Not a doubt!" Buddy exclaimed as he scribbled more notes on his pad.

"And I know we talked about having a snack time for the kids each day, but a lot of them are on free lunch at school, but since they'll be on vacation I was thinking it might be nice if we could provide a full lunch for them, too."

"I'm on it!" Buddy flipped a page and added some notes to a previous list. "You know...," he looked up and paused. "I remember you were kind of discouraged about the lack of parental involvement before. Do you think we could do anything to reach out to them?"

Jake pondered the suggestion silently. He was pretty cynical in that area, but it couldn't hurt to try. "Free food tends to work with any age group. What if we had some kind of special exhibition game the last day and then fed everyone a free dinner?"

"Now you're talking!" Buddy slapped Jake on the shoulder and then went back to work on the same list. "What else?"

"So," Jake began hesitantly, "I know that by having all the Grace Fellowship volunteers out there we're sending a good message to the community. But I've been thinking, what if that's not enough? Maybe some of these kids will be interested enough to check out church as a result, maybe come to VBS or something, but probably most of them won't do anything about it, especially if their parents don't want to drive them. So where are they ever going to hear about Jesus then? I know that we have to be careful since the University's name is associated with the clinic and all, but...I just don't want this whole thing to be a waste...in the eternal scheme of things, you know?"

Buddy looked up at Jake and tears glistened in his eyes. "So what are we going to do about that?" he asked with a grin.

"I don't know. Maybe we could get some kind of big speaker to come at the end."

"That's great. Any ideas?"

Jake wracked his brain, trying to think of his possible connections. "Do you think we could find a pro player to come out here for an afternoon?"

"Come on, they're Louisville fans," Buddy chided. "They don't need a pro."

"I guess I could talk to one of the local FCA coaches," Jake suggested.

"How about someone who almost went pro?"

"Yeah, I met a guy who played for Louisville and then had a tryout with the Denver Nuggets like ten years ago!"

"Eh..." Buddy wrinkled his nose. "How about someone younger?"

"Uh..."

"Someone who is really passionate about them...someone who has already earned their trust..."

Jake stopped staring out the window and turned to Buddy who was smiling from ear to ear. "Wait a minute." His eyes widened as Buddy just kept grinning at him. "Come on, I play basketball; I don't give speeches."

Buddy patted him on the back. "There's no time like the present for trying something new."

JAKE RACED OVER TO THE RUNDOWN PARK after his morning class hoping an hour would be enough time to set everything up before the kids were scheduled to arrive at one. He and Grant had canvassed the neighborhood with Debron last week, passing out flyers to whoever would take one, but people had seemed pretty disinterested so Debron's bold claims that they'd have at least fifty kids seemed like quite a stretch. They'd been averaging about twenty-five kids during their weekly Friday night pickup games lately, so Jake figured he'd be happy with thirty.

Nothing prepared him for what he saw as he pulled his truck up to the curb by the basketball courts. Clusters of pop-up shade tents were already set up on every side of the asphalt. Underneath the northernmost ones were tables overflowing with hot dogs, chips, tubs of sliced watermelon, and plates of cookies. Behind the tables, a dozen white-haired grandmas served a steady line of kids their lunches, while others kept bringing out more food. The ladies of Grace Fellowship had outdone themselves!

Jake's eyes followed the flurry of activity all the way around to the tents at the far side of the court, where a growing line of kids and their parents snaked all the way out to the street. Jake estimated that Debron's fifty had already arrived, and more kept coming. A handful of volunteers from church manned the registration table, giving the parents forms to fill out while their children selected a shiny red, black, grey, or white practice jersey. Jake would have never thought about organizing the kids into color-designated teams, but fortunately somebody had. *Brilliant!* he celebrated as a growing smile spread across his face.

"Your church is amazing," Grant's voice sounded at Jake's elbow. Nomis, Tyler, Travis, and Jadon walked up beside him.

"This is pretty legit, man," Nomis agreed, knocking knuckles with Jake.

"Seriously." Jake shook his head and gave his teammates each a man-hug. "Thanks for coming out."

Jake hoisted a bag of practice balls out of the back of his truck. Grant grabbed the megaphone and stack of clipboards with one hand and bag of whistles and stop watches with the other. The other guys picked up cones and the rest of the gear Jake had hauled over. Coach had shown his support of their efforts by hooking them up with a ton of equipment to use.

"So, are we ready?" Jake asked, inhaling deeply.

"Let's do this!" Travis cheered.

Keeping the kids off the courts while they were setting up proved to be an unexpected challenge, but at five minutes before starting time, everything was finally in place and the guys were ready to go. Jake had planned on each of his teammates taking a group of kids through a set series of stations. But as Jake scanned the crowds, he suddenly wondered how they were all going to fit—and even more importantly, how they were going to be able to maintain control.

Jake walked over to the registration tables to get an accurate count, bumping into Buddy on his way. While Jake was struggling to avoid slipping into panic mode, Buddy looked like he was enjoying all the craziness.

"Isn't this great!" he exclaimed. "Yvonne would have loved this."

"Buddy, there's too many kids. What are we going to do?"

"Too many?" He laughed loudly. "That's not possible."

"But how are we going to have enough food...or jerseys? And we definitely don't have enough coaches."

"Don't you worry. Some of our gals are already working on the first two. How many more coaches do you need?"

Jake scanned the massive throng of kids scampering everywhere. It seemed like there were close to a hundred of them. "Uh, I don't know. Maybe five more?" That would divide out to about ten kids per coach, which still left a lot of room for chaos, but it was better than nothing.

Buddy winked at Jake. "Consider it done. I've still got a few connections from my days of playing."

The next three hours were a crazy mix of pandemonium and downright comedy as Jake and his teammates did all they could to teach these kids how to play ball. They started out doing basic conditioning and fundamentals drills as a big group for the first half hour, by which time four of Buddy's old teammates arrived to help manage the mayhem.

Jake paired Buddy and his cronies each up with one of the current Cardinals, and they broke the kids up by their jersey colors (including a group of no jerseys). The older guys might not be able to get down in defensive stance as well as they used to, but they could teach a proper bounce pass as good as ever, and by the end of the afternoon, the cycle of drill stations Jake had envisioned was going almost as smoothly as he had hoped for. Court space was limited, and the rusty old rims and backboards made shooting drills difficult, but somehow they made do with what they had.

By 5:30, all the kids had finally gone home, all the tents and tables had been loaded into the ancient church van, and Jake and his friends sat exhausted in the grass at the edge of the courts.

"You know, I grew up in this neighborhood," Jadon said out of nowhere. "Until my mom remarried and moved us across town. This is the coolest thing I've ever seen down here. Thanks for inviting me to do this, Taylor."

Jake didn't know how to respond.

"Me, too," Nomis piped up. "There was lots of street ball in my hood, but nothing organized like this."

ALL or **NOTHING**

"Organized?" Jake laughed.

"Nah, I'm serious," Nomis continued. "Sure, this ain't perfect, but these kids don't know any better. This would have been the highlight of my year if I'd had something like this growing up."

"Well, you have no idea how much I appreciate you doing this with me...with us." Jake looked at Grant and smiled.

"You know, some of my girlfriend's friends are sticking around for the summer," Travis offered. He was dating one of the girls on the women's basketball team. "I bet I could get them out here tomorrow."

Jake and his teammates looked at the freshman.

"Duh!" Tyler exclaimed in a funny accent.

They all bust out into laughter as they pulled each other up and walked to their cars. Jake looked around him and sighed contentedly. Life was good. And God was even better.

As the week went on, more kids joined every day and somehow more food and jerseys kept showing up to meet the need. Jake felt like he was in the middle of one of Jesus' feeding-the-multitudes miracles. The force of volunteers kept growing, too. As it turned out, Jadon's mom was involved in a church across town, and when she found out how things were going, she mobilized another whole army of volunteers to serve alongside Grace Fellowship's squadron, including a troop of men who could help with the coaching.

On the final afternoon, Jake took a thirty-second breather and surveyed all the activity going on around him. Four enormous color-coded groups spread out over the entire park supervised by an odd mix of volunteers serving as coaches. Curious parents mingled throughout and heaps of hot dogs and burgers and tons of other food waited under the shade of half a dozen tents. Several local news stations had even set up camp and had been shooting footage for the last hour or so, much to the delight of the camera-happy kids. Jake roughly estimated that there were over two hundred people gathered, and everyone looked like they were having fun. This was all more than he could have ever dreamed of, and he knew he owed all the credit to God.

Based on the sheer number of kids who had been coming, Jake had scrapped the idea for a final exhibition game. So now all that was left of the week-long clinic—besides the final feast, of course—was his little closing talk. The weather had started to cool off a little, but Jake was sweating more than ever. He hadn't been this nervous in a long time.

Jesus, help me, Jake breathed as he blew his whistle and sounded the horn on his megaphone for extra measure. Each group met for its final cheer before converging en masse on the asphalt and Jake started blasting out some fun party music on the sound system brought by Jadon's mom's church. The atmosphere was electric, and Jake couldn't help but feel energized in spite of his wearying week. *God, this is what it's all about. Please speak through me now.*

Within a few minutes, everyone had gathered and sat as quietly as a large, unruly crowd can be expected. Jake looked out at the sea of people, the news cameras, his teammates all staring at him waiting for him to speak and suddenly his mouth felt full of cotton balls. "Ah, hi," he stammered into the microphone, his mind completely blanking on what he wanted to say. Crickets chirped in his mind as he fought for control, and sweat flowed out of his pores. *God, help!* he pleaded.

Out of the corner of his eye, he noticed a small cluster of people from his church gathered away from everyone in the field. Their posture conveyed that they were praying, and suddenly a wave of peace washed over him. With renewed confidence, Jake spoke into the microphone.

"Thank you all for coming out this week. When I first dreamed up the idea of this basketball camp, I thought having fifty kids here would be miraculous." Laughter traveled throughout the crowd. "Never in my wildest dreams would I ever have imagined this." Jake waved his hand around the entire area. "And none of this could have ever happened without a ton of help from all these volunteers. Thank you, Grace Fellowship Church and New Life Christian Church for sponsoring this camp. Before you take a bite tonight, I ask you to find at least one of them to hug." Rousing applause quickly spread, and some of the kids nearly tackled their coaches in appreciation.

"You know, none of this could have happened without a lot of help from God, too," Jake plunged. The atmosphere turned slightly awkward, but Jake breathed deeply and kept on going. "I know God gets thanked in tons of speeches, but I mean this. I know that I for one would definitely not be out here today if it wasn't for Him.

"All I ever wanted growing up was to play basketball. For some reason, my mom brought home a Louisville T-shirt when I was little and from that day forward I bled Louisville crimson red. The day I received my scholarship offer to play here was the best day of my life. I was living the dream, getting everything I ever wanted... And then my life fell apart." Jake cleared his throat and shot a quick glance over to Buddy who gave him a nod of confidence like only he could.

"My childhood best friend committed suicide right in front of me. And I knew that if I'd been a better friend it would have never gotten to that. My girlfriend of three years broke up with me... and then told me she was pregnant. And then just when I thought my life couldn't get any worse, my mom walked in on my dad with another woman and everything else in my perfect little world fell apart." Jake looked around at the crowd around him and realized that for the first time all week, it was quiet enough to hear a mouse squeak. It was almost eerie how quiet it was. Taking comfort in his audience's attention, Jake kept on going.

"Somehow in the midst of all this, Jesus Christ swooped in and saved me. He threw me a lifeline in the form of a pastor named Chris who walked with me through all my pain. He helped me fix what I could and learn from what I couldn't. God restored my broken life and set me on a path of new purpose and new hope. And he even gave me back my dream of coming to Louisville." Jake took another deep breath and smiled.

"I wish I could tell you my life has been perfect since then, but it hasn't. In spite of everything God gave me, I still found ways to mess it up. I've made some big mistakes and brought a whole heap of troubles on myself." Jake looked at Grant. "But God still never gave up on me. Nothing I could do could ever make Him love me any less than He already does. And that goes the same way for you.

"You see, God created us to be His friends. And He's the best friend there is. He's the kind of friend who is always there, any time of day or night, any time we need Him. But there's a problem. The Bible calls it sin. Sin is anything we do that isn't perfect. Like if we're jealous, or we steal, or we say a bad word, or we get angry at someone. Everyone sins. And as we all know, there's consequences for it. Unfortunately, since God is perfect, He can't be in a relationship with imperfection, so the ultimate consequence for sin is eternal separation from God in a very real place called hell. Now God doesn't want us to go to hell, but consequences are consequences.

"So as God was sitting in heaven, watching everyone He wanted to be friends with sin, He thought, 'That's not cool. I've got to do something.' So, that's why He sent Jesus down to earth as a man. Since Jesus was perfect, He was able to take the punishment in our place. His death on the cross clears our record so that we can get back into that perfect relationship with God. We don't have to *stay* perfect, because Jesus' death cleared our record both for the past *and* the future. All we have to do is tell God we're sorry and He wipes our past off the books. That's some pretty good news.

"The trick is that we have to actually accept the deal. It's kind of like a plea bargain. We have to admit we're guilty and accept God's offer of life with Him, otherwise He is forced to punish us to the full extent of the law. God offers us salvation, like a life raft to a drowning man, but we have to actually grab it. So many people ignore it, because they'd rather try to swim to the other side on their own. But it's impossible. No one can do it. It's logically impossible for an imperfect person to somehow achieve perfection.

"I don't know if you've ever felt like you were drowning, alone in the difficulties in your life. If you haven't yet, you probably will sometime. Let me tell you, just grab a hold of Jesus. He loves you and He wants to be your forever friend. He wants to give you a second chance. He wants to give you strength. And He wants to use you then to reach out to others who are hurting around you."

In what seemed like an out-of-body experience, Jake heard himself coming to a close and looked at everyone staring at him. He had no idea where most of his words were coming from, but somehow, it seemed as if everyone was still paying attention. *Land the plane, Jake,* he heard Chris's voice in the back of his mind. In all his efforts to glow for God, he'd never once actually led anyone in a prayer to ask Jesus into their life. A flood of nervousness started seeping back into his heart. *You can do this*, echoed through his thoughts, staving off the growing apprehension.

"So that's my story, and I'd love for it to be your story, too," Jake concluded. "I'm going to pray for our meal real quick, but before I do that, I want to give you all an opportunity to ask Jesus into your life. The words aren't magic, but your intentions are what counts. Would everybody please bow their heads and close their eyes with me?"

Jake desperately tried to remember exactly how Chris did it, but he could only remember bits and pieces. "If you're ready to grab hold of Jesus, all you need to do is tell God something like, 'Jesus, thanks for dying on the cross to pay the consequences of my sins. I'm sorry. I'd like you to be a part of my life from here on out. Amen."

In a sudden moment of inspiration, Jake quickly added, "Uh, with everybody's eyes still closed, if you just prayed that for the first time would you raise your hand so I could see it?" *Please let there be at least one*, Jake said quickly in his own brain as he hesitantly opened one of his eyes.

Looking at the packed basketball court, Jake nearly lost his breath. Hands were raised everywhere, by tons of kids and even a few adults. Both his eyes popped wide open and tried to take it all in. At the right, a skinny kid with a 'fro held his hand up proudly. Debron flashed Jake a winning smile, and it was all Jake could do to hold back the tears. *Thank You, God!* Jake celebrated as his eyes continued to scan the crowd. Suddenly his gaze was stopped by another unexpected confession of faith—the adult hand raised tentatively in the very back belonged to none other than Nomis. The two teammates made eye contact and both broke out into huge grins. Tears spilled over onto Jake's cheeks and he struggled to gulp down the lump that had formed in his throat.

"I know You're happy to be reunited with all these friends, God," Jake finally brought his prayer to a close. "Thank You for this week, and thanks for this food we're about to enjoy...Amen."

A spontaneous cheer erupted as everyone opened their eyes and Jake just had to laugh. "That's right. The Bible says that when new people join God's kingdom, the angels celebrate in heaven. Let me tell you, there's a major party going on up there right now. And we get to celebrate down here as well. It's been a great week. Let's wrap up the fun with some dinner!"

Another cheer rippled through the large group, and Jake dismissed the grey team to get their food. As everyone else waited to get in line, Jake was about to turn the music back on, and then had another sudden thought. "Hey, one last thing as you're all waiting so patiently. Those of you who prayed with me today, let me tell you, it's a lot more fun to walk with God in the company of others. We've got two great churches out here this week that would love to help you get plugged in to their families. Please talk to one of the volunteers to find out how."

Jake turned the music up loud and sat down on a nearby cooler as all organization broke down and a frenzied herd made their way to the food lines.

"I'm so proud of you, Jake," Buddy whispered in his direction as he hustled over to the food lines with another tray of hot dogs.

Jake smiled. *Thanks, God. That was pretty awesome.* Jake knew he had bumbled through his whole speech, but the fact that God had used his feeble words to bring at least fifty people into a relationship with Him astounded Jake. This had to be unequivocally the greatest moment in his life thus far. He couldn't wait to tell Amy all about it.

"Hey, Jake. That was amazing."

The unfamiliar voice startled Jake and he looked up to see a burly guy in his early thirties with biceps nearly as big as his waist. "Uh, thanks." Jake stood up to face the guy eye to eye.

"I'm Kevin Ross. I'm a big fan." He grabbed Jake's hand and pumped his arm vigorously. "And after that, I like you even more." He smiled.

Jake smiled back.

"I'm one of the regional directors for Fellowship of Christian Athletes. Have you ever considered coaching at one of our camps?"

"Uh..."

"Do you have any free weeks this summer?"

44

Dear Amy,

I was most overjoyed to receive your letter about how you would like to help me with my doll project. I am truly humbled that you would even remember me, let alone care so much as to want to help. Jodi told me all about your fundraiser idea, and I can't believe it. I know that it is still many months away, but every day I wake up thinking about it. The other girls here at our home are excited to make dolls, too. You are the answer to my prayers and I hope God remembers you much in His blessings.

I am just heading into my finals, so please to keep me in your prayers. I pray for you much, too. I am hoping that you have a very good summer.

Love, Bogdana

AMY READ THROUGH the letter from Bogdana at least three times on the way from her mailbox to her car and her eyes were more than just a little misty. Encouragement like this made her want to work that much harder to make the Christmas Tea a success. In the months since the idea for "Bogdana's Dream" had sprung to life, not a day had passed since she'd asked God for help, and she couldn't wait to see what He was going to do.

Amy hopped into her already-loaded car and eagerly pulled out of the parking lot to start the long trek from Stanford to Oceanside. *Lord, this fundraiser is in Your hands,* she prayed once more. *But I'd sure love to see it bring in a ton of money.* As much as she knew that God was more than able to do anything, in her mind, $60,000 was still a goal too lofty to comprehend. Even a third of that seemed miraculous, but that was what she was hoping for. She'd be satisfied with anything, but who knew what God would pull out of His sleeve.

The money was yet to roll in, but the potential was already getting bigger than she'd ever dreamed. Here it was, only August, and already six other churches had signed on to host similar events for "Bogdana's Dream." Four of them were recruited through Chris and Cari's influence and two of them came on board thanks to Amy's stepmom's connections. Meanwhile, Amy's own mom was using her shrewd business skills to lure in other donors, and who knew what Jake's mom would come up with next? It was all so crazy!

Initially, Amy had just assumed that all money would go through New Song before being sent off to Heart to Heart Ministries on behalf of Bogdana. But as more churches and businesses got involved, that option got more complicated. Enter Edward Cunningham, one of her dad's friends who was a self-professed philanthropist who loved connecting worthy causes with significant sums of money. He hadn't volunteered any actual financial contributions but he had stepped in and propelled Amy down the path of turning her simple idea into an actual non-profit charity. Having done this countless times before, he handled all the paperwork and lawyer's fees and every other detail, and before Amy knew it, she was the founder of a 501(c)3 charity on its way to a tax-deductible status.

Amy pulled onto the freeway and shook her head. God was so incredible! She thought about the other blessings in her life: her friendship with Renee, her top-quality nearly-free education, her

Saturdays with her family...her growing correspondence with her uncle. Okay, she had to admit that one was a little bizarre.

After her initial letter, Amy hadn't heard back from Harold until after her return from Romania. His letter was clearly apologetic and over-the-top thankful, but it had still been a little creepy for her. She'd let it sit at the bottom of a pile on her desk until after finals when she finally had no more excuses to avoid it. After reading it again, she decided to write back, keeping her personal details brief but filling it with all kinds of Bible verses and thoughts she'd been learning at Intersect and church. Harold had written back promptly, again filled with gratitude for her words. He shared about his own life in prison and she had to admit it sounded pretty grim.

All she had originally intended to do was write him that once to convey her forgiveness and then be done with it, but something compelled her to write back. In the two months since then they had exchanged letters several more times, and with each one Harold became less and less the monster who deserved punishment for the horrible things he had done to her and more and more a man in need of Jesus' love. It was a strange transformation, and sometimes it still weirded her out that she was corresponding with the man who had molested her, but in her case, it just seemed like the right thing to do. And therein lay the blessing: God had healed her completely, so much so that she was able to be a blessing to the man who had hurt her. Talk about loving one's enemies! That complete healing was definitely a huge blessing.

Of course, Amy's biggest blessing of all was Jake. Every day with him was a beautiful reminder of how marvelously God works to bring good out of hardships. As much as she would never want to go through their rough times again, she clearly understood how valuable those times had been in the formation of their character and how much better suited for a life together they were now. And now she was fortunate enough to be heading home to spend the next two weeks with Jake. What more could she ask for?

Oh yeah, an amazing paid position at PACS this summer that had given her two weeks off in the middle of her service.

She still couldn't believe that Dr. Teddy and his staff had so graciously given her the time off to make the visit to Oceanside. With all the competition out there for jobs, she was sure they didn't need to be giving a lowly intern such a generous vacation. This was just one more example of God's incredible favor in her life.

She drove along with the windows down, relishing the warm air that whipped around her. It was four o'clock, which meant if she made good time she'd be home by midnight. Originally, Amy had looked forward to stopping by Jake's house for a few minutes upon arriving in Oceanside, but Cari had strongly advised against that. She said nothing good happened at that time of night when a couple was alone, especially a couple who hadn't seen each other for a long time. Jake had agreed, so instead they had decided to simply talk once more on the phone and then spend all day tomorrow together. Amy couldn't wait.

Knowing the two weeks would fly, they had intentionally tried not to over-schedule their time. Aside from speaking to the youth group next Tuesday night and spending Friday with Jonny and Andrea—who had just become an official couple last month—their schedule was relatively open. They had plenty of loosely made plans to spend time with family and friends, but nothing was set in stone and that sounded delightful.

Cari had warned Amy against leaving their time too unstructured, however, cautioning that those moments of unsupervised freedom would become the times of greatest temptation. It didn't matter how strong their relationship had been growing during their months apart; hormones mixed with pent-up passion were definitely not a good combo, and if Jake and Amy weren't careful, they could easily end up doing something they regretted later, especially since they'd raised the bar for themselves to not even kiss again until their wedding day.

In some ways, Cari said, it made it worse that they'd been apart for so long, because their defenses had likely turned a little lazy. Her suggested solution was to talk about it a bunch in advance, find people to keep them daily accountable, and avoid opportunities to be alone in private. Constantly remain in the presence of friends or other public places, especially after dark.

Amy knew Cari was right—she'd been down this road before with Jake. But she hoped that they'd matured enough and learned enough to simply enjoy being near each other without even worrying about boundaries. They weren't going to kiss. They weren't going to have sex. And that was that. Nevertheless, she took Cari's wisdom to heart. In the previous few weeks, she and Jake had talked extensively about their boundaries and committed to be strong when the other person was weak. They resolved to keep their activities to public places. And they agreed to nightly calls with Chris and Cari, sharing how they'd each done every day.

Lord, I know You'll always be there. Help us to glorify You in our time together, Amy prayed as she smiled and sighed. She glanced at her clock. Jake should probably just barely be getting home right now after volunteering all week at the Southern California FCA camp. It had ended earlier this afternoon and then his mom had picked him up since he'd left his truck in Louisville for the quick trip out to California.

Amy had felt like her summer had been busy working full-time at PACS, but Jake's schedule made hers look like a vacation. After pulling off his amazing basketball clinic, he'd aced all three summer courses on top of keeping up with the work of a last-minute online course he'd added to get three extra units. That class ended next week and, assuming he finished the final paper okay, that would leave him a mere two classes behind schedule for a graduation next spring. He'd already looked up his options and found two more online courses he could take to satisfy that deficit, including one he could polish off before basketball season geared up in October. Amy didn't know how he'd done it, but she was so proud of him.

Brake lights started glowing ahead of her and Amy groaned. *Not traffic!* she complained. But what was another hour when she had to wait until morning to see Jake anyway? Bumping up the volume of her stereo, Amy sang along proudly with the catchy song on the radio. She was going home to see her boyfriend, and nothing could get her down.

WHAT A GLORIOUS DAY! Amy rejoiced as her eyes adjusted to the sunlight streaming in through her window. She glanced over at her bedside clock wondering how late she had slept in. *6:30?* Obviously her 1:00 a.m. arrival home hadn't tired her out as much as she'd expected.

Not wanting to wake Jake up quite this early, she tried to go back to sleep but her eyes kept popping open in anticipation. Today was the day she got to spend with her boyfriend, and she just couldn't wait. Finally surrendering to wakefulness, she sat up in bed and tried to read her Bible, but that wasn't so fruitful either. All she could think about was seeing Jake.

Seven o'clock finally rolled around, and Amy reached for her phone immediately. Whether Jake was awake or not, she just couldn't wait any longer.

She need not have feared—his bright voice indicated that he'd been up for awhile, too. "Hey, Ames! I can't believe you're up already!"

"I know," Amy groaned. "But I just couldn't wait to see you." Just the sound of his voice spread a smile on her face that couldn't be erased.

"You wanna meet me at the trails for a run?" Jake suggested. "Or are you too tired from your drive?"

"No, no. That sounds great. I can probably be there in fifteen minutes."

"I can't wait."

Obviously, Amy couldn't either. She couldn't get dressed or drive over fast enough. But when she arrived at the regional park by Jake's house thirteen minutes later, Jake was already there, early as usual. Sitting at a picnic table, dressed to workout in basketball shorts and a T-shirt, Jake didn't look as polished as he normally did for their Skype calls, but there was just something about seeing him in person that made him cuter than ever. Amy felt like her heart might drop out through her stomach and she ran over to throw herself into his embrace.

It was amazing how intimate hugging could be when kissing wasn't an option, and after twenty minutes of simply holding each other close, Amy felt more bonded to Jake than ever.

"Maybe we'd better start running," Jake eventually said with a grin. "Or else my knees might get so weak you'll have to carry me. Amy Briggs, you are beautiful."

"You're pretty attractive yourself, Mr. Taylor." Amy smiled back and poked him in his ticklish spot in the side.

They set off at a decent jog, and their five-mile loop flew by like nothing while they filled in their steps with playful banter. Since their entire recent relationship had been based completely on long-distance conversations, they'd become pretty good at talking with each other, and sharing what was on their hearts and minds had become as second nature as breathing.

"You ready for breakfast?" Jake asked as they slowed down to a walk and headed back toward the table to stretch.

"Dressed like this?"

"Sweat and all." Jake grinned.

"You that hungry?"

"Hungry for you." Jake winked playfully. "But pancakes will do."

"Ooh, listen to you, Mr. Poet. Okay, I'm game."

"Unfortunately, without you I'm stranded. You mind taking your car?" Jake asked shyly.

"Ah, men. What would you do without us?" Amy teased. She threw him her keys. "But you're driving. I've had enough of that to last me awhile!"

Jake drove them over to a part of town Amy didn't usually frequent, but for some reason it instigated feelings of déjà vu. They stopped in front of a little café inside a run-down strip mall, and instantly Amy knew where they were. This was the place where they had mended their relationship at the end of their senior year, the morning Jake had convinced her not to go in for her abortion. So much had happened between them since then, but if Jake hadn't surrendered everything to her that morning, she was pretty sure she wouldn't be here today.

"Jake?"

Jake squeezed her hand and then ran around to open her door and led her into the tiny restaurant. Seated at a cute little bistro table, they placed their orders and then just sat staring at each other.

"Last time we ate here, neither of us was looking our best then either." Jake smiled and took Amy's hand. "Amy, I promised you a lot that day, and I know you gave up a lot when you trusted me with those promises. I'm sorry I didn't hold up my end of the bargain. I'm sorry how badly I let you down. When I look back at my journey from this point, I'm embarrassed."

"Jake," Amy interrupted. "That's all in our past. You know I forgive you."

"I know," Jake continued. "Because you are so amazing. But as much as I wish I could redo all the events that brought us to this place and everything that happened after, I wouldn't trade that morning here for anything. I may have failed—grossly—but I just want you to know how proud I am of who you've become since then."

Amy remembered shedding her share of tears that morning over three years ago, but the ones stinging her eyes today were full of so much more hope and joy. "Jake, you may have made your share of mistakes, but if it wasn't for you, I'd never have gotten started."

"Well, I guess it's good that God's been working all along, huh?"

They both smiled in agreement as their fingers intertwined across the table...just as the waitress brought their overfilled plates to the table. Amy jumped back to leave room.

"Oh, don't you mind me, sweetie. I'll get out of your hair just as soon as I get this handsome young man here a refill on his OJ," the waitress said jovially.

Over pancakes and eggs, Jake and Amy reminisced back to their senior year and all the drama that had unfolded. Several times they imagined how things could have been different, but those optional roads never seemed to bring them back to the present moment. For all the difficulties, God had brought them to a really good place and they wouldn't trade it for anything.

Two hours later, they finally left and stopped at Amy's house so that she could shower and change.

"You know what, I think I'll just wait in the car," Jake suggested when he saw that her mom wasn't home.

Amy smiled and squeezed his hand. "I love you. I'll try to hurry."

Wanting to waste as little time with him as possible, Amy ran to the bathroom and turned on the shower and then scampered to her room to grab a clean change of clothes. Immediately, she realized a predicament. Eager to enjoy the benefits of free laundry, the only clothes she had brought home were dirty.

Crap! she exclaimed silently. Her first day together with her boyfriend and she had nothing clean to wear.

She rushed over to the closet that she had severely purged last year, hoping there would be something to get her by. Nothing caught her attention except for a little ruffled white skirt. It would have to do. She rummaged through the few tops remaining but found nothing that worked with it. *Shoot!*

Suddenly she had an idea. She ran to her mom's room and checked out the options in her closet. In days gone by, this would have never been acceptable, but since they'd been growing closer the past year, Amy hoped she wouldn't mind. The first thing that caught her eye was a cute grey tank top, and she grabbed it without second thought.

The bathroom was now steaming hot and Amy jumped in and out of the shower as quickly as she could. A little makeup, a little work on her hair, and she slipped on her sandals and was ready to go. She was definitely dressed a little nicer than she intended for a casual day hanging out with her boyfriend, but given the circumstances, she was quite happy with what she'd found. And she was sure Jake wouldn't mind.

Grabbing her purse, she ran out the door and noticed that Jake was chatting happily on the phone. But by the time she was sitting next to him in the passenger seat, his attention was all hers.

"Wow!" Jake grabbed Amy's waist and leaned forward as if he was going to kiss her.

Instinctively, Amy turned away. "I forgot I didn't have any clean laundry, so I had to hunt through my mom's closet," she quickly explained.

Jake blushed and promptly pulled back. "Your mom has good taste," he mumbled and stared straight ahead. After a few seconds, he cleared his throat and turned back to Amy. "Well, lest anyone wonder why such a beauty is hanging out with such a beast, do you mind heading over to my house so that I can try to clean up a little? My mom is home, and she'd love to hang out with you."

"That sounds great!" Amy exclaimed. She'd been looking forward to spending time with her.

For all the years that Amy and Jake had dated the first time, Pam had never been in the picture much. Once Jake had gone off to college, Pam had started getting more involved at New Song, which gave Amy opportunities for brief conversations. But once Amy and Jake broke up, that had started feeling awkward and Amy tried to avoid it as much as possible. Now that they were back together, however, Amy couldn't wait to get to know her better, especially in light of all the help she'd been contributing to the fundraiser for Bogdana.

The moment they walked into Jake's house, Amy felt inundated with love. Pam treated her like a long-lost daughter and they started talking as if they'd been close friends for years. After a few pleasantries, Pam led them into the living room, and they immediately started talking about new ideas for the Christmas Tea. Amy was so engrossed in the conversation that she hardly even noticed when Jake slipped out to take his shower and she had no idea how much time had passed until Pam looked at her watch and gasped.

"Oh my! I completely forgot about my 3:30 meeting. I'm supposed to be at the church in seven minutes." She jumped out of her seat and grabbed her purse. "Amy, I am so sorry to rush out on you like this, but I'm sure you'll be around, right?"

"Of course, Mrs. Taylor." Amy grinned. "Thanks for taking my dream so seriously."

"Amy, you are a gem. Thanks for giving my son a second chance."

"Well, I didn't just give it to him. He earned it." Amy winked at Jake who was just walking in.

"Bye, mom." He gave her a hug and a kiss on the cheek.

"Bye, guys. Have fun." She whisked out of the room and slammed the front door behind her.

"Hey, babe. Long time no see." Amy grinned as she gave her boyfriend the once over. Dressed in a loose button up shirt with rolled up sleeves, cargo shorts, and flip flops, Jake exuded coolness from head to toe. If Amy didn't know any better, she'd think she was staring at an Abercrombie ad.

"I know; I missed you." Jake slid onto the couch next to her and pulled her into his strong arms.

Amy leaned back against the armrest and Jake leaned in on top of her. As they lay there staring at each other, a tantalizing moment passed where they both seemed to realize that they had the house to themselves. Old habits return to haunt long after they've been broken, and as Amy gazed into Jake's alluring blue eyes, she couldn't help but think about all the fun afternoons they'd spent in Jake's bedroom back in high school. Her head fogged by emotion, she traced her finger down Jake's forearm trying to remember the reasons why going back there would be a bad idea.

Suddenly, Jake jumped up and pulled her to a stand. "Let's get out of here!" he said and tugged her toward the entry.

Once in the safety of her car, they both looked at each other bashfully.

"Sorry about that." Amy grimaced, grateful that Jake was sticking stronger to their convictions than she was.

Jake shook his head. "No, no, it's my fault. I'm the one that can't keep my head straight. I apologize." He looked at Amy with soft eyes. "You're just so gorgeous; your beauty is intoxicating."

Amy rolled her eyes at the cheesy pickup line.

Jake chuckled. "I know, that sounded lame. But I'm really serious." He brushed a stray strand of hair out of her face. "Anyway, uh, you want to go to Costco? I hear they've got great samples today."

"Where'd you hear that?"

"Chris. I was talking to him while you were getting ready earlier, and he'd just been there with a student."

Amy smiled, amused by Jake's second choice of dining today. "Seems like that's another spot we have some history."

Jake smirked knowingly. "You think we'll see Doug there today?"

"I hope not."

"Really?" Jake asked. "You seemed pretty happy to see him last time. You have no idea how much I'd love to tell him that yes, we really are together."

Amy laughed. "I was pretty rough on you last time, huh?"

"Shoot. Did you hug him so tightly on purpose?"

"You noticed, huh?"

"Uh, yeah!" Jake diverted his gaze from the road and looked her in the eyes. "I know; you had to. You had a boyfriend and didn't want to lead me on. You were honorable in every way, and I would have expected nothing less from you."

Amy rested her hand on Jake's knee and thought back to that afternoon at Costco last summer. So much had changed since then and she couldn't be happier. "Jake, I tried to deny it, but that was the day I knew I wanted to spend the rest of my life with you. Thanks for being so respectful, but thank you also for not giving up on me. I know it must have been hard."

Jake just smiled.

"But was it worth it?"

"You have no idea." He picked up her hand and brought it to his lips. "I deserved a million times worse than what you gave me. I'm just glad it turned out this way."

A couple of hours later, Jake and Amy walked out of Costco hand in hand, stuffed beyond belief. In addition to the hot dogs and ice cream bars they had enjoyed when they first arrived, the samples had been unbelievable. Cheesecake, steak sandwiches, pizza bites, chocolate, ravioli... They could have enjoyed an entire meal simply by sticking to the bite-sized morsels. They didn't end up buying anything, but it was fun to just walk the aisles and watch the other customers.

When they finally left, it was after six, and Jake looked up at the waning sun. He draped his arm around Amy's shoulders. "I haven't seen a beach sunset for a long time. You have any interest in watching one with me?"

"Romantic sunset at the beach with the hottest guy on the planet? What more could I ask for?"

They drove down to the harbor and parked facing the water. Sitting in silence with fingers entwined, they stared out at the crashing waves.

"Jake," Amy murmured contentedly. "I think this has been the most perfect day of my life. Thank you."

"Hey! It's not over yet. We've got at least another hour until the sun says goodnight. Let's go for a walk."

Definitely wanting to heed Cari's advice about not being alone after dark, especially after their near compromises all day, Amy balked. "I don't know... Are you sure...you know?"

"Yes," Jake answered resolutely and ran around to open her door.

The August air was balmy and the water was pleasant, so it didn't take too long until Amy and Jake were frolicking along the water line, splashing in the waves, skipping rocks, chasing each other with seaweed, and searching for interesting shells.

They had walked quite a way and left all the other beachgoers far behind before Amy finally looked around her to see where they were. Suddenly, she stopped cold in her tracks. About twenty feet ahead was the hidden little cove where she and Jake had shared their first kiss back in ninth grade and enjoyed plenty of other intimate times since then.

Amy could think of no more romantic place to watch the sunset than "their" spot, but at the same time she could think of no more tempting place than the secluded inlet that held so many memories.

"Jake…I don't know if this is such a good idea." Amy hesitated.

"Trust me." He came back and laced his fingers through hers and led her closer to the outcropping of rocks.

They rounded one huge boulder and Amy's breath was taken away by what she saw. Hundreds of candles flickered in jars everywhere, propped on rocks, tucked into crevices, and littered all over the beach itself. Dozens of velvety red roses were scattered along the perimeter, and in the middle, a nest of pillows was draped by a fluffy down blanket.

"Jake." Amy gasped as she slowly spun around, taking it all in. "I think we're interrupting some—" But her voice caught in her throat as she came full circle to Jake, who was suddenly carrying a guitar and strumming out some resonant chords. His face beamed with pride and Amy didn't know whether to laugh or cry. *Is this what I think it is?* she asked herself incredulously. But before she had time to think any more, Jake started singing.

"It's been a long, long road," he crooned with a surprisingly smooth, deep voice,

"But we've made it this far, baby.

I've definitely been a toad

ALL or NOTHING

But you've forgiven me, maybe.

And I just want to say I'm grateful

For having you in my life

And now I want to spend the rest of my days loving you.

"Who knows where we'll go

But we're gonna have fun, baby.

NBA or Palo Alto

Or even Romania, maybe.

And I just want to say I'm happy

To have you by my side.

And now I want to spend the rest of my days loving you.

"You've given me new life,

And I owe you so much, baby.

But if you'll be my wife

I can make it up to you, maybe.

And I just want to say I love you.

You're the best thing in my world.

And now I want to spend the rest of my days loving you."

As the final notes drifted away on the salty air, Jake dropped to one knee and pulled a box out of his pocket. Prying open the lid, he revealed a gorgeous solitaire ring whose diamond must have been at least a carat. Catching the rays of the setting sun, it sparkled like a dewdrop on fire, and Amy was mesmerized.

"Amy, you know we've talked plenty about the rest of our lives, but I'm tired of just talking about it, like something vague in the distant future. Ten months from now, come what may, I want our long-distance relationship to end and our future together to begin. I cannot wait to spend every day with you, to dream with you and laugh with you and serve with you and play with you together, in person. You're my best friend, and I love you. Amy Briggs, will you marry me?"

There may not have been fireworks in the sky at that moment, but the explosions in her chest more than sufficed. Amy pulled

Jake up off his knee and hugged him over his guitar. "Of course," she whispered, unable to find her voice. Tears streamed down her face, and she couldn't stop smiling.

Jake slid the ring onto her finger and then unhooked his guitar strap and set the instrument down on the blanket. He sat down next to it and drew Amy down beside him. The sun loomed heavy over the horizon and it was just a matter of time until it plunged into the watery depths below. Surrounded by flickering firelight, Amy snuggled up next to her fiancé—oh, how she loved the sound of that!—and watched the Earth's giant candle spin its unhurried magic in front of her. She thought back over their day with new appreciation for every stop, marveling over how Jake had managed to capture the essence of their story in such a nonchalant and unsuspecting way.

"Jake, this entire day has been too wonderful for words. And now this. You are brilliant, and caught me completely by surprise." Amy rested her head on his shoulder and tried to absorb her fairytale surroundings. "How in the world did you pull this part off?"

Jake chuckled softly. "Jonny and Andrea. They were here all day, protecting the spot and setting it up."

"Wow." Again she was speechless and merely tried to soak it all in. But again she had another thought. "And the guitar?"

"I didn't want Steven to have anything on me, so I had a friend from school teach me a few chords. It's become one of my new hobbies." Jake chuckled again and buried his face in her hair.

Amy wrapped her arm around his torso. "I really want to kiss you right now," she whispered in his ear.

Jake turned and pulled her into a hug. "Please don't," he whispered back. "I'm pretty sure I couldn't resist."

The sun dipped down into the Pacific. Slowly, slowly, the vibrant red orb sank lower and lower until it was nothing more than a glowing crescent over the flat surface of the sea. Soon, even that was swallowed by the ocean and the sky imploded in deep shades of indigo, pink, and purple.

FALL

OCTOBER HAD COME AND GONE and Jake found himself once again in the midst of the flurry called basketball season. Tonight was their season opener and Jake sat on the bench absorbing the roar of the sold-out crowd. As he waited for the announcer to call his name, he marveled at the fact that he was sitting here in a Cardinal uniform living out his dreams. It was so surreal.

On his drive home from Buddy's the other day, he'd counted his mug on no less than seventeen different billboards and banners. The preseason polls were predicting him to be Big East MVP this year. And Louisville had come out ranked seventh in the nation. Expectations were high. And his goals were even higher.

This was it, his final season, his final chance to win a championship, his final shot at securing a place in the NBA. Sure, he had that extra year of eligibility, but in seven months he was going to marry Amy, and coming back to Louisville wasn't even a consideration. It was now or never, and he was ready to give it all he had.

The past couple months, Jake had worked harder than ever before. Between classes and homework, he'd spent nearly every waking moment either in the weight room, the gym, or Coach's office studying film. He'd gained ten more pounds of muscle, an extra inch on his vertical jump, and more consistency on his outside shot. His confidence as a playmaker had skyrocketed, and Jake couldn't wait to test things out.

As exciting as his prospects were this season, he still couldn't shake the nagging doubt that maybe he should have just taken the plunge into the NBA. The draft had turned out softer than predicted and guys he had taken to school last year were picked up easily in the first round. Jake knew that logically he had made the best choice at the time, but with hindsight, he couldn't help but wonder if maybe his decision to wait a year might end up being his downfall. If something went wrong, would he spend the rest of his life looking back at the year he gave his future away?

Voicemails from Jordan and his dad replayed over and over in his mind. *Take the money and run. Don't pass up the best deal you may ever get. Do you want to regret this decision for the rest of your life?* But this was Jake's life, not Jordan's, his dad's, or even Jamal's. And most sports commentators agreed, unless an athlete is slotted to be picked up in the lottery, he should stay in school. Jake tried to take the smart road and he couldn't wait to prove to them that he was right.

Besides, it wasn't only about basketball. Jake scanned his teammates lining the court and couldn't help but feel awe toward the breakthroughs God had given him with them. Since the summer clinic, Jadon had started joining his mom at church again and his life had turned around 180 degrees. Whereas last year, his foul mouth and propensity for drinking and drugs had landed him in various forms of trouble, this year Jadon had transformed into a model citizen, quick to share his story of redemption with anyone who would listen. Nomis, too, had become a new person since raising his hand during Jake's prayer. Nearly every day, he came to Jake with new questions about what he was reading in the Bible, and within the first three months, he had already read God's Word from cover to cover once.

The two of them now joined Jake and Grant in their weekly visits to the park, which had generated an even larger throng of kids. Jake had started seeing some of the kids and their parents at Grace Fellowship, and Jadon reported that at least a dozen had started coming to his church. Jake couldn't believe that his one simple idea could have such an impact.

Jadon and Nomis had also started joining Jake in his weekly lunches with Buddy. Grant had started coming more regularly again, too, although he still made it clear that he was nowhere near ready to cross the bridge. Jake had asked him about his hesitation one night in their apartment, and Grant had basically said that while he loved the idea of God and all that a relationship with Him had to offer, he knew that his lifestyle was expressly condemned in the Bible and he wasn't ready to give it up. Jake wished that he'd just give it a chance, but he respected that Grant didn't take God's expectations lightly.

One of Jake's favorite areas of impact was Debron. Jake watched him as he now crouched at the end of the court, ready to engage in his ball-boy duties. Since raising his hand, the kid had blossomed. He still had a mouth that wouldn't quit, but rather than using it to constantly tear others down and build himself up, his growing relationship with God had triggered a switch and now he was one of the most encouraging people Jake knew. Debron was also now the youngest usher Grace Fellowship had ever had, and Jake had a ton of fun greeting people with him every Sunday. Jake loved that kid and wanted to pour as much into him as possible this year before he left.

The impact of that neighborhood basketball camp had even spread beyond Jake's immediate circle of concern. Jake had never for one second done it to receive any recognition, but this summer, the NCAA had recognized his and Grant's efforts and had honored them with a Humanitarian Award for their passion in pouring into the next generation. FCA had also recognized his work and Kevin Ross had already lined up five schools that wanted Jake to come speak to their campus club at lunch as part of a big outreach. Jake knew his schedule was already way past packed but how could he refuse? God was opening up opportunities and Jake was thrilled.

The noise in the gym had grown to a deafening roar and Jake wondered if he'd even be able to hear his name when it was called. He watched to see Nate Williams jump up and run on the court, and then, finally, it was his turn. The crowd went wild and Jake did all he could to stay focused on the game.

"Are you ready?" Jake yelled to his teammates as they converged onto the middle of the court. "Let's do this!"

Heart pounding and adrenaline pumping, Jake lined up for the opening toss. Tyler dominated and scooped the ball right into Jake's waiting hands while the rest of the guys raced down the court. Jake tossed a perfect alley-oop to Grant for a sensational slam in the first five seconds of the game. They were off to a beautiful start.

WINTER

AFTER MONTHS OF PLANNING, the day of the New Song Christmas Tea had finally arrived. Thanks to some promotional airline rates her mom had discovered, Amy had been able to buy a round-trip ticket to San Diego and back for less than a hundred dollars, which sure beat making the long drive herself during this short weekend. So now she stood in the back of the large New Song auditorium, watching the flurry of activity all around her with humbled awe. Beyond Cari, Jake's mom, and her own mom—women who all had a vested interest in helping her—scores of ladies she'd never even met before scurried to and fro to lend a hand with the setup.

Each table had been adopted by a different hostess who went out of her way to decorate it as beautifully as she could imagine. Along the back wall, elegant stations were covered with delectable pastries and desserts donated by several local bakeries in town. The front of the room was lined with an enticing variety of baskets up for raffle. And out in the lobby, a veritable marketplace of fair-trade gifts and handmade goods had sprung up, giving guests an opportunity to do some ethical Christmas shopping. The entire atmosphere was festive, sophisticated, and uplifting, and Amy was blown away.

A choir started singing joyous Christmas carols, and Amy made her way to Cari's table at the front where she had a seat reserved next to Pam and Cari and Melia and Jan and Emily—who at three years old had begged her mom to come so she could sit next to Amy. Needless to say, Amy was touched. But her highlight by far was seeing her mom surrounded by all these quality new friends. Since agreeing to help with this event, her mom had started coming to New Song occasionally and Amy was so excited to see what God was going to do in her life.

After a few more jubilant tunes, the choir stepped down and Cari got on stage.

"Welcome, ladies, and Merry Christmas! I don't know if you've had the chance to look around you, but are we in a winter wonderland or what?" Ladies everywhere cheered with shrill voices. "Much thanks goes out to everyone who played a part in bringing this spectacular event together—" More applause interrupted her. "And thank you to all of you. With over three hundred women in attendance this afternoon, your presence here makes this the largest women's event our church has ever seen." Again, giddy celebration broke out.

When the clapping finally died down, Cari continued. "And while it's fun to get into the spirit of Christmas and start our celebrating early, don't forget we're also working to make a young woman in Romania's dream come true." Her tone turned a little more serious and a pervasive hush followed.

"Thanks to the vision of a woman I have come to know and love over the past few years, we are changing not just one life today, but many. To tell us a little more about that, Amy Briggs has come to share a little of her passion. Amy was a student in our youth group three years ago. Through many trials of her own, she discovered God and His boundless love, and she has been spreading that good news to others ever since. I've witnessed her pour into the lives of several young ladies in our youth ministry, and now she is ministering to abused children while getting her education at Stanford. Please join me in welcoming Amy Briggs!"

Amy climbed the steps timidly, bashful from the glowing introduction from her mentor. But she knew this wasn't about her; she was merely a piece in the puzzle of God's great plan. Feeling the prayers of her family and friends, including Jake who was getting ready for a big game on the other side of the country, Amy approached the podium with confidence and quickly glanced at her notes.

"Let me tell you about a girl I've recently come to know and love." A picture of Bogdana appeared on the screen behind her. "Bogdana is a victim of abuse and neglect, both from her family of origin as well as the child welfare system that stepped in to supposedly protect her. I met her on my recent trip to Romania, and she changed my life."

Amy continued sharing about Bogdana's horrific past and within minutes there wasn't a dry eye in the room. Of course, what did she expect from an estrogen-filled environment like this? But then Amy turned the story to describe Bogdana's radical transformation through the love of Christ. She described in detail her doll-making aspirations and explained how the Bible verse attached to the dolls so aptly communicated God's unwavering love toward them.

"And that's where Bogdana's dream is so unique," Amy said. "While other organizations attempt to meet these children's physical needs for things like food and shelter, Bogdana has discovered a brilliant way to concretely meet these children's intangible need to love and be loved while introducing them to the perfect love of the Savior."

This provided the perfect segue for Amy to convey the beautiful truth of God's unwavering love toward everyone there as well. She described the glorious gift God offered to all, and challenged them to unwrap the presence of Christ in their own lives in the midst of this season celebrating His birth.

"Many of you came here today to give hope to a girl in Romania. But maybe you also came here needing your own dose of hope. Well, you are not alone, and I would love to talk to you more and introduce you to the Author of unfailing love." Amy paused and took a deep breath.

"Bogdana is a girl with a dream," she concluded. "She wants to share the love of Jesus with every single orphan in the dysfunctional Romanian orphanage system. Recent statistics show there are about 20,000 of them, so obviously Bogdana can't do this alone. But with our help, she can do more. Thank you."

The room erupted in applause and ladies jumped to their feet. Amy had never asked for additional donations—she merely meant to explain where the proceeds from their tickets were going—but she noticed women rifling through their purses and pulling out wallets and checkbooks everywhere. *Is this for real?* she marveled as she headed off the stage. Whatever God was doing, she felt honored to be a part.

By the end of the event, Amy's face hurt from smiling so much and she was exhausted from talking to so many women. But all of that paled in comparison to the joy welling up inside of her. In addition to all the support generated for Bogdana, she had prayed with at least a dozen ladies to receive the gift of Christ in their life, and that was her highlight by far.

She hitched a ride with Cari back to the Vaughn house where a dozen or so guys had already gathered to watch Jake's weighty game against Butler. While Cari tallied up all the contributions gathered from the ticket sales, raffle, proceeds from the vendors, and general donations, Amy sunk into their couch and basked in the pleasure of watching her fiancé play basketball. This day was going better than she could have ever imagined, so it was no surprise to her to see that the Louisville Cardinals were leading by nine with twelve minutes to go and Jake was having a spectacular game.

Amy knew Jake still sometimes wondered if he'd made the right call in avoiding the draft, but based on his play so far this season, the answer seemed a resounding "Yes!" Stronger than ever and full of poise, he was leading his team with an average of nineteen points a game and a stellar twelve assists. He'd carried them to a 7-0 record and they'd come out ranked fifth in the nation just this past week. Jake's numbers were at the top of the charts, and there was no way more scouts weren't going to recognize his growing potential. Amy was so proud of him.

Absentmindedly, Amy studied the rock on her left hand and whispered for no one to hear, "My fiancé is going to play in the NBA." The words sounded too good to be true, but she liked the sound of them.

"Yes, he is," Cari whispered back as she sank onto the couch next to her.

Embarrassed that she had been caught in her daydreaming, Amy blushed.

"I just thought you might like to know the total brought in today," Cari said. "But if you'd rather keep talking about Jake, I understand." She gave Amy a playful nudge with her shoulder.

"Of course! I didn't think you'd have it so soon."

"I got a five on the AP Calculus exam back in high school. I've got mad math skills."

Amy laughed. "So what is it?"

"Well...how much were you hoping for again?"

"Oh man, you're going to draw this out?" Amy shook her head. "Um, I told God I'd love to see twenty thousand when all is said and done, but that includes everything from the other churches, too. So from New Song, I guess I'd be blown away by five thousand."

Cari remained silent and just looked at the numbers on her paper dubiously.

"Oooh, is that too much? I'll be happy with anything!"

Cari looked down at her paper and then back up at Amy.

"Cari! Tell me already!"

"I'm just thinking you need to renegotiate your plans with God. 'Cause girl...He just gave you twenty-two thousand dollars today!"

"What!" Amy gasped. "That's impossible! Are you serious?" Amy felt like she might start hyperventilating.

"Nothing's impossible with God, my friend. And I think He's trying to prove that to you."

"Wow." Amy leaned back and closed her eyes, trying to let the magnitude of this moment sink in.

"OH!" Chris's voice shouted in horror on the other side of the room, instantly drawing everyone's attention to the television. There on the forty-two inch screen in front of them lay Jake clutching his knee in agony as teammates and coaches rushed to surround him.

"What happened?" Amy bolted upright, her eyes fixed on Jake's pained face.

Chris started to explain but the announcers beat him to it with a slow motion replay of the injury. As Jake had juked by his defender en route to the hoop, a hulking Butler forward had tried to clog the lane but had only succeeded in kicking his leg out into Jake's path. Momentum had carried Jake's body forward even while his lower half had been rendered stationary, and the opposing movements had tweaked Jake's right knee and sent him tumbling to the floor. Over and over again, the sportscasters replayed a close-up of the unnaturally twisting knee, and Amy felt suddenly squeamish.

"Stop showing us that already. Just show me Jake," she begged, but instead they cut to a commercial break. "Nooooo," she moaned, desperate for hope.

Cari pulled her into a tight, motherly embrace and Chris immediately started praying. "Lord, Jake's hurting. Please let him know that You're right there. And please let him be okay." He, too, stood up and surrounded Amy with loving arms. "It's going to be alright, Amy. It's going to be alright."

The commercial ended and the station cut back to the game, where Jake was being carried off the floor directly to the locker room.

"Man, you hate to see that," one of the announcers sympathized.

"I know. You just gotta hope it's not an ACL tear. Those are season-ending, and you just never want to see that for a promising guy like Taylor."

The two guys on the television kept going about how bad the injury looked, but Amy couldn't focus on anything past the words "season-ending." *God? That's not what you want, is it?* This was Jake's final season. It couldn't be over yet.

With nothing else to do, Amy dialed Jake's number. She didn't expect to get through to him, but she just wanted to hear his voice, even if it was just a recording. "Jake, I love you," she spoke into the phone after the beep. "And we're all praying for you, here. Cari and I, and Chris and Billy and Jonny and Danny and a bunch of the other guys. Hang in there, okay, babe?" Amy's voice started to quiver and she knew she needed to get off so that he wouldn't hear her break down. "Call me back when you can."

She clicked to end the call and stared numbly in front of her. Suddenly, her perfect day had turned into a nightmare.

FIFTEEN HOURS LATER, Jake sat in the examination room of the orthopedic surgeon, anxiously awaiting the results of his MRI. Since the collision last night, his knee had ballooned out to nearly three times its normal size, in spite of his liberal use of ice and ibuprofen, and it throbbed with pain. Sleep had been nearly impossible, giving him plenty of time to scrutinize every worst-case scenario, and he was pretty much a basket case.

God, what are you doing? he prayed in desperation. Things had been going so well—better than he could have hoped, even—and now this. Was this some sort of punishment? Had he missed God's guidance and now this was a drastic redirect? *If there's some sort of lesson You want me to learn, Lord, help me to master it quick. But please don't take away basketball,* he pleaded.

Jolting him out of his introspective gloom, the doctor burst into the room looking grim. "Well, I have good news and bad," he began. "The good is that your ACL is only strained. The bad is that your meniscus is torn. Classic basketball injury."

"So what does that mean for my season?"

The doctor chuckled. "Maybe the better question is what does this mean for your knee?"

"Okay?" Jake asked carefully, trying not to slip into despondency.

"Your meniscus isn't pretty...but I've seen worse. You have a couple of options. Surgery isn't necessary, and you can rest it for a few months to see if it will heal on its own."

"A few months? But the season will be done by then."

"Or you can elect for surgery to trim out the damage. Ironically, recovery from surgery tends to go faster."

"What exactly does faster look like for me?"

"There are so many factors involved in the healing process, but I'd say if everything goes well and you stick to the therapy regimen like a full time job, we might be able to get you back on the court in six to eight weeks."

"Whew," Jake exhaled as he contemplated the significance of his options. Eight weeks would leave him only the last few games in February...but that was better than nothing. "How soon can I schedule the surgery?"

Two weeks later, Jake awoke in the post-op room of Tri-City Hospital back home in Oceanside with his leg braced and elevated. Groggy from anesthesia, he lay staring at the ceiling trying to remember where he was.

"Hey, baby. You made it," Amy's voice said softly right next to his head.

He turned to see her and tried to speak, but words refused to form.

"Just rest." She caressed his forehead. "The doctor said the surgery went as well as expected. Everything's going to be okay."

Jake closed his eyes under her tender touch and focused on trying to clear his head. At least his knee didn't hurt. Slowly his thoughts regained coherence and after laying there for what seemed to be a very long time, he decided to sit up. The abrupt movement didn't sit so well with the anesthesia, and his stomach lurched. His face must have registered the sudden queasiness because Amy jumped up.

"Jake! What are you doing? Take it easy."

"It's okay. I'm fine. Is the doctor around?"

"Uh, yeah. He said he'd be back in a few minutes to check on you." Amy looked concerned. "Babe. You can't start rehab this second. Relax and enjoy this little break. You just finished finals. You get to be home for Christmas. You get to be with me."

Jake didn't miss her emphasis on the last sentence. "I know, I know. I just got tired of laying down...Wait, did he say anything about rehab?"

"No, Jake. I just know you're raring to get back on the court."

"How's my boy doing?" a familiar booming voice sounded around the corner. A second later, Jake's dad pulled back the curtain and lumbered in. "You're sitting up. Good job. Don't want to be lazy for too long. It makes you soft."

"Hi, dad." Jake was surprised to see his dad here, but he had to admit he much preferred Amy's gentle company.

"So I just got off the phone with that Spiro guy. He sends you his best regards, and says not to worry. Depending on how quick and strong you make your comeback, he thinks he can still get you picked up pretty high this summer thanks to your compelling start of the season."

"Really?" Jake asked, thrilled by the first dose of truly good news he'd heard in awhile. The pressure his dad always put on him was usually intensely irritating, but today it sounded like music to his ears. There was hope, and he was ready to rise to the challenge.

"Hi, Jake!" The surgeon walked in with a smile. "Looks like someone's ready to get out of here."

Jake smiled back.

"Well, we cleaned your meniscus up real nice. By the time it's done healing, you should never know the difference. I do want you to be careful of that ACL, though. The strain should heal up just fine on its own, but it is weak right now, so we don't want you to push yourself too hard too soon. We found some other bits of scar tissue here and there, so we cleaned that up, too. It looks like you've been pretty hard on those knees of yours over the years. I guess that goes with the territory, huh? Basketball's a rough sport on that joint with all the fast starts and stops and twisting and pivoting, not to mention those fouls. For a non-contact sport, it's pretty rough."

"So when can I start playing again?"

"Whoa-ho there, cowboy. Let's take first things first. You ready to start talking rehab?"

Jake nodded. The doctor proscribed him some minimal strength- and mobility-promoting exercises he could do on his own for the next few days before Christmas, and then daily physical therapy sessions at his sports-injury clinic until Jake returned to Louisville after the New Year. Jake consented whole-heartedly, vowing to himself to go above and beyond what the doctor asked of him. If God was willing to give him a second chance, there was no way he was going to waste it.

His dad pushed his wheelchair to Amy's car and helped him into the passenger seat before dashing off to another meeting. Amy seemed more silent than usual, but Jake didn't have the chance to ask her about it before his phone rang.

"Buddy!" he answered as soon as he saw the caller I.D.

"Jake, how are you?"

"I'm really good. The doctor just gave me some exercises I can already start doing, and he said things look good for a speedy recovery. And my dad talked to Jordan Spiro, and he said things still looked okay for the draft, too."

"Wow. Well, I've sure been praying for you."

"Thanks, man. I think God's been listening."

Buddy laughed gently. "He's always listening Jake, whether things go the way we want them to or not. Well, hey, I don't want to keep you. I'm sure you have plenty of family and friends who want all the time they can get with you. But I read this verse this morning and claimed it for you. Psalm 37:4 says, 'Delight yourself in the Lord and He will give you the desires of your heart.' Keep focusing on God, Jake, and He won't fail you."

"I love it."

"Say hi to that pretty lady of yours for me."

"Will do." Jake hung up, a big smile on his face. "Buddy says hi."

Amy smiled but remained silent.

"Is everything okay, babe? You're awfully quiet."

"Yeah, yeah."

"But...?" From all their countless hours of talking, Jake was pretty good now at knowing when something wasn't quite right.

Amy looked at Jake and grinned. "It's no big deal, babe. I just don't want you to set your expectations too high, you know, and push yourself too hard." She laced her fingers in with Jake's and sighed. "Things happen for a reason, you know, and I'm just wondering if maybe God has some other plans."

"Other than basketball, you mean?"

Amy must have detected the edge in his voice because she quickly pulled his hand up and kissed it. "I don't know what I mean, baby. It's just all this talk about you returning so quickly makes me wonder if we're racing ahead of God."

"Amy, why wouldn't God want me to keep playing?"

"I'm not saying He doesn't. But have you asked Him?"

"Yes!... Kind of." Jake had to admit his asking had probably sounded a lot more like begging...for what he wanted.

"All I know is you were willing to give up basketball pretty easily for me; it just seems like God deserves at least that much."

"Is this about us, Amy?" Jake said, getting a little annoyed. "Is it all the notoriety? All the publicity? Are you feeling left out? If *you* don't want me to play anymore, just tell me."

"Jake. This has nothing to do with me. This isn't about what I want—"

"Well, it sure seems like it. I thought you were excited about me going pro."

"I was! I am.... If that's what God wants."

"Whatever."

"Jake, listen to yourself—" At this point, Amy pulled into the Taylor driveway and Jake opened his door to jump out. "Jake, wait! You need my help." She slammed the transmission into park and yanked on the brake.

Jake just huffed. "I'm tired of being told what I can and can't do." He hobbled out on his good leg and tried to situate himself on his new crutches.

Amy ran around and tried to steady him. "Jake."

Jake knew he should listen to her, but he was irritated and didn't feel like it. There was no way God was trying to stop him from playing basketball, not after he gave up the draft last summer for the sake of Amy and Buddy and Debron and his teammates. He'd given God one more year of ministry in Louisville. It just wouldn't be fair if God didn't hold up His end of the bargain and let Jake realize his dreams this year. Jake was determined to make it back on the court, whatever it took. He'd already put too much hard work into this to back down now.

Jake hopped upstairs to his room and slammed the door behind him. He cranked up his stereo and flopped on the bed. Amy must have got the point, because she didn't follow him. He lay motionless, staring at the ceiling. *Buddy said You'd give me the desires of my heart, God. Well, this is what I really want!*

The dull ache in his knee started growing stronger. Too bad he'd forgotten to grab the pain medication from Amy. There was no way he was going back down there now. *Pain is just weakness leaving the body,* he thought with gritted teeth as he rolled over and tried to sleep it off.

JAKE KNEW THAT IF THERE WAS EVER AN EXCUSE

to cancel a commitment, knee surgery was surely as legitimate as it comes. Nevertheless, only a few days after returning to Louisville, he somehow still found himself riding in the back of Kevin Ross's minivan on the way to another FCA club speaking engagement. Knee still braced, it stretched stiffly across the middle of the van as Jake awkwardly leaned forward to participate in the conversation.

His operation had been almost three weeks ago now, and thanks to rigorous and persistent physical therapy, he was virtually pain free and felt almost as strong as before. The doctor here in Louisville had insisted on him wearing the brace and avoiding basketball-specific drills and exercises for one more week, but he was positive about Jake's progress so far and hinted that Jake's return to the hardwood might come sooner than anticipated. Jake took that good news and ran with it, setting his sights on Louisville's big game against Syracuse—at home—on February 2. What an exciting return to his fans that would be!

Amy hadn't mentioned her concerns again, and that whole incident in the car had blown over like a piece of pollen in the wind. Jake knew he should have probably apologized for his attitude with her, but since she had never mentioned it, he never got around to it, and it seemed like a moot point now. Things were going well, she was supportive of his rapid improvement, and he felt vindicated by his speedy recovery that God really was on His side.

"Right, Jake?" Debron turned around and smiled at him winsomely.

Jake shook his head to refocus on the conversation happening up front. Debron had the day off from school for some kind of teacher work day, and since Jake had been trying to invest as much time in the kid as possible, he'd figured this experience would be good for him. Debron, of course, was thrilled.

"I was just telling Mr. Ross here about how much bigger this year's basketball camp is going to be."

"Bigger? Don't you think a hundred is big enough? That had to have been virtually every kid from the neighborhood, plus some. I'm okay with getting *better*, but bigger...?"

"Nah, there's a whole lot more of us in the projects. And a ton of kids from my school said they wanna come this year."

"Sounds like you've started something, Jake," Kevin said from the driver's seat.

"Don't you remember how crazy it was last year?"

"Yeah. Crazy awesome. But obviously we're gonna need to expand. I figure we'll need at least two more courts. Those tennis courts that nobody uses will work great. Whose stupid idea was it to build those in the hood, anyway? Everybody knows poor people don't play tennis. We'll definitely need more coaches, too," Debron chattered on. "Jake, I'll let you handle that, but hey, Mr. Ross, you probably got some connections, too, right?"

Jake saw a smile appear on Kevin's face in the rearview mirror.

"Yeah, I think I could help you find some more guys to help."

"Coo'. And the jerseys were cool from last year and all, but I think we should all get a T-shirt, too. You know, the official looking ones like what the rich kids get at their camps. That would be awesome."

Jake chuckled. "Okay, okay, dreamer. And where are we going to get the money to do all this?"

"I don't know. I've been talking to God about it. I'm sure He can figure something out," Debron said matter-of-factly.

Jake leaned back listening to Debron prattle on about his dreams and he smiled. Talk about speedy progress. Jake loved how far this kid had come in the six months since he'd raised his hand to invite Jesus into his life. Whereas before he would just roll his eyes any time Jake brought up God, now he ate up anything Jake told him and was a walking example of the kind of childlike faith Jesus spoke so passionately about. The kid who never stopped talking actually listened!

At the high school, Jake hobbled into the classroom he was scheduled to speak in and immediately students started whispering and staring. When the bell rang for lunch, many of them stuck around, and more and more students quickly trickled in. By the time Jake was introduced to speak, the room was so packed that there were people sitting on the ground in between desks, all along the back and side walls, and anywhere else there was an inch of space. Jake figured he had less to do with the huge turnout than the free pizza, but it was exhilarating nonetheless.

Sitting in the teacher's big swivel chair and propping his leg up on a desk, he started his spiel while nearly a hundred young people munched on the free lunch.

"The day I received my scholarship offer to play at Louisville was the best day of my life," he began. "I was living the dream, getting everything I ever wanted: popularity, success, and even a hot girlfriend..." By now, he'd shared his story so many times that he could do it without even thinking. But today, the cumbersome brace covering his once nimble right leg added the perfect extra touch.

"I know you've all probably heard about Jesus before. Maybe some of you pray a quick prayer before your games that you'll win or that you won't get hurt." Jake looked down at his knee.

"I guess I didn't pray hard enough." Muffled snickers sounded throughout the room. "Here's the deal, though. You don't really know what your faith is about until you're taken through a storm. As you can tell, I'm learning that all over again right now. But ultimately, the only thing that really matters in life is your faith. Without faith, we're toast."

Jake pulled a few permanent markers out of his pocket and started unfastening his brace while talking. "So I want to make you a deal. Wherever you're at in your walk with God—whether you're still just checking Him out or you're already all in—I want you to go even deeper. Psalm 34:8 says, 'Taste and see that the Lord is good.' So go ahead; dig in. See how much richer He makes your life.

"They say it takes twenty-one days to start a habit. Give God your next three weeks, and just watch how your faith grows. Read your Bible every day, get involved in your youth group, reach out and share God's love with others. The more you do it, I guarantee you, the more you're going to grow." Jake lifted up his knee, which was now simply covered in a tan cloth wrap. "So here's the deal. I've got three weeks left of recovery until I make my comeback. While I'm working through my storm for the next twenty-one days, will you commit to working out your own faith? I often get asked for my autograph, but today I want to turn the tables. If you're willing to step up to my challenge, then could you come up here and give me yours, right here on my bandage. If you do, I commit to praying for you by name every day until I get to throw this dirty thing away."

The students laughed and almost immediately started flocking to the front of the classroom. They gathered around him long after the warning bell rang for them to get to class, until finally the teacher had to shoo them all out. Finally, Jake stood up, his leg a colorful patchwork of different names. His message sure seemed to have struck a nerve. Now he just needed to remember to follow through on praying for them every day.

"That was a pretty clever object lesson you used in there," Kevin said as they walked out of the school to the van. "It's such a powerful reminder to these students how fleeting athletic stardom can be...and that life is about so much more. Win or lose, succeed or fail, the only thing that really matters is our relationship with God. Sometimes we forget that, you know? Thanks for the reminder."

Debron grabbed a pen from Jake's pocket. "Yeah man, I wanna sign my name, too. 'Tho' you might not want to throw mine away, cuz it'll definitely be worth money someday." He laughed, a charming smile turning his usual arrogant banter into something much more endearing. "Just kidding, man. I think I wanna start reading my Bible every day. Buddy said the book of Mark is a good place to start. There's a kid named Mark at my school that's real mean, but maybe I can learn something..."

Debron chattered on, but Jake's mind slowed down to a crawl. He found himself bristling at Kevin's compliment but gripped by Debron's commitment. How many sixth graders out there would be interested in reading their Bibles every day? Jake was pretty sure this was not the norm. And to think that he'd played a role in bringing Debron to that point...It was mind-blowing! Jake wondered if this is how Chris felt every day in youth ministry. *No wonder he loves his job so much!*

50

AMY ENDED HER NIGHTLY CONVERSATION
with Jake, enamored as usual with her fiancé. She was so proud
of how hard he was working to get back to full health, and even
though she sometimes wondered if he was pushing it too hard,
God seemed to be definitely working alongside him. Tonight, she
had been thrilled to hear about his speaking engagement at the
FCA club. Jake's idea to have the kids autograph his bandage was
brilliant. What a great way to use his trial as an object lesson.

Amy was also completely impressed by Debron. What a special kid! He had such a noble goal to spread the love of Jesus
through this basketball camp. He reminded her a lot of Bogdana.

Bogdana's Dream had sure been going well. In the month
or so since all of the Christmas fundraising events, money had
not stopped rolling in and Amy was flabbergasted by the support people were showing. Not only had they surpassed her far-
fetched hope to reach the $20,000 mark, they had also blown her
$60,000 fantasy out of the water. At last count, contributions
had exceeded $100,000, and they just kept coming. Thanks to
Mr. Cunningham's connections, more fundraisers were in the
works, and he was also teaching her how to find and write grants
to procure additional funds.

"So what's next?" he had asked after the doll-making dream was fully funded. The question came with a promise of an additional $100,000 if Amy found a worthwhile venue for his generosity.

Amy had never thought beyond raising what seemed to be the impossible sum required to make all of Bogdana's dolls. And it wasn't like she had the time to just sit around all day making up new ideas. She felt like she was just barely scraping by in her studies this semester. While the honors research program was an incredible opportunity, it was certainly not a walk in the park. Add to that all of her other responsibilities and she felt like she was barely keeping her head above water.

Just last night, she had written desperately in her prayer journal, "Lord, You obviously are thinking way bigger than me in this. I need Your help! If You want me to do something else, then give me some extra time, and give me an idea."

Sitting at her desk now, thinking about Bogdana and Debron and Jake and her crazy life, she suddenly was struck with an idea. The more she thought about it, a marvelous plan started unfolding in her mind. She quickly opened a new email to Edward Cunningham and started typing feverishly away. *Well, that's a great idea, God; now I just need the time!*

AS TOUGH AS THE PHYSICAL THERAPY had been for Jake, the worst part by far of this whole ordeal with his knee had been the separation from his team. He still showed up for the first few minutes of practice every day, but as soon as they started doing drills and running plays, that was his cue to hit the pool or the weight room or therapy. Working out on his own had its benefits, but basketball is a team sport and he missed the guys.

Even worse than missing out on practice was missing out on games. Watching from the bench was sheer torture, especially as the team started falling to their tough opponents in the Big East. What started off as a 9-0 season before Jake's injury quickly disintegrated to 13-5, and their top-five ranking plummeted nearly off the charts. Barely hanging on at number twenty-five for the past two weeks, they desperately needed a miracle to pull their wonder season back together, and Jake was desperately hoping that miracle could be his knee.

While restricted from the court, he was determined to improve his game in every other way, and as the weeks progressed, he intensified his film analysis even more than before. Jake studied the top teams in the nation with a vengeance and passed on his copious notes to the guys. He found himself enjoying this mental side of the game, fascinated by the strategy teams used based on their strengths and weaknesses and intrigued by the idiosyncratic tendencies even the best players often fell into. The more he scrutinized their soft spots, the easier it appeared to capitalize on them, and Jake couldn't wait to apply his new findings to the game himself.

February 2 had been circled on his calendar ever since his surgery, and as Syracuse continued charging undefeated through their season, Jake grew more and more eager to topple them. That's all he could think about today as he walked into his afternoon follow-up appointment.

"Wow," was all that the doctor said as he walked Jake through a battery of tests and measurements.

"Is 'wow' a good thing or bad?" Jake clarified.

The doctor sat back on his stool and looked Jake in the eye. "Definitely good. I can tell you've been working hard."

"I have!"

"Well, good job. I'm proud of you. Your range of motion is one-hundred percent, the swelling is completely gone, your support muscles are strong...your knee looks great."

"Really? Does that mean I can start playing again?"

"Yes. Slowly. Your ACL is still a little weak, leaving your knee a little less stable and still prone to further injury, but if you ease into it, it will continue to heal up nicely and be ready to perform when you need it."

"Won't the brace help?"

"Yes...and no. I want you to keep wearing it for the next few weeks, but it isn't a miracle worker. It will give you a little extra support, but more than anything, it will slow you down and keep you from doing anything too crazy."

That made sense. Jake couldn't imagine being very quick and nimble while wearing the cumbersome apparatus. "So...," he began hesitantly, "do you think I'll be ready by the second?"

The doctor smiled and patted him on the knee. "Keep doing what you're doing, Jake, and I think you've still got a little bit of season left in you."

Cherishing those words like a pot of gold, Jake walked out of the office feeling like a new man. That night after dinner, Jake convinced Grant to join him for their first jog together in months.

"Are you sure you're supposed to be running the streets? All that pounding can't be good for your knee."

"Grant. The doctor cleared me to go back. How am I supposed to play basketball if I can't run? Besides, we'll go slow." He ducked into his room and quickly brought out a ball. "And I figured you could be the first to run me through some drills." He tossed Grant a firm chest pass with a smile.

"Okay, man, but you better not hurt yourself out there. Coach would kill me."

"No one will ever know."

Of course, that promise was impossible. The moment they arrived at their favorite neighborhood court, the word spread like wildfire and kids poured out of their homes.

"Hey, man, why didn't you call me?" Debron walked up with a little attitude.

"Sorry, bro," Jake apologized sincerely. "It was a spontaneous decision. The doctor cleared me today to start practicing again, and I thought I might test it out here."

Debron looked at him with narrow eyes, then broke out in a smile. "Sure thing, man. Hey guys!" He turned to the gathering throng and started shooing them back with his arms. "Let's give the man some space. He ain't played in awhile, though, so cut him slack if he sucks." He glanced at Jake over his shoulder and winked.

Jake started with a series of layups. He intentionally didn't go up too high in order to avoid putting much weight on his right leg, but it was feeling pretty good. Then he moved to short jump shots around the key. Grant shagged the rebounds that were mostly nothing but net. Again, Jake kept his hops low out of caution, but his legs felt fresh and wanted to soar. Getting bolder, Jake moved a few steps back toward the invisible three-point line. With a little more force on his knee, he knocked down shot after shot like he had only dreamed about the last couple months.

Grant knew his roommate well and began to commentate. "Jake Taylor, the newly-healed Louisville star makes his comeback in style. Knocking down threes without effort, he wows the packed crowd..." —the kids started cheering enthusiastically— "and proves that he most definitely hasn't lost his touch." Grant tossed Jake the rebound.

Feeling better than expected, Jake crouched down a little to test out his knee. It still felt perfect. He slowly dropped the ball and caught it with his left hand. Dribbling between hands, he absorbed the power of each recoil, feeling more and more energized with each bounce. Slowly, he started to move forward.

Grant stepped up to lightly cover him. "Undaunted by the formidable defense, he charges to the hoop."

Jake leaned right and then pushed off of his right leg to go around Grant.

"He fakes right with a head nod and goes left, breaking his defender's ankles like a number-two pencil." Grant glanced over to Debron and winked.

"Oof," Jake grunted as he stumbled. He'd felt a little click and his knee had just sort of given way, but now he was fine...mostly. A dull throb started to pulsate at the front of the joint, but it was nothing bad enough to make him quit.

"Jake! You okay?" Grant ran up behind him.

"Yeah, yeah, I'm fine," Jake lied as he jogged easily to the hoop and laid the ball up. "I must have just slipped on a pebble or something. This crazy court with all its cracks, you know," he called back over his shoulder.

Grant looked at Jake suspiciously, but backed away as Jake dribbled the ball back to half court and then drove the lane for another layup.

The slight discomfort wasn't going away, so after a few more minutes of play, Jake knew he needed to call it an evening. They bid goodnight to their young fans and jogged slowly back to their apartment, where Jake promptly made up a bag of ice and settled on the couch to treat his knee.

Aside from that one little hitch, he'd felt great all night, which filled him with hope. But as he lay back trying to rest, he just couldn't shake the foreboding feeling of dread that kept trying to creep back into his mind. What if his knee didn't heel in time? What if he reinjured it? He was doing everything the doctors and trainers told him to—everything and more. But what if all that just wasn't enough? *You're fine!* he scolded himself. *It was just one little bump. Don't be so worried!* He leaned his head back and closed his eyes, trying to focus on how good the three-pointers had felt. Suddenly, his phone rang.

It was Chris.

"Hey, Jake!" his youth pastor's voice sounded through the phone's speaker.

"Hey! Guess where I just was?"

"Uh...the bathroom?"

"Ha. Good guess." Jake laughed. "Nah. Grant and I just jogged down to Debron's neighborhood and I made my debut back to the court."

"No way! How was it?"

"Awesome! Seriously, Chris, I have missed it so much, and it felt so good to be out there again."

"Jake, that's great. I'm proud of you. I know you've worked really hard."

"Yeah." He shook his head and exhaled. Unfortunately, the hardest part might just be starting. Getting comfortable with the ball again and refusing to be tentative in his cuts and pivots...that was going to be tough.

"So how's your goal of praying for all those students going?"

Jake chuckled. Chris always knew how to keep him challenged. "Pretty good, actually." He smiled.

"Tell me about it."

"Well, I'll admit I had a tough time getting going. A lot of kids signed their names, and it was hard to keep track of them all. Not to mention just *reading* through their names extended my prayer time by a ton."

"I'll bet."

"But I told them I'd do it, so I felt bad every night that I never got around to it. So I decided to get creative. I rewrote all the names in alphabetical order and had the card laminated so I could carry it with me everywhere—including the pool. That way I can double up praying for them with working out."

"That's brilliant!"

"You think? I don't know. It's worked, though. And it's been so cool. God keeps reminding me of who different students were, so I have faces to match with the names. I've never been good at remembering people, so that's just been crazy. And He's making me really care about them. I keep picturing myself back in high school, and what an impact you had on me. They're in such a pivotal time in their lives, and it feels almost like a privilege to have a part in praying for them as they try to head in the right direction. I don't know; does that even make any sense? I know I'm just rambling here."

"Absolutely, Jake. That's why I do what I do."

"I don't know, though. Sometimes I wonder if just praying will really make any difference. It just seems like there's more I could do."

"Maybe so. But God's far more concerned with your obedience than your impact."

Jake chuckled. "That sounds like something Buddy told me when I was thinking about going for the draft. 'God's far more concerned with your conduct and character than your vocation and location.'"

"He's a wise man." Both guys were silent for a few moments before Chris spoke up again. "Jake, there's something I've felt like God's been wanting me to ask you for awhile now, but I've just been too chicken to do it."

ALL or NOTHING

"Okay?" Jake asked cautiously.

"What if the NBA isn't in your future? Would you be okay with that?"

Jake exhaled slowly, feeling the same irritation he had in his tense conversation with Amy after the surgery. "Uhhh...," he started, unsure how to respond.

"Look, I don't mean to put a damper on things, and I couldn't be happier that your recovery is going so well. But sometimes, we just have to ask ourselves the tough questions."

"Yeah," Jake replied curtly, his head boiling with emotions.

Later that night, he lay in bed, still unable to fall asleep after hours of tossing and turning. Chris's question was just the icing on top of layers of other doubts people like Amy, Buddy, Kevin Ross, and even his own mom had raised. Jake didn't want to listen to them, because in his mind it admitted defeat, but God wouldn't seem to let him run away.

All right, God, is that what You want? Jake fumed. *You want me to give up, just like that. It just doesn't seem fair that You'd let me get this far only to pull the rug out from under me. I don't know, God. People keep raising these doubts in my mind, but You're the one allowing my knee to heal so quickly. I want to do what You want; I really do. But I love basketball. And imagine how much good I can do for You from the pros.*

Jake flopped over onto his back and stared angrily up at his ceiling. A quiet impression filled his brain. *Jake, I can use you for a lot of good anywhere.*

Ack! Jake bristled. *But why not use me where I'd most enjoy it?*

Are you sure that's what you'd enjoy most?

Sighing, Jake relented. Who was he to tell God the facts? *Fine. Whatever You want. Just know that I think I'd like to at least give the NBA a try.* He twisted vigorously to his left side and slapped his head on the pillow to find the right spot.

As he lay there pouting, he could have sworn God's voice was nearly audible. *Thank you.*

52

FEBRUARY 2 ARRIVED BEFORE JAKE KNEW IT, and sitting on the bench waiting to be introduced at the start of the game felt surreal. Several times already he had shaken his head just to make sure he wasn't dreaming. After working through his comeback with Coach, it had been decided that Jake would resume his starting position, but for this first game at least, his minutes would be minimal. Jake hated the kid-glove treatment he was getting, but anything was better than nothing, and he figured the harder he could play, the more Coach—and the scouts—would see that he was completely back to health.

The fans roared when his name was called, and posters and banners welcoming him back waved vibrantly all around the packed arena. Jake tried to keep his ego in check, but he couldn't deny that the appreciation felt unbelievable.

The ball was tossed into play and Tyler flipped it to Nate who passed it to Jake who started running it down the court. Nomis cut toward the basket and Jake hurled it to his ready hands with perfect accuracy. Nomis skied toward the hoop and dunked the ball with a resounding thud. *Not a bad start.* Jake grinned at his friends and backpedaled onto defense.

His matchup was an all-star senior who had also chosen to defer his entry into the draft. He obviously knew that Jake was fresh off an injury and tried to capitalize on that potential weakness by cutting and weaving all over the court. Jake caught himself responding tentatively a few times, but the longer his opponent did it the more it fueled Jake to annihilate him. It was the thrill of Jake's night when the Syracuse coach pulled him out for a breather before Jake was relieved.

By the time Coach finally did call him out, Jake had scored eight points and four assists. Not bad for his first ten minutes. Jadon, Jake's replacement at point, seemed to step it up a notch once he got into the game and by halftime, the Cardinals were leading the Orangemen 44-41. The game was far from over, but everyone was energized.

Coach was far more conservative with Jake the second half and signaled him out after only four minutes. Jake was bummed, but his knee was starting to feel a little tender, so he jogged off the court with as good of an attitude as he could muster.

"Stay ready for the end," Coach called out to him. "I want you to remember what it feels like." He smiled briefly then quickly turned back to the action on the court.

Jake joined some of the freshmen at the end of the bench and gingerly massaged his slightly swelling knee.

"You okay?" one of them asked.

"Yeah, yeah." Jake smiled. "Just working it back into shape."

The rest of the half was a battle, with Syracuse pulling itself into the lead momentarily until Louisville grappled back to the top, and back and forth and back and forth like an erratic teeter-totter. Engrossed in the action, Jake almost didn't hear Coach's call with two minutes to go. But when the freshman next to him nudged him, Jake sprung into action, tossing the heat pack he was using aside, and running over to check in. This was it—his opportunity to help the team, his shot to see if he still had it, his chance to shine.

Jake inbounded the ball with a minute and forty-three seconds to go. Immediately he noticed that Syracuse's defense was stretching out pretty wide. "Card-Four!" he quickly shouted and held up four fingers. Instantly, Nomis set a screen for Nate and Tyler set a cross-pick for Grant while Jake raced to the other side. Grant's man recovered too rapidly but Nate had a split-second opening at the top of the key. Jake flung him the pass and Nate caught the ball and shot it in one fluid motion. Swish! Louisville was up by one.

Syracuse inbounded the ball without hesitation and their big man cut loose toward the basket. Jake was the only one in his vicinity and he sprinted to thwart the open shot. Tearing down a straight course toward collision, warning bells went off in Jake's head, but he knew that if he heeded them, he'd be that much more timid the next time, and fear had no place in an elite athlete's mind. So he pressed forward, discerning that the Syracuse passer's arm was sending the ball in a slightly different trajectory than the big man was heading. Jake slightly corrected his path and a split-second later intercepted the pass. The crowd erupted in approval, and Jake couldn't help but smile. All that studying of film was paying off!

He brought the ball back to half court and called for his team to set up Three High. Tyler popped up to the free-throw line just in time to receive the pass. As anticipated, Jake's defender dropped back a few steps to collapse on the threat, wherein Tyler popped the ball right back out to Jake, who sunk an easy three-pointer from the wing. Louisville led by four.

Syracuse took their time setting up with this possession, but the Cardinals did their job in sticking to them, and ultimately they had to settle for an ugly shot without a look just before the shot clock sounded.

The ball bounced hard out to Jake's waiting hands and immediately two Syracuse men clobbered him. With less than thirty seconds to go, a foul was their only option, even if it was their twelfth one of the half. Jake stepped calmly up to the free-throw line. Until he'd been cleared to start practicing again, this had been his sanctuary and he'd faithfully shot at least a hundred baskets a day to keep his form sharp and his muscle memory fresh. The referee handed him the ball and he slowly bounced it once, twice, three times, then cocked the ball and released it in a single graceful motion. Louisville was up by five. Jake sank the second free throw just as easily, extending the Cardinal's lead to six with twenty-seven seconds remaining.

Syracuse inbounded the ball once again, and Louisville met them with a full-court press. Jake ran over to trap the point guard with Nate and took advantage of his opponent's characteristically high bounce when looking for an outlet to strip him of the ball. Streaking back to the basket, Jake felt so good that he contemplated dunking, just for fun. But reason prevailed and, remembering how far down the landing would be, he settled for the easy layup. Nineteen seconds to go and Louisville was sitting pretty at 76-68.

With one more possession, Syracuse gave it all they had, but the Louisville men stayed tough and the ball careened off the backboard without scoring as the final buzzer sounded. Louisville had broken Syracuse's undefeated season, and Jake had played better than he could have ever dreamed. Nineteen points and six assists with a rebound and two steals to boot would have been a great game before his surgery. Tonight, it felt exceptional.

Jake couldn't wipe the smile off his face as he jogged back to the bench amidst plenty of slaps on the back from both his teammates and even his opponents. Nights like these were the reason he couldn't imagine giving up this sport he loved, and he was so grateful that God had helped him make this comeback.

At the sideline, he was suddenly barraged by a horde of reporters clamoring for his attention.

"Jake, your return to the hardwood tonight was pretty remarkable. How do you feel?"

Jake shook his head with a grin. "I begged God not to take basketball away from me, and it looks like He gave me a second chance," he panted. "I can't thank Him enough."

More reporters closed in around him, but Jake had said all he needed to say. He pushed his way to the locker room, tucking in between Grant and Tyler as soon as he had the chance.

✚ ✚ ✚

The rest of the month of February looked just about as good. Jake averaged eighteen points and bumped up his assists to nine per game. Coach still limited him to about twenty-five minutes of play each night, reminding him that they still needed him in the post-season. With six more wins and only one loss, they ended the regular season with a 21-8 record, which had bumped them back up to seventeenth in the rankings. It was a far cry from their beautiful start, but rankings didn't mean anything anyway once the post-season began.

Louisville ended up losing to Syracuse by four in the Big East championship game, a tough loss but not the end of the world, since their season continued in the more-important NCAA tournament. Seeded fifth in their bracket, they breezed through the first three rounds into a Sweet Sixteen game against seventh-ranked Texas A&M. They ultimately emerged victorious from that hard-fought battle, but were exhausted in the process. Hobbling into the Elite Eight round two days later, they buckled down to business, however, and were pleased to bring the unlikely Cinderella-run of eleventh-seeded Gonzaga to an end.

The Cardinals' dream season that had temporarily spun into an unexpected nightmare was back on track, and they eagerly set their sights on the illustrious Final Four the following weekend. Just being there was an amazing accomplishment, and they all tried to soak up as much enjoyment as possible from the publicity-filled event. But what they were really gunning for was the Championship game, and "all" they needed to do was unseat top-ranked Kansas to get there.

The game was physical from the start, and by halftime, Jake was really starting to feel worn down. He'd tried to ignore it, but the sporadic clicking and sticking in his knee that he'd been hiding from everyone—including himself—all month was really starting to hinder his movement. His agility severely diminished, he overcompensated with effort, but all the energy he was expending to keep up was taking its toll on him. Nevertheless, he'd been having a tremendous night. Fourteen points were already notched onto his belt, and his eight assists were setting him on pace for a career high. The whole team was rising to the challenge, and with three other players approaching double-digit scoring, they led Kansas 43-35 going into halftime.

Jake stood up from their midgame pep talk, and his knee buckled causing him to fall over into Nate.

"Whoah, you okay dude?"

"Sorry. Just lost my balance for a sec."

Nate bought the line, but Jake was a little worried. Sitting still for that long had allowed stiffness to settle in, and he wondered if he'd be able to warm his knee up in time. He tried not to limp, but couldn't figure out how not to, and before he made it out of the players' tunnel, Coach had seen him.

"Jake, you're playing phenomenally tonight, but I think we should let Jadon start the half."

"No. Coach, I'm okay. I just need to warm up a little again."

"I agree. And let's let Jadon fill in while you do that. If the team needs you, I want you to be ready."

With no other recourse, Jake fell into step behind Coach. He immediately got to work with the heating pad, and once the game started, he watched from his perch on a stationary bike, hoping the constant motion would loosen his joint up.

Sure enough, five minutes later, the Louisville lead had crumbled to one and Coach signaled for Jake to jump in. Jake didn't waste any time, attacking the Kansas defense as if they were made of straw. Within five more minutes, he had bumped the lead back up to six and earned three more assists in the process. The Cardinal offense was running like a well-oiled machine, and Jake was having the time of his life.

For the entire second half so far, Jake had favored his knee by avoiding the inside traffic himself, choosing instead to dish out well-timed passes to his unstoppable teammates. But this time down the court, after some great fakes and a couple of beautifully executed picks by his guys, the key was wide open, and Jake just couldn't resist. He charged the lane and launched himself into the air just as a Kansas big man recovered in time to throw his body into Jake. At once Jake heard a pop and felt a piercing pain tear through his leg. He released the ball and crashed to the floor, reactively clutching his knee in agony. The Kansas forward toppled over him and his hulking frame landed on top of Jake's leg, while the ball, which somehow miraculously fell through the net, thud-ded mere millimeters from Jake's face before bouncing off toward the sidelines. Jake groaned as the commotion all around him faded to an excruciating white fuzz.

When Jake regained consciousness, he was lying immobilized in an ambulance. He tried to lift his head and speak, but it took too much effort and he succumbed to another blackout.

The next time Jake came to, he found himself in a hospital emergency room, alone behind a curtain. He heard the hustle and bustle of motion all around him, but inside his little "room" all was quiet. Taking advantage of the tranquility, he did a grad-ual self-evaluation. He rolled his neck and shoulders, wiggled his fingers, and tried to sit up...which immediately sent shocks of pain shooting up and down his right leg. He strained his neck to see what was going on down there, but the only thing he could see was a giant bag of ice. He didn't need to know any more.

He'd been banged up plenty of times before, not the least of which was his recent debilitating injury, but this felt different. It was the same knee, but this time it felt like it was barely hanging on by a shoe string to the rest of his leg. This was definitely not a re-injury of the same problem. This was something worse.

Jake dropped his head back down and choked back tears. Chris's words echoed through his mind. *What if the NBA isn't in your future? Would you be okay with that?* A million differ-ent angry rebuttals tinged with self-pity, regret, and devastation raced after the questions, but they didn't help. With no one but his thoughts to keep him company, Jake turned to the only friend available.

God, I don't really want to talk to you right now...but I have no one else. I don't get it. Why is this happening? How can this be your plan for my life? Everything was going so perfectly and...and I gave You all the credit. What more do You want?

The curtain was yanked open and in hurried a harried-look-ing nurse.

"How are you feeling, son?" he asked as he checked Jake's vitals and jotted notes on a clipboard.

"I've been better," Jake responded even though he was pretty sure the guy wasn't even listening.

"Well, they're ready for you in Imaging, so we're going to wheel you over for your MRI."

Another nurse walked in pushing a wheelchair and the two of them hoisted Jake down into it. Whizzing past doctors and patients, they headed down a hallway and through some swinging doors before entering a room with the large MRI machine. Having gone through all this a mere four months ago, Jake was only too familiar with the routine and unenthusiastically endured all the jostling and rigmarole. They slid him into the cylinder and the loud whirring began. Trying to drown out the racket, Jake's thoughts once again turned to self-pity and resentment.

Long before he was done with his internal ranting, the scanning was done and he was wheeled to his own private room. Jake had no idea how much time had passed, but he was sure the game was over. He wondered if they'd pulled out the victory. And he wondered how long it would take for Coach or some of his friends to come see him. He felt so alone.

Wallowing in his misery, Jake was completely taken by surprise when the door opened and in walked Amy and his mom.

"Jake!" they both exclaimed in unison as they rushed to his side and smothered him with hugs.

"Amy! Mom! How—? What—? When did you guys get here?"

"Here, as in the hospital, or here, as in Atlanta?" Amy asked with a smile.

"Uh...both?"

"There is no way I was going to miss my son's appearance in the Final Four!" His mom began getting a little teary. "So, last minute, we decided to come out here and surprise you."

"We barely made it like fifteen minutes before the game," Amy added.

"You played so well, Jake!"

"And then..." Amy's voice trailed off and her eyes brimmed over with tears.

"When you hurt yourself, it took us forever to find someone to tell us where they took you—"

"But we rushed here as fast as we could. Sorry you had to be alone for so long."

Both women's eyes were red and teary, and Jake wondered if they'd had a harder time of it than him. "It is so good to see you." He grinned and grabbed both of their hands, but he couldn't take his eyes off of Amy. "So good."

"So are you doing okay?" his mom asked tentatively, brushing the hair off of his forehead.

Out of nowhere, Jake felt his own eyes getting watery and a lump forming in his throat. He tried to force another grin but it turned into a grimace and all he could do was shrug. "I'm kind of having a tough time with this," he finally whispered and averted his eyes.

As his mom continued stroking his forehead, Amy rubbed his arm. His knee was still very much a problem, but just having the two most important women in his life beside him made things feel a whole lot better.

"It just doesn't seem fair," Amy murmured.

Jake had no problem running down that road on his own, but with them in the room, he suddenly wanted to jump out of the mucky pit he had dug for himself. "So, did we win the game?" he asked abruptly.

"Always the competitor." His mom chuckled.

"We didn't watch the end," Amy said. "But with all the delays in trying to find you, we heard that the final score was 68-65... Louisville!"

"What? No way!" Jake let out a huge holler. They had done it! They had made it to the Championship Game. Jake only wished he could have been there with his team to celebrate. But still, he had been a part of that win...*God let me play a part in it.* The realization dawned on Jake and filled him with new appreciation.

"Apparently Jadon Williams stepped up to lead the team pretty well. But you were the one who got them into position." Amy smiled and chucked Jake on the shoulder.

"I knew I liked that kid." Jake grinned.

Suddenly, the door flung open again and Coach walked through, followed by the entire squad. Coach patted his star point guard on his good leg while the rest of the team crowded around his bed, clearly unsure of what to say. Then Nomis stepped forward and handed Jake an Elmo-playing-basketball get-well-soon balloon.

"What's a hospital visit without a balloon?" He shrugged.

"Thanks, man. I love Elmo." Jake grinned then turned to Jadon. "So I heard you partied like an all-star after I left." He held up his hand for a high five. "Thanks."

"Hey, you were the one who got us there," Jadon replied. "I just held on for dear life." The guys all chuckled.

"Well, hang on for one more game...'cause we're playing for the championship, baby!"

Everyone cheered and started talking about their final game against Ohio State. With over a dozen big guys in the room, it was definitely pretty crowded, and Amy and Pam excused themselves to go find some coffee.

As soon as the door clicked behind them, several of the newer guys let out whistles.

"Whew, now we know why Taylor isn't interested in any of the girls at school!"

"How'd a guy like you end up with a girl like her?"

"Mmhm! I don't know how you survive without getting any action... I wouldn't last a night with a girl like that."

"Seriously! Man, how you do it?"

Jake just shook his head and smiled. His teammates couldn't fathom how—or why!—he'd decided to wait until marriage to have sex again, but they were definitely intrigued by his unusual choice. And since he defended it with confidence, they even seemed to respect it. "From what I hear, married sex knocks what you guys are doing out of the water. Let's just call this my long-term investment. I'm going to be having fun long after you guys are washed out and alone." He grinned.

"Shoot, I ain't never gonna be washed out."

"You sure about that? Meet me here in fifty years and let's see whose getting it more then."

"Ohhhhh!" came the resonant reply.

Jake could only hope that some of them might take his example to heart.

Amy and Pam eventually returned and the conversation stayed light for the next twenty minutes or so until a doctor came in to check on Jake.

"Well, Mr. Taylor, we're sending your MRI results to your doctor in Louisville, and that's about all we can do for you here. Until he examines them, there's nothing more for you to do besides staying off your knee and managing the pain. We'll send you home with some prescription ibuprofen to reduce the swelling and ease the pain, and I recommend using plenty of ice."

"So, you think I'll be all healed up for the big game?" Jake asked with a smirk.

He looked at Jake with a glimmer of sympathy. "I'm afraid you're going to have to sit this one out, son. Best of luck to you." And with that, he breezed out of the room.

The atmosphere instantly dampened and finally Coach spoke up. "Well, Jake, I guess we'd better be heading back to the hotel. I'm assuming you'll want to stay with your mom and...future wife?" He gave Jake a wink. The guys responded with good-natured catcalls and whistles, and Amy playfully flaunted her ring.

Jake grabbed her hand and winked back. "Thanks, Coach."

The guys started trickling out, but Coach lingered behind. He leaned over to take Jake's free hand and patted it. "You've had a good run, Jake."

Jake sighed. "I'm sorry I couldn't take us all the way. I—"

Tears glistened faintly in Coach's eyes as he cut Jake off. "Don't be sorry for anything you've done, Jake. You have led our team to more than just victories—your very presence leads us to becoming better men. You have inspired me and encouraged me and even taught me a few things." He paused for a second and then added, "And if this setback makes you want to come back for another season, it would be my pleasure to coach you one more year." Standing back up straight, he looked Jake in the eyes. "I want you sitting next to me during our big game in two days. Who knows what good ideas you might have after all that studying film you've done." He turned to Amy and Pam. "Ms. Taylor, Ms. Briggs. Take good care of this guy."

Soon after he left, a nurse walked in with a wheelchair and a bag of information for Jake. He signed some paperwork and then was released. Pam went ahead to pull their rental car up while Amy pushed him toward the exit, and he couldn't do anything but go along for the ride. Today had started off with such great hope and anticipation, and now, just like that, it was over, with only a throbbing damaged knee to show for it.

God? I could kind of use some help here, he begged as the cool evening air stung his eyes.

Two nights later, Jake joined Coach at the front of the bench as requested, and watched his team give their all against a superior Ohio State squad. His guys had surrounded him in the locker room before warm-ups and told him they were dedicating the game to him. Jake was floored by the honor and used all his strength to keep himself together in front these mighty men, but when he looked around he realized that his were far from the only moist eyes in the room.

Every guy dug deep on the court and gave the Buckeyes a run for their money, but ultimately the Cardinals fell by twelve. It was a heartbreaking loss at the end of a tumultuous season, but they all knew they had every reason to be proud of themselves. They had beaten the odds and held nothing back, and while their team might not be listed in the record books as champions, they all knew that being number two in the country is not an accomplishment to scoff at. Losing never feels good, but falling in the final round was an achievement no one but them could claim this year.

Jake hugged each one of his teammates, knowing that regardless of his future, this group of guys would never play together again. After redshirting his freshman year, Nomis had finally expended all of his eligibility, and while his prospects in the NBA didn't look so promising, a stint playing overseas had potential. Nate, too, was graduating, and he was already looking forward to the NBA combines starting next month. Tyler had stuck around for a surprise second season, but wasn't likely to skip the draft this year. With those three gone, all that was left was Grant, finishing off his fifth year, and the slew of current freshmen. Next year definitely wouldn't be the same.

Jake tottered on his crutches down the corridor to the locker room, pondering how anticlimactic this end had turned out. In his dreams, it had always seemed so much more...fantastic.

SPRING

53

THE SPRING DAY WAS BLUSTERY, with clouds overhead threatening to burst at any moment. Jake hobbled into the sports injury clinic that he had come to know and...not quite love...with Amy by his side. His mom had flown out two hours ago, but Amy had five more days before she had to return to school. Unlike her spring break visit three years ago, Jake had found her a place to stay with Travis's girlfriend, and thanks to the searing discomfort of his knee, physical boundaries weren't likely to be an issue.

Amy had done a great job of creating structure for their time together—or in other words, she had assembled a rigorous study schedule with which she would help Jake get caught up in all his classes. In their free time, she was excited to discuss wedding plans with him. While the activities—or lack thereof—didn't thrill Jake immensely, the unexpected opportunity to do the mundane with the girl he loved was better than a dream come true.

Their big day was approaching steadily, and while they still had three months to go, Amy kept reassuring Jake that the time would fly by. Gazing at his beautiful beloved now, he doubted it could go fast enough, but listening to Amy's endless list of preparations—in the midst of finishing her senior research and getting ready to graduate—reminded him that there were other important parts of a wedding beside the honeymoon.

Making the most of their wait in the doctor's office, Jake and Amy held hands and rested their heads against each other. If it wasn't for the unpleasant nature of the cause of their wait, it would have almost felt sublime. But all too soon, Jake was startled into reality when his name was called to head to the back. Amy helped him up and then gave him a shoulder to lean on as he hoisted himself onto the examination table in preparation for the doctor's assessment of his MRI.

It had been five days since his injury, and without the help of painkillers and ice, Jake didn't know how he would cope. The swelling wasn't going down, and the minute the medication started to wear off, the pain was excruciating. Based on his previous journey through physical therapy, he had attempted various exercises to regain range of motion, but beside the unbearable pain, sometimes his knee would just lock into place. Bottom line, he was pretty grim about what the doctor might tell him.

"Hello, Jake! Long time, no see." Dr. Gruber entered jovially. "You missed me that much, huh?"

"Something like that," Jake attempted to joke back.

Dr. Gruber pulled some transparent sheets out of a folder and pinned them up on the light box. He then turned to Jake looking serious. "Well, I can't tell you how much I wish I didn't have to see you under these circumstances. I'll cut to the chase. These look pretty bad." He uncapped a pen and circled several spots on each scan.

"If there's any good news in all of this, it's that your meniscus has remained intact. But that ACL you strained last time...it's gone. Completely ruptured. And it took a chunk of your bone with it."

Jake exhaled rapidly trying to take in this devastating news.

"And that's not even the worst of it," Dr. Gruber continued. "There's another piece of your bone missing that isn't anywhere near your ACL. We'll have to do some more tests to confirm, but it seems very likely that you've been hit by *Osteochondritis Dissecans*."

"Osteo-what?"

"It's a disease of the bone and cartilage that is most frequently seen in active young males. You're a little on the old side of the common spectrum, but given your lengthy involvement in sports, I'd say chances are high that you've been affected unknowingly with this problem for awhile. Causes aren't always known, but repeated trauma to a joint is a widespread culprit. Reduced blood flow to the tip of the bone causes it to die, and what you're left with is an increasingly sensitive joint surface. Sometimes, if the damage is minor and the joint is given rest, it can heal on its own over time, and sometimes there won't even be symptoms. But in the case of most athletes, it just gets worse and worse until a doctor finally catches it."

"So..." Jake started, unable to figure out where to start. Panicked questions bounced around in his brain, all pleading for a happy twist.

"So what are his next steps?" Amy jumped in, much to Jake's relief.

"The million dollar question." Dr. Gruber looked at both of them sympathetically. "Surgery is the first step. We'll have to reconstruct your ACL, probably using a graft from your patellar tendon. While we're in there, we'll remove the other loose fragment and possibly perform another graft to stimulate new bone and cartilage growth in the lesion caused by the OCD."

Jake felt like he was gasping for air. "Wow," he finally uttered, dreading the recovery those procedures must require. Despite his stellar comeback earlier in the season, he knew his draft stock had dropped to nil for this go around. But Coach's offer of finishing up his eligibility next season had started him thinking. What if he and Amy did move back to Louisville after the wedding? That wouldn't be the worst thing ever. If that's what it took to realize his dream of going pro, then it was totally worth it. What was one more year in the grand scheme of things? "So, like, what are we looking at? Six to nine months?" That would get him back in the action just as the season was heating up.

"It depends on what your goals are."

"Uh, like get back in the game."

Dr. Gruber almost laughed. "I was thinking more in the realm of walking, Jake. I know you're willing to work hard. I saw it last time. But these things just take time to heal. With an ACL tear like yours, most people take *at least* twelve to eighteen months to get back to normal, and the osteochondritis usually takes even longer to heal correctly. But that's just returning to everyday activities. At this point, I'm not sure if your knee will ever be ready for the rigors of twisting and pivoting and reacting that elite basketball requires."

Those words hit Jake's heart like a razor-sharp icicle.

"Plus, thanks to the OCD," Dr. Gruber continued, "you're now at risk for early-onset osteoarthritis." He paused and looked at Jake with kind eyes. "Bottom line, Jake: think about your future. We all know how hard you're willing to work. You beat the odds last time, and I'm sure you can do it again. If professional basketball is the only thing that will satisfy you, then hey, slow down your goals and let's get you started on this implausible uphill climb. But if you want to be able to take a walk with your wife,"—he nodded in Amy's direction— "if you want to be able to play ball with your kids, ten, twenty years from now, do yourself a favor and find a new dream."

Unable to breathe, Jake closed his eyes and braced himself on the table. Amy grabbed his hand, but it didn't help. The whole world felt like it was crashing down on him and he didn't know how to stop it. He'd had a hard enough time swallowing Chris's inquiries about abandoning his dream of the NBA, but this was even worse. Dr. Gruber was talking about never playing ball again. *God? Why are You letting this happen?*

"Jake, I'm sorry." Dr. Gruber patted his leg and stood up. "Figure out what you want, and I'll be here to help. Let's get your surgery scheduled right away, and we'll see what we can do." He turned to leave and then paused with his hand on the doorknob. "For what it's worth, you've sure had an exciting stint here in Louisville. Most guys would give anything to have a run in your shoes."

＋ ＋ ＋

The rest of the afternoon passed in a fog. Everything except for his knee felt numb, and Jake kept hoping this was all just a really bad nightmare. Unfortunately, he couldn't figure out how to wake up.

That night, they met Buddy for dinner, and Jake finally started figuring out how to put his seething emotions into words.

"After all I've gone through, after all I've done for Him, I just can't believe God is doing this!"

Buddy paused for a moment before answering. "Jake, I don't know why God *let* this happen but I know for a fact that He didn't do it *to* you."

"But He's God. Isn't He in control?"

"Yes. He is. And He will bring good out of it like He has with every other painful tragedy you've gone through."

Amy rubbed Jake's hand and nodded.

"Well, whatever happened to Him giving me the desires of my heart?" Jake argued back.

"Delighting yourself in the Lord means tuning yourself in to His desires, so much so that you start wanting what He wants," Buddy clarified.

"So I guess He doesn't want me to play basketball anymore." Jake shrugged resentfully.

"This is going to sound harsh, but honestly, in the grand scheme of things, I'm not sure God really cares."

Jake looked at him curiously.

"Remember what I told you? God doesn't care so much about your vocation and location, but rather—"

"My conduct and character," Jake completed the well-worn wisdom and rolled his eyes.

"Jake, that is truer now with your knee immobilized than ever before." Buddy pulled a greenish bouncy ball out of his pocket and tossed it across the table to Jake. "You've got the choice to glow and bounce back or whine and get stuck. If you refuse to let circumstances dictate your attitude, just watch and see how God will use you. If not, then you just get depressed. Up to you, bud," Buddy said with a mirthful wink.

"My dad's going to be so disappointed."

"You never know. He might surprise you. But it's not about him anyway."

"And you know we all support you no matter what," Amy added with a squeeze to Jake's arm.

Jake knew their words were right. This definitely wasn't the first challenge he'd faced in his life. Watching Roger die, getting blindsided by his dad's affair and all the drama that ensued, losing Amy—twice!—and their baby, too... Each of these events had shaken him, but each time he came out of the trial even stronger. And the greater his faith grew, the more courage he had to face the next obstacle in his path. He had seen God do so many things in and through his life over the past several years. But it still hurt to lose his dream. He was a basketball player, and a really good one at that. Basketball was his identity. How could he just give it up?

Jake sighed and furrowed his brows. "It's just so hard, you know? I love basketball...and playing in the NBA was such a nice dream. I mean, what am I supposed to do with my life now? Basketball is the only thing I've ever been good at."

"Jake, who says you have to give up basketball completely?" Buddy consoled. "What if God put you on the planet to work with young people, using your love of basketball to pour into their lives and lead them closer to Him?"

"I don't know..."

"Jake," Amy piped up. "Basketball is definitely not the only thing you're good at. I've seen you work with those freshmen boys at New Song. And I've heard your stories about Debron and your speaking at different schools."

"And don't forget VBS!" Buddy chimed in.

"You've got a gift, Jake," Amy affirmed.

"And you just might find that you enjoy working with young people far more than you ever would playing in the stinky ol' NBA."

"That paycheck sure would have been nice, though, you gotta admit." Jake smiled wryly.

"What's money when you're surrounded by love?" Amy winked.

Later that night as he got ready for bed, Jake looked at himself in the mirror. He reminisced over all his successes on the basketball court and then walked through the victories he'd had in other realms. Truth be told, those stood out a lot brighter in his mind. For the first time in months, his injuries—and his decision not to enter the draft last year—didn't seem as much like tragedies as potentially divine interventions leading him to something better. Closing the door on professional basketball still required some grieving, but now at least he was open to plan B.

SUMMER

54

THREE WEEKS AFTER his reconstructive surgery, Jake limped across the stage to receive his diploma, the succinct end to his three and a half years at Louisville. After less deliberation than expected, he'd agreed with most of the people that cared about him that returning for his final year of eligibility just wasn't worth it in the long run. Even if he was able to make a total comeback to basketball, future injuries were virtually guaranteed, and Jake didn't want to further jeopardize his later enjoyment of life. Dr. Gruber was right; he'd had a good run. In spite of his difficulties, he'd been given the chance to live out his dream here, and he was so grateful.

Jake allowed his eyes to linger on the people around him, and he knew it would be sad to leave. But he looked forward to the next chapter in his life. Graduating with a degree in Physical Education, he planned to enroll in San Francisco State University's teacher credentialing program next year, while Amy pursued her post-graduate work while working full-time at PACS. Thanks to connections through Renee's boyfriend Brian, Jake even had a teaching/coaching job lined up in one of Oakland's toughest neighborhoods, assuming he got accepted into the

SFSU internship program. Growing up, Jake would have never envisioned himself working in the inner city, but given the recent rollercoaster ride God had been taking him on, Jake was excited to embark on this next leg of his journey.

As he gazed out over the mass of his fellow students, a commotion in the section to his left caught his attention. His own personal fan club—consisting of his mom and dad, Amy, Buddy, some of his teammates, and Debron and some of the other kids—blared fog horns and cheered with reckless abandon. Jake laughed and waved at them. It felt good to be loved.

Suddenly Jake noticed his dad put his arm around his mom... and even more remarkably, his mom hugged her ex-husband back. The impromptu display of affection could have simply been a spontaneous expression of the pride they felt in seeing their son reach such a valuable milestone, but even from a distance, Jake recognized a certain spark in the exchange. *Hm...* he thought with a smile. Could God still be working there, too?

His father had been acting differently lately, ever since Jake's career-ending injury. When Jake had first shared the devastating news with his dad, Glen had lashed out in denial. But since then, as Jake had grown more at peace with his NBA-less future, that calm acceptance seemed to rub off on his dad. At least four times in the past few weeks Glen had reiterated how proud he was of his son and had repeatedly expressed admiration at the way Jake was handling this catastrophic twist of fate. Jake had used those opportunities to explain to his dad about the peace that God offers that transcends understanding and the hope that God extends for an even greater purpose. Jake never knew if his words had any effect, but perhaps his dad had indeed been listening.

After a celebratory lunch at the local buffet, Jake's dad was ready to get started on his long drive. Even though Jake had just been cleared to drive, it certainly wasn't recommended for him to make the trek himself and so his parents had decided that his dad would bring his truck back to California. When his mom started gathering her stuff to leave, Jake realized that she would be joining Glen on the drive and he was stunned. With a smile playing on his lips, he hugged them goodbye and couldn't help but hope that their journey together would be as healing as his own journey with his dad three and a half years earlier.

Amy left soon after them, flying back to Stanford for her last month of school, and as much as Jake hated to see her go, he was consoled by the thought that this would be their last goodbye before spending the rest of their life together. That alone was motivation to get him back in his room to study for his final class as a U of L student. With all the activity surrounding his knee rehab, Jake had never got the chance to polish off that last online course and so now he was enrolled in one more condensed summer session to meet his undergraduate requirements after he walked.

Doing homework while all his friends were free for the summer felt like a pretty lame way to celebrate his graduation, but Jake buckled down and opened his textbook. After all, he had a lot to look forward to!

BACK AT STANFORD, Amy sat at her desk trying to study but her mind was swimming with the million-and-one things she needed to do in the next six weeks. Finals were obviously a high priority but other things were jockeying for position, not the least of which was planning the final details of her wedding. And wedding planning was so much more fun!

But the most important project at hand was completing her honors research. What started as a study of how helping others could aid in abuse recovery had morphed into something even more personal and practical when her advisor had suggested that she use her non-profit organization as a component of her research. Being able to work on Bogdana's Dream for a school assignment had been the most enriching part of Amy's education thus far.

Just last week, she had sent off several boxes of fabric and stuffing and laminated Bible verse cards and other materials which would be difficult to procure in Romania, along with a generous check that would cover a year's worth of salaries for the girls in the transition program. Jodi promised she would take lots of pictures for Amy to use in her final presentation.

Now, Amy's efforts were focused on finishing off Debron's project—which was turning out far bigger than she'd anticipated, but also a lot more astounding. She couldn't wait to unveil it!

And, oh yeah. As if she didn't have enough on her plate already, tomorrow she was going to visit her uncle in prison. It was a step she had kept putting off, but in spite of everything else she was juggling, it was something she felt like she needed to do before moving on to the next chapter of her life. Her dad was going with her, and she had one particular goal in mind: to lead her uncle into a healing personal relationship with Christ. Prison had done its duty and Harold was a completely broken man, but Amy knew that brokenness was worthless unless he let God take the pieces and turn them into a brand new masterpiece. She was both excited and nervous, as this would be the first time she'd come face to face with him since the abuse. But she felt a peace and strength from God that this would be a valuable experience, and so she was charging on.

"AHHHHHH!!!" A scream down the hall startled Amy out of her contemplations.

Pounding footsteps ran toward her room and suddenly the door burst open revealing an ecstatic Renee.

"I'm engaged!" she yelped and started jumping up and down.

"What? No way!" Amy jumped up to celebrate with her roommate. Amy had been wondering how long it was going to take Brian to pop the question. She knew he still had an extra semester of school left, but it would make planning her own wedding so much more fun if she could do it together with her best friend here at Stanford. Amy sat down on her bed and patted the spot next to her. "Okay, girl, tell me all about it!"

BESIDES COMPLETING HIS COURSEWORK—

with flying colors!—and giving his all to rehabilitating his knee (after surrendering basketball, Jake had quickly adjusted his goals to simply being healthy enough to fully enjoy his honeymoon!), Jake had also kept busy after graduation working on last-minute preparations for his second annual basketball clinic. After months of planning, the week had finally arrived and so far it had gone without a hitch.

He and Grant, with the help of Nomis, Jadon, Tyler, and Travis, had persuaded most of their teammates to either stick around or come back to participate, which had turned it into a fun last hurrah. Meanwhile, Jadon had recruited even more helpers from his church and Buddy and the faithful senior citizens of Grace Fellowship had been more committed than ever.

Being on crutches limited the amount of actual coaching Jake had been able to do, but as much as he liked working with the individual kids, he found he was enjoying just walking around and supervising everything, too. The atmosphere was electric and everyone was having so much fun.

As anticipated, the number of kids this week had nearly doubled last year's unexpected crowds, but the number of volunteers had tripled so the stress had cut in half. To manage two hundred kids, the Grace Fellowship seamstresses had sewn practice jerseys in ten different colors and some generous contributors from New Life had pitched in to buy portable hoops to transform the neglected tennis courts into useful space.

Debron and Jadon had really stepped up into leadership, which encouraged Jake to no end. The fact that he was leaving had weighed heavily on him, and he hated to think that after he was gone, all of the progress here would simply fade back to the way things were. But Jadon had really come a long way since last year and now he was almost more passionate than Jake about reaching out to the kids in this neighborhood. Last week, he had asked Jake to meet with him to talk about continuing this ministry for the long haul.

The team of volunteers Jadon had recruited was willing to make this an ongoing commitment and they already had plans for monthly outreaches at the park. Jake couldn't be more thrilled and had simply asked him to look after Debron. Jadon said he was already on it and expressed excitement about raising him up to be a leader in this community. As much as Jake knew he should expect it, once again he was blown away by God's faithfulness.

Today was the final day of camp, and from the moment he'd arrived, Jake had struggled with annoyingly raw emotions. He had never been one to cry much, but for some reason today he felt just a little more sensitive. Everywhere he turned he saw reminders of how much God had blessed him and how much he was going to miss these people and places he had grown to love. Buddy had just caught him getting a little teary at the refreshment station and had simply patted him on the back and whispered, "Congratulations. You're becoming a real man."

The irony of that encouragement did not escape Jake, and he chuckled as he walked over to where the purple squad was learning how to do jump-hooks. Watching tiny boys and girls soaring in the air with perfect form was a beautiful thing to behold, and Jake just stood back and smiled.

He looked forward to the day when he would have his own brood of tiny ones to play ball with in the driveway. He pictured Amy sitting on the porch watching as he taught his sons and daughters their own special moves. Jake suddenly realized that all of the kids in his mind's eye had darker skin, and again he smiled. Amy obviously had a huge heart for orphans, and after working with these kids and talking to some of the New Life volunteers about the foster system, Jake, too, was starting to love the idea of growing their family the way God does, through adoption. Given his history with Amy, it kind of seemed like an appropriate full circle.

Jake's thoughts drifted on to the joys of being married to Amy, and he grinned to realize that the wedding countdown was now down to fifteen days. After his final service at Grace Fellowship on Sunday, he'd fly out to northern California where he and Amy would spend the week searching for apartments before her graduation that following Sunday. Then they would fly down to Oceanside for a crammed week of wedding activities, and then they would be joined in holy matrimony on June 23 and whisk away to Cancun for a blissful, uninterrupted week of togetherness and s—"

"Excuse me, Mr. Taylor?" a newspaper journalist interrupted his fantasies. "I was wondering if I could ask you a couple of questions."

Jake shook his head and smiled. Dreaming about Amy was far more enticing, but he was more than happy to comply, figuring that this was probably the last time in his life he would be at the center of so much attention. By the time the interview was concluded, Jake looked at his clock and realized it was almost time to bring the week of fun to a close.

He sounded the horn and waited for everyone to gather. A moment of déjà vu washed over him and he remembered back to that meaningful final day last year when so many people's eternities had changed thanks to God working through him. *Lord, please do it again!* he prayed, feeling a whole lot less nervous. Of course, it helped that this year he had a partner emcee. Jake handed the microphone over to a sweaty Debron, who took over without hesitation.

"Yo, yo, yo!" he called out, looking quite like a rapper with his jauntily-cocked hat and his sideways grip of the mic. "Y'all have fun up in here this week?"

A roar of cheers answered.

"Well, let me see you give some love to all these volunteers!"

The kids started applauding raucously, and some of them even jumped up to give their favorites hugs right then and there.

"That's right," he encouraged. "They gave up a week of their time to hang out with all of us, and you know why?" Debron paused for effect. "It's 'cause they love us." He paused again. "And you know who loves even more? Jesus. Can I hear you say, 'Je-sus!'"

The kids echoed back, "JE-SUS!"

"That's right. Let me hear it again. Say, 'Je-sus!'"

"JE-SUS!"

Jake wasn't sure where all this was coming from—it definitely wasn't what they had practiced! But he was sure getting a kick out of it, and he couldn't wait to see where Debron took it.

"So me and my main man Jake Taylor here have a few words we want to tell you about our best friend, Jesus. Jake, take it away."

Jake couldn't help but laugh at the transition, but he promptly launched into the story he'd shared so many times before, closing with, "Debron is right. Jesus is the best friend I've ever had, and I couldn't imagine going through life without Him. But don't just take it from me. Debron, you've got your own story to share, right?"

Debron took the microphone back and proceeded to share with insight that exceeded his years how God had transformed his life. He described his insecurity and loneliness that had made him want to die, and then shared about the hope that had saved him the moment he raised his hand to invite Jesus into his life last summer.

"Some of you remember what a punk I used to be. I'm sorry if I hurt you. I was only lashing out to protect myself. But I hope you can tell that I've changed. I'm still not perfect, but I'm growing. And you can, too. My friend Buddy over there" —Debron waved and smiled at the old man standing in the back— "taught me that it's as easy as A, B, C.

"A—Admit that you've messed up. B—Believe that God forgives you because He paid for your punishment by dying on the cross. And C—Choose to live your life for Him. It's a deal too good to pass up, and I hope a bunch of you will accept it today. If you want Jesus to become your best friend today, just pray these words with me."

Debron began to pray and Jake marveled at the words coming out of his young friend's mouth. He even dropped his slang in the sincerity of the moment. Debron's awareness of the difference God had made in his life was priceless and it made his message so powerful. Jake had thought it was amazing to get to lead people into a relationship with Christ last year, but that was nothing compared to watching his young mentee follow in his steps.

Debron ended the prayer and asked everyone to look up. "Now I know that last year Jake kept everyone's eyes closed when he gave us the opportunity to share that we'd prayed, but that just seems like we're hiding the most amazing thing we could ever do. There ain't no shame in it, y'all! If you just prayed with me, you just made like the smartest decision of your life. So who wants everyone to know that now you're on Jesus' team?" he shouted.

Hands started popping up everywhere and then not just hands but entire bodies. Kids and parents started hugging and dancing and celebrating their new life and the joy was infectious. This year, the churches had gotten smarter and had "new believer" packets to pass out to everyone who raised their hand, but with all the festivity, volunteers were scrambling to reach everyone and write down their names and contact information. Ultimately, Jake thought he counted over sixty people who gave their life to Christ, and his heart felt like it would burst with happiness. He pulled Debron into a side hug and ruffled his fluffy 'fro.

"Way to go, man," he said. "You're a natural."

Debron smirked good-naturedly, and pulled the microphone up to his mouth again. "Hey. If you prayed with me today, it ain't gonna do you no good unless you do something about it. You should have all received an envelope with a Bible in it and invitations to our churches. We better see you there on Sunday!" He winked. "And if you need a good place to start reading, the book of Mark is pretty tight. So Jake, tell us what's next." He handed the microphone to Jake and started scanning the crowd with an intent look on his face.

Jake assumed he was looking for a friend or something and started to describe the lunch procedures. "So if you're wearing a—"

"Whoah, whoah, whoah! Hold up, my friend." Debron reached up and pulled the microphone out of Jake's hand. "There's one more thing we need to do before we eat."

A sneaky grin was plastered to Debron's face and Jake looked at him in confusion. He tried to send a message with his eyes: *What are you doing?*

"As many of you know," Debron started, "this is Jake's last time with us. He's about to move back to California and get *married*."

The way he said it made Jake laugh, and Jake wondered what this kid was up to now. He'd had more than his share of recognition lately and he'd really rather just get out of the limelight.

"So some of us started thinking, trying to figure out what we could get him as a going away present." Debron motioned to Grant, Jadon, Buddy, and Kevin Ross, and they started walking up front as a cluster. "He's done so much for us here, and we wanted to leave him with a little memento to always remember us by. So with a lot of thought...and a little extra help...we think we figured out the perfect thing. Miss Amy, can you come up here and show it to him?"

Amy? Jake thought. *Amy who?*

Suddenly, the cluster of men split apart and out walked *his* Amy, carrying a cumbersome flat object covered by a red cloth. Sporting a Louisville jersey with Jake's number, she looked amazing and even Jake's healthy knee went weak.

Amy took the microphone from Debron and gave Jake a wink. "First, let me say how excited I am for all of you who just started your new life with Christ. I, too, made that choice just a few years ago, and it has made all the difference in the world! Second, this camp is amazing. I've been watching you guys all morning," —she looked at Jake and grinned apologetically— "and you guys have got skills!" The kids cheered enthusiastically until Amy began to speak again.

"This year, I started a nonprofit organization to empower young people to live out their dreams of making the world a better place. My initial goals started small, but God had bigger plans, and after hearing Jake here talk about Debron's goals to expand this basketball camp, I had a new idea. Since then, Debron and I have been working with a ton of others to turn a dream into reality. Thank you, Buddy and Grant, Jadon and Kevin, and a ton of other people who have helped us in our quest. Thanks to some generous contributors and some liberal matching grants, we have raised sufficient funds and procured the necessary permits from the city to upgrade this park into the nicest basketball facility in Louisville. I present to you..." With a flourish, Amy yanked the crimson sheet off of the board and revealed an elaborate drawing of a state-of-the-art park. "...the future Jake Taylor Community Park!"

Kids and parents erupted in excitement and Jake simply lost it. Buddy brought him a chair to collapse into and Debron gave him a gigantic hug.

"I wanted to name it the Jake Taylor Memorial Park but—"

"Memorial?" Jake interrupted with a laugh. "Isn't that for people who are already dead?"

"That's what Amy said. So we went with my second choice. But I wanted you to know, we'll always remember you. You've been like a dad to me, you know. Thanks."

Unable to speak, Jake just shook his head. "I love it," he finally whispered. "You ready to take over the reins here?"

"Don't worry." Debron smirked. "I'll make you proud."

"You already have, Debron. You already have."

Amy started tapping on the microphone to get everyone's attention again. "There's one more small matter I need to take care of," she said. "Debron, could you come over here?"

Debron looked at Jake in surprise and Jake just shrugged.

Putting her arm around the little man, she continued, "There's one more thing our dreamer wished for that I forgot to mention. He thought it would be cool if everyone got official camp T-shirts to remember their week by. Well, with some help from the Louisville athletic department, we thought that these might do the trick."

Buddy threw her a red blob and she unfurled it to reveal the Louisville Cardinal logo surrounded by the words "2nd Annual Taylor Community Basketball Camp."

"No way!" Debron hollered and started jumping up and down. Now it was Amy's turn to receive a gigantic hug.

Jake sat back and surveyed all the joy gushing all around him. His teammates, his church friends, his kids from the neighborhood...his entire life at Louisville all together in one perfect celebration. And just when he thought it couldn't get any better, Amy showed up to fuse his dreams with hers. He was a truly blessed man.

SUMMER

(FIVE YEARS LATER...)

57

FIVE YEARS LATER...

"ARE YOU KIDDING ME? You got another chick flick? I thought it was my turn to pick," Jake complained as Amy put in the movie. He loved his wife more today than the day they had said their vows but that shouldn't mean he had to give up on action movies altogether.

"Oh, was it your turn? Sorry, I forgot." Amy laughed with her flirtatious giggle that somehow always excused her of everything. "But after Rog falls asleep I was thinking we could make our own little romance, anyway." She traced her finger down his cheek and gave him the eye.

"Mommy, mommy! I can't find Alfredo!" three-year-old Roger exclaimed as he ran into the living room.

"Wait a minute," Jake said as he pretended to intently search for his son's favorite stuffed monkey. "What's this under the blanket? Aha!" He pushed Alfredo out of the blanket into his son's waiting arms.

"Alfredo!" Roger yelled and smothered his toy with hugs and kisses.

The family of three piled onto their hand-me-down couch from the Vaughns and cuddled up under the blankets as the previews started. Roger started chowing down on the popcorn in front of him giving Jake and Amy the perfect space to smooch above his head.

"Did you miss me?" Amy whispered as her lips lingered on her husband's.

"You have no idea," Jake whispered back with a grin. He'd just returned from a week-long visit to Louisville to help coach at the seventh annual Taylor Community Basketball Camp, and while he'd had a ton of fun revisiting his old stomping grounds, he was more than happy to be home. Amy usually joined him each summer, but being eight and a half months pregnant this year, her doctor had insisted that she stay at home. Jake leaned over to kiss his wife's belly. "I missed you, too, little Christopher Jonathan Taylor," he said, and the little boy inside kicked heartily.

"What about me? Did you miss me, daddy?" Roger asked earnestly.

"I must have thought about you like a million times a day," Jake replied and tousled his son's kinky curls.

The movie started and as they quieted down to watch it, Jake's thoughts quickly drifted away. With one arm on his son and the other around his wife, he knew he must be the happiest man in the world. God had given him so much.

He loved his job teaching PE and coaching boys' basketball at the challenging west Oakland school he had started at. Just last year, he and Amy had pulled together all their pennies and purchased a home in the neighborhood. It wasn't big and it wasn't beautiful, but it was theirs and they were excitely turning it into their own do-it-yourself masterpiece. Renee and Brian lived just down the street, and together they felt like they were really starting to have an impact on their community.

Last summer, Jake and Amy had eagerly welcomed their first child into their new home. Neglected and abused, the tiny two-year-old had come to them through the foster system, and the instant they saw him, they fell hopelessly in love. They had named him Roger and he was a daily reminder of God's transforming grace and love. His adjustment to stability hadn't been immediate, but now a year later, his cheerful smile could light up a room and his pleasant personality provided constant entertainment.

Upon entering motherhood, Amy had promptly given up her full-time job at the clinic, but she still volunteered as many hours as she could providing free counseling through their church. Bogdana's Dream was still going strong and the nonprofit gave her another outlet for her talents.

They both volunteered in the youth ministry at their church, and Jake had started an FCA club on his campus. Much to his surprise, he was still a favorite speaker at local events. His story had changed a little, but it still boiled down to the same important thing: without God, nothing really mattered.

Even his trip to Louisville had been a blessing. After all these years, seeing the neighborhood ministry going strong was an encouragement beyond belief. Jadon Williams had graduated from Louisville two years ago and had taken a position with the local Boys' and Girls' Club. His work was inspiring and Jake was so proud to be a part of it. Debron was now a strapping seventeen-year-old getting ready to enter his senior year of high school. He already had several recruiters looking at him, but his goal was to make it to UC Berkeley—so that he could spend the next four years near Jake again. Jake tuned back in to the movie, content beyond belief with his wonderful life. Roger, who had long since drifted into dreamland, sighed deeply and twisted his arms around his daddy. Jake smiled and ran his fingers through Amy's hair. She looked up at him and smiled back. Their life was hectic and full and far from easy, but most nights when they finally crashed into bed in each others' arms, they both felt the same way: They were living the dream.

As Amy snuggled in closer, Jake suddenly felt his cell phone vibrate. As much as he wanted to ignore it, curiosity won over and he quietly looked down at the incoming call from an unfamiliar number.

"Who is it?" she asked sleepily.

"I'm not quite sure," he responded as he pulled the phone to his ear. "Hello?"

The voice on the other side was instantly familiar. It was Dante, a kid Jake had met at the neighborhood basketball courts just before he left for his trip. "I'll be right there," Jake responded after Dante had explained his predicament. He hung up and sighed and then pried himself loose from his son.

"What's up?" Amy asked.

"This kid I met the other day is at some party that's getting out of control. I told him to give me a call any time, and he's taking me up on the offer."

Amy shook her head and smiled and reached into a basket on the shelf. Tossing Jake a glow-in-the-dark bouncy ball, she said, "I'm proud of you, babe," and winked.

Jake smiled. He walked out the door, got into his car, and slowly drove down the street. *I feel like I've been here before.*